THE
HUNTER'S
DAUGHTER

THE HUNTER'S DAUGHTER

Nicola Solvinic

BERKLEY
NEW YORK

BERKLEY
An imprint of Penguin Random House LLC
penguinrandomhouse.com

Library of Congress Cataloging-in-Publication Data

Names: Solvinic, Nicola, author.
Title: The hunter's daughter / Nicola Solvinic.
Description: New York: Berkley, 2024.
Identifiers: LCCN 2023034751 (print) | LCCN 2023034752 (ebook) |
ISBN 9780593639726 (hardcover) | ISBN 9780593639740 (ebook)
Subjects: LCGFT: Detective and mystery fiction.
Classification: LCC PS3619.O4396 H86 2024 (print) | LCC PS3619.O4396 (ebook) |
DDC 813/.6—dc23/eng/20231002
LC record available at https://lccn.loc.gov/2023034751
LC ebook record available at https://lccn.loc.gov/2023034752

Printed in the United States of America
1st Printing

Book design by Alison Cnockaert

For Jason, who understands my fascination
with the snakes in the garden.

THE
HUNTER'S
DAUGHTER

1

AWAKENING

The first time I killed a man was on Tuesday.

I thought I could get through my whole life without killing someone. I thought I could be virtuous. Peaceful. That I could broker treaties among evil men and shattered hearts. And I thought wrong.

I'd been driving home from work. It was late summer, when the skies become silver around dusk and the leaves begin to curl yellow at the edges. The sun was up, and I had the windows down, trying to absorb that last bit of heat on my skin before cold winter settled into my bones. Wind slid through my blond ponytail with invisible fingers while I squinted at the sunset through sunglasses. The falling light painted the two-lane country road in flashes of gold and shadow. My elbow rested on the window and my fingers combed through the air, feeling the swish of it against my palms. The police radio in my car hummed along at medium volume, and I was only half paying attention to the radio traffic. Though I was officially off duty, I was curious to hear if Sergeant Calvert was finally going to take the chief's car to the car wash after losing a bet on a high school football game.

"This is S12. C1 is out of service," a voice announced glumly. That was Calvert, admitting defeat. Finally.

"Acknowledged, S12. C1 is out of service," Dispatch chirped merrily.

Someone keyed their radio and a burst of applause echoed in the car. That was probably Chief Nelson. He'd already left the office, but I was pretty sure the chief of the Detective Bureau listened to the radio in his sleep.

The dispatcher broke in, her tone all business. *"Code 20 at 7071 Stroud's Road."*

I glanced at the road. I was only about a mile away. That was a domestic call, and I was likely closest. The county was seven hundred square miles, and it would take a while for backup to arrive. But I didn't like the idea of anyone getting their teeth knocked out when I could help it.

I keyed the radio. "This is L4. I'm at Sunday Creek and Route 6. En route." I flipped on the lights on my unmarked Crown Victoria and stepped on the gas, soaring over the blacktopped roads as the radio chattered.

"Acknowledged, L4. D2 is at 442 and Coffrey."

I thumbed the radio again. "Thanks, D2. I'll wait for you." I didn't hesitate because I was a woman in plain clothes. Departmental policy was that no one went to a domestic alone. Domestic violence cases could be unpredictable as fuck.

Adrenaline twitched through me as I drove down a hill and the sun slipped behind the trees. I pulled up before a dented rural mailbox with *7071* painted on the side. A gravel driveway wound into forest, and I couldn't see the house through the trees. I reached into the back seat for my vest, shrugged it on over my

T-shirt, and tightened the Velcro straps. I put my detective's badge on a lanyard around my neck and buckled on my utility belt. I checked my cuffs, gun, and Taser, then pulled a radio out of its charging station. I tucked the base into my belt and threaded the toggle control up to the collar of my vest.

A shadow swept across the hood of my car. Reflexively, I reached to my belt. But it was only a bird sweeping low across the road, so low that its feathers nearly brushed my windshield. My heart rose in my throat at the magnificence of it: a great blue heron, wings moving in slow motion as it flew across the road and vanished in the forest.

A gunshot rang out in the direction of that gravel driveway winding down into a shady valley.

I sucked in my breath. "Shit."

I lunged out of the car, drawing my gun with my right hand and keying my radio with my left. "This is L4, 52A, 52A at 7071 Stroud's Road."

"Copy, L4. Hold your position. Backup is five miles away."

Five miles was an eternity. Some unlucky woman could be bleeding out on her kitchen floor while her husband was booking it out the back door. That vision was clear for me, clear as a movie playing out behind my mind's eye: a woman lying on a crusty linoleum floor, fingers twitching as the last of her air whistled through her ruined lungs.

I gritted my teeth. I couldn't let that happen. I tried to be a good cop who always followed the rules, but someone needed me more than the rules needed me to follow them. Aiming my gun at the ground, I stalked down the gravel drive. My boots crunched in the pale gray rock while the birds screamed around me. The canopy of the forest closed over my head, casting me in shadow. Sweat prickled on my brow as I came into view of a tiny yellow bungalow with algae-streaked siding. Its roof was covered in moss. A brand-new pickup truck was parked out front, and I scanned the area for a propane tank. If I had to use my weapon, I sure as hell didn't want to hit that.

I advanced upon the shiny red pickup, approaching the driver's side. I saw no movement in the mirror. I drew down and aimed my gun into the cab. The window was down, but no one was there. Keys dangled in the ignition. I didn't know what kind of clusterfuck I was walking into, but I didn't want any perps or witnesses to drive off.

I stepped up on the running board, reached in, and yanked the keys out of the ignition. I bumped my head on the visor, and a cloud of white dust rained down on me. My sinuses were flooded with the acrid smell of a Magic Marker. A plastic bag landed on the floorboards.

I swore silently and rubbed my arm across my face. The powder was all over the seat and over me. No telling what it was yet: could be cocaine, PCP, or, worse, fentanyl.

I keyed my radio: "Base, this is L4. Suspected drugs on scene with exposure. Backup should have PPE and request medic." Whatever this shit was, I wanted someone with Narcan en route . . . for myself and whoever had driven that truck.

I pocketed the keys and ducked behind the truck's front fender. I slipped my hand up to the hood. It was warm. Likely, the conflict inside hadn't been going on long . . . but long enough for a gunshot to punctuate it.

I projected my voice toward the house. "Bayern County Sheriff's Office. We need to talk."

I was hoping that would startle the perpetrator; that he—and it was statistically most likely to be a "he"—would go flying out the back door into the woods. If he came out the front, the truck was between him and me. Worst-case scenario would be him taking a hostage. Best case . . . he thought the woods were crawling with cops.

The screen door banged open, and a mid-thirties man in jeans and a black T-shirt strode down the slimy wooden steps. He held a shotgun in his hands. He was breathing fast, glowering, panicked.

"It's all right," I called. "Put down the gun and we'll talk, okay?"

My radio chattered but I wasn't listening. I was watching the guy pump the shotgun. I sucked in my breath, hoping to hell he wasn't going to shoot at his shiny new truck. His shoes crunched in the gravel. I backed up and scuttled around the edge of the bumper, gun raised. My pulse was pounding in my forehead, and I flipped the safety off.

"She fucking cheated on me," he was muttering. "She fucking cheated . . ."

And I was all of a sudden face-to-face with this wild-eyed man with a shotgun. His black T-shirt was wet, and a spatter of blood stained his arm.

I lifted my hand. "It's okay," I said soothingly. "It's okay . . ."

He aimed at me and pulled the trigger. Hundreds of pieces of birdshot rattled into me, and the shotgun blast rocked me out of my crouch into the gravel on my back. Pain seared me, and I gasped.

My pulse pounded harder, faster than the panic. I hadn't let go of my gun. I pressed both my fists around the grips, sighted through my bloody sunglasses, and fired.

I hit him in the gut. He was on the way down, but I kept shooting. He dropped to the ground, still clutching the shotgun.

I climbed, wincing, to my feet, supporting myself on the back fender of the truck. I felt surreally calm as I took a step toward him.

I fired. I hit him in the shoulder, and he shrieked.

I took another step.

I fired.

Another step.

Another bullet.

Gunfire rang out around me, deafening me. All I could hear was my blood thumping evenly in my ears. I was staring down at him, his fingers tangled in the shotgun's trigger guard. He wheezed, his mouth speckled in red, and his lips were moving, but I couldn't hear a thing.

I stood over him and shot him in the neck. His throat blossomed into red, and a piece of gravel, shattered, bounced back against my shin.

I collapsed to my knees beside him. Leaning over him, I watched his face intently. I knew he was dying. He gasped, gaping like a fish on land, as blood pumped through his shredded shirt and poured out of his torn-open throat. Bubbles emerged from the wound. He gurgled, his teeth stained red, and he twitched. His eyes rolled right and left, his pupils dilated, and his lower lip trembled above his sparse beard, sticking to it with a red string.

He looked up at me, gaze focused on my face. A drop of red dribbled down my chin and landed on his forehead.

And I felt it then . . . that moment where he was living and then not living. His chest stopped rattling, the blood slowed, and the twitching and fluttering faded. The focus of his gaze slackened, and I watched it like a voyeur, connected and yet disconnected to this vanishing of a man I didn't know.

He was dead.

I sat back in the gravel. Sound rushed back into my world, and I felt nauseous. I turned my head and vomited before collapsing in the gravel, overcome by the hundreds of piercing wounds burrowing into my body like hot worms. The shaded driveway felt cool against my body.

My radio buzzed distantly at my shoulder. I fumbled to key it.

"L4, 44," I whispered. *Officer in trouble . . .*

My radio squawked at me, but it sounded like a bird on my shoulder. Through my broken sunglasses, I stared up at the trees. I smelled metallic blood, leaf mold, and moss. Blood dripped into my right eye, and it stung. Disturbed by a pleasant breeze, yellow sugar maple leaves drifted down and stuck to my wet bulletproof vest. I stared, fascinated, as a whirligig seed pod spun down and stuck to my lip.

I exhaled, and its skeletal wing shuddered like a creature reborn.

2

THE FALL

Sound roared around me. Sirens, yelling, and the squeal of radios. I was conscious of my sunglasses pulled from my eyes and a plastic mask fitted over my face. I stared up, up at the trees and the silver sky, as I was carried up the narrow gravel drive to an ambulance. I searched the sky for the heron but didn't find it.

I was still, croaking one-word answers to the fingers paramedics put in front of my face, tasting blood. I didn't know if I'd bitten my lip or bloodied my nose or if it was a sign of much worse.

"Do you know your name?" one paramedic who looked to be barely out of high school asked me.

I paused for a moment before answering, and he and the other paramedic exchanged worried glances.

"Anna Koray," I said finally.

"Good." The paramedics nodded as they stabbed my arms for IV lines. They cut my bulletproof vest off with scissors at the straps and cut away my T-shirt. I lay quietly, listening to the blood thumping evenly in my skull. It ticked like a metronome, a regular thud under the churning lights and motion and distant sirens. I felt myself moving quickly, hurtling over dips and valleys in the road. I knew we'd reached the hospital when white fluorescent light washed over me. I closed my eyes because the light was too bright, bright as noonday sun shining on water. Behind my eyes, I saw the life draining away from the man I killed, feeling that last instant as something ephemeral escaped him, an unseen exhalation . . .

"Anna."

I opened my eyes. A man leaned over me—a man I knew. His brow was creased as brown eyes stared down at me.

"Nick." My lips were dry, and the mask over my face fogged. I hadn't seen him since we'd broken up six months earlier. He'd pursued me hard with his wit and his charm, and I'd slowed down long enough for him to catch me. It was . . . too good. He was attentive, appreciative. We never argued; to him, my happiness mattered more than whatever petty thing we could ever find to argue about. I felt safe with him. The sex was the best I'd ever had. Unlike the men I'd known before, he didn't diminish me in any way. He and I, somehow, were more together than the sum of our parts. He'd wanted more. I . . . didn't know what I wanted. I think I was afraid to fully open up to him, to be vulnerable. I'd felt trapped in a way I didn't want to admit, like I did now, pinned under his dark gaze that searched my face for truths I couldn't give him. There were shadows beneath his eyes that I didn't remember from before.

Mercifully, he looked away from me to bark orders at the nurses. It figured that I would wind up in his emergency room, and during one of his shifts. I closed my eyes and listened to the regular beeping of the machines.

I felt a hand slip into mine before I drifted into darkness.

———

I dreamed I was a nine-year-old girl walking in the woods with my dad. His calloused hand was in my left hand, and we walked through a summer field. My right hand gripped a sticky dandelion. My cheeks felt warm with sunburn.

"Are we going to see the tree houses?" I asked.

He smiled, his face crinkling around his gray eyes. "You mean the tree stands?"

"Yes!" I tugged him toward the line of trees at the edge of the field.

He let go of my hand, and I ran. The grasses whipped my arms as I pumped my fists. The dandelion dropped from my grasp, forgotten, and I plunged into the shade of the forest. My mom would've told me to look out for snakes; she was terrified of snakes and bees and pretty much anything that crawled or flew or swam. But my dad seemed to live in the woods, disappearing there for long days and coming back at dark. He'd return with a deer carcass in the back of his pickup truck that he'd string up, slice open, and bleed out over a bucket in the backyard. I remembered staring into those soft brown deer eyes, sad that the deer had died, but also fascinated. Mom would shoo me away into the house, try to distract me with a doll or a cookie. I'd sneak out later at night, listening to the tap-tap of blood draining into the bucket and gazing at the reflection of the moon in the blackness.

Mom found me there one fall night, barefoot and in my nightgown, stroking the velvet above the deer's nose and whispering to it: "*You can't be dead. You're too beautiful.*" Something moved at the edge of the woods, and my breath caught in my throat. A flick of a white tail, and I spied a deer, his antlers silvery in the moonlight. He could've been a brother to the one my dad killed, or his ghost.

My heart swelled. The deer was alive!

My mom sobbed behind me. I turned to her joyously and pointed into the dark. "See? The deer came back!"

But the deer was gone. Mom grabbed my hand and dragged me into the house. I didn't understand why she was crying. The deer—the deer was alive, and she didn't need to be sad. It had transformed, changed.

But my mom knew. How much, I wasn't ever certain. She saw my dad in me. I had her blond hair, but I had his nose and his gray eyes. But I think she saw beyond that, to what we really were underneath our skins.

And that terrified her.

Dad took me to the woods often, and I could see the pain in her eyes every time we left. But I wanted to run through fields, climb trees, and track prey with my father. I didn't want to sit at the kitchen table and snap beans or scrub the oven. Who would?

I'd rather sink into the woods with my dad, who told me stories of spirits who lived among the trees. He'd tell me that everything was alive and listening in the forest: stones, trees, and especially animals. Everything I saw was magic: crows mimicking human speech; mirages of puddles that vanished when I approached; sticks that turned into snakes when I tried to pick them up. Nothing was as it seemed, but I accepted this, the brutality and the wonder of it.

I found the oak with the tree stand effortlessly. I climbed the tree quickly, noticing how the bark smelled like meat. I'd told my dad about this, how peeling bark smelled like hamburger. He said that was because trees were living things, and flesh was flesh.

I loved this tree because an owl nested in it. I scrambled up to the rickety wood platform that my dad hunted from. It had rained the night before, and the shaded wood was still damp. The stand was barely four feet square, but it seemed a whole tree house to me. There, Dad would wait for deer, getting up at four a.m. and crouching in the cold November mornings in deer season, waiting for prey. I would look up for white owl droppings that would show me where the barred owl in this tree roosted. The leaf canopy was thick, but sometimes I could glimpse it sleeping, its eyes closed and blending in with the tree bark.

I couldn't see the owl that day. I decided to climb up higher to look, but my attention was snagged by something shiny glittering on the grayed wood platform.

Forgetting the owl, I dropped to my hands and knees to examine it. It was a necklace on a chain . . . a heart-shaped locket. The chain slipped through the wood slats, threatening to slide away.

No one else knew about my father's tree stands, my tree houses. Someone else had been here. Who was she? What was she doing here?

I lunged for it, trying to capture it in my grubby fingers.

But I slipped. I slipped on that mossy, damp wood, sliding beneath the two-by-four guardrail, and fell.

For an instant, I was frozen between earth and sky, shade and sun flashing over me, air caught in my hands and hair . . .

. . . until I crashed to the ground, gasping, as the wind was driven from me in a sickening crunch. Pain glittered through me, and I drew breath to call for my dad. But my breath was shallow, and all that came out was a thin whistle. I'd heard it before: the whine of a shot deer.

Disturbed by my crash to the forest floor, the owl took flight.

I tried to get up. My hand slipped in the mud, but I couldn't push myself upright. I'd really hurt myself, and I hoped Dad wouldn't be angry. I swallowed blood that welled up in my throat.

I saw his boots before me, and he wordlessly gathered me in his arms. He carried me away in long, silent strides. The weight of his disappointment was crushing. I tried not to whimper, biting my lip as he put me in the passenger side of the pickup truck.

He drove me to the hospital. I remembered little of that time, only that a plastic tube was installed between my broken ribs to blow my lung back up. There was a head injury, too. The doctors didn't really tell me; I only know what I overheard my mom sobbing about in the hallway.

"How could you do this to her!" Mom sobbed.

Dad's voice was low. "She fell from the tree stand. She just fell."

"You have no business taking my daughter out there. None." The way she said "my daughter" . . . Later, I would look back on this as if she were trying to take some kind of psychic custody from him, a custody that he would never give up. My parents rarely fought; Dad wasn't home often enough for that to happen. But there was no doubt as to who ruled the house. It was him, and the shadow he cast.

Dad didn't say anything, but I heard a soft, startled squeak from my mom. I opened my eyes to see him grasping her wrist tightly.

"She is *my* daughter." He glared at her with such fury. I'd never seen this in his eyes before, that faraway darkness. It was as if his skin had split and I saw the bloody red pulp that lay beneath.

It scared me, and I closed my eyes, but the image of my father's wrath burned behind my eyelids.

I didn't know who he was then. How could I?

But I would learn that I was his daughter—in all ways.

I woke up the next morning to find that necklace fastened around my neck. It lay at the hollow of my throat, smelling like metal and green. When I opened the locket, it was filled with moss.

I didn't take it off . . . not until I was forced to, years later.

———

"You're gonna be all right."

Nick sat at the edge of my bed, sounding reassuring. I wasn't sure if he was being truthful or if this was his professional bedside manner. I'd been in the hospital for a few hours, I estimated, drifting in and out of consciousness. They must have put me under for a while. I remembered counting backward, but I had no way of telling how much time had passed, since there were no windows in ICU.

They'd hooked me up to a drip that I suspected contained morphine, since I was hallucinating here and there. Just then, a blacksnake slithered beneath my hospital bed. And I didn't look at the stain on the ceiling tile that was growing moss. Those things weren't real, so I focused on Nick.

"You're lucky, you know," he said. "The wad from the shotgun hit your vest, and your vest took most of the impact of the blast. The spread of the birdshot, though, peppered all over you, and we had to dig those out."

I looked down at my bandaged arms. Gauze pressed on my face and upper thighs. There was a bandage over my right eye. My fingers crawled up to it in panic, and the heart rate monitor bleeped loudly.

"Your eye is fine." He grasped my hand before I could pull away the bandage. "You were wearing sunglasses, which protected you some from the impact. Just a shard of plastic that got embedded above your eyelid. It's been sutured, and no one will notice the scar."

I nodded, noticing he didn't release my hand.

"You also got exposed to a shitload of PCP. Fortunately, you didn't overdose, but you're likely to be prone to hallucinations for the next few hours. It could be longer, but that would be really rare."

Ah. That explained the snake and the moss.

"Thank you," I said, meaning it. "This had to be hard for you."

"Don't worry about me," he told me firmly. "You just have to worry about getting better."

"Will I? Get better?" Fear twitched through me. I had a hard time being truly honest with Nick, but I was depending on him in this moment to be brutally honest with me.

He nodded. "Yeah. We need to keep monitoring your heart for tachycardia as a result of the drug exposure. We got all the shot out. You'll have some scars, but over time they should fade and look pretty much like freckles. They bled like hell, but like I said, you were lucky." I believed he was telling me the truth.

Below the bed, the blacksnake hissed.

"I'm lucky you were on duty." I smiled at him, feeling a pang of sadness for the circles under his eyes. Clearly, he hadn't slept. My lip ached, stretching into the smile. I suspected I'd bitten it.

"Anna." He took a deep breath. "I was nervous when the squad said they were bringing in an injured deputy. But when I saw it was you . . ." He slid his hand over his mouth. He had long, intellectual fingers capable of incredible gentleness. "I was afraid. Really afraid."

"I'm okay," I said. My eye trailed to the corner of the ceiling, where the moss carpet was growing.

He seemed to get himself together then, placing both his hands around mine. "I'm gonna be here for you, Anna. I swear. But only if you want me to be."

The snake hissed below my bed and the moss crackled in the corner. I strained to hear Nick above those sounds; I wanted his voice to blot out the seethe of the forest. His hands were warm, and they were real. I wanted that reality.

"Yes," I said at last. "I want you to be."

He kissed my knuckle, and warmth flooded through me. My chest swelled and I felt alive, even a little hopeful. Or maybe that was just the PCP burning little holes into my brain.

The snake crawled up the foot of the bed and under the blankets, then coiled around my ankle. I couldn't stop it. I couldn't tell anyone about it. I just had to pretend it wasn't there.

I was good at pretending.

3

THEY NEVER LOOK LIKE KILLERS

I didn't want visitors. I wanted to go home, but Nick insisted on keeping me overnight. No one really says no to cops wandering hospital halls, so a steady stream of deputies trickled in to check on me. Or gather fodder for departmental gossip. Could've been both. But they did a good job of keeping the local news crews out, and I was grateful. They didn't say much about the shooting, just made awkward get-well comments. Nobody turned the TV on for me.

They asked if I had family to notify. I told them my family was out of the country and I didn't want to scare them.

The sheriff trucked in to make a display for morale. He appeared to be a dotty old man who kissed a lot of babies at reelection time, but he was cagey enough to know where all the bodies were buried. Bayern County was a rural county not far from a large Midwestern city, where he'd grown up and served as a police officer before running for office here in the boonies. He knew things but rarely said things.

I was still high on PCP and just nodded as he nattered about good cops keeping the two-lane roads of Bayern County safe for law-abiding citizens. I didn't really listen to him; instead, I looked over his shoulder at a hallucinated chrysalis dangling from my IV pole. I watched, fascinated, as a pale green luna moth crawled out, flexing damp wings. I watched the moon eyes on its wings twitch, slowly unfurling, and realized the sheriff had left. By then, more chrysalises began to speckle the ceiling, wobbling and twisting with each exhalation I took.

I slept, dipping into hissing darkness.

When the chief came by, I was awake and mostly sober. Or at least, able to act like it. The snake living under my bed was dozing, and all seemed a little sharper around me.

He pulled a chair up beside me, heedless of the snake on the floor. He was a tall man with a barrel chest and a haircut last seen on *Miami Vice* when spiked hair had been in vogue. "How you feeling, Koray?"

"I've been better," I told him. "But not bad, considering."

"Yeah." He frowned. "Are you up to talking about what happened?"

I nodded. I'd have to do an official interview at some point. Explain myself. I waited patiently for the chief to speak.

"You received the call. What happened then?"

I took a deep breath. "I went to the residence, heard a shot fired . . ." I told the chief everything. Almost everything. I told him that a shot had been fired and I went down the drive to investigate. I took the keys from the truck, and he nodded at my quick thinking. The perp headed out of the house and shot me first. And I shot back.

"How many rounds did you fire?"

"I don't remember. He didn't let go of the shotgun, and I didn't trust him not to get up again."

I didn't tell him about how I'd watched him die.

"What's his name?" I asked.

"Tom Sullivan. He worked at the aluminum plant. Was dating Cecily Owens, the homeowner. Two priors for DV, one for possession, and one for aggravated assault at a bar in town."

"Did he make it?" I felt like that was the appropriate thing to ask, though I already knew the answer.

"No."

"Is she okay?" I couldn't forget the image my brain had conjured up of a woman bleeding out on a linoleum floor.

"She died before paramedics got on the scene. They tried to resuscitate her, but . . ." Chief lifted a shoulder. "Close-range hit. There wasn't much to work with."

"I'm sorry for that," I said. "For both their deaths."

"You should've waited for backup," Chief said. "That guy was high and not feeling any pain. His glove box was stuffed with PCP, ketamine, and prescription painkillers. He was clearly into distribution."

"Yeah," I admitted. "I messed up."

"I don't blame you for what you did, though. In your shoes . . . I would've done the same thing."

I smiled at him. "Thanks, Chief."

"Internal Affairs is going to do their own investigation, of course. But I don't see this being a problem for you. We gotta dot the *i*'s and cross the *t*'s. Get letters from your doctors and a shrink that you're fit to return."

"I understand."

"In the meantime, don't worry about anything. Rest up. You'll be on admin leave until you're cleared to return to duty. Go binge some Netflix or whatever people are watching these days."

"I will." I was honestly too sore to contemplate anything else. The places where Nick had dug the birdshot out of my skin felt as if I'd been hit with a nail gun. My bandages seeped and wept, even though they were changed often. Looking down at my arms during one of those changes, I saw dozens of tiny holes closed with one or two stitches each.

I was lucky, right?

I asked one of the nurses for a remote control for the TV. I caught a report about the shooting on the evening news. Tom Sullivan's mug shot was displayed under a red banner that announced, OFFICER-INVOLVED SHOOTING. It was actually one of the better mug shot photos I'd seen. Though Sullivan was sporting a black eye, he had a lopsided grin and a certain charm to him. He didn't look like a killer, but then again, they never do.

The picture of the victim, Cecily Owens, was next. It looked like a photo from social media. She was a slight woman of maybe thirty, her hair dyed purple. She wore cat-eye glasses and a silver nose ring. The newscaster said that she worked at the county library. The newscaster interviewed some of her coworkers, who said she was a wonderful person who brought in baked goods when she worked the reference desk. Her ex-boyfriend had been escorted off library property several times. They never imagined he would do something like this.

Last, my photograph was shown. The news must've gotten it from the department's yearbook. I looked serene and confident, smiling quietly at the camera with my father's gray eyes in my dress uniform with the American flag behind me. My shoulder glittered with medals: a commendation medal for resuscitating a woman who had a heart attack; another commendation for rescuing a truck driver from a fiery accident; and the department's Person of Steel Medal for having run a warming shelter for people who lost power in the prior year's blizzard.

Yeah. They never do look like killers.

———

When I fell out of the tree stand when I was nine, the doctors said that I'd punctured a lung and broken a few ribs. I'd also broken my mom's heart, though I didn't understand why.

I stayed in the hospital for a few days, and then Mom came to get me. She'd brought a change of clothes in a duffel bag, swept me up, and took me to my grandparents' house to "recover."

We didn't visit my mom's parents very much. I only saw them a few times a year when they'd drive up from Florida. My dad would sit in his chair and silently stare at them. Eventually, they got so uncomfortable they'd leave. Or else he wouldn't be there at all, and they'd have awkward conversations with my mother about how beautiful the ocean was at sunset. We should see the ocean, I was told.

I'd never seen the ocean. Not until then.

Mom drove all night to Florida. Woozy with pain, I slept stretched out on the back seat of her station wagon, watching the moon pursue us in the rear window. When she stopped for fast food, I excitedly stuffed myself full of chicken nuggets and then slept some more. The whistle in my breath faded. I could take deep breaths even though it hurt.

Early in the morning, before the sun rose, my mom pulled into the driveway of a tiny house painted bright peach. A palm tree swayed in the front yard, and it seemed very bright and cheerful, like something from a cartoon. Grandma and Grandpa were surprised but happy to see us as Mom carried me inside. She put me to bed in a twin bed in the guest room with pictures of seagulls hung on the walls. The adults whispered in the kitchen, but I drowsed, ignoring them, listening to the waking cries of gulls in the distance.

I grew stronger, enough for my grandparents to take me to the beach. I remembered the warm bathtub water of the ocean dragging seaweed to curl around my ankles and squealing at jellyfish that washed up. My grandparents were leathery and tanned, as if they'd spent their whole lives flying close to the sun. Mom seemed to relax here as the sun turned her pale skin golden.

"We should enroll you in school," my mom said. "I think you're well enough."

I frowned. I thought we were here for a visit, and I missed my friends and school. But I also missed my dad. I knew I couldn't speak of him, though.

"We're not going back?"

She took my face in her hands. "No, dear. We're not going back."

I spent two weeks in the sun, building sand castles and collecting shells in an empty jar. The sun beat down on me, warming me, healing me, but I didn't belong here. Not really. I was too easily burned, too unfamiliar with the jellyfish hazards with their trailing tentacles the ocean hurled my way. There was no magic here, like in the woods. This was meant to be a vacation.

And that's how my dad saw it, too.

Mom and I slept in the same bed in the guest room. I awoke in the middle of the night to find myself alone in bed, with shouting echoing in the living room. I heard my granddad, roaring.

I shrank back, terrified by the conflict. I grabbed my blanket and rolled under the bed, among the dust bunnies and a spider living along the baseboards.

The door opened, and footsteps entered the room. I heard my dad's voice, soft and insistent.

"It's time to go, Elena."

Summoned by his voice, I crawled out from under the bed. He smiled at me. I flung my arms around him. His stubble pricked my cheek like needles. He smelled like my beloved forest.

He picked me up and carried me to the living room. To my shock, Grandpa lay on the floor, pressing his hand to his bloody mouth. Grandma hovered over him, shrieking at my father.

Mom stood blocking the door. Her voice trembled. "You can't take her. I won't let you."

"She's mine," he said. "Don't ever forget that."

Her gaze fell to the floor, where my granddad sprawled. Her eyes met my dad's.

"Get in the car," he said.

She was still for a moment, but only a moment. She stepped aside, and my dad carried me out to his pickup. He placed me in the middle seat, and my mom climbed in beside me. I rode back home between them in total silence.

Mom loved me. I knew that. Dad loved me, too. But I couldn't understand what was between them. I only knew that they both wanted me and hated each other. And that my mom was afraid of my dad.

I didn't understand this. He'd always been my hero. How could anyone be afraid of him?

We returned home, and my parents never spoke of Florida again. They didn't speak much to each other ever again, either. Our house was so silent, I could hear the ticking of a clock and the hum of the refrigerator over everything else.

I felt Mom pulling away from me. She often didn't hear me when I spoke to her, and with my dad's extended absences, it was as if I were a shadow in the house, like I didn't really exist without my father's presence. To amuse myself I'd go out to the woods, the only place I could escape that tension. I felt less and less like a girl, more that I was part of the seething world of the forest. I combed the grass and whispered into the ear of the earth, collected chestnuts, and searched for salamanders in shallow creeks. I'd return home with a pocket of stones or acorns that I'd leave on my windowsill. To my fascination, they would vanish at night nearly as fast as I could replenish them. Squirrels, probably. But I imagined the spirit of the forest visited me and that I gained its favor with my gifts.

Mom didn't want me in the forest. Maybe some part of her gave up. She read and sewed and watched television, in between her work as a medical secretary. She didn't listen for bird calls or puzzle over the subtle differences between raccoon and opossum tracks. She was still and boring.

Except for those brief flashes of rage. Shortly after we'd come back from Florida, I went back to school. My dad had vanished for work, and I'd dressed myself, wolfed down some cereal, and was heading out to catch the bus.

She caught my arm as I was on my way out, gripping it hard.

"What is that?" she hissed at me.

I blinked, unused to her speaking to me. "Um . . . what . . ."

"That." She pointed at the necklace my father had given me. I'd forgotten to hide it in the collar of my shirt, like I usually did. "Where did you get that?"

"Dad gave it to me."

She sucked in her breath and extended her hand, palm up. "Give it to me."

My hand slipped up to my neck and covered the pendant. "No."

I never said no to either of my parents.

"Elena, give it to me. Now."

"No," I whispered, twisting out of her grip, running to the bus.

Then I thought she'd just been jealous that Dad gave me gifts. Usually, they were things he'd found in the forest: moths, holed stones, a snakeskin. Now that he'd given me something pretty, I thought she was jealous. I don't remember him giving her jewelry.

She wasn't jealous. But I was too young to understand the necklace that would become a collar, tethering me to my dad's dreams.

———

"You've been sprung. I can take you home."

Nick smiled cautiously at me, and I mirrored his smile. I was ready. I didn't like the incessant light of the hospital from bleeping machines and filtering in under the door. It was impossible to sleep with the noises, the clatter of gurneys in the hall, and the din of voices. The hallucinations had died down. The moss and chrysalises withered from the ceiling, and even the snake under my bed vanished, unable to keep me company.

Nick brought me clothes. Not clothes from home—I'd never given him a key to my house—but hospital scrubs and slipper socks. I imagined the sheriff's office had taken my clothes as evidence, to swab for gunpowder residue and the like. I was discharged with bottles of antibiotics and oxycodone.

Outside seemed incredibly bright after the artificial light of the hospital. I climbed into the passenger seat of Nick's silver sports car, wincing as the bandages tugged my skin.

"I can stay with you," he said after he got me settled and started the ignition. He said it very neutrally, so I wouldn't read too much into the offer.

"I appreciate that." I tried to make my voice sound warm. "But I think I need to spend some time alone. Get a real shower. Sleep."

If that hurt him, he didn't react. That was one thing I thought I really liked about Nick. He was unfazed, seemingly invulnerable. I'd come to know, far too late, that was the surface. He would never show when he was hurt. When I hurt him.

He guided his car down two-lane country roads ten miles above the speed limit, gliding unerringly like a bat in the dark. I never chastised him about his speeding. Part of what he liked about this and ER medicine was the thrill.

"How about I order some food? We can have dinner, and then I'll take off."

I nodded. I didn't have much in the refrigerator. "That sounds good. Thanks."

He wound deeper into the forest, to my house. It had been a farmhouse a long time ago, a one-level bungalow that had seen better days. On one side, abandoned horse pasture stretched. On the other side, the woods. I had no neighbors within two miles, which was one of the things I liked about it. The white clapboard siding was in need of replacement, turning green at the bottom with mold. The gutters needed cleaning: maple saplings had begun to grow in them, seeds cast by the sugar maple in the overgrown front yard. My sheriff's office car hadn't been returned to me; only my beat-up SUV was parked in the shade of the maple.

I walked up the two steps to the wooden deck, digging for my keys in the plastic bag the hospital had given me for my personal effects. The sheriff's office hadn't confiscated my purse for evidence, but I could tell they'd been through it: the bills in my billfold were organized by denomination.

"Let me." Nick took the keys from me and opened the door.

I followed him into the darkness of my house.

He took two steps in and stopped, peering into the shadows.

"You haven't changed a bit, Anna."

4

BELONGING

I didn't need to flip on the light. I slipped past Nick, into the darkness of the house. I could navigate this space with my eyes closed.

But my world wasn't his world. I had to remind myself of that. So I turned on the light.

My house was furnished in odds and ends from garage sales and thrift stores. A tufted green velvet couch pressed against the tall windows of the living room. It and the matching chair had come from the estate of a lady who'd been wealthy in the seventies but who'd fallen on hard times before withering away. I slipped my fingers into the back of the couch every so often and came up with odds and ends: a bobby pin, coins, and once part of a postcard from Las Vegas. *Wish you were here.*

The coffee table held a collection of found stones in a candy dish: bits of milky quartz, a shiny piece of green slag, and a handful of flint arrowheads. I would run my fingers over their serrated edges and contemplate how much blood they'd touched.

A vase held a bouquet of bones and lost feathers. I had found them here and there on the property: a crow's feather, a jay's feather, the light bones of a sparrow's wing unfurled. From behind the feathers peered the skull of an opossum. Bones of a pigeon rattled in the bottom of the vase if I picked it up. I remembered the thrill of discovery as I found each item, as if the land had accepted me and willingly gave up its treasures. We conspired together, the land and I, creating this haven.

Looking over the room was a mounted deer head from a garage sale. The wife of the man who'd shot it sold it to me for twenty dollars, ready to have the remains of her ex-husband gone. I took the buck home, lovingly brushed the dirt from his fur, and cleaned his antlers. His glass eyes gazed down at me beneath his long lashes. I talked to him sometimes, imagining him in frost-kissed fields in November, beneath skies speckled with geese flying south.

Below the deer on the fireplace mantel stretched a series of knickknacks. Diplomas. Commendations. A framed crayon drawing a child made for me when I'd rescued her dog from drowning in a pond. She'd drawn me in uniform with an improbably large yellow ponytail and big sunglasses. There was a picture of me with the local Girl Scout troop celebrating Career Day. And another with the high school girls' softball team, where I was assistant coach. I didn't care for publicity, but I liked helping people. I tried to be a good cop. I believed I was a servant of the public, and it was important to approach the job in that spirit of humility.

Nick's observation echoed in my head: *You haven't changed a bit, Anna.* I lifted a shoulder and grimaced as the stitches pulled. "I guess not." Why would I? I was safe here. Happy. Wasn't I?

His expression was wistful. He and I both felt powerfully motivated to help people. We'd seen the dark side of human nature, too, and didn't censor our dark humor. I listened to his stories of the ER and made love to him when he came to my door smelling like death. He accepted that I sometimes needed long stretches of quiet to digest what had happened at work, and he could exist in companiable silence with me. I missed that silence.

"I'm going to take a shower," I said, half expecting him to leave.

"Do you need help?" If anyone else had asked me that, I would have been insulted. He was honestly assessing the situation, and I appreciated that.

"Maybe with the bandages later. If . . ." *If you're sticking around.*

Nick didn't skip a beat. "Okay. I'll order delivery. What would you like?"

My stomach growled. "How about veggie lo mein from Ying's?"

"Still vegetarian?"

"Yep. Thanks." I threaded my way through the small living room to the kitchen. The layout of the house was awkward, but I liked the close feeling of it. It felt safe. I grimaced at a bowl of foraged chicken of the woods mushrooms on the counter that had gone bad during my absence. Regretfully, I dumped them in the trash.

I fished some clothes from the dryer: yoga pants and a T-shirt. I took them to the small bathroom and set them on the sink. I stared at my reflection, at my bruised face stippled with red. My eyelid with stitches in it itched.

Taking a deep breath, I pulled off my clothes. My skin caught and pulled in odd places. I stared down at the bandages and bruises crossing my body. A violet-and-red bruise spread over my chest like a nebula exploding across my ribs. The bulletproof vest had protected me from the worst of the shotgun blast, but injuries peppered my body. Hissing as I pulled bandages from my legs and arms, I saw a constellation of stars wrapping around my body, fastened to my skin by black knots of surgical thread.

I sighed as I stepped into the shower. I wasn't vain and wasn't particularly worried about scars. But seeing these injuries, feeling them, I felt fragile. I'd never gotten hurt in the line of duty before. I winced as hot water pelted down on me, causing those wounds to ignite.

It would get better. It would. I took in a shaky breath and exhaled. I would heal, and things would be exactly as they had been before. Nothing would change. I would feel strong and confident again, I vowed. This was just a fluke. A once-in-a-lifetime incident that I'd quickly put in the rearview mirror.

When I got out of the shower, I wrapped a towel around my torso and called for Nick. He arrived with fistfuls of bandages and antibiotic ointment. He dotted the ointment on the wounds and wrapped them in fresh bandages. I stared down at the trash can containing rusty blood on old bandages.

"Am I going to be okay?" I asked softly. "Like I was before?"

He paused, his finger lingering on the inside of my right elbow. "You're not going to have lasting physical effects. You'll heal."

I nodded, not trusting myself to speak. I worried this experience had changed me, in a way I didn't want to contemplate.

He cupped the back of my head in his hand and enfolded me in a hug. I pressed my cheek against his chest, listening to his heartbeat.

Nick would never lie to me. I wanted to believe in him.

He stayed over, by silent agreement. We ate lo mein in front of the television, watching a comedian complain about modern weddings. I didn't take the pain medication Nick placed on my plate. He saw but didn't comment. I needed to be alert. In control. Not sliding away to that hallucinogenic place of PCP-fueled snakes seething beneath my bed. My hold on reality felt too tenuous.

And when I went to bed, he crawled in beside me, on the right side of the four-poster bed that he used to occupy.

My heart hammered. We'd slipped back into the shell of our relationship so quickly. I told myself that it was because of this unusual circumstance. I could've died. It was understandable that we would both be rattled, that we would want some comfort from each other. Nick had come back, with gentleness, with compassion, even though I'd hurt him. But I didn't deserve that from Nick. Not after how we'd left things. It was my fault, all my fault, and I didn't want to hurt him again.

I stared up at the ceiling. The four-poster bed had come from an auction, dark walnut and smelling faintly of lemon oil. In the middle of summer, when the room was closed up while the air conditioner ran, a faint whiff of tobacco smoke exuded from the pores of the wood, and I imagined a man smoking his pipe in bed until his lungs gave out.

I'd opened the window beside me a crack, so that the night sounds slipped inside. I couldn't sleep. Instead, I listened to the cicadas and crickets calling me in the dark.

———

Nick got paged in the middle of the night.

He always did.

He lurched out of bed, slapped around for the lamp, searched for his shoes, and got ready to head to the hospital.

"Your scrubs are still in the bottom drawer," I said from the bed.

He broke out in a grin. "Really?"

"Yeah." I hadn't exiled him from this place. Not really.

He changed clothes quickly and kissed me on the forehead the way he used to when he was called away. My heart flip-flopped in the cage of my chest to feel that once again.

He must've been operating on autopilot because he jerked back. He flushed and started to mumble an apology. "Look, I'm sorry. I didn't—"

"It's okay," I said, meaning it.

He gave me a hesitant smile.

"There's an extra key on the hook by the door," I told him. I wanted him to have it now when I never had before. Maybe it was because he'd saved my life. Maybe it was because I missed him. I wasn't sure.

"I'll be back later," he promised.

I nodded and smiled, knowing I'd be lucky to see him before noon.

I listened to the screen door swing shut behind him and turned off the lamp. Gravel crunched in the driveway, and I was alone with the dark.

I couldn't sleep. I got out of bed, put on socks and shoes, and a jacket over my T-shirt. Internal Affairs had taken my service 9mm, and I realized how much I didn't like the idea of going out unarmed. I felt vulnerable at the thought. I'd been armed 24-7 for years. I felt naked.

But also oddly exhilarated.

I let myself out of the house and got into my SUV. The moon was heading toward the western horizon, and I nearly forgot to turn on the headlights. Sketchy figures of deer waded in the meadow. I paused for a moment as something pale flickered past my vision: an owl.

I remembered when my dad had driven with Mom and me one winter night. We were traveling down silvery gravel roads like this when something flashed across the windshield. I only caught it out of the corner of my eye, but my dad spun my mom's car out on the gravel, swinging us perpendicular to the road. Mom squeaked and clutched the dashboard. Our headlights silhouetted a tree in the field behind barbed wire.

An owl perched in the tree, wide golden eyes and wings spread. In its talons lay a twitching rabbit, stretched long over a branch.

"That's a great horned owl," he said quietly.

I crept forward, pressing my hand and nose to the back windshield. My breath fogged the glass, and the owl seemed some monstrous, beautiful spirit of nature.

"It's the greatest predator in these woods," he said.

And I believed him.

5

THE SCENE OF THE CRIME

I drove with the windows down, feeling cool night air on my face. I wound over the roads, not seeing a human soul. A fox crossed my path once, pausing to look up at me before he vanished with a flick of his tail into a culvert.

I followed that black ribbon of asphalt to Stroud's Road, to the place where something in me had cracked open. I'd killed a man here. I'd almost lost my life, but I'd taken one, too. I'd faced death and been victorious. My body was battered, but something uncoiled in my gut and slithered up my spine: a sense of power. I had taken a life. I'd chosen to do that. It didn't matter whether I was right or wrong or what the shades of gray were. I was a killer, and that knowledge buzzed in my veins.

I clicked off my headlights and let the pickup drift down the driveway. There were no lights here, no vehicles; the perpetrator's pickup must've been towed for evidence. The night sang quietly around me.

I shut off the engine. I remained still, letting the radiator tick.

I could turn around now. I could crank the engine, turn on the lights, go back out on the main road, and go back to bed. I could be who I'd been days ago. I could go back to being Anna Koray, the good cop who did everything by the book. And I did a good job of being her. I'd worked hard. I'd been of service. I'd put awful people behind bars. I'd saved lives, even. I was a good person and a good cop.

But as hard as I tried to be her, I was afraid I wasn't. Deep down, I was afraid I was my father's daughter.

I reached into the glove box for a pair of gloves. I popped open the door and stepped out, pulling on the latex. I walked lightly, making no sound, as my father had taught me. The gravel shone white, stained in spots by blackness. Crime scene tape on stakes blocked my path.

I peered over the cordon at the first dark spot. That was where I'd been shot, a small, uneven smear. I followed my dried bloody footsteps over to where Tom Sullivan had fallen. This puddle yawned black ink, with a smaller one beside it where I'd collapsed. It was like a black hole, seething, moving . . . I saw beetles within it, crawling over the rough gravel.

I gazed skyward. It hadn't rained yet. And no one had ordered a crime scene cleaner from the nearest city. The rain might wash some of it away, but they'd still have to rake the gravel over, dilute it in this sea of white. There was some disturbance of the stones already. Probably a curious animal, not so different than me, come to investigate the smell of death.

I crouched painfully beside this spot, but it felt inert. I'd already witnessed Tom Sullivan's death, seen that ephemeral something—I guess it was what religious people would call a soul, or scientists would call electrical activity in the brain—slip away. I pressed my gloved palms to the stones and felt only the slightest resonance of it here, now, some low humidity clinging to the ground. It vibrated softly, in a way I couldn't explain.

I stood, inhaling sharply and wincing. I'd almost lost my life here. That hadn't disturbed me nearly as much as what I'd felt when Sullivan died, the ticking of the clock that wound down to silence before my eyes. Alive and then not, that imperceptible shift that meant everything and awakened something in me, a fascination I thought locked safely away and buried. I tried to chalk it up to an overdose of PCP, a chemical warping of reality. But I felt it still, slowly unfurling in my body.

I glanced at the front door, locked up tight and wrapped in yellow crime scene tape. By now, evidence would've been collected. It was unlikely there was anything I could do that would screw things up, but I wanted to be careful.

I went around back, testing windows. My hands were sweating inside the gloves. I came across an unlocked basement window next to a dryer vent.

I crouched before it, wincing. I was in no shape to be stuffing myself into dark holes. But I jammed my feet into that window and slipped through. Stitches pulled, and I felt a couple pop, weeping. My feet landed on top of the dryer, and I scrambled painfully, gracelessly, inside.

My ribs throbbed, and my pulse pounded loudly in my ears, a low steady drumbeat. I smelled fresh blood seeping on my jacket sleeves. I jumped down to the floor, giving my eyes a moment to adjust to the thicker darkness of indoors. I could make out boxes, a furnace, and the smell of mildew.

I climbed the basement stairs to the kitchen. It was hot here. Someone must've turned the air-conditioning off. It smelled of old blood, the way it curdled in heat and began to sour.

My nostrils flared.

I hadn't smelled this much blood since I was a child.

The kitchen was cluttered, with groceries still in bags on the countertops. Dishes lay in the sink. A chair from a dinette set was overturned. And on the floor a black stain spread.

It had been smeared and moved, maybe by paramedics, before it dried. I approached and crouched down before it, imagining the dead woman. Speckles of putrid black ink splattered up on the white-painted cabinets with adhesive markers placed beside them, no doubt indicating the direction and velocity of blood spatter.

The pool moved, seething with buzzing flies. The victim, Cecily Owens, was still alive in that way. She had died and something fed on her death. With gloved fingers, I touched the pool. I closed my eyes, seeing that image of her from the news. She was alive and then gone. What had Tom Sullivan felt when she died? Did he even keep watch? Likely, he was overcome with rage when he pulled the trigger, not focusing on her at all as the blood ticked away and her heart ground to a stop. She might have still even been alive when he darted out of the house to confront me.

Such a waste.

I knew nothing about her, really, only what I'd learned on the news. A stack of library books stood at eye level on the kitchen table, their plastic-wrapped spines glistening. *A Forgotten History of Rome. Subversive Knitting. Mycology for Beginners.* Every word she'd burned into her brain had been lost.

My fingers buzzed, and a flicker of that life moved through me. Maybe some cells in the blood were still bursting, some electron orbits decaying. But I felt it, that power.

I snatched my fingers away, disgusted at myself. I listened to my breathing and the buzzing of the flies in this fetid place.

What had I hoped to find here? I told myself that I probably wanted closure, to feel that what I'd gone through was really over.

Some other part of me probably wanted to confront my mistakes, the deaths I might have been able to prevent.

But the real reason I was here was that I wanted to feel what I'd felt when I'd killed Tom Sullivan. That rush of dark power that moved through me felt so foreign, even though I lived with power. I wore the mantle of societal authority every day, carrying a gun and a badge. But this was a different sort of power.

I wanted to feel the presence of Sullivan's death, and his victim's. I wanted to see if I had hallucinated it all, or if the shadow of death I'd felt there still lingered. I wanted to know if it was real. If this place was haunted or if I was.

I let myself out through the back door, locking it behind me. Cool forest shadows washed over me as I walked around to the front.

A buck stood before me in the darkness. His antlers spread out like hands, ghostly white.

I stopped and gazed upon him, the hair lifting on the back of my neck.

He was unconcerned with me, bending down to chew at grass on the edge of the driveway. He stepped noiselessly back into the forest. He saw nothing out of the ordinary with me being here.

I belonged here, in the dark and the forest and reeking of sticky death.

———

I got home without remembering the drive. I knew only that the moon had set. I scrubbed my hands in hot water until my knuckles were raw. Somehow, my hands were filthy. I hoped to hell I hadn't contaminated that crime scene. It honestly terrified me that I didn't remember the drive back. I hoped that PCP exposure wasn't burning holes in my brain.

38

I got a shovel and dug in a spot outside the southwestern corner of the house. The effort hurt, but I eventually came away with a metal box wrapped in a trash bag.

I took the bundle into the house, unwrapped it, and sank before the cold hearth of the fireplace. I stared at the old ammo box I'd picked up at an army surplus store, too shiny and new to have seen action. I shouldn't have kept anything that was in it. The things inside belonged to Elena, not Anna.

Elena was dead.

Right?

These were things I'd found a couple of years ago, when I started to remember. I'd made copies of microfiche in dusty libraries and clipped pages from old magazines. Yellowed newspaper smelled vaguely moldy. My research was here, gathered in one place and locked away. I buried it outside because I instinctively didn't want it in my house, the way one doesn't store gasoline indoors. But I wanted to know it was there if I wanted it, if I needed it.

There were a few orange-tinted Polaroids. My mother holding me as a baby. A picture of me in a softball uniform. And there were photographs that would've looked like normal family snapshots if they hadn't been printed in magazines. My parents' wedding photograph, them feeding each other cake in a wood-paneled basement. My mother was wearing a short lavender dress, and my father was wearing a suit. Her hair was long, past her waist, and she looked happy. Another picture showed him dressed in camo, kneeling and holding the antlers of a limp deer. The deer's tongue lolled free of his mouth.

I quickly sifted through them and the newspaper clippings. My father's mug shot appeared in many of them, in black and white, showing no expression whatsoever. His eyes were hollow and gray-black, below letters proclaiming THE FOREST STRANGLER

CAPTURED. I knew there were other eyes in the pile, eyes of dead women.

This knowledge pounded behind my temples. I tried so hard to forget. Panicked, I riffled through the contents of the box, searching . . .

There. A plain business card.

I sat back and reached for my cell phone. I dialed the number on the card without looking at it. I had it memorized.

The phone rang. I glanced at the time on my phone. Three fifteen a.m.

My heart pounded. Maybe the number had changed. Maybe it was too late.

A female voice answered, muzzy in sleep. "Hello?"

"Dr. Richardson. It's Anna Koray."

There was a pause.

I closed my eyes and my mouth was dry. "It's Elena Theron."

6

GODS AND MONSTERS

"Where are you?" Dr. Richardson asked, her voice now crisp and awake.

"I'm in Bayern County. At my house."

"What happened?"

I took a deep, quavering breath. "I killed a man."

Silence thundered for a beat before I amended it: "In the line of duty. It was on the news."

"Can you be at my office at eight a.m.?"

"Yes. Are you at the same place?" I stared at the yellowed card.

"Yes." She read me the address.

"I'll be there."

"Good."

The line was disconnected, and I stared at the phone. This was the right thing to do, I told myself. I glanced up at the mantel, looking at the pictures of Detective Lieutenant Anna Koray, smiling. That was the real Anna Koray, and I needed to keep from losing her.

I heard gravel crunching, and headlights washed across my windows.

I scooped the contents of the box back inside and jammed the box into the fireplace, behind some logs half burned to ash. I drew the chain curtain and glass doors shut over it.

I rose to my feet when the door opened and the light flipped on. It was Nick.

His brows drew together when he saw my face. "Anna. What are you doing up?"

I slid my dirty hands behind my back. "I couldn't sleep. Why are you back so soon?" I hadn't been expecting him until noon. Usually when he got called into work he got pulled into extinguishing an ever-escalating list of fires. He never said no to work.

"I took care of the one thing they needed me for. Everything else they can deal with. I needed to be back."

He moved across the floor and touched my face. My face was wet and I hadn't noticed.

"Come here." He pulled me to him, and I rested my head on his chest. He smelled like antiseptic and death.

"It's going to be all right," he murmured.

"It will be," I agreed, because it had to be.

"Come to bed," he invited me, drawing me to the bedroom.

I slid away to wash my hands before climbing into bed beside him. Nick could fall asleep anyplace, at any time. I expected him to be snoring by the time I got comfortable, but he turned over in bed, kicking the covers off his feet. Nick had apparently never been a child who was fearful of monsters grabbing his limbs at night.

I closed my eyes. I envied Nick. I envied that he knew who and what he was, every moment of every day. He was the hero, a doctor.

He saved lives. And when he failed, it wasn't his fault, because he had tried. He and death were well acquainted, but he knew which side he was on.

I thought I knew what side I was on. I thought I was, in my way, on the side of law and light and saving lives in my own small way. I had to make reparations for what my father had done. I was on the right side.

But was I really? The shadow of father's blood ran in my veins.

———

I had no inkling that my dad was a killer.

I only knew that I idolized him.

I was twelve when he took me out on one of our many hikes through the woods. It was early spring, and the earth still smelled like wet snow and mud. The redbuds were almost ready to bloom, and other trees sprouted green. We walked in silence for miles, taking a ridge trail around a ravine.

We took a break on a rock outcropping. Dad removed his rifle from his shoulder and folded his hands in his lap.

"Elena. I'm going to be leaving you soon."

I blinked at him. "Leaving? For a trip?"

"Something like that. But it's likely to be for a very long time."

My brow creased. "Is it for work?"

He shook his head. He placed his hand on my back. "It's something else. Something . . . a lot of people will tell you about. But you'll know the truth."

I didn't like his speaking in riddles. And I didn't like the idea of his leaving me. "I want to go with you."

His hand pressed on my back, and I glanced down at the forest below, my legs swinging into space. I thought I slipped forward, but he caught my collar and drew me back.

43

"No," he said, seeming to be talking to himself. "You can't have her. Not yet."

I blinked at him in confusion. He smoothed my hair back from my face and smiled. "You're the best part of me."

"I don't get it."

"You will." He spread his hand out, scraping the forest horizon. There was brown beneath his fingernails. He must have killed a deer recently. "All of this, the woods . . . it's a living thing."

I squirmed. I knew it was alive, from the microbes in the soil to the salamanders hiding under rocks in the creek to the squirrels nesting above us.

"It's also a dead thing. Eggs hatch and flesh rots. All in service to the spirit of the forest."

I struggled to grasp what he was saying. "Like God?" I didn't know much about a Christian deity. My parents weren't religious. But I'd gone to church a couple of times with one of my classmates and listened to a man in a pulpit recite orders from the divine to the congregation, as if a supreme being whispered directly into the pastor's ear.

"Men don't really understand God. The only god there is is the order of the forest. The coyote hunts the rabbit, devours it, becomes stronger. You understand?"

"I think so. It has to eat."

"But more than that. It takes its strength, but also its spirit. It crunches down its blood and bones and the rabbit becomes its blood and bones."

My brain wandered. "Then . . . what happens when people die?" We didn't eat people, after all.

"When people die in the forest, their spirits go to feed the Forest God, Veles." He watched me carefully.

He'd always talked about spirits of the forest, of fairies and unseen things, so this wasn't too strange. I screwed up my face, trying to understand. "The Forest God eats people?"

"He doesn't consume their flesh. He consumes their spirits. They sustain him. And from him, all of this grows." He spread his hand out below us, at the teeming forest. "From death comes life."

This didn't really sound much different from church, where they muttered about consuming the body of Christ, which tasted bland and papery. "Does the Forest God have a church?"

"No. Wild places are his church. Here, everywhere in the world." His gaze was cloudy, as if he remembered something distant. "I first met Veles many years ago, in a place very far from here. And when you look at him, he looks deep into your soul. He sees you for what you truly are. And you serve."

I was silent, listening to the forest. There was something there. Something otherworldly. I just hadn't been able to put a name to it until now.

His gaze fell on me. "Do you understand?"

"I think so." I thought that this Forest God must've been the spirit that took the acorns from my windowsill, the antlered shadow I glimpsed sometimes in the dark. It wasn't fairies; it was something else.

"Good." He rested his hand on my shoulder. "I'm glad you understand. Most people don't. They think nourishment comes from meat, not from the death. Veles, the old god, understands this."

I felt plenty well fed by the venison my father provided. I looked down at my dirty sneakers. "Is this why you're leaving? The Forest God wants you to go?"

"I've overhunted this place. It's time to find someplace new." His gray eyes crinkled kindly as he smiled at me.

The freezer went empty by February this year. This past fall, he had only brought two does home.

"But you'll come back?" I leaned into his side. He smelled of woodsmoke and dirt.

"I'll always be with you," he promised. "I swear. I'm part of the forest, and I will be part of you."

He sent me home then, alone. I knew the way back; I knew these woods by heart, and he'd taught me to navigate by sun and stars in case I ever got truly lost.

I let myself into the back kitchen door just after sunset. Mom was making soup. She didn't look up at me when I came home.

"Where's your father?"

"Still in the woods."

She nodded once, then reached for the bowls. She didn't care where he was. I resented her for that. She hated him and I didn't know why. Not then. Maybe she did, or maybe she didn't. It was hard to tell what she knew and when she knew it. I didn't know what she suspected or even if she thought much of him at all.

We ate with the television on to fill our silence. The evening news had been full of scary stories for several months. A woman's body had been found in fall, in a nature preserve across the state. She was young and blond, a college-age girl, found murdered. Police called it a ritual murder but provided few details.

Like a trickle, over the next months, more bodies turned up on this side of the state. The police thought they were connected: the women were all blond, young, and posed in strange ways. One was found beside a river, another near an old canal. Police speculated that the killings were connected.

No one knew who the last victim was. They offered a sketch and called her the "Snow Angel." Hikers in a state park found her covered in a blanket of snow at the bottom of a ravine. One of the hikers, a young man, was telling the newscaster:

"Our dog found her . . . and it looked like she'd been there for some time. I brushed the snow away from her face, and . . . her eyes were gone. It looked like hickory nuts in her eye sockets. We took off and called the park rangers."

I shuddered.

Mom watched the news, her spoon clicking against the bowl. "I hope they catch that son of a bitch."

I did, too. Who would do such a thing?

My father remained missing. When he didn't show up to work, his boss called my mom. Mom said he'd left us, and that was that. Word got around my school. Kids made fun of me for not having a dad anymore, especially the boss's kid, Jeff. Once, when I was being taunted at recess, I grabbed a handful of poison ivy and smeared it in Jeff's face. I was immune to the stuff, and he developed a rash that got so bad, he had to be hospitalized.

Mom was furious. She grounded me, the worst punishment she could've chosen. I sat in my room, my fingers winding in the necklace dad had given me, thinking that he wouldn't have allowed this to happen.

But he'd left me. And I was alone.

Mom snatched that necklace from around my neck and threw it in the trash. Late at night, I dug it out and hid it in the loose seam of a teddy bear. I wouldn't allow her to erase that memory of him.

I would open my window a few inches at night to listen to the sounds of the dark. I'd sometimes hear footsteps outside and I'd rush to the window, thinking it was my dad. But there was nothing there.

Not even the acorns.

Just sets of wet footprints that trailed off into the woods. I tried to follow them, but they dissipated like fog.

In the middle of a late spring night, I awoke to knocking on the

NICOLA SOLVINIC

front door. Mom went to answer it, and I heard male voices. I cracked my bedroom door open to listen.

Police. There were men in blue uniforms and dark suits that looked like cops in television shows.

"Mrs. Theron, my name's Agent Chandler. Is Stephen home?"

"No. He hasn't been home for a month," she murmured.

One of the cops talked into his radio about "relaxing the perimeter."

"Do you know where he is?"

"No. He just didn't come home." I heard her take a deep breath. "What's this about?"

"We found some evidence that suggests your husband might be involved with a murder."

7

POISON IVY

I peered through the cracked door, down the hall, and saw my mom standing rigidly, her arms crossed over her robe.

"Who was it?" she whispered.

"Her name was Emily Marsh. She was a waitress at a truck stop in the northern part of the state."

Mom sank down to the plaid couch, her face unreadable.

"Mrs. Theron, did you know this woman?" Agent Chandler showed her a picture I couldn't see.

Mom shook her head. "No. How . . . how did this happen? Did he kill her?"

The agent took a deep breath. "Trace evidence suggests he did. And not just her."

I burst from my room, my hands curled into fists. "My father would never do anything like that. Get out!"

I stood in the living room, surrounded by all the cops staring at me. I think they expected my mom to comfort me, but she sat woodenly on the couch. My voice echoed against the stamped ceiling, and no one spoke. Until a man with brown hair and FBI letters on his jacket knelt before me. He had a German shepherd wearing a vest with him. The dog sat and watched me, still as a statue.

"I'm Aaron Parkes. Would it be all right if I talked with you?" He glanced at my mom, who gave him a curt nod.

Adults rarely asked me what I wanted. Maybe this was my chance to set the record straight. "Yeah," I said, at a lower volume. "If I can pet your dog."

The adults began to speak again, in low voices. Agent Parkes whispered a command to the dog, and the dog approached me, tail wagging and tongue lolling. I rubbed the dog's ears and grinned at it.

"What's your name?" he asked.

"Elena," I said, focusing on the dog. If he thought I was going to tell him my father was a monster, there was no way I would. "What's the dog's name?"

"His name is Percival."

"Like the knight?"

The agent seemed taken off guard, but I was a kid who had read every book in the school library. "Yes. Like the knight. Do you have any pets?"

I shook my head. "No."

The men behind me were asking my mom if my dad cheated on her, if there was a girlfriend he might be holed up with.

Parkes flinched and said, "How about you show me your room?"

I led him down the hallway. Other cops were filtering into my parents' bedroom, the bathroom, down to the basement. Someone pulled down the ladder to the attic in the hallway and I heard footsteps banging above us. Past the windows in my bedroom, flashlight beams bounced.

I sat on the edge of my bed. Percival lay down beside me and rested his head on my knee. Parkes pushed the door shut, and the sounds of my house being ransacked were muffled.

He sat on the floor beside my closet and gazed around my room, taking in the lavender paint that Dad had allowed me to pick out. His gaze slipped over the posters on the walls, the books stacked on the dresser, and the mason jars on the windowsill containing stones, pieces of antlers, and feathers. His gaze stopped there.

"He's not a monster," I said. "He's my dad."

"Nobody said your dad's a monster. We just want to find him. And get him some help."

My gaze narrowed. "Help for what?"

"Help for why he ran away. For whatever reason, he left."

"He's never been around much. But that doesn't mean he hurt anyone."

"We need to talk to him. If he didn't, then he can clear this up. If he did, he needs help."

I rubbed my eye, stubborn. "My dad never hurt anyone."

"We need to find him before he hurts himself or someone else hurts him. Do you know where he is?"

"No," I told him quickly, petting the dog.

"I get the sense that you and your dad were close."

"Yeah." My chin jutted out defiantly.

"What kinds of things do you guys talk about?"

"We go on hikes in the woods. We talk about animal tracks, how to tell opossum from raccoon tracks. Those are tricky."

"I can't tell the difference," he admitted. "What else do you talk about?"

"Stars. Constellations. Phases of the moon." I was eager to tell Parkes that my dad was a gentle and smart man, not a killer.

Parkes paused. "The moon, huh?"

"Yeah. The full moon this month is the Hare Moon."

"Cool. I didn't know that."

"My dad knows lots of cool stuff. All the names of the moons. Where the deer sleep." I looked down at the dog leaning against my leg and rubbed his ears.

"When was the last time you saw your dad?"

I closed my eyes. "Four weeks ago. Right after the Worm Moon."

"Where did you last see him?"

I didn't say anything.

"Elena, I don't want you to tell me where he is. Just where he was."

I stayed quiet.

Parkes crouched before me. "I'm not going to lie to you, Elena. If I find him, I'll arrest him. It's my job to learn about men like him, to get into their heads and track them down. I won't hurt him. But I can't make that guarantee if anyone else finds him."

I looked at him. I was aware, on some level, I was being tricked. But he seemed nice enough.

"I've haven't fired my weapon once in my whole career." He raised three fingers of his right hand. "Scout's honor."

I listened to the boots pounding on the ceiling above us and the violent crash of a lamp hitting the floor in my parents' bedroom.

"I can show you where I last saw him," I said quietly.

Parkes sat back on his heels. "You're a good girl, Elena."

At least, I thought so at the time.

He left the room so I could dress, but Percival remained. I pulled jeans on, put on a sweatshirt, and dragged my hiking boots and socks out of the closet. I reached for a camo jacket that belonged to my dad. I shrugged into it, and tears sprang to my eyes as I thought of how it smelled of him: woodsmoke and leaf mold.

Percival cocked his head and whined at me.

"You're not going to hurt him, are you, Percival?"

Percival gazed at me with solemn eyes. I felt like I could trust the dog.

I opened the door to find Parkes talking into his radio. He stopped when I came out and looked at me. "Is that your dad's jacket?"

I sank into it. "Yeah."

He nodded. "Okay. Why don't you show me and Percival where you last saw him? Do you think you can do it in the dark?"

"Yeah," I answered crankily. I knew the woods inside and out, by sun- and moonlight. I wasn't a baby.

"Okay." He reached into his pocket for a flashlight. "Show us."

On our way out, he paused in the living room to speak to my mom. She still hadn't moved. Her gaze slipped from him to me. She nodded.

And we headed out the back door, into the dark.

Well, it should've been dark. Red and blue strobe lights cast jumping shadows through the trees. Overhead, a noisy light churned, one that thundered away scraps of conversation among the people milling around the house: a helicopter, I realized. It felt surreal, swimming in light and shadow, way past my bedtime. I froze.

Parkes's hand rested on my shoulder. "It's okay. Just ignore them."

I took a deep breath and turned toward the woods, into that welcoming darkness.

The trees closed over me, and I walked fast. I wanted to get away from all the churn and the haze of accusations against my father. I plunged into the night, running, tears streaming across my cheeks. I'd considered running away before, especially when it was clear my dad had left me alone with Mom. I knew all the caves for miles and miles, could forage mushrooms, wild onion, berries, sunchokes, and fiddleheads. I could escape, the way my dad had, never to return to civilization.

I ran until the breath burned in my throat and the stars careened dizzily overhead. I was beyond the reach of the helicopters and police lights now. I was alone with the bats, an owl, and mice skittering through the leaf debris.

I was far past the spot where I had that last conversation with my dad. I paused, taking a deep, ragged breath. I heard nothing around me. I continued onward, pushing into the night and my freedom.

I was well off our property now, and I moved for hours, sliding among the branches and brush. I was on the edge of state land, but I moved west, into private land. Based on what I'd seen on television, I figured the cops couldn't come here without a warrant, right?

This place smelled green, like the earth twitching life forward. Grass blades pushed through the mud, and the tree buds had unfurled. Fragrant redbud branches stretched overhead as I climbed over the remains of a fallen apple tree. Once, long ago, this tree had belonged to someone. With years of neglect, it had collapsed under the weight of its own apples in the fall. But it was still alive, soft leaves emerging from the scaled bark.

There.

A small house stood, barely. Nobody had lived in this house for decades. The windows were long shattered, and the roof had caved in. The wooden siding had rotted, buckling and bowing as it softened. Pitcher plants surrounded its rotting foundations, their glistening mouths open to the sky.

The front door didn't fit the frame anymore. I pulled it open, tugging hard as the corner snagged on the ground. I made just enough space to worm in and push the door closed behind me. My breath echoed in my head, and I wrapped my arms around myself.

No one knew this place existed. Not the absentee landowner. Not the local hunters, who likely obeyed the NO TRESPASSING signs posted at the edge of the property, miles away.

No one knew about it but me and my dad.

We'd found this place when I was eight. Well, Dad found it. I'd skipped on by, intent on following deer tracks. I realized he wasn't following me after a few moments, and I turned back. He was squinting at something in the summer greenness. I peered in that direction and saw what he was looking at: a shack with a carpet of leaves covering the dented roof, walls covered in moss. A blackened chimney reached a finger to the sky, charred as if it had been struck by lightning.

He forced the door open and we went inside. There was peeling wallpaper here, speckled with black soot and mildew, and a rusted cast-iron stove. The area around the stove was burnt, as if it had caught fire when lightning struck. The floor was rotted, and saplings grew up from the floor to a hole in the roof, through which the sun shone.

"Is this a fairy house?" I asked, my head full of stories I'd read in a library book.

"Yes," he said, decisively.

I looked around nervously. "Fairies can be mean." I knew they stole children; the books said so.

He laughed softly. "They can be mean, but I'll protect you.

Look." He pointed at the rusted red stove. A forgotten pot sat on it, growing poison ivy.

"That's what they eat," he said.

I eyed the poison ivy. I didn't get a rash, but I still wouldn't eat it. I screwed up my face.

"It won't hurt you. You're immune, remember?"

I nodded.

"That means you've got the fairy blood."

I looked up at him. "You do, too?"

He chuckled. "I suppose so."

I knew he was telling me a story then, like the stories he spun when we walked in the woods, about how trees whispered in the summer. How talking catfish swam in the rivers. How opossums danced under full moons, and how bees made hives only in stumps that belonged to trees struck by lightning. It had that same cadence, then, that gauzy substance of a lie made for my entertainment.

Funny that his story about the Forest God didn't sound like that. It didn't sound like a lie.

Now that house was still. The hole in the roof had widened, allowing moonlight to beam in. And it stank, I realized. Like roadkill.

I let my eyes adjust, making out the sagging walls and the rusted stove.

And I realized that I wasn't alone.

8

FASCINATED

I climbed out of bed before dawn. I picked stained bandages from my skin, showered, re-bandaged, and dressed in black yoga pants and a loose black tunic. My skin was tender today, and I didn't want my blood to seep into lighter-colored clothes.

I padded back to my bedroom to find Nick awake in bed, watching me.

"You should be resting," he said.

"So should you." My gaze settled on the circles under his eyes. His lack of sleep worried me.

"Where are you going?" he asked, brow creased.

I lifted my chin. "I'm going to an appointment with my therapist." I hadn't seen her in years, but she was still my therapist.

"Oh." He ran his fingers through his hair. "I didn't know you were seeing a therapist now. But that's good, you know?"

"Have you ever seen one?" He flinched when I asked.

"Yeah. A long time ago, though. I lost a patient, and it stirred some stuff up." He met my gaze. "I think it's good that you're going."

I nodded. I didn't need his approval for this, but was glad he was supportive.

"Let me find my pants and I'll drive . . ."

I shook my head. "Her office is a couple hours away."

"I don't mind."

I smiled, bent, and kissed his forehead. "I know you don't. But I can do this, truly."

"I don't love the idea of you driving on pain meds." His brow creased in concern.

"I've just taken ibuprofen. Nothing else."

He frowned at me. "Anna. You should be closely observed. You're wounded, and you got exposed to enough hallucinogenic drugs to fell an elephant. I want to be there for you."

I took a deep breath and reached for his hand. I knew what it cost him to be in my life again. I'd hurt him badly, and he still trusted me. But maybe he shouldn't. "This is something I need to do for myself, okay? And if I wanted anyone to come with, it would be you."

He nodded. "I get it. Text me when you get there?"

"I will," I promised.

"I'm off tonight. I'll bring dinner."

I kissed him. His mouth was warm, and I wanted him there. In my bed. Getting crumbs in my couch. Dressing my wounds.

But I did not want him in this therapist's office.

I left when the clouds still gathered close to the ground, a dense mist. My SUV climbed up from my gravel drive to a two-lane road, then to the interstate. I had to stop for gas; my tank was nearly on E, though I swore it was full just yesterday. I tapped on the gauge, frowning. The mileage looked weird to me, too. I decided to cut myself some slack; I wasn't firing on all cylinders, and that was okay.

When I got out to the open road, I rolled the windows down and let the wind roar in my ears. It distracted me some from the aches in my body.

Nick was probably right. I had no business, from a physical standpoint, haring off across county lines to the city.

But I needed to go. Even though sunshine warmed my face now, darkness gathered in my head. Before, I'd felt the echoes of my father's crimes in my life, just a soft reverberation. There was nothing new animating those shadows. But now . . . now, everything had changed. That soft whisper had become a roar, and I needed Dr. Richardson to help me.

Traffic thickened the closer I got to the city, and I plugged Dr. Richardson's address into my GPS. I wound around construction, a traffic jam, and managed to get into the parking lot of the bland building in an office park with five minutes to spare. I shut off the ignition, texted Nick that I'd arrived safely, and winced when I stepped down to the pavement. I dumped some ibuprofen into my hand and swallowed them dry. When I got home, I promised myself, I would take the oxycodone tablets Nick gave me. But, for now, I needed to be in control to drive, and pain kept me sharp.

But now . . . I faced the concrete office building. It had been built in the midst of some brutalist architectural period, devoid of organic lines or personality. I let myself into the empty lobby, then moved down a hallway on the first floor.

Dr. Richardson was waiting, her door propped open. She was a petite woman with silvery-blond hair cut in a bob, and she was dressed in a sweater and tailored jeans. She looked much the way I remembered her, perfect eyeliner and glasses resting on the bridge of her nose.

"Anna. It's good to see you," she said.

I nodded and followed her to her office.

A desk and chair were pressed against the wall beside an ancient file cabinet. There was no computer here; I remembered that she always preferred paper files. There was a leather couch along the opposite side of the room, while abstract paintings adorned the walls. A white noise machine played in the other corner, masking our voices from any eavesdroppers. A coffee table before the couch held a bottled water and an Ansel Adams photography book.

I sat down on the couch and watched the bottle sweat onto the glass.

Dr. Richardson settled into her chair and turned toward me. "It's been a long time since I've seen you."

"Two years," I said. I had stopped going to her when I started remembering my childhood. Dr. Richardson was too tangled in the past, and I needed space from it.

She nodded. "I hoped you were doing well."

"I was. I was doing well." I took a deep breath. I thought briefly of Nick. I was better with him than without him, but I couldn't really be with him. Not all of me . . .

"Still at the sheriff's office?"

"I was promoted last year, to lieutenant."

"Congratulations."

She leaned forward in her chair and rested her elbows on her knees. "But that's not why you're here. You said there was a death."

I sank back against that familiar couch. I closed my eyes and told her what had happened. I told her how I had killed that man, and how I felt, and the acrid smell of white dust in my sinuses. I told her that I'd returned to the house the previous night, feeling fresh death swirling around me. I told her about the buck I'd seen, watching me in the moonlight.

When I opened my eyes, she was watching me, a faint wrinkle forming between her brows. "And you're concerned that your reaction to this event is not normal?"

"Yeah." My shoulders sagged. "I'm afraid that I'm . . . fascinated. Like something in my head is going to come spilling out and I won't be able to control it."

"Take a deep breath," Dr. Richardson said, and I obeyed. "You've experienced a psychologically traumatic event, compounded by exposure to a foreign chemical agent."

"But I should get over that, shouldn't I? It's worn off."

"Not necessarily. The trauma of causing a death lingers. And as for the hallucinogen . . . that can linger in your mind, too, even after you pass a drug test. You might experience effects from it months from now, flashbacks that we can't predict from this vantage point."

I shook my head. No. I was not willing to relinquish control of my life to memory and fear.

She gave me a reassuring smile. "I've been treating you since you were a child. You were a kind, conscientious girl. You've grown into an empathetic, responsible adult."

I released the breath I'd been holding. "I'm trying."

"You're still a vegetarian?"

"Yes."

"You're serving your community and doing a good job. How's your romantic life?"

I twiddled my thumbs. "There's someone. I care about him. But I'm not sure what the next step should be."

"Well, that's a refreshingly common enough relationship issue." A smile played at the corner of her mouth. "Another cop?"

"No, a doctor."

"Someone else with empathy who serves." She nodded sharply. "That could be very good for you."

I looked away. "I can't be myself with him. Not all of myself."

"It's an act of vulnerability to be authentic with another person. And even more so for you," Dr. Richardson observed. "But you're not here for that. You're here about last night."

I took a deep breath. "What I felt last night . . . it's not normal."

"No one ever has a normal reaction to death," Dr. Richardson said. "Some people cry. Some are sickened. Some feel nothing at all, for a little while or a long while. This is the first time you've been so close to death."

I paused, looking at her. "That's not true though, is it?"

She seemed to stop breathing. "Anna, how much do you remember from your childhood?"

"Bits and pieces." Some were soft and distant; others were sharp and proximate. "I remember my father and my mother."

"What else?"

"I remember what he did."

Dr. Richardson's face was a mask. "I'm surprised you recall that."

I crossed my arms over my chest. "I know you tried your best to erase that."

Dr. Richardson leaned forward and rested her chin in her hands. "To be honest, I don't know if that was the right thing to do."

I said nothing. I wasn't sure, either.

"Your mother asked me to try to block out the memories of your father," she said slowly. "She explained it to me, and at the time I agreed that a child shouldn't be subjected to the weight of such horrible things. And you . . . you were faltering. I remember seeing a girl in the institution who was completely shattered. I told your mother there were no guarantees, but I did my best."

"And it worked, for many years," I said softly. "The memories started coming back about two years ago."

"I didn't know."

Because I didn't tell you.

"I wasn't sure they were real." I clasped my hands around my knee. "But I did some research. And my adoptive mother gave me some pictures that my biological mother left for me at the time I was adopted." Slowly, I had gathered articles and newspaper clippings and put them and Dr. Richardson's business card into the ammo box and buried it. These things grew into a collection of evidence, things I couldn't ignore even though they were out of my sight.

"I'm so sorry, Anna."

We sat in silence for a few moments.

"What did you do to me?" I asked, my voice sounding small. But bile rose in my throat.

9

BURGLED MEMORY VAULT

She rested her hands, palms up, in her lap. "Your mother came to me and told me who your father was. I placed you under hypnosis and asked you to remember him. As each memory came forth, I asked you to lock it away in a sort of memory vault."

"'Memory vault'?"

"It's my own experimentation with the method of loci. The ancient Greeks organized memories in an imagined physical terrain to enhance memory. A very elaborate mnemonic device, actually. I tried the reverse with you. We placed the memories of your father in a physical structure in your head, locked it up, and threw away the key."

I frowned. "I don't remember any vault."

"It wasn't a mental bank vault, in your case. And I won't tell you what it was, unless you want to access all those memories and you instruct me to. But it seems ghosts are leaking out of that vault." She steepled her fingers together. "What do you remember about him?"

"That he was the Forest Strangler. That we spent time hiking in the woods. That my mother tried to keep me away from him, but she just . . . gave up after a while." I told her what I recalled, trying to be as factual as possible. I didn't want to be mired in emotions of those memories.

"Do these recollections happen spontaneously during your day? Or in dreams?"

"Both. Once they started surfacing, I did research, too. Just what was available in the press."

Dr. Richardson's mouth flattened. "Did you use law enforcement resources to find more details?"

I shook my head. "No. That would've been a breach of ethics that could get me fired. We're not allowed to dip into LEADS or records unrelated to our own cases for any reason." The Law Enforcement Automated Data System logged everyone who accessed it. If someone abused it, there would be a trail.

She smiled and nodded at me. "You're following the rules. Which is more than many people in your position do."

"Yes." Cops often dug into records for information on ex-partners, family, and out of pure nosiness. When one of the patrol deputies pulled over a politician last year, I didn't look at the file. It was none of my business. But others did. I was trying—*trying*—to be a good cop.

She asked: "What would you like for me to do now to help you?"

I blinked at her. I suppose I'd come to her for help, right? But I had no idea what kind of shape that kind of help might take. "Um. What are my options?"

She leaned back in her chair. "Well, you could report me to the board, and I would likely be stripped of my license and retire early. That would be entirely justified and would ensure that I never experimented on anyone's memories again. Or I could transfer you to another psychiatrist's care."

I shook my head. I wanted neither of those things. "You know me better than anyone else does. I . . . don't have the energy to start over with someone else. And I've got no desire to punish you."

She folded her hands. "We could work to uncover more memories of your father. Open up your memory vault. Or I could put you under hypnosis again and try to lock those stray memories away from you again, to reinforce the walls of that vault, and you could go on as you were before, remembering nothing."

My mouth went dry. "I didn't know that was an option . . . to try and bury him again."

I felt a moment of elation, of power, of fear. I could remove my father from my life, entirely. I just had to choose to do it. I could make this all go away.

She lifted a shoulder. "There's been more research in hypnotherapy, and with hallucinogenic substances. Much of it with mixed efficacy. But there's no reason to think that what we did with you as a child couldn't be reproduced again. We'd just have to be careful to maintain the results to prevent relapse."

Relapse. Remembering my whole life was a relapse. I closed my eyes.

"Or we can deal with things as they come up."

"I'm not sure what I want to do. I just . . ." I looked down at my hands. "I just need to know that I'm not going to become what he was."

Dr. Richardson shook her head and placed her hands around mine. She smiled at me reassuringly. "You won't. You are your own person. Remember that."

———

Dr. Richardson had confidence in me—more than I had in myself. Perhaps she knew me better than I did. She knew those locked-away nooks and crannies I was now excavating. Somehow they existed in her memory and undoubtedly in her notes.

But did I want them? Did I want to know everything, or did I want to go back to where I was before, living an ordinary life?

I paused when I reached my SUV in the parking lot. There was something underneath my windshield wiper. I plucked back the wiper and pulled out a sprig of poison ivy.

I stared at it, then scanned the empty parking lot. I twirled it in my fingers. Perhaps it had just gotten caught under my wiper blade and I hadn't noticed it until now. Probably.

But it still made me shudder, remembering that I was immune to it. No one would know that.

Just a coincidence, I told myself.

I chewed my lip on the drive home, dipping into my memories that I hadn't locked away. I remembered college clearly, picking criminology as my major. When my adoptive mother asked me why I chose that, I wasn't sure what to tell her. I told her I wanted to help people. That was true; I felt it in my bones, even now. But I didn't know why.

Maybe . . . I was trying to atone in some way for what my father did. Perhaps subconscious guilt chewed away at me. Or perhaps I was determined to be the opposite of what he was. I didn't know the answer, only supposed that it worked at a subconscious level, an undercurrent I hadn't been fully aware of.

I would have to talk to Dr. Richardson about this.

Tired of my eddying thoughts, I flipped on the radio. I zipped around the radio stations until I paused on the local news when I got in range:

". . . body of an unidentified young woman found along Route 80 and Churchwell Road."

I frowned. That was a remote corner of Bayern County. Not much there but farms and woods.

"Sources say the woman was found by hunters in a dry creek bed. The men who found the woman's body reported that it was mutilated. Her hands were reportedly folded on her chest, holding a bouquet of goldenrod, and her eyes were removed and replaced with chestnuts . . ."

Oh, God. My heart pounded. That sounded like my father's work.

A horn blared at me, and I realized I'd veered across the double yellow line. I yanked the steering wheel back just in time to avoid striking a truck head-on.

I clutched the wheel and hunched over it, my wounds screaming.

"What the fuck?" I whispered to myself, wondering how the hell they'd managed to leak those salacious details to the news.

I took the back way in to Bayern County. I took Route 80, through flatter farmland that met late-summer forest. I wound down dirt roads until the road was closed by a roadblock. A news van was parked by the black-and-white sawhorses. I nodded when I saw the local news team there.

But I suppressed a grimace when I saw a gray van parked next to it. Cas Russo glanced in his rearview mirror at me, not a hair out of place from his K-pop style and his shiny jacket. Cas ran a YouTube channel, fancied himself to be a ghost hunter on the weekends and an investigative journalist on weekdays. He popped his door open and stepped in front of my truck. He lifted a small camcorder in his fist the way a soldier might hold a grenade.

"Lieutenant Koray. Surprised to see you up and about." He grinned at me.

I nodded at him behind my sunglasses.

"Care to comment about the shooting on Stroud's Road?"

I shook my head. We had a media spokesperson for this stuff. Someone more gregarious than me who could think on their feet.

He wasn't deterred. He approached the driver's-side window. "I hear you overdid it when you shot Tom Sullivan. Panicked. Filled him full of lead until your clip went empty."

My mouth flattened. I wasn't going to take the bait. Panicked was not what I'd felt. Bizarrely, I was peacefully in control, listening to blood ring in my ears.

"No comment at this time," I said. Though I really wanted to tell him to shut his piehole.

"Are you here on official business?"

I didn't say anything but rolled on past him to the deputy manning the roadblock.

I heard Cas shouting behind me: "Aren't you supposed to be on admin leave?"

I flashed my badge at the deputy and she let me pass. I saw a couple of sheriff's cars with the evidence van pulled off by the side of the road. I parked behind the van and winced as I got out of the SUV. My hand slipped to my elbow, which had become sticky. *I should go home*, I told myself. *I should . . .*

"Lieutenant Koray?"

I looked up to see another deputy approaching me. He was one of the shiny new deputies from last year's class. He looked like he was about twelve to me.

"Deputy Detwiler," I acknowledged. "I heard you got some action on the radio. I was in the neighborhood and thought I'd drop by to see if you guys needed anything."

"Lieutenant, I thought you were still in the hospital—"

"I got sprung. On my way back from a doctor's appointment." I glanced into the forest. "What've you guys got here?"

I shouldn't have been here. But I knew that even though it was against the rules, cops often were lookie-loos at gruesome scenes.

"Weird shit, El-Tee," he said. He looked a little green and he smelled like vomit.

"Who's the CO on the scene?"

"Captain Wozniak, ma'am."

Captain Wozniak had been my field trainer back in my patrol days. She was the only other woman at lieutenant rank or above in the department. I was pretty sure she'd humor me.

"Can you take me to her?"

"Of course, ma'am."

I minced over the ditch and followed Detwiler into the woods. A deer path had been matted down by many sets of boots. After about a mile, my wounds were screaming. I didn't show it to Detwiler, though he kept it slow going, for which I was grateful. I owed the kid a favor.

Finally, we reached a dry creek bed covered in leaves. Yellow crime scene tape tangled around trees, and two evidence technicians combed the forest floor. My attention was arrested by a tarp covering what was presumably a body cradled in the creek. The scene smelled like vomit. I wondered where Detwiler had barfed so I could avoid it.

But there was something about this place, something familiar. It felt secluded, protected from the outside world, shielded from

70

the sun with the shiver of leaves. Warm breeze stirred my pony-tail, and I was overcome for a moment by a woozy sense of déjà vu. I'd spent a lot of time in the woods as a girl. Maybe they all looked the same after a while.

Monica Wozniak stood on the creek bank, outside the yellow caution tape, smoking a cigarette. She turned at my approach, and her red lips twisted in concern.

"Girl, you should be at home resting up."

"Yeah . . . probably. But I was in the neighborhood and got curious."

Monica tapped ash from her cigarette. "You know what they say about curiosity and cats and shit."

I jammed my hands in the pockets of my track jacket. "The news said some hunters found something weird."

Monica took a deep drag. "Really weird. Two hunters were looking for squirrel, stumbled across a body. They gave a vague description of a figure in a hoodie retreating from a distance—no specifics on age, sex, or other identifying characteristics. They lost their shit and called 911. Then deputies came out and lost *their* shit."

My least favorite deputy, Corporal Rollins, elbowed Detwiler. "This fucking pussy barfed so hard he almost passed out."

Detwiler flushed red.

"Knock it off, Rollins," I said. As the owner and operator of a pussy, I really wanted to tell him to fuck off, but I restrained myself.

Rollins sneered and stalked off.

Monica blew out smoke that clung in a menthol-scented halo around her dark hair. I thought she'd quit, but she was going at it like a dragon. She continued, "One thing I can say for certain now: it's murder."

We all stared at the tarp.

I shifted my weight from foot to foot. "Can I, uh, take a look?"

She glanced sidelong at me. "You're supposed to be on leave, Anna."

"Mmm, yeah. I am."

"I'll make a bet with you," she said at last. "You take a peek. If you barf like Detwiler, you owe me a steak dinner and first pick of positions on the department softball team. If you don't, I'll buy and you get first pick."

That was fair. "Sure."

I stepped forward, toward the crime scene tape.

"Hey," Monica said, kicking at a plastic bucket. "Take this with you."

I grabbed the bucket and headed toward the scene. I paused and made eye contact with the nearest evidence tech. He waved me through.

"Just don't touch anything," he warned.

I followed behind him, holding the bucket. My heart pounded. His shoes crunched on the ground, but my footsteps made no sound.

He knelt beside the body, pulled back the tarp, and looked away. The soft smell of decomposition wafted up.

I stared down.

A nude woman lay in the creek bed. She hadn't been there for long; her body didn't show any obvious signs of decay. She was nude, with her hands arranged over her chest. She held a bouquet of wilted goldenrod limply molded to her breasts like a plate of armor. Something had chewed on her leg. More flower petals were stuck to her body in curling designs.

I looked at her face. A crown of limp asters circled her head.

72

Her face was swollen, and she gazed back at me with dark chestnut eyes. The eyeballs themselves were gone, but the lashes framed the chestnuts in an unsettling way, wide-open and curiously alive looking. Her lips were purple and slack. Below her chin, her throat was blackened—whether from injury or the beginnings of decomposition, I couldn't tell.

But I felt death, heavy and clinging to this place. Just like it did when I killed Tom Sullivan. I stared into those dark chestnut eyes, feeling the stillness settle over her.

My heart beat, slow and steady. I took a step back and nodded at the tech, who covered the body back up.

I turned and trudged back to Monica and Detwiler with my empty bucket. Detwiler had his back turned. I didn't comment on it and placed the bucket down on the ground.

Monica nodded at me. "You're tough, girl. Tough enough to earn a steak dinner."

Steak held no appeal for me. "How about Indian?"

"That's good, too."

Monica ground out a cigarette under her heel and tapped another out of the crumpled pack in her jacket pocket. She was halfway through the pack. She took the cigarette between her lips and lit it. I saw her fingers shake for only a moment before she put the lighter away.

"Any idea who she is?" I asked.

"Techs should be able to get some DNA from her to make an ID. Whoever she is, this is beyond my pay grade. I'm gonna ask Chief to call in the state Bureau of Criminal Investigation for assistance. This is all kinds of fucked-up."

"What the actual hell happened to her?" I glanced over my shoulder.

Monica exhaled more smoke. "It sure as hell looks like something the Forest Strangler woulda done, doesn't it?"

"That's not possible," I said quietly.

"I know." She looked up at the sky. "I think what we've got here is some kind of fucked-up copycat, and I sure as hell am not gonna put up with that kind of monster in my jurisdiction."

10

PAINKILLERS

My hands shook. I stuffed them in my pockets so no one would see. I took off quietly, winding my way back to my SUV. Detwiler came with me, no doubt relieved to have escaped. I wasn't certain if Rollins or the crime scene itself was the worst of the evils for him.

Cas was waiting for me, leaning up against the roadblock. "The hunters that found the body said it was all kinds of fucked-up. Like the Forest Strangler." His eyes glistened, and I couldn't imagine how gruesome his videos were going to get.

I lowered my head, refusing to respond, and looked ahead of myself with that thousand-yard stare behind sunglasses that all cops perfect over time. I wouldn't let him see how rattled I was. I made a beeline for my SUV.

Detwiler came between me and Cas. "Simmer down, Mr. Russo."

"You know you're bleeding, right?" Cas called.

I paused and glanced down, a reflex. The top of my right thigh, covered by black yoga pants, was shiny.

"You get hurt as bad as they said? Or is it that time of the month?"

I wasn't going to reward him with a reaction. Guys like Cas ran their mouths until someone clocked them, then cackled about it on their video feeds while the pennies rolled in.

Detwiler ordered him to leave, and Cas argued about public roadways belonging to the public. The local news crew stayed at a respectful distance and sipped their coffee. I had no doubt they were listening closely, though. The local news station was more respectful than Cas, and that was why they got invited to press conferences and Cas didn't. But they still had their ears to the ground.

I climbed into the SUV and I backed out, white knuckling the steering wheel. My hands were shaking too hard. I was sweating and my clothes stuck to me. I didn't know what was sweat and what was blood. I hurt, and I felt like I was drowning. I cranked up the AC.

I had no business being out of bed.

I drove straight home, chewing my lip until I tasted blood.

It's a copycat, I told myself. Some sick fucker dying for attention. Somebody who would bring Stephen Theron, the Forest Strangler, back into the public eye. Didn't that happen with the Zodiac Killer? Wasn't there a copycat?

My breath echoed in my throat. I got home without remembering the drive. Nick's car was gone, which was good. I couldn't deal with his kindness right now.

I let myself inside and locked the door. I dropped the keys three times, finally got my shit together, and blew out my breath.

Get a grip, Anna.

I made it to the bathroom, pulled my hair back, and washed my bruised face. I looked up at the medicine cabinet, seeing my father's eyes staring back at me.

It couldn't be my father who'd killed that woman in the forest. But it sure looked like his work. At a gut level, I didn't think anyone could ever duplicate it. No one else had an eye for such detail.

I grabbed the bottle of painkillers Nick had prescribed for me. I tapped out a couple pills and swallowed them. Then I began peeling away my clothes, letting them fall to the floor in shadowy puddles that smelled like copper.

I groaned when I saw I'd popped a couple more stitches. I dabbed at those with gauze and tried to put the edges together with butterfly bandages. Those didn't hold and popped off immediately. With a growl, I put antibiotic ointment on them.

I dumped my clothes in the bathtub and ran cold water on them to get the blood out. I swished them around with my toe before I let them soak.

I grabbed a fluffy robe from the back of the door, wrapped myself in it, and climbed into bed. I texted Nick that I was home and pulled the covers up to my chin.

For the first time in a very long time, I felt unsafe.

I could accept the idea that someone would copy my father. I could even accept that it could happen in this jurisdiction, near my father's regular hunting grounds.

But a small, selfish, terrible part of me hoped it was him—that he was back with me once more.

———

I wasn't alone in that fallen-down house in the woods.

My eyes adjusted to the darkness. Thin moonlight sketched out the vegetation, the walls, the rusty stove . . .

. . . and a woman lying on the floor. Long blond hair covered her face, rendered stark white in the dark. She was curled on her side.

My heart froze at the sight of the intruder. Only my dad and I belonged in this place. No one else. I was torn between the urge to run away . . . and the need to see who this intruder was and what she wanted here.

Curiosity won. I knelt beside her and touched her bare shoulder. It was cold. I realized she was nude, and ivy was braided in her hair. My heart kick-started once more, pounding.

I pushed away the curtain of hair. She was curled around an empty bird nest. Her hands and feet were bound with the ivy.

I shook her shoulder.

A mouse crawled from her mouth.

I gasped, rocketed to my feet, and stumbled backward. I became aware of the soft smell of rot . . . not just from the floor, but all around me.

I looked to my right. A woman was pinned to the wall, her head bowed. Her short, curly blond hair fell forward in a mop that hid her face. Her neck was wreathed in a garland of poison ivy. Her skin was speckled with rot, and I saw with horror that her hands had been nailed to the wall. Poison ivy was wrapped around her, obscuring her nudity.

A blacksnake slithered across the floor in pursuit of the mouse that had escaped the lips of the woman on the floor.

This couldn't be. It couldn't be.

No one knew about this place but me and my dad.

And my dad was not a monster.

I whirled, panicked, the landscape of my childhood turned into a decaying nightmare. I bolted toward the door but scrambled back when I saw a figure in the corner, crouching down. Her blond hair cascaded over her bare shoulders and legs, brushing the floor. Her skull was crowned with deer antlers.

I fell to my hands and knees before her, this strange fairy goddess of nightmare. I saw black eyes . . . river stones, I thought, staring blankly back at me from the pile of limbs. Her mouth was slack and dark . . . whether from lipstick or blood, I couldn't tell.

I covered a silent scream with my hands.

"I didn't mean for you to find out like this, Elena."

A soft voice echoed from the other side of the house. I turned my gaze to a pile of rotted fallen beams. My dad sat there quietly in the dark, perched as he would in a tree stand in the forest. His hat was low over his head, and his rifle was slung over his shoulder.

"I didn't mean for you to find out at all."

I whimpered.

He sighed.

"Are you a monster?" I demanded. The word didn't seem adequate. "Monster" sounded like a word for fairy tales. Not my beloved dad.

He looked at the bodies arranged around the room. "Maybe."

He stretched his legs and slid down the pile. I backed up against the rusted stove. Liquid sloshed, and something cold and wet splashed down my side. I recognized the smell immediately: curdled blood. A metal bucket turned over and crashed on the floor, spilling the rest of the blood over my sneakers.

I was frozen. I saw the outline of the door, and I should've run. But I was rooted in place, as motionless and helpless as any of these women.

My dad loomed over me. His face was strange, his eyes too dark and still. This man who stood over me was not my dad. He was

79

some changeling who had come to take him, leaving an evil shell in his place. A monster.

"What have you done with my dad?" I croaked.

He reached out to touch my cheek. I flinched.

"Your dad is gone." His voice was a low hiss, like rain in a gutter.

And I knew then what I saw. It was my dad's Forest God, the one he called Veles, dark and terrible and devouring everything under this roof. He wanted me. I didn't know if he meant to consume me like those other women or if the Forest God was wanting to do to me as he was doing to my dad, wearing my skin like his own . . .

The door crashed open. The Forest God spun, reaching for his rifle, but he was tackled by a snarling dog. Percival.

An armed shadow stood in the doorway. Agent Parkes. "*Freeze*," he ordered.

The Forest God had no intention of obeying anyone's orders. He wrestled with the dog, and the rifle went off. A new hole was blown in the roof, and I was partially blinded by muzzle flash and deafened by a gunshot in a closed space.

"Drop it!" Parkes commanded. His voice was faint and tinny over the ringing in my ears.

The Forest God scrambled away from the dog, kicking Percival in the chest. He sighted his rifle on the dog.

I screamed.

The Forest God hesitated for an instant—only an instant.

It was enough.

More gunfire, muzzle flashes. The Forest God tumbled across the floor. Parkes advanced on him, shouting, his shoes slipping in the blood. Percival was growling, clamping my dad's right hand in his jaws. The rifle spun out on the floor, the barrel skidding up against my sneakers. It was hot, and it singed the rubber of my shoe.

"Put it down!" Parkes yelled.

The man who had once been my father had gotten his hunting knife loose from his belt and was slashing at Percival. He'd pulled himself up into a half crouch, dripping on the floor, snarling like a cornered animal.

"Put it down now!"

I knew Parkes was going to kill my dad.

Trembling, I reached down for the gun at my feet.

———

I heard the front door open and sat up in bed. Behind my blackout curtains, the last orange fingers of sunset crept down the walls. I felt foggy, and the room swam. I didn't remember getting in and out of bed. Wet footprints crossed the floor.

Nick shuffled into the bedroom, bleary-eyed. "How are you feeling?"

He placed a bouquet of flowers at my bedside, daisies and goldenrod and purple asters. I stared at them, remembering the browning asters and limp goldenrod from the crime scene. These were local flowers in season, I reminded myself. I reached out to touch them.

"Anna?" he asked again. "Are you okay?"

I ran my hand through my hair. "Those painkillers gave me a helluva headache." I didn't want to tell him about missing time.

"They can do that. And give you vivid dreams. And also make you constipated." He came to sit on the edge of the bed. "Have you had anything to eat?"

I shook my head. It honestly hadn't occurred to me.

"Let's get you up and order something for dinner. How about the deli?"

I nodded. I had no appetite, but Nick liked the deli.

I pulled back the comforter and sheets to get out of bed, and Nick's face settled into a carefully neutral expression. A clinical expression, the kind he wore at the hospital. We were doing this awkward dance around the light bulb of our relationship, the two of us moths, neither wanting to get burned.

But his expression was too distant even for that as his gaze settled on my chest.

I looked down. The bed was covered in blood, and so was I.

I felt nauseous. The sight of blood had never made me nauseous before, but it had to be the painkillers. I leaned over the edge of the bed and threw up in the general direction of a trash can. There wasn't much to throw up, just a terrible-smelling black ichor.

Nick was unfazed by blood. Even mine. His cool fingers worked over my stitches. He grabbed a cold washcloth from the bathroom and dabbed at my wounds.

"Your stitches," he said. "They've pulled out."

I stared down at my leg and my arm, and my gaze landed at my hands against the sheet. Rusty half-moons were embedded beneath my fingernails. There was dried blood there and dark crumbles resembling dirt.

I pressed the heel of my hand to my head. "I don't remember—"

"Shh. It's going to be okay." He kissed my forehead.

He bundled me up and put me in his car. I muttered about ruining the leather seats, but he shushed me. We zinged down the curving country back roads, and my stomach flip-flopped. I retched once or twice. It felt as if everything inside me were being pulled out. I hung my head out the window like a dog, desperate to feel the cooling night air on my face.

We pulled up to the back of the hospital. Nick disappeared and returned with a wheelchair. I protested, but he made me sit. I closed my eyes as we moved down the halls. I didn't want to meet gazes. I let voices wash over me.

Ambient noise was soon sealed behind a door. Overhead, a fluorescent light buzzed. I was playing opossum. Maybe better that everyone around me thought that I'd passed out.

Nick's voice rumbled over me: "Thanks for helping. I'd appreciate if you'd keep this quiet for her privacy."

A female voice answered over the sound of running water. "Sure. I owe you for covering for me last Sunday."

"How's Clark?"

Something cool and stinging pressed against the wounds on my abdomen. It smelled like antiseptic.

"He's better. Got him on methadone, but it seems like a whole helluva lot for a sixteen-year-old."

"They start younger and younger. He's got you. He'll be okay."

"I should've seen the signs earlier." More stinging. "He's my son, you know?"

"No one ever knows the secret lives we lead," Nick said soothingly.

"What happened to her?" the female voice said, moving the stinging around my body. "I thought she was on the mend."

"She had a bad reaction to the pain meds. Pulled her stitches out."

"Damn. That's rough."

The sharp antiseptic pain moved to my arm. I flinched and knew I had to open my eyes and act like a conscious person. The light shone bright over me, like the headlights of a truck. Nick's gloved hands were pulling open a suture kit while a redheaded

83

physician's assistant leaned over me. I think I remembered her from Nick's holiday party. Trina, I thought.

"Hey, hon. You're gonna be okay," she said reassuringly.

"We're gonna get your wounds cleaned and stitched back up," Nick said. "And no more painkillers for you."

I watched Trina clean the dried blood and mud from my skin while Nick poked me with local anesthetic needles. He began to pluck out the ruined sutures.

I looked from her to him. She was a couple of years younger than Nick and me. Smart. Cute. Had a son from a previous relationship. She would be a better woman for Nick. They worked in practiced concert the way a long-married couple dances around each other in a familiar kitchen. I lay on the table between them, a project for them to work on. A recipe to complete.

Tools clinked in a metal tray as Nick sewed me back together. I closed my eyes, feeling the tug and pull of my skin as he closed me back up.

"You'll be good as new," Trina assured me.

Soon I was sewn up and tucked back into Nick's car. The anesthetic was wearing off, and my skin beneath the bandages was beginning to itch.

"I'm sorry," I said as he pulled out of the parking lot. I spotted a bloodstain below the window. Feeling guilty, I licked my thumb and wiped it away.

"Don't be," he said. "You're gonna be fine. When you pulled them out in your sleep, you didn't do much damage to the lower structures of your skin. I just trimmed the edges and made new margins. But you're gonna have to keep them covered to avoid infection and take some more antibiotics."

I sank into the seat. He was giving me an out, but I was determined to pick at it. "I don't remember pulling them out," I said slowly.

"They probably itched in your sleep, and the pain meds dulled the sensation. That, and the half-life of PCP can be anywhere from fifteen hours to a day. That kind of thing happens."

It felt like more than that. That I'd somehow tried to rip my skin off in my sleep. And neither of us said anything about the dirt.

I stared at my wan reflection in the dark window.

"No more painkillers," I whispered. But there was nothing to be done for the half-life of PCP.

My fingers curled around the wood stock of the rifle, and I braced it against my shoulder. I stared down the barrel first at Agent Parkes, then my dad.

Parkes lifted a calming hand. "You're gonna be all right. You're gonna be all right." He kept repeating that like a mantra, staring at the black blood I'd spilled on my clothes. He thought Dad had hurt me. "Just put the gun down."

My dad slowly climbed to his feet. I aimed the gun at him. But it wasn't him—not really. It was the monster. Wasn't it? I could see his eyes shining in the darkness. They were my dad's eyes. My eyes. Not the eyes of a monster. Weren't they?

His face was sunken, pale. Those eyes turned toward me as if they saw me for the first time.

Terrified, I backed up toward the door, holding the gun out in front of me. My hands shook. Cool night air and the song of crickets pressed against my back.

I dropped the gun.

It went off with a deafening roar and a shout from inside the fallen house.

I turned and ran into the dark, away from that thunder and flash of light, away from the intruders in my sanctuary, away from this nightmare.

I ran until my breath burned my throat and my tears spangled the darkness. If I could make it to the river, I could follow it downstream, away, maybe find a boat. I sensed something following me, my dad's nightmare, the Forest God. Instinctively, I ran for the river. Perhaps it couldn't swim . . .

I lurched down a hill, gathering speed. From there, I could smell the muddy water. I flew over the brush and stones, soaring effortlessly. For a moment I believed I could run from this. For a moment I believed I would wake up in my own bed, that this dream would fade . . .

I tripped. I smacked down to the forest floor on my elbows. The wind was knocked from me and my palms were skinned. I was stunned. Through the trees, I could see the muddy track of the river. I began to pull myself toward it . . .

Something crashed through the forest. I rolled over, shielding my face and closing my eyes. I knew the Forest God was tracking me. It had released my dad and had found me.

I squeezed my eyes shut. I refused it. I refused to look upon it. If it meant to kill me, it could. But I would not let it stare deep into my soul, rip out my eyes, and wear my skin.

In the distance, I heard rustling. Something running, then barking.

The Forest God swept over me, barely brushing my body, and slipped away. I lay there, frozen.

When something furry and smelling like blood pounced upon me, I cried out. A warm tongue washed my face.

Percival stood on me, panting. He'd tracked me all this way and chased away the nightmare of the Forest God.

Sobbing, I wrapped my arms around him.

That was the way the FBI agents' flashlights found me: within a stone's throw of the river, embracing the dog. I was all cried out by then and refused to let go of the dog.

Percival was real. And I held on to that touchstone for all I was worth.

11

INTERROGATION

"Tell us what happened when you shot him."

I sat in the chief's office on the first floor of the county jail, on a mercifully squishy leather couch. Opposite a coffee table from me sat the two IA detectives, Cassidy and Vernon. The chief's office was shaped like a bowling alley, with his massive desk and bookcases at one end and a conversation area on the other. There was a U.S. and an Ohio state flag for him to stand between for photo ops, but this end of the room was cooler, quieter, with worse lighting. The leather smelled vaguely of tobacco, and there were ring stains from glasses on the lacquered wood. Framed pictures of the chief with celebrities and government officials hung on the walls, along with a rare pistol that once belonged to Eliot Ness, the greatest lawman of all time, in a shadow box.

The chief had made IA interview me there, where it was clear I was under his protection. I was grateful not to be sitting in a hard plastic chair in an interrogation room, or the ridiculously squeaky chairs in the conference room. He had me arrive an hour early, then offered me coffee and asked how I was doing. I told him I was feeling sore but was getting along all right. He had me sign some forms for FMLA.

"Do you want me to stay while you talk to them?" he asked me, pushing up his glasses with his middle finger.

"I think we'll be fine," I assured him, knowing full well that Chief was going to do whatever he wanted.

"This shitty thing that happened wasn't your fault," he said. I genuinely liked Chief. He was fatherly; he had daughters only a few years younger than me.

I sank back into the couch. "It just feels . . . wrong. Like none of this is real."

"It's always gonna feel like that, kiddo," he said, and I believed him. Chief had gotten in a couple of gunfights in his salad days. "It was him or you. Sometimes it's just as simple as that. You'll drive yourself nuts if you start second-guessing yourself."

I nodded and pressed my clammy palms onto my pants.

A knock sounded at the door. The two IA detectives, Cassidy and Vernon, were invited in. Cassidy was short, with his hair in a crew cut, and a tie the color of fresh blood. Vernon was tall and quiet, in a short-sleeved dress shirt. His tattoos, angels and devils, curled up and down his arms. Vernon ran most of our IT, and I was pretty certain he read everyone's email in his downtime. He'd made a lieutenant who had a thing for looking at clown porn retire quietly.

We stood and shook hands politely. They sat down opposite me, and the chief sat down in a tufted leather chair at the end of the coffee table.

Cassidy raised a brow. "You sitting in, Chief?"

The chief settled back in his chair. "Yup."

I could see Cassidy's objections running behind his brow. "You're the boss."

He and Vernon opened their notebooks.

The chief winked at me.

"Let's go through a timeline of that day." Cassidy clicked his pen while Vernon set up a recorder.

I recited what had been a very boring day up until the time things had gone all pear-shaped. I'd caught up on some paperwork, investigated a complaint about cemetery desecration near the abandoned church at Township Road 12. I'd met with the nearby municipal department on a task force about illegal drug trafficking, standing in for the Vice guys, who were out on a stakeout that day. A car loaded up with prescription drugs and a few gallons of homemade PCP had been intercepted, and the driver was one of our locals. City Vice had caught this action on an anonymous tip, and they were understandably perturbed. We were in talks to run down the driver's contacts and figure out if we had a full-scale drug ring operating in Bayern County.

"I was on my way home when I heard the call go out on the radio." My hands, laced together, rested lightly on my knee. "I was closest, so I took the call."

Cassidy looked up at me. "You didn't wait for backup."

"I heard gunfire. I assumed—correctly—that a civilian was in danger. I informed Dispatch and went."

He scribbled something on his notepad. "You walked down the drive?"

"Yes. I positioned myself beside the suspect's truck, took the keys, and . . ." I paused. "The sun visor fell open, dumping what I later learned was PCP on me."

"Did you feel any negative effects from that exposure, then or later?"

"No. I spent most of the time unconscious at the hospital." I certainly wasn't going to confess to any hallucinations.

"What then?"

"I announced my presence."

"What did you say?"

"I identified myself as an officer and told whoever was in the house to come out with their hands up."

"Then what happened?" He scribbled on his paper.

"Then Sullivan came out of the house with a shotgun in hand. I hid behind the truck, but he rounded the fender. And he shot me." I flinched slightly as a twinge slipped through my upper thigh.

"Can you show us?" Vernon pushed a piece of paper to me. I sketched the truck and drew an O for Sullivan and an X for myself.

"Then what happened?"

I was relieved to have the paper to focus on. "I shot him." I moved the pen from the X to the O.

"Where were you standing when you shot him?"

"I was trying to advance on him, but I was stumbling." I moved the X closer to the O.

"How many times did you shoot him?" Vernon was now doing the questioning. Of course he knew how many times I'd fired; they'd collected the bullet casings. He was fishing to see if I knew.

"I don't remember. Maybe three? Four?"

"Did he return fire?"

"No."

"Why did you keep shooting? Were you under the influence?"

Chief made an audible creak in the leather chair to remind them of his presence.

I sucked in my breath. "No. I knew I was hurt and that I had to stop him. If I didn't stop him, he was going to shoot someone else."

"What was your goal?"

"To separate him from his weapon." That was the correct answer, but the answer I truly felt was different. I wanted to put him down so he wouldn't get back up again.

"Did you do that?"

"No. I saw him down in the gravel, holding his weapon. And I just . . . passed out." I remembered the trees above me. "I thought I was dead."

The only sound was Cassidy's pen scraping paper. And someone's stomach growled.

Vernon turned the diagram toward himself and seemed to study it.

"Did you at any point think you'd killed him?"

"I wasn't sure. I saw him fall. I thought I'd hit him, but I didn't know how bad it was."

"Was there anything you would have done differently?"

I stared at Vernon in silence for a few heartbeats. "No." My voice sounded hollow.

"I think that's enough for today," the chief said.

The IA guys exchanged pleasantries and saw themselves out. I remained stuck to the chief's leather couch.

"You all right?"

"Yup." I nodded vigorously.

"You did fine." He took a drink of his coffee. "But there are rules to follow."

"I understand."

"One of those rules is that we have to have medical and psychological certifications that you're fit to return to duty. A drug test, all that. You don't need to rush anything," he amended. "Take some time. Rest up. Watch shitty television and pick up a hobby. I hear the kids these days are doing shit with TikTok."

I glanced at him from the corner of my eye. "I'd like to get back to work."

"So I heard from Captain Wozniak." One corner of his mouth quirked up.

"What's up with that?" I asked, as if we were talking about any other investigation.

"I have no clue." His mouth turned down. "The FBI is dying to look at what happened, though."

"It's kind of their bailiwick, though, right? Serial killers?"

"It's our backyard, though. Our jurisdiction." He tapped his thumb against his coffee mug. The chief liked the limelight. He managed cameras well. There might not be another case like this for the rest of his career.

"Right."

"They'll send down some of their people to look. Same with the state crime lab." He shrugged and set the mug down. "It made the cable news networks, after all."

"What do you think?"

He looked at me directly. "You want to know if I think it's the Forest Strangler?"

"I mean, it can't be." My pulse thudded evenly in my throat. I said it with such certainty . . .

"Right. So it's some copycat. Some fucking incel who saw this shit on the internet and decided to romanticize it. But this isn't the eighties. We've got DNA databases and cameras everywhere." He settled back in his chair, an expression of anticipation on his face. "I'd like for us to be the ones who chase him down."

I saw then what the chief wanted, in the shadow of those two flags for television. He wanted to be the man whose department caught a serial killer. That was, in its own way, a certain immortality.

Eliot Ness, after all, never died.

12

SNAKESKIN

I wanted to do something for Nick, to thank him for what he had done. Anything I came up with felt woefully inadequate, but I stopped by his favorite pizza joint on my way home from work. I snagged a pie and headed to the ER.

Security waved me through, and I headed up to the registration desk. The waiting room was empty, and two RNs were shooting the breeze with the clerk.

"Hey," I said. "I wanted to leave this for Dr. Kohler. Is he busy?"

Their eyes lit up. One of the nurses said: "We'd love to take that off your hands. But Dr. Kohler hasn't been in for the last couple of days."

"Um. Okay." I handed the pizza over awkwardly, and they ripped into it like raccoons at a buffet.

I felt a little naïve. I assumed Nick was where he said he was. But . . . he could be seeing someone, for all I knew. He had a life that was no longer entangled with mine. As kind as he'd been to me, I had no right to expect anything else of him. No explanations were owed, and I wouldn't ask for any. I'd given that right up when I pushed him away.

Still, I felt a red spasm of fear. It surprised me with its intensity, this fear of losing him. I think I had assumed that he'd remained who and where he was, suspended, when he was out of my sight. And he very well might have moved on, and I couldn't blame him.

I returned home to find Nick snoring in my bed.

I stood over him, watching him sleep for a moment. So strange the way we'd fallen back into the patterns we'd had before we'd broken up. I assumed that was normal in times of crisis . . . but what now? A pang of longing thudded through my chest. I felt gratitude, but also an undercurrent of sadness. If I had managed to become Anna Koray fully, I would've crawled into bed beside him and slept with him. I'd run from him, in many ways, because I thought I could never be myself with him. I expected he would never understand or be able to accept Elena. He would view me as broken. Until Elena was gone, I couldn't fully let myself belong to him.

Instead, I went outside. I took my shoes off and walked into the woods. Feeling the wind in my hair and the dirt against my feet, I took a deep breath.

As a child, I had thought my father was haunted by something monstrous, something separate from him. My belief in the Forest God had been a child's coping mechanism, a way to explain how my beloved father had done the unthinkable. I didn't believe that anymore. I believed my father was that monster and that he was gone.

Right?

I dug my fingernails into my palms until they bled.

I was here, and I was real, and he was gone.

I listened to the leaves conspire over me, felt the prickling of grass against the soles of my feet and the humidity gathering against my skin. Absently, I chewed sassafras root as I walked. It chased the metallic taste of drugs from my tongue.

I should've gone home. I should've gone to bed.

But I walked until the sun dipped below the horizon, and the forest swelled with the sounds of crickets and the calls of an owl. I drank iron-tanged water from a stream and stared up at the sky. I wanted to melt into the woods and vanish from the sight of everyone: the sheriff's office, the psychiatrist, even Nick.

My toes stepped in something squishy and brittle at once. I knelt down to look, stitches pulling my skin. It was a snakeskin, diaphanous as an onion peel but as soft as velvet. It was nearly perfect. Holding it up to the sky, I could even see the scales that once covered the snake's eyes. As I turned it over in my hands, I couldn't feel a tear in it.

I pressed it to my chest. This was meant for me. I knew it. I didn't know what it meant, but I knew it was part of the forest, and it welcomed me back.

I combed my fingers through my hair with my free hand, feeling the night slide through it. I'd missed this. I would break open my memory vault if I could have this feeling of freedom back.

I'd been away from myself for too long, and I wanted all of me back.

Even if that meant inviting my father back in.

———

I returned to the house, climbing up on the porch. The porch light was on, but I shaded my eyes.

The door flew open and Nick's silhouette stood before me.

"Anna! Where have you been?"

"I went for a walk." It took a lot of effort to get those words to come out in a way that sounded like my voice.

He grabbed my hand and pulled me indoors, into that blinding light.

He looked me up and down, at the mud streaked on my bare feet and clothes, at the leaves in my hair, at the snake skin wound around my neck.

He took me by my shoulders. "Anna! You have to keep those wounds clean or you'll get an infection."

His brown eyes fell on me; then there was a moment of distance between us.

I took a deep breath, wanting to close that distance. I'd always been so controlled, so civilized with him. "I needed to clear my head. I used to take walks in the woods when I was a little girl." I looked up at him with eyes that I knew shone with childlike wonder. "I found an owl and this . . ." My fingers twined in the translucent snake skin. "And you should see the stars tonight. They're beautiful. Capricorn rose and . . ."

Nick was silent. I'd shown this to him, this flicker of myself, this grubby girl from the forest and her treasures, this girl whose heart leapt at falling stars and who kept holed stones in her pocket. I'd taken this risk, opened up to him the way I knew he wanted me to, the way I'd refused to do six months ago.

He was going to drag me to the shower and leave. I just knew it.

Nick reached out to touch my brow. His fingers were cold, but they lingered. His expression was inscrutable: longing and memory and sadness mingling together. He kissed me, hot and tangling in the dark. I leaned into it, wanting the connection, wanting him . . .

But he gently put his hands on my shoulders. His voice was tight, as if he struggled to hold himself back. "We can't. Not now. We've got to wait until you've recovered."

I whispered against his mouth, "I don't want to wait."

Finally, he said: "Let's get you to bed."

I let him take my hand and lead me to the bedroom, to the waiting.

———

When the agents found me with Percival in the woods, covered in blood, they took me to a hospital.

I was frozen, unable to answer any questions they asked:

"Do you remember your name?"

"How many fingers am I holding up?"

"Where are you hurt?"

They took me to a sterile white room. I was poked and prodded and light was shone into my eyes. There were no windows, only plastic and machines. I was moved from that blank room to another, then another. I curled up and pulled the covers over my face. I slept off and on, each time hoping I would truly wake up from this nightmare. There were no clocks in any of these rooms, and I was tempted to believe that none of this had really happened.

Mom was brought to me. Her clothes were wrinkled but her eyes were dry. While the police were watching, she reached out to shake my shoulder.

"Elena."

I flinched and turned my face to the wall.

They sent in more people in white coats who tried to talk to me. And they sent in people in plain clothes: cops. They all brought teddy bears and candy and comic books, trying to tempt me to speak. But I had nothing to say.

And I didn't ask any questions. I truly didn't want to know the answers. When the rifle went off, did I kill my dad? Or Agent Parkes? Did I miss them both, and did they fight it out? Did Dad get arrested, or did he kill Agent Parkes and run?

I should've wanted to know, but I didn't. I wanted to go back to who I had been a few days earlier, a girl with a normal past and an ordinary future.

I was curled up in bed when I heard the click of toenails on the floor. I turned over to see Percival trotting toward me. He was wearing a cast around one of his front legs and was limping. I slipped from the bed, flung my arms around his neck, and sobbed into his shoulder. He leaned into me, and we had a moment of wordless understanding. A sigh rumbled deep in his chest, one echoed in my own body.

When I looked up, Agent Parkes sat in a chair by the door. His arm was in a sling, and his face was crossed with stitches. Part of his hair had been shaved.

I sat back and stared.

"I thought you might like to see Percival," he said quietly.

I nodded at him while I became very interested in stroking Percival's back.

He stared down at the floor. "The veterinarian says his leg will heal, but he's gonna have a limp. He's retiring from service."

I looked up at Parkes, alarmed.

"Don't worry," Parkes said. "He's going to continue to live with me. He just won't be in the field anymore. He'll be fat and happy. He's been eating a whole lot of takeout lately."

Percival looked at Parkes. His canine eyebrows worked up and down. When Parkes reached for him, he shied away and leaned harder into me. Percival's heart pounded against my fingers, fast, like a rabbit's.

"I also wanted to come to tell you I was sorry." Parkes leaned forward and rubbed his brow. His words came out in a flood. "I never should have put you in that position. I put you in danger, and I had no business on earth doing that. I was so ready to catch your father. I wanted to be the one . . . the hero . . . and I nearly got you killed. I exposed you to horrific things no child should ever see. I'm sorry, and I'll never be able to make that up to you."

His eyes were glassy, near tears. An adult had never apologized to me for anything before. I wasn't sure how to react. I thought I was supposed to be angry. I thought I was supposed to accept this apology. Maybe I was supposed to be relieved he was still alive. Instead, I just felt numb.

"What happened to my dad?" There was no television here; there were no newspapers. I didn't know. I wasn't sure I wanted to know. But I knew Parkes would tell me the truth.

His mouth flattened, and the fingers of his uninjured hand slipped to his arm. "After you fled, we fought. He got the upper hand, shot me. And he escaped."

I sucked in my breath. My dad was alive. And free.

I hiccupped a sob and leaned into Percival.

Something in me broke, but it also sang.

Agent Parkes came by every day after that. I didn't know if this was something the people in white coats made him do, or whether it was his own guilt, but he brought Percival for me to pet. He brought checkers to set up on a side table. There was a mirror on the wall bordering the hallway. Parkes never looked at it, but my skin crawled when I did. We were being watched, but there wasn't anything I could do about it.

I spoke rarely, mostly about the game or the dog. Parkes accepted this, and we played. Percival was always unwilling to leave and would reluctantly go to Parkes's side, his tail held low. Percival played with me, wholeheartedly, but dodged Parkes's hands.

Once, while studying the board, I told him, unbidden, "I'm not going to talk about my dad."

He looked up at me, his fingers hesitating on a black plastic checker. "What do you mean?"

I shrugged. "I'm not gonna tell you anything about him. I'm not going to tell *them* anything, either." I flicked my gaze over his shoulder, to the one-way mirror.

He nodded. "I don't think you should. This is about you, not your dad."

I blinked, startled.

"I'm here to help you. And these people are, too. You don't have to talk about your dad. You have no responsibility whatsoever to do that, to help people catch him, to help them find evidence. You're a child. You shouldn't have anything at all to do with this."

I chewed my lip.

"This is about you. Your trauma. Your recovery and you being able to grow up and get on with your life without that shadow hanging over it."

A lump rose in my throat. It had never been about me.

I pressed the heels of my hands to my eyes and cried. Percival laid his head in my lap, and I felt Parkes hug me.

I was released. I was released of responsibility for my dad.

Wasn't I?

Once I was eating and talking, my mom came to get me. She was thin, gray-looking, with two red spots of anger on her cheeks.

"It's time to go," she said. I thought she was going to bring me home.

I dressed and followed her down the green-tiled hallway. I'd figured out long ago that this place wasn't a regular hospital. It was too full of screams and locked doors and soft corners. I felt afraid out in the hallway, and I pulled my jacket tighter around my body. It wasn't my dad's jacket that I'd been wearing in the woods but a pink one Mom had bought for me that I hated.

We paused in the lobby. Mom tugged my hood over my head and grabbed my arm. She nodded to a pair of policemen.

"We're ready." She put on a pair of sunglasses.

A police officer pushed through the doors of the hospital, out into the glare of day. Even though it was cloudy, it felt blinding after being indoors for so long. Flashbulbs went off, and a roar of sound washed over me. Bodies crushed around us, and I dimly realized that these people were shouting questions at us, questions about my dad.

"Has there been any contact from your husband?"

"Did you know what he was doing?"

"How did you marry a monster?"

"Are you afraid he'll come back?"

"Did he abuse you and your daughter?"

Mom flung her arm around my shoulders to keep from being separated from me. The cops closed around us, marching us toward a waiting state highway patrol car. They put my mom and me in the back, struggling to close the doors against the press of people. The doors slammed, and hands pounded on the door. The trooper who was driving put on his lights and flipped on his siren to get them to move away enough to pull out of the parking lot. The lot was full of vans with television antennae and people clutching microphones.

I sank down in the seat, trying to become invisible. Mom sat beside me, wooden. I stared through the cage at the driver as he pulled out onto the road. Cars followed us, but he plucked up his radio and spoke an unintelligible stream of letters and numbers.

Within moments, other patrol cars appeared and blocked the street behind us, thwarting our followers.

"Are we going home?" I asked.

Mom shook her head. She hadn't taken off her sunglasses.

We changed cars in a parking lot behind a building, getting into an unmarked car. That car drove us across state lines, far away. We drove into the night, where headlights washed over us. It reminded me of driving to Florida, though we were driving east.

Lulled by the sound of the engine, I fell half asleep. I hadn't dreamed in the white rooms of the hospital. But here, in the dark, I dreamed of the smells of moss and blood and running in the woods.

Late that night, the car parked before an apartment building. Groggily, I stumbled out behind my mom. The driver pulled a couple of bags from the trunk and led us to the front door. He thumbed an intercom button and told the person on the other end that "Grandma's visiting." The heavy door opened, and we climbed steps to the third floor.

The place reminded me of a hotel, with the same kind of loud patterned carpet hotels had. The driver knocked on a door, one of many in a hallway, and it opened after some shuffling within.

A man beckoned us inside. He was wearing a gun holster, so I assumed he was another cop. So many cops. I plodded inside the beige apartment.

"Let's get you to bed," Mom said. She pulled one of the bags down a very short hallway. There were three doors. One was a bathroom, the two others bedrooms. The bedroom she showed me was beige, with a bed and a lamp on a nightstand. The only other furniture was an empty dresser.

My mom put the suitcase on the bed and zipped it open. There were clothes there, my size, with the tags still on.

"There's toothpaste and toothbrushes in the bathroom," she said.

"Where are we?"

"There's soap in the bathroom, too."

I nodded. I went out into the hallway to find the bathroom. The low-toned conversation in the living room stalled.

I dutifully unwrapped a toothbrush and brushed my teeth, staring into the mirror at my dad's eyes. I wondered where he was.

I went to bed as instructed and my mother tucked me in. She leaned over to kiss my forehead. I don't know why she did that; she hadn't done that before. Maybe because we weren't really alone. I wanted to believe she missed me.

She closed the door and went to join the voices in the living room. We were here because the police thought we were in danger. I didn't want to believe that Dad was a danger to us, but after what I'd seen in the broken house, I wasn't sure. Maybe it was because of all the people around the hospital. Maybe it was both.

I lay in the dark, staring at the mini blinds. The voices in the living room were unintelligible.

I slipped out of bed and padded, barefoot, to the far wall. I pressed my ear to it, hearing nothing.

I gently opened the closet door, sliding it carefully open just enough for me to get inside. It was empty of everything except the smell of paint. I crouched at the back of the closet and pressed my ear to the wall.

"He'll turn up," a male voice said. "His picture is on every television screen and newspaper from New York to Los Angeles. Someone will see him."

My mom's voice was robotic. "And then what?"

"And he'll stand trial for those murders. He's going to get the death penalty. You won't ever see him again."

"But what about me and Elena?"

"We'll see if we can put you in the witness protection program, assuming you don't want to go back . . ."

"No," she said firmly, with the most emotion I'd heard in her voice. "I never want to go back."

I slumped against the wall.

I knew what was behind us, but I had no idea what was before us.

13

THE STAG

"I saw what happened, on the television."

Dr. Richardson sat in her chair, her hands folded over a plain legal pad. I sat on the couch opposite her, hunched over a book open on the coffee table. She was having me page through books of Rothko art as we spoke, to see if that triggered some emotion. The book was open to an untitled rendering of a horizon line below a red sky and a black underworld.

I turned my gaze back to the Rothko. "It can't be my father. It can't. No matter how much this looks like his work."

"It's a disturbing coincidence that someone is copying his murders," Dr. Richardson said.

I tapped the dry page, imagining moist soil under my fingertips. "I worry that this has something to do with me. That someone, somehow, knows who I really am." There. I'd said it out loud. It sounded terrifying and paranoid.

"I understand how it might feel that way. But these are the

Forest Strangler's old stomping grounds. If someone is copying him, it makes sense that they would return here."

I turned the page to a triptych painting. I thought of heaven, earth, and the underworld. I didn't believe in a benign, all-powerful God, but I suspected there were mystical things in the world, things beyond my understanding, above and below. Things my father told me about. Like the Forest God.

"I suppose that makes sense." I wanted to believe it.

"You know, you don't have to deal with this at all," Dr. Richardson said. "You could quit your job and move. There's nothing stopping you."

I frowned. "There's the guy I'm seeing."

"What does he know about your past?"

"He doesn't know about Elena." It felt better to refer to Elena as her own person, not part of me.

Dr. Richardson tapped a pen on her notepad. "Do you want him to know?"

My finger traced the orange sky of the Rothko. "I don't know. I'd like to tell him, for him to accept me, the whole me. But I don't think he's capable of that."

"Why not? Are you afraid he would tell someone?"

"No. I don't think he would. I just don't think he would be able to wrap his mind around it. I think he would feel like I've lied to him. And I sort of have. I think that's why I broke up with him in the first place. I felt bad, lying to him."

"Tell me about the breakup."

I inhaled, flipping the page to bright slashes of red. "He made me dinner, brought me flowers. We made love, and he asked me to marry him."

"You said no."

"I said no."

"How did you feel when he asked you? First flash of emotion."

I chewed my lip, remembering. "Fear."

She nodded. "If you told him, though, what would you have to lose to be seen like that?"

I stared down at the red. "Someone would know. I would be . . . naked, I guess."

"If you would like to bring him here, we could do couples therapy."

I shook my head. "No."

"All right." She scribbled down a note. "Let's move back to this murder. You're not working this case, right? That would be a clear conflict of interest."

"No, I'm not. I understand that. I'm still on leave. Pending a whole lot of stuff . . . investigation by IA, passing a drug test, and a letter from a physician showing I'm fit for duty." Nick had written a letter and taken my blood, telling me that a blood test would only pop positive for PCP if it was administered within a day of exposure. He felt it was a meaningless test, since the effects of PCP could linger in my body much longer. But he still signed off.

"That sounds like quite a process."

I flipped the page, scanning brilliant sunset oranges. "My boss also needs a letter from a therapist to let me go back to work. Prove I'm stable and sane and all that."

"Do you want to go back to work?"

"I feel like I can go to work." I wanted that letter, so I didn't mention missing time.

"But do you want to?"

"Yes."

"Okay. I can send one." She tapped the cap end of her pen on the page. "Have you given any thought to what we talked about last time? About opening your memory vault or closing it for good?"

I leaned forward and cupped my chin in my hand. "I think I would feel safer now, knowing everything. Then I'd know, on a gut level, that this copycat murder isn't him, that this isn't about me, so I can move forward."

She nodded. "I can understand that."

"What about if I change my mind later?" I asked, looking her in the eye. "Can you zip that memory vault back up again?"

Her brows drew together. "Theoretically. But as you've seen, over these many years, things leak through. You would probably have to commit to maintenance treatments."

For a moment I thought about it. If Dr. Richardson could erase my past, then I could move forward with Nick. I could shed this once and for all, the darkness and the smell of leaf mold and clawing at my skin in my sleep.

Maybe someday. But not right now. I was never one to leave stones unturned. I wanted the truth, the whole truth, always. Now I felt a haze of danger at the edge of my vision, and I wondered how much my child mind might have misinterpreted or magnified things. I didn't want to be afraid. I wanted to face it.

And I wanted to feel alive, the way I did in the forest. If I didn't do this, I might lose that forever.

I nodded sharply, having decided. "I want to see what's in the rest of my head. What do I need to do?"

She glanced at her watch. "Are you free for the rest of the afternoon?"

I lifted my brows. So soon? But I leaned forward in anticipation, wanting to begin. "Yes."

"Good. I'll cancel the rest of my appointments." She stood and nodded at me. "Please get comfortable on the couch and I'll be back in a bit, all right?" She turned the lights off and left the room.

I took my shoes off and stretched out on the couch. I sank into it and stared up at the drop ceiling. I had no idea what was going to happen in this session. I heard Richardson's voice in the next room, unintelligible over the white noise machine. She was canceling her other appointments, so maybe this would be involved.

Dr. Richardson returned after about thirty minutes. By then I was feeling sleepy.

"Are you warm enough?" she asked.

I nodded, but she tugged a blanket down over my feet. "In case you need it." She bent to light a candle.

"I'd like for you to take a deep breath and focus your gaze softly on that candle," she said.

I turned my head to look at the flame. Gradually, as I watched it, the black room around me receded, and the flame itself grew dim and fuzzy. I had the sensation of falling, of moving away from it. Soon the flame disappeared, and I was in the dark.

"This is Dr. Richardson," a distant voice buzzed. "Can you tell me where you are?"

"I'm in the dark," I answered.

"Good. Please look around and tell me what you see."

I let my eyes adjust. I was on the crest of a grassy hillock on a moonless night. Just downhill sprawled a massive, dense forest sparkling with fireflies.

"I'm on a hill, looking down at a forest."

"Good. I'd like for you to walk down the hill into the forest."

I descended, feeling the grass prickle the bare soles of my feet. I moved on, into the forest, to a soft dirt path rippled with tree roots. I smelled pine and soft rot.

"Do you see the path?" Wet footprints stretched ahead of me on the dirt.

"Yes."

"Follow it."

I moved down the path, listening to the tree frogs, my fingers brushing the sharp edges of dog roses shedding their petals on a bed of pine needles. The path wound down into a valley, ending before a stone wall.

"Where are you now?"

"Before a rock outcropping." I pressed my hand to the cool stone. This place felt familiar somehow.

"Is there a stone covering a passage?"

I examined the rock more closely. It was gritty sandstone under my fingertips, but I found a larger stone pressed up against a cleft in the wall. Cracks fractured the stone, and lichens and rainwater leaked from it. Maybe at one time this cave had been an impregnable fortress, but no longer.

"Yes."

"This is where we left your memories, Anna. If you want to meet them, you'll need to push that rock out of the way."

The rock was large, perhaps too large for me to move. But I put my shoulder to it, toes clawing in the dirt. I shoved it as hard as I could, and it began to roll out of the way with a grating sound. A black hole was exposed, and cool mineral-laden air blew into my face.

I peered inside, stooping to enter. The stone was cold under my toes, and I straightened up, sensing a tunnel before me where red light emanated at the end. The tunnel was well-worn, as if many creatures had passed through there, pacing, and it smelled of lichen.

My heart drummed slowly, evenly, as I moved toward the red light. Soon the light intensified, and I found myself in a vast chamber of stalactites and stalagmites. Dripping water echoed, and bats scuttled in the vaulted ceiling.

"Where are you now?"

"In a cave . . ." I turned my attention to a still pool of water on the floor of the cave. I crept toward the water and peered in.

I expected to see my reflection, but my father's stared back at me with his silent gray eyes. Startled, I jerked back.

"What do you see?"

"It's him," I whispered. I reached forward to touch the reflection. My father mirrored my gesture, touching his index finger to mine. The water rippled, then churned.

I snatched my hand away. The water continued to roil, splashing and dampening my knees. I scrambled back as a huge shape burst forth from the underground lake, spewing cold water that glittered like stars.

It was a massive stag, antlers gleaming white and thrashing in the water. It climbed out, flinging stinging water at me, clambering up the stone bank and bellowing a deafening roar. I clapped my hands over my ears. It fixed me for an instant with a dark eye, then thundered past me, down the path, plunging into the night.

I paused, breathless.

"Anna. What happened?"

"The deer—it . . . came out of the water." I crawled on hands and knees to the pool and peered in. In the broken water, I saw a pale face with black eyes glaring back at me, the thing I'd seen in my father's face when I'd confronted him in his house of death. The Forest God.

I scrambled back, heart pounding. I climbed to my feet and ran, following the damp path the deer had taken, my heels pounding on the cold stone, the shock reverberating up my spine.

I burst out into the dark, breath burning. I thundered down the path, in the wake of the stag, which was long gone. I ran until I reached the crest of the hill, turning, and finding nothing there, only trampled grass.

———

"Anna."

My eyes snapped open, and I was once again in the darkness of Dr. Richardson's office. The room swam around me, and I lurched forward, trying to focus on the weak candle flame before me.

"Anna, breathe."

I sucked in lungfuls of air and sat back on the couch. My legs were tangled in the blanket, and I struggled to orient myself. Dr. Richardson turned on the light, and that helped.

"Are you all right?" She came to sit beside me on the couch.

I nodded. I felt clammy all over, as if I'd been underground. She awkwardly patted my shoulder. "You did well."

"What happened?"

"When you were a girl, we established a place in your mind to lock away your memories of your father and your life with him."

"The cave."

"Yes. The vault. You've opened it now, and you should begin to be able to access your full memories."

I thought back to my childhood but couldn't remember more than before. "I don't feel any different, and I can't remember more." I was afraid it had failed.

"That's normal. Those memories will gradually come back to you. They might come in flashbacks, dreams, or daydreams. Or you may wake up one morning and feel they've always been there. Believe it or not, your exposure to a hallucinogen might ease this process."

I took a deep breath. I had asked Dr. Richardson to release my memories. I only hoped that we'd released the stag and not the monster at the bottom of the pool.

14

MEMORY LEAKS

My father was back in the news. His gray eyes peered at me from every cable channel. I watched with the sound off. Images flickered across the screen: pictures of my father from long ago, his gaze hard and cold. One of them might have been a driver's license photograph. Others must have come from family members at some time or another, since I recognized our house in the background. His family was cropped out, but my skin crawled to think that my picture was still out there, circulating in the possession of people I didn't know.

Then there were the pictures of his victims. I turned up the volume. I didn't know any of these women, though they were all of a type: women with blond hair. Their smiles flashed through high school yearbook photos and shone beside Christmas trees. They ranged in age from eighteen to thirty-two. There were twenty-seven victims they knew of. I winced when I saw the photos of the last three victims, remembering them posed like discarded props from *A Midsummer Night's Dream* in the ruined house. But I forced myself to look at their photos and recite their names: Danielle Goss, Rebecca Rae Solon, Christy McCormick. Danielle was a waitress. Rebecca was a stay-at-home mother of two, and Christy was a student at a nearby college. They seemed so ordinary and alive in those photos, nothing like how I'd seen them. I wondered if their families knew the details. I hoped not.

A reporter held a microphone to a pair of young women on the street: "How does the knowledge that a serial killer might be on the loose in Bayern County make you feel?"

The first wrapped her arms around her elbows as if she were cold. Her hair was pink, but it had to have been bleached to blond to achieve that color. "It's creepy. Real creepy. I'm not taking any evening shifts anymore."

The second shook her head. "I don't go anywhere alone. Not until that maniac is caught. My mom told me about when he was here the first time, that nobody was certain who he would take next."

I clicked the television back on mute and opened my laptop. I did a dive on my father, searching for recent articles. I skimmed through the local and national news, then reluctantly headed over to Cas Russo's YouTube channel. I hated giving that guy any clicks, but I needed to know what the fuck he was up to. His channel was full of gruesome true crime retellings mixed with some ghost hunting in which a group of men taunted supposed spirits and demons. The guy liked to collect artifacts from famous killers. He reportedly owned one of John Wayne Gacy's paintings and had conducted a séance on it in which he scared himself and his friends shitless. That one had circulated around the sheriff's office for much merriment.

I grimaced when I saw his latest upload. Two hundred thousand views, and it had only been up for two hours. Steeling myself, I clicked.

"Welcome, fellow ghouls, to Cas Russo's Dark Misdeeds Podcast." Cas grinned at the camera. He was dressed in black, and his backdrop looked like a basement wall with water damage. "If you've been following the news, you're certainly aware of a fascinating new murder . . . one that seems to follow the Forest Strangler's modus operandi."

A picture of my father flashed across the screen.

"I've done several shows about Stephen Theron before: Click here for previous visits I've made to his dumping grounds." Cas pointed at a cartoon box that popped up in the corner. "Anyway, he's my local serial killer and one of my favorites. So imagine my utter delight when I got an exclusive anonymous tip that someone was copying his work . . ."

The video switched to shaky cell phone camera footage. A pair of feet in black boots moved noisily through a forest.

"God damn it," I breathed, watching as Cas swept the camera before him to a pale pair of women's feet sticking out of a creek bed. The victim's body lay in the cradle of the dry creek, her hands folded over flowers and her eyes black chestnuts.

"Oh my God," someone could be heard breathing. "She's gorgeous."

The camera operator knelt before the body.

I leaned forward. I knew something of the awe Cas might have felt here, this reverence at coming upon a body recently drained of life. My hand slipped over my mouth.

I assumed that Cas had been listening to the police scanner and that was why he'd showed up. But he knew before . . . he'd either been told or he had created this scene.

The camera panned over the body. But then the camera jerked dizzyingly as footsteps crunched in the other direction. The camera turned, joggled, as the operator ran, before the image went black.

"There's no information yet on the victim's identity." Cas zoomed in on a still of the body. My hands balled into fists. If the victim's family saw . . .

"But this looks just like a Forest Strangler victim, doesn't it?" Cas pointed to the body. "She's been ritualistically posed, with flowers, like Stephen Theron did. There's been a lot of speculation, none of it confirmed, about why he staged the crime scenes like that. In most of the killings, it was assumed that he abducted the women, brought them to remote locations, and killed them there. But he picked uninhabited places where he could do this sort of funereal decoration to them. This place is like that, not a place where one would be disturbed. And it's very similar to other locations where bodies were discovered . . ." The video switched over to still photos of a gravel riverbank, a wooded thicket, and the ruined house where my father had fought Agent Parkes.

"Rest assured that I'll be following this case closely," Cas said. He leaned forward, and his face filled the screen. "Confidential to my anonymous informant . . . Get in touch with me. I admire your work."

He gave the camera a knowing grin.

That shitheel. He was getting off on having the attention, the connection to the killer. If he wasn't the killer himself, he was engineering this situation for the likes.

I stopped the video. For spite, I clicked the "thumbs down" icon below the video. I got a sting of anonymous satisfaction from that.

I glanced up at the television, and my boss was on camera, standing out on the steps of the courthouse in his dress uniform, with a bouquet of microphones in front of him. I unmuted him.

"... received word from the coroner's office that the victim has been identified as Rachel Marie Slouda, of Maysville. Rachel had been missing since Friday, when she was driving to her sister's house. We ask that you grant the family privacy in this time of their grief."

Cameras flashed and shouted questions could be heard.

"Chief, can you comment on the similarity of this murder to the Forest Strangler?"

The chief shook his head regally. "We don't have any information to share on that at this time. Next question."

"Is the FBI involved in this case?"

"FBI and the state Bureau of Criminal Investigation are assisting. Next."

"Are you aware that the crime scene was compromised by the podcaster Cas Russo? Is Cas Russo a suspect?"

I rolled my eyes so hard, they almost fell down the back of my spine. Great. Now his name was on the national news.

The chief fixed the questioner with a look that could cut diamonds. "The evidentiary value of our crime scene was never compromised. Participants who interfere with our investigation will receive all applicable criminal charges."

"What about Cas Russo's video of the crime scene?"

The chief stepped down from the podium as questions roared, and the newscast went back to a talking head.

I did a quick search for Rachel Marie Slouda. Her social media profiles showed she was a nurse at one of the local hospitals. Judging from her photos, she had a group of young women she hung out with, a boyfriend, and a shiny new engagement ring.

I frowned. I didn't remember seeing a ring at the crime scene.

I reached for my phone and texted Monica.

Hey. You need a drink?

I didn't expect her to respond today. This case was a total nightmare, and it was her baby.

To my surprise, she replied within minutes.

You're buying.

———

I met Monica at our favorite dive bar pizza joint. Sparky's was tucked away in a Victorian-era building near the local college, with street parking. I fed the meter and pushed through the decrepit door. My feet stuck to the floor. On a weekday night, it wasn't busy. I slid into a booth in the corner of the room where I could watch the door. The vinyl upholstery had been fixed with duct tape, and graffiti declarations of love had been cheerfully scrawled on the wall above me.

My gaze drifted up to a security camera mounted above the cash register and aimed at the door. Behind my head on the wall was the alarm system panel. My gaze roved over it. I could guess the alarm code by which four digits were worn away. Only twenty-four permutations. That brand of alarm allowed forty-five seconds between entering and an alarm triggering. If a person wrote all the permutations out, they had more than enough time to enter each one before the alarm sounded.

Cop brain. Cops often sussed out how hard any given target was. And honestly . . . it was sometimes a challenge to figure out how a criminal might get in. Sparky's was easy. I still hadn't figured out the hardware store down the street.

I didn't need to see a menu. When the waitress came by, I ordered a beer. I wasn't much of a drinker, and I was pretty sure my latest encounter with legitimate and illegitimate drugs meant that I should be taking it easy. Ordering a skunky beer would ensure I'd never finish it.

I scanned the patrons. Mostly college students. As a somewhat rural county not too far away from the city, we had a small liberal arts college with a pretty good academic reputation. We had a couple of streets of funky thrift shops, cafés, and bars—just enough to keep the student body entertained and mostly out of trouble. My gaze fell on a girl with a blond ponytail. She was thin, pretty, with a dancer's posture. Just the kind of girl the Forest Strangler liked.

Above the bar, a television droned. The news anchor murmured over a picture of my father.

". . . citizens are encouraged to be cautious about their surroundings in the face of this threat . . ."

The blond girl looked up at the screen and shuddered. The girl sitting beside her, a brunette, had put her keys on the table with a brand-new can of pepper spray on the key chain.

My cell phone dinged. I saw a brief text from the chief:

Got the letter from your psychiatrist, doc, and IA's final report. Take a couple weeks off to rest up but come back when you're ready.

I grinned and texted back: I'm off admin leave?

Yes. Jesus christ take some time off or I'll just assign you to desk duty. You have 240 hours of banked sick leave.

I wrinkled my nose.

Yes, Chief. Thank you.

YW.

The door opened and I glanced up to see Monica. She was wearing dress pants with a rumpled blouse and a reptile-print jacket. As she slid into the booth, her shoulders slumped. She smelled of cigarette smoke.

I noticed she was wearing more makeup than usual: a red lip plus a smoky eye. "You got tarted up to get on the news?"

She made a kissy face at me. "Thank God not. Chief likes to do the talking." She ordered a beer, and we put in an order for a garbage pizza with just about everything on it, no meat on my half.

I told her the chief had taken me off AL. Monica grinned and clinked my beer bottle with hers. "That's gotta be a load off your mind. Not that there was any question, but having your career hanging over your head has to be stressful."

I took a swig of my beer and made a face. "How's it going in your world?"

Monica put her head in her hand. "That poor girl in the woods. We ID'd her right away with fingerprints from the state nursing board database. I talked to her family and fiancé earlier today. She was a good girl. Did all the right things. Graduated top of her class. Was working as a nurse. Just got engaged."

I lifted my eyebrow at the obvious. Whenever a woman was killed, money was always on the boyfriend or husband, even in weird circumstances like this. "What's up with the fiancé?"

"As near as I can tell, nothing. She met the guy in college, and they've been dating since. He works in finance. No record. When I broke the news, he just dissolved."

"Yeah?"

"Yup. Those were real tears. Very convincing. That guy is devastated."

"Well, fuck. I was hoping this was gonna be open-and-shut."

"Oh, hell no." Monica sat back in the booth. "We've even got an FBI profiler down here, looking at the evidence at the state crime lab."

"Any good prints?"

"Hopefully we'll get something back. She's being swabbed for DNA, too, so fingers crossed we'll get a hit."

The pizza came, and I pulled a piece out and spoke around mouthfuls of gooey cheese. "You think she was raped? I seem to recall that the Forest Strangler didn't rape his victims."

"Right. I didn't see any obvious bruising or signs of forcible attack, but that doesn't mean anything. We'll see what comes back from the swabs. But I'm pretty sure I know the mode of death."

"Yeah?"

Monica pulled a cheese string into her mouth. "Lots of bruising around the neck, and I'm guessing her hyoid bone is crushed. In keeping with the Strangler's MO. We'll know more after the lab has worked through everything."

I chewed thoughtfully. "Any other evidence show up?"

"We saw some cut foliage in the area that we assume was used for decoration. We haven't found her car yet. I'm guessing she was abducted on her trip somehow, the car was hidden, and he transported her who knows where. I don't yet know if he killed her in the car, or if she was killed somewhere else and then transported to the woods . . . or if there was an intermediary stop . . ." Monica rubbed her brow. "Anna, I'm used to dealing with cases where some guy gets high and shoots his ex. Like what you walked into."

"Well, sometimes greatness is thrust upon us." I gave her a wry smile. "I have no doubt you'll rise to the occasion."

Monica stared up at the ceiling. "It may not be up to me. The Feds are all over this. Not sure how that's all going to play out. It's our jurisdiction, for sure, but they're crawling all over the place and wanting to put a task force into place. Maybe that's for the best."

"You're the best investigator I've ever met," I told her. "You got this."

She made a face. "Enough about me and my hassles. How're you doing?"

"Okay, I think. Mostly tired of sitting around the house. I'd like to get back to work."

"You recovering okay?"

"I've got antibiotics and things seem to be healing up." I rolled up my sleeve and showed her a constellation of stitches.

"You got lucky," Monica said solemnly. "How are you feeling about how it went down?"

I frowned. "I'm not sure. I never really thought I'd have to kill anyone." And I certainly hadn't been anticipating that trill of thrill I felt at seeing the life fleeing the perp's face.

"That can totally mess you up. I had a roommate in the Army who woke up screaming after she lost someone in a training accident. She eventually took a bottle of sleeping pills and almost killed herself. It's not anything to fuck around with."

"I know. I'm seeing a shrink."

She nodded. "Good. Don't get stupid, because stuff like that can sneak up and bite your ass later on, sometimes years later. That shit goes dormant in your brain, but it rots there and can contaminate stuff you can't see now."

"I've got it under control." It was a lie, but I was really good at lying.

Monica's cell phone went off. She fished it out of her pocket, stared at it. "Fuck."

I concentrated on my pizza. Monica rubbed her brow, making affirmative noises and grimacing. She finally set the phone down on the table, sighed, and released a beautiful string of expletives that described the current state of the world sculpted in the language of shit.

"Yeah?" I said.

"Fucking Cas Russo. I sent out a deputy to tail him until I could get an arrest warrant for interference. But he lost the tail."

My brow knit. "Who was tailing him?"

She rolled her eyes. "Rollins."

"Ugh. Why did *he* get assigned?"

"Apparently, I needed to specify that he be tailed by someone competent. A judge just issued the warrant. Sheriff's deputies went to serve it at his apartment but he's already cleared out. Fuck."

"Fuck," I agreed.

"I want to go look at his place."

I lifted an eyebrow. "Yeah?"

"The apartment and its technological contents are named in the warrant." Monica shrugged and reached for the check. "Wanna ride along?"

I thought about the chief's text. "If Chief finds out I'm not taking it easy, he's going to be pissed."

"Pfft. He's got enough on his plate. If anybody makes a deal of it, we just tell him that you and I were gonna go see a movie and I thought I was only going to be fifteen minutes." Monica stood. "C'mon. You really want to look in Cas Russo's drawers and giggle at his Underoos."

15

THE LOCKET

I had to admit that I did want to see Cas's lair. Monica texted me the address, and I climbed into my SUV to follow her.

We drove west, toward the exurbs of the nearby city. Out here, car dealerships, drive-through carry-outs, and occasional new-build apartment complexes sprawled. The sun had set, and a few streetlamps illuminated new streets carved through former cow fields. The landscaping around the apartment complexes looked like twigs jammed in seas of mulch, and mayflies swarmed the lights. Monica stopped in an apartment complex parking lot, pulling in behind a sheriff's cruiser.

I met Monica at her car. She was rummaging through her car trunk and tossed me a pair of latex gloves and a pair of booties.

"You're prepared," I observed.

"Yup. Dotting my *i*'s and crossing my *t*'s. Plus, I don't want to leave any of my own damn prints behind for Cas to do a podcast on," she muttered. "Last thing I want is to be doxxed and deal with his fans."

That sounded eminently reasonable. I followed Monica up an external staircase to the second floor. A door was slightly ajar, and Monica nudged it open with her bootie-covered shoe.

I looked past her and stifled a groan. Corporal Rollins was standing in the center of the floor, talking with a guy in a maintenance uniform. I noticed he hadn't bothered to glove up or put on booties.

I glanced past him to the alarm panel on the kitchen wall. It had been silenced with a master code, likely provided by the alarm company or maintenance. Interesting that Cas felt like he had valuables to protect, or else felt he was at risk of physical harm.

Monica nodded at Rollins. "You can return to your post outside."

"I was just—"

"To your post, Corporal. And I don't want to see you back here without proper PPE."

"Yes, Captain." Rollins reluctantly headed outside, but he kept the door ajar. Probably so he could hear everything.

Monica closed the door and began chatting with the maintenance guy. I took a moment to take in the whole room. It was a lot.

The small apartment was completely stuffed full of crap. A sagging couch sat against a wall before an altar of media that probably cost more than my annual salary. With those speakers, I was sure his upstairs and downstairs neighbors were plotting to kill him. My gaze skimmed video game consoles, a desk with a computer, the largest television I'd ever seen, but froze on the walls and shelves.

Flanked by posters from horror movies, a painting of a sad-looking clown hung on the wall, signed by John Wayne Gacy. It didn't look like a print but the real thing. Animal skulls decorated the shelves. In between were a collection of odd items: a folded ornate pocketknife, a rusty bayonet, and a framed postcard signed by Ed Gein. Lower bookshelves were loaded with true crime books.

I glanced at his desk. His computer lock screen demanded a password. With gloved fingers, I flipped through a notepad beside his mouse. Mostly video game cheat codes, but I found a hand-drawn map of the crime scene, with GPS coordinates. He might have scribbled that down while talking to his informant.

"Hey, Monica," I said.

I glanced back to see her opening the door to let the maintenance guy out. Rollins must have had his ear pressed tight to the door, because he nearly stumbled inside. Monica glared at him while she watched the maintenance guy leave.

She crooked a finger at Rollins. At least he was wearing gloves and booties now. He came inside, and she shut the door behind him.

"Is there a problem, Corporal?" she asked.

"I just wanted to make sure you asked the maintenance guy if he's seen Cas."

"You seem to have a misapprehension of the chain of command, Corporal. Wouldn't you think a detective would ask that?"

"Well, I just thought—"

"Your job is to stand guard outside this door and apprehend the suspect if he should appear. And not contaminate a potential crime scene by stomping around here, flouting evidentiary rules and inviting third parties to the scene. Understand?"

"Yes." He gave her a sulky look, then glanced at me. "But if she gets to be here, then—"

"Go to your assignment or you'll be charged with insubordination. Is that clear?"

He turned, mumbling something that sounded a lot like "Bitch."

He slammed the door on his way out.

Monica rolled her eyes. "That fucking guy. Whatcha got?"

I showed her the notepad, and she paged through it. "Hmm. I don't like this." She picked up the notepad and dropped it into an evidence bag.

She hooked a thumb toward the bedroom. "IT's en route to take that computer. I'm gonna look for more evidence."

I nodded and turned my attention back to his trophy case. A fine layer of dust had accumulated on these treasures, but I noticed a couple of blank spots. Maybe Cas had taken some things with him. I frowned.

My heart froze when I spied a small acrylic case. A heart-shaped gold-tone locket hung inside. It looked identical to the one my father had given me, once upon a time.

I picked up the case. It was the same one: I remembered the scratch on the face.

I turned over the box. A label read: **Trophy from the Forest Strangler, Victim #18, Teresa Stanger.**

My pulse pounded. Where had he gotten this? Some auction site? He had no right . . . My hand closed around it, and I slipped it in my pocket.

I heard footsteps in the hallway and turned. Monica was busily taking pictures.

"Any sign of him packing to leave?" I asked.

"That's the weird thing. I found a suitcase in the back of the closet. He's left some things here that I'd expect a man on the run to take with him: prescription medications, cell phone charger, cash." Her mouth turned down. "I'm betting he guessed we were coming and didn't come home. Maybe he saw Rollins and split, or he knew we'd be on his six the instant that video dropped."

A knock sounded on the door, and Monica opened it to the IT

techs. I was glad it wasn't Detective Vernon but two of his techs I was friendly with, Saxon and Solomon. I nodded at them, and Solomon told me: "Glad to see you back, El-Tee."

"Glad to be back," I said truthfully.

Saxon grinned at me. The petite woman with purple hair stepped into the room with paper-covered Doc Martens. "Oh, this is so fucked-up."

"You should see the bedroom," Monica said.

I couldn't resist. I went down the short hallway and peered inside. An unmade bed stood in the center of a bank of monitors and wires. Some of it was ghost-hunting equipment he'd used in his podcasts. The walls were painted black, featuring a neon-green silhouette of Bigfoot wading through a fluorescent forest.

"Somebody ain't getting his deposit back," I said mildly.

"Check this out." Monica flipped out the light switch. "It glows in the dark."

True to her word, Bigfoot shone like a neon ghost in the dark.

"Awesome." The techs cackled.

It was getting pretty crowded here, and I was conscious of the fact that I had the necklace burning a hole in my pocket. Monica walked me out. Rollins was leaning up against the wall, staring daggers at us.

A moment of rage lit in me. Rollins had been a pain in my ass and Monica's since he'd been hired. I was tired of his bullshit, no matter how petty it might be.

I paused, looked him in the face. He sneered at me.

"Corporal, turn out your pockets, please."

He froze. "What?"

"Corporal, that's an order. Turn out your pockets."

"I'm not—"

"I won't tell you again."

He huffed and began to walk away. I blocked his path. I exchanged glances with Monica. She grabbed his right arm as I grabbed his left, turning him so that his face was planted against the apartment wall. Rollins squawked, but Monica already had his arms behind his back.

The techs came rushing out, and before Rollins knew it, four people were on him. Monica patted him down and came up with four small items: a lock of hair, labeled as being from Charles Manson, embedded in acrylic; a kitchen knife purported to have been owned by Jeffrey Dahmer; a piece of brick from Dennis Rader's house; and a picture of Ted Bundy after his execution.

"What the hell, Rollins?" Monica squawked.

"You've got no right," Rollins hissed. "The union isn't going to let you get away with this."

"What kind of a total sociopath steals shit like this from a bottom feeder like Cas Russo?"

Rollins refused to answer. "I want my union steward and a lawyer."

I stepped back. Now that the adrenaline had begun to fade, my arm hurt. I looked down to see blood trickling down my forearm.

"You all right, Lieutenant?" Solomon asked, his moustache turning down with the corner of his mouth.

"Yeah." I pressed my hand over the wound. "Just overdid it."

Monica glanced at me. "Go home, Koray. I'll get your statement later."

Saxon walked me to my car. "How did you know he stole that stuff?"

"There were a few areas clear of dust on Cas's shelves," I said. "Cas wasn't a great housekeeper. Either he took those with him or someone else took them. And since he hadn't been back . . ."

"What a slimeball," Saxon said. "Who does shit like that?"

"Rollins, apparently." I unlocked my SUV. I watched Saxon wave and head back to the apartment complex.

I reached into my pocket for the sharp box there.

Slimeballs like Rollins and me.

I cranked the ignition, but quickly shut it down. Solomon was hauling ass down the steps with a computer tower in his hands. Monica was behind him, shouting into her radio and waving Saxon back.

I grabbed my radio and lunged out of the SUV. Monica started pounding on doors, ordering residents to come out.

I jogged toward Solomon, who was loading the computer tower into the back of his car.

"What's going on?"

Solomon grimaced. "I opened his hall closet. There's buckets of something that smells like ether in there."

My brows drew together. "That shit's flammable."

"Incredibly so."

He could be using it to drug victims. Or . . . more likely, we'd stumbled upon a drug lab. Ether was a critical component in PCP. If it could be smelled, one spark would be all it would take to send the whole building up.

I sprinted to the apartment complex and started pounding on doors as fire truck sirens sounded in the distance.

The fire chief evacuated everyone from Cas's apartment building until further notice. Monica praised Solomon's quick thinking on snatching up Cas's computer. At least we could begin on that part of the investigation.

Pissed-off residents milled in the parking lot, talking on their cell phones.

"Do you have any idea when we can get back in?" Monica asked the fire chief.

The chief and his volunteer firefighters cordoned off the parking lot. "Not until I get that clear. Bomb squad's en route from two neighboring counties. From what I saw in there, he's got buckets of unknown chemicals stashed in closets, under the kitchen sink, and God knows where else. We're shutting down pilot lights and everything that can cause a spark in the meantime. Lucky thing the whole building didn't go up."

And Cas, indirectly, could've been responsible for my own PCP poisoning. Small world.

I exhaled. Cas was involved in more shit than I'd anticipated, and we could be well and truly fucked.

16

SUMMONING

It had been years since I'd seen that locket.

I'd assumed the police found it when they searched our house, that they tore it apart looking for evidence. I certainly didn't tell them. I imagined that it sat in the bottom of an evidence box or was returned to the victim's family. I just assumed that it was from one of the dozens of blond girls who blurred together.

I arrived home in darkness. I never left my porch light on, but something rested on the step, right before the door.

At first, I thought it might be some kind of wounded animal. I crept toward it, wary and gentle.

But it was a bird's nest, beautiful and intact. I crouched and lifted it in my hands. It was the sort that would belong to a medium-sized bird, like a catbird, with a thin film of gray feathers clinging to the interior.

Logically, it could've blown here or been dragged here by a predator. Logically.

But my skin prickled. I felt as if I were being watched.

I circled the house, drawing my gun, feeling silly for doing so. I saw nothing out of the ordinary, only startling an opossum in the woodpile.

I told myself that I was easily triggered by the soup of memories, PCP, and emotions swirling in my head. It was a nest. That was all.

I took it inside and locked the door behind me. I grabbed a kitchen chair and pulled it to the deer mounted above the fireplace. Gently, I placed the nest within the antlers. It felt like it belonged there. At any other time in my life, I would've been delighted to find such a treasure, and I clung to that.

After I kicked my shoes off, I got to work. First, I did a search for Teresa Stanger, victim #18. A photograph I'd seen before came up: a tall, willowy blonde with shoulder-length hair and glasses. She was standing with a horse and wearing equestrian gear. She was tan, her teeth were straight, and she had the look of a woman certain about who she was and where she was going.

"She was the mother of a ten-year-old boy," her mother tearfully told a reporter. "She was working on her PhD in English. We were looking forward to her becoming an English professor. She wrote the most beautiful poetry."

At the woman's side stood a young boy staring into the distance. He looked numb, confused. My heart ached for him.

I skimmed through the articles. Teresa Stanger's car was found in a ditch after an accident, but she was missing. Police suspected another car was involved but had only paint scrapings to go on. She'd simply disappeared, only to resurface in a river. Her death was considered to be one of the Forest Strangler's more elaborate works: he'd created a raft of lashed branches, placed her on the raft with her arms laden with dogwood blossoms, and sent her downstream to be discovered by kayakers. Investigators speculated that the Forest Strangler had seen her and had run her compact car off the road to abduct her.

I stared into the acrylic box. It felt as if a forgotten part of myself had been returned to me. This was Teresa's, to be certain. But it was also mine, in a strange chain of provenance. I felt the way an adult does when she finds a toy she used to play with at a rummage sale: that warmth.

But also the horror. I closed my eyes. How could my father have done that? Did he see me as a victim, too?

And how could I steal this? If I were found out, I'd be fired and charged with a crime.

I thought about returning it surreptitiously. No one would ever need to know. It wasn't too late to do the right thing.

But it was. I knew it, on some level, ever since I'd looked into Tom Sullivan's darkening eyes in that driveway. I had started to creep beyond the bright line separating right and wrong.

I placed the case on the floor and stomped on it with the heel of my boot. It fractured open, and I fished the necklace out of the shattered pieces. It felt immediately warm in my palm, as if a part of me had returned.

I fastened it around my neck, relishing the familiar weight of it. I fed the paper label to the garbage disposal, then swept up the acrylic pieces. I took them outside, to a rusted burn barrel the prior residents of the house left behind. I flung the pieces there, then dumped my trash on top. I squirted some lighter fluid in the barrel, then lit a match.

As the plastic dissolved, the smoke became acrid, and I hated the artificial smell of it. My fingers traced the pendant glittering on my collar. I opened it, and brittle pieces of brown moss were still inside.

I knew this was wrong, so wrong.

But it felt right, in a way I could never explain, as if I were re-trieving parts of my past, calling them home.

———

The safe house the FBI had put Mom and me up in after my fa-ther's arrest could never be home.

We were at that apartment for two weeks. A plainclothes agent was always watching television in the living room. Mom and I rarely spoke.

Plainclothes agents rotated in and out. I asked about Agent Parkes but was always told that he'd come visit with Percival when he could. I began to doubt that as the days slipped by. Maybe he'd lied to me. It had happened before.

But the agents were nice to me. While my mom stayed in bed, the agents taught me to play card games. I leafed through the magazines they left. These were carefully curated glossies that mentioned nothing about my father, instead describing makeup techniques and wildlife on far-distant savannas.

I went to my mom once when I woke up with a nightmare about the women in the house. I crept into her bedroom and tried to climb in bed with her.

She shoved me away. "You're too old for that."

I went back to my room. I knew the agent on duty had heard everything, and I was ashamed. My mom had rejected me. What kind of an awful kid gets rejected by her mom like that? My cheeks burned and I held my tears in until I got back into my own bed.

I heard my door open. It was one of the agents, a woman with short, highlighted brown hair. She told me her name was Margie.

She sat on the edge of the bed and stroked my hair. "You okay, kiddo?"

I could only shake my head, tears trickling from my eyes.

She held me until I was sobbed out, hiccupping. And she brought with her a magazine with a story about the pyramids in Egypt. She read it aloud to me until I fell asleep. I woke up a few times in the night and saw she was still in my room, her shadow flipping the pages of a fashion magazine she read by flashlight. We didn't speak of that night again, but I noticed that the agents were considerably colder to my mother afterward.

"Have you caught him yet?" I asked Margie. We were sitting on the carpeted living room floor, speaking in low voices so as not to disturb Mom, asleep in the next room.

"I'll tell you if you drink some juice." She nodded at my mostly full juice box.

I slurped it down and showed her my purple tongue.

"Good." She looked over her cards at me. "No. Not yet. Go fish."

I fished.

"Do you think you'll ever catch him?"

She paused, frowning. "I don't know."

I stared down at my cards.

"Do you want to talk about it?"

I clamped my lips together and shook my head. A big part of me wanted him to escape, to run away to Canada or wherever people went into the wilderness to disappear, never to be seen again. Another part of me wanted them to catch him. I was afraid of him now, and my dreams woke me often, screaming, envisioning the horrible scene in that fallen-down house.

Margie handed me an apple. "You want some fruit?"

I looked down at it. I wasn't ever really hungry anymore, but this lady always insisted I eat the snacks she brought, fruit and string cheese and carrots and celery with peanut butter. I took a bite to be polite.

She nodded. "Good girl."

A sob caught in my throat. No one had ever called me that before. The piece of apple stuck in my throat, and I began to choke. The agent swore, leapt up, and gave me the Heimlich maneuver. I spat the piece of apple out on the beige carpet and started to sob.

She wrapped her arms around me. "Shh. It's okay. It's okay."

But it wasn't, and she couldn't make it okay.

Later that night, I lay in bed next to a window with the stripes of blinds cast across the wall and the floor. I stared up at that streetlight, feeling lonely. I could've gotten out of bed to go flip through magazines with Margie, but I didn't want to be a pest. It didn't occur to me to go to my mom at all.

A deafening crack sounded, and glass shattered above me. I screamed and rolled out of bed, pulling my blanket over myself.

Margie thundered into the room, gun drawn, and shoved me under the bed. I heard her shouting at her radio, then the door opening and feet clomping through the apartment.

I rolled under the bed and pushed myself toward the wall.

Margie slithered under the bed. "Are you hurt?"

I shook my head.

"You have to come with me." She extended her hand to me and pulled me out from under the bed. We crawled through the broken glass, staying low, reaching the door. Agents flooded in, and shouting echoed from the parking lot.

Mom was in the hallway, slurring, "What happened?"

No one answered. Someone threw a blanket over her head an instant before one was tossed over mine, and we were whisked down the steps. My feet never touched the ground; an agent lifted each elbow. We were shoved into a car, and that car peeled out of the parking lot.

I peeped back, seeing red and blue strobe lights through the blanket weave.

Mom lay on the back seat and hissed to Margie in the passenger's seat: "Was it him?"

"No." Margie's mouth was pressed into a hard line. "It was a paparazzo."

I didn't know what a paparazzo was, but I was pretty sure my job was to hunker down and keep quiet.

"I don't understand . . . Why would they do that?"

"They wanted to get pictures of you." Margie rubbed her temple.

"Is it always going to be like this?" Mom demanded.

Margie met her gaze. "No. Eventually they'll lose interest. After they catch him, they'll focus on him. I swear."

Mom slumped against the seat, pulling the blanket away. I looked down at my hands. I was bleeding.

"Let me see," Margie ordered. I dutifully extended my hands, palms up, to her. She delicately plucked out slivers of glass and put them in the ashtray.

Mom popped a pill and closed her eyes.

I watched Margie work, wondering if she had children. "You're good at this."

She gave me a half smile. "I was an Army nurse once upon a time."

"Did you get to go anyplace interesting?"

She winked at me. "Can't tell you, kiddo. That's classified."

I sighed.

"But let's just say that one of the places I got to go to was Alaska. There are all kinds of cool animals there. Eagles. Bears. Otters. Got to watch the otters sled on the snow, on their bellies." She made a zooming motion with her hand.

I knew she was trying to distract me, to help me.

But I felt beyond all help, hopeless, and staring into an uncertain night in my pajamas with no shoes and an unconscious mom.

We were moved to another safe house, this one a house at the end of a dead-end road in another state. Undercover cops in a pickup truck were stationed at the end of the road by the mailbox.

I liked it better there. I could walk through the backyard, and I found acorns to place on my windowsill. Maybe I put them there to ward off the press. Or my father. Or the Forest God, who had taken him. *Take the acorns and leave us be.*

Agent Parkes came back, with Percival. I knew that when I saw him it was because they'd found my father. I had no way of knowing how the investigation had gone; there was no television there, and no one brought any newspapers. I assumed they kept my mother updated, but I existed in a limbo of not knowing, of counting blades of grass and dimples on the popcorn ceiling.

When he came into the sparsely furnished living room, he sat in a dusty armchair. Mom and I sat on the couch, and Margie leaned in the doorway to the kitchen. The clock on the paneled wall ticked loudly. Percival edged away from Parkes and came to sit beside me.

"I wanted to come tell you in person," he began. "They found your husband."

My mom sat on the couch, her hands clasped around each other, so tight her knuckles were white.

"Is he alive?"

"For now, but it doesn't look good. He was trying to steal a car at a truck stop south of the state line. Someone saw him and he took off. But some truckers chased after him. One of them shot him in the back."

I blinked. This wasn't the end I imagined for my dad. I'd expected him to melt away into the woods, never to be seen again. A truck stop wasn't where he belonged. This was why he was caught. I closed my eyes and listened to the adults talk. I concentrated on the feel of Percival's fur under my palm.

"He's hanging on, but he might not ever wake up," Parkes said.

"What happens if he wakes up?"

"Then he gets the death penalty. There's no escaping it. He's never going to be able to hurt anyone ever again."

I listened to my mom's shallow breathing.

"Can I see him?" I asked, opening my eyes.

Parkes looked to my mom.

"No," she said. "No, you can't."

"I just want to say goodbye."

"No." Her voice grew shrill: "*No, no, no, no . . .* "

Margie drew her away to the kitchen.

I stared at Agent Parkes.

"Your mom is in charge," he said.

Percival sighed and laid his head in my lap.

My mom had never been in charge of anything before. And I feared that, more than I feared my father.

———

I awoke in darkness beside Nick. He snored softly. He'd once told me he didn't dream at all. Sometimes I envied him that. Other times I pitied him. I always dreamed, a second life full of strange symbols and conversations. Even now, with memories of my father creeping to the surface, I looked forward to mining that darkness for answers, for connections I couldn't make in conscious life.

I slipped out of bed and through the front door, to the porch. It was too late for the frogs to be singing, and the moon was tangled in the western tree line. The fireflies had faded into the stillest part of the night. I reached into the pocket of my lounge pants for the locket, feeling the metal warm against my palm.

I stared at the driveway. Nick's car wasn't there. His silver sports car had been replaced by a glossy black SUV. I paced around it. It was next year's model year, brand-new, with tinted back windows. I peered in the driver's side, squinting in the dim light. I made out hand-stitched leather and the fancy custom floor liners that were advertised on TV.

I didn't expect Nick to clear his life decisions with me, certainly. But I'd had an image of him fixed in my brain, a sports car–loving guy who liked the thrill. Maybe he'd changed.

I walked out onto the grass, cool against my feet. I picked violets, just white ones. When I had five, I carried them back to the porch and placed them on the windowsill, as I'd placed findings as a little girl.

Were they offerings? Wards? A gift in exchange for the nest? I didn't know. I just felt compelled to do so, to reenact that memory of being a child in the woods, back when I had nothing to fear. Back when the Forest God kept his distance.

I stared into the woods. Something moved, a shadow in the dark. I held still, holding my breath, watching.

The shape paused, seeming to peer at me. I couldn't fully define it, except it made my heart thunder. It looked like a man with antlers, soundless and staring at me with those bottomless black eyes I'd seen haunting my father's face at the house in the woods.

My heart pounded.

The moon passed behind a cloud, and the light shifted. When it peeked again through the tree branches, a buck glided serenely through the underbrush. His antlers shone in the moonlight.

He paused a moment, making eye contact with me before fading away into the dark.

17

THE LYSSA VARIANT

"Saddle up, girl. We're heading out to the crime lab."

I glanced up from my desk in the bullpen. I'd been put on light duty, and that meant reviewing time sheets and dodging dark glares from Rollins's buddies. The thin blue line got pretty squiggly sometimes.

I realized I'd been staring at my monitor for so long, the screen saver had kicked in. I frowned and glanced at my watch. I'd been there for two hours, and I'd blanked it all out. I blinked and stared down at my notepad. There was only a scribble of a daisy on the paper, one I didn't remember making. *I really should talk to Dr. Richardson about this*, I thought. *But she might pull me from duty.*

Monica stood in front of my desk, popping a piece of nicotine gum into her mouth. She offered me a piece, but I refused.

"What's with this 'we'?" I took a swig of cold coffee and made a face.

"I asked Chief to put you on the murder investigation." She popped her gum and grinned. "Beats time sheets, am I right?"

I had to agree. I grabbed my bag and followed her out of the office, relieved. Rollins wasn't especially liked, but shady guys had shady friends, and I was quickly becoming aware of who was who. Like when a deputy wordlessly slapped his time sheet down on my desk with a grimace. I was too close to the chief for them to pull any major shit, but it was still annoying as hell, and I was glad to get some air.

And even more intrigued to get closer to the case. I was certain Dr. Richardson would call this all kinds of a conflict of interest. But I didn't want to step away. I wanted—no, I needed—to watch.

"Any word on Cas's little drug setup?"

"He's apparently got shit stashed everywhere. Might have also been in on it with the maintenance guy . . . A firefighter followed his nose and found more materials in the maintenance shed. The maintenance guy's in the wind, but we've got an APB out for him, too."

"What about the people who got displaced?"

"Red Cross set up a temporary shelter in the high school gym. Everyone's accounted for, and nobody got hurt. But nobody can get back in unless there's some serious decontamination. A couple of the buckets leaked into the closet of Cas's downstairs neighbor. And she had a toddler."

"Jesus." Cas was one busy dude.

We climbed into one of the office's Crown Vics and headed down the road. Monica put the windows down to chase out the smell of smoke.

"The state crime lab's started looking at the body," she said. "And, honestly, I'm glad they have it. They'll dot all their *i*'s and cross their *t*'s. If there's evidence there to be found, I'm sure they'll get it."

"No doubt. Anybody seen Cas?"

"There's an APB out for him and his van. We're monitoring his ATM and credit cards and waiting to see if his cell phone pings off a tower. I figure he's hiding out in one of his buddies' basements, but that's gonna end when the cops start knocking on doors. He might have enough internet contacts to find a place to hide for a couple of days, but he's going to have to come up for air sooner or later."

"You're banking on the cops scaring him? I dunno. It seems like he might crave that kind of attention. I don't think he'll keep silent for long. He's gonna pop up online."

"Could be. How in the hell did Cas pick up such a weird hobby, anyway? I hear K-pop is big now. Why couldn't he be more into K-pop and less into PCP and serial killers?"

"This morbid stuff feels like more than a hobby to me. I mean . . . killer memorabilia?"

Monica rubbed her temple. "I don't get it. Maybe his parents didn't love him enough or something. But he dropped some money on that shit."

"Speaking of someone who didn't get enough love as a child, Rollins was sure looking to cash in."

"Ugh. That guy." Monica rolled her eyes. "Chief was pissed. I don't know what IA's got cookin', but if I were them, I'd be really curious to see if Rollins has swiped any other evidence from crime scenes. As brazen as that was, I'm sure it's not his first time."

I looked out the window. It was *my* first time. And hopefully my last. I fully knew Rollins was going to take the fall for that locket—if and when Cas ever discovered it missing.

But I didn't care.

Did that make me any better than him? Maybe. I liked to think that I did what I did for non-assholey reasons, but that was a slippery slope these days.

We took the interstate north to what was lovingly called the state's "prison-industrial complex." Out in the middle of nowhere, a town had sprung up around two prisons and the state crime lab. One prison was a brand-spankin'-new medium-security prison, and the other was an older facility that had originally been constructed with the intent of using agriculture to rehabilitate prisoners. At one time, that facility generated all the food for the state penal system. It had been greatly scaled back and just did butchering now. I personally thought it was a shitty idea to let even minimum-security inmates kill cows all day, but I was certainly no expert on mental health.

We headed down the road to the state crime lab, a one-story brick building surrounded by a large parking lot.

We were buzzed through a door in the lobby and followed it down the tiled hallway. To the right and left, through windows in doors, I saw technicians working with microscopes and paper files. There was a bewildering plethora of equipment set up here, thanks to federal grants; I had no idea what most of it was used for. We passed a humming server room where they maintained the state fingerprint database and where cold leaked from under the door.

We paused before the morgue. Monica knocked.

The door opened, and a man in his sixties wearing round glasses peered back at us. "Detective Captain Wozniak?"

"Yes. This is Detective Lieutenant Koray."

"Pleased to meet you. I'm Sam Constantine, the ME. Please come in and get suited up. I have some interesting things to show you."

Despite the vigorous air-conditioning, the place smelled like death. Metal cabinets lined the walls, and three stainless steel tables perched above floor drains on the tile floor. Two tables held body bags. One was about the size and shape of a woman, while the other was more sunken and amorphous in shape. That one smelled like it had been in the water for some time.

"So, what did you find?" Monica asked Sam, who was pulling down the zipper of the first body bag. Rachel Marie Slouda looked gray and quiet in repose. She didn't look alive; she wasn't fresh enough for that. But there was something peaceful about her. Still . . .

Constantine pointed to the red marks around her neck. "Cause of death was manual strangulation. Judging by the age of botfly larvae, we think she was killed around twenty-four hours before she was found."

So if Cas killed her, he went back to the crime scene to admire his work.

I leaned closer, seeing something wiggling under her eyelid. Summer was hell on corpses. "Any other injuries?"

"No signs of sexual assault. Her fiancé reports that they hadn't had sex in a couple of weeks. We also found amphetamines on her tox screen."

"Amphetamines?" Monica echoed.

"We thought she might be medicated for ADHD, but the levels seemed excessive for a prescribed dose. We were able to check with the state reporting system and there are no prescriptions for ADHD medications or similar on file for the subject."

I looked up. "She seemed like she was on the straight and narrow. That sort of thing could've jeopardized her nursing license."

"Maybe she was trying to stay awake for her shifts," Monica offered. "It's not unheard-of for people in that line of work to do that."

I frowned at Rachel Marie Slouda. She was a woman with secrets, and I could sympathize.

The ME continued: "Otherwise, it looks like she fought hard against her attacker. Bruises on her knees and hands, scrapes on her knuckles. Those small cuts were washed out after the time of death."

"Do you think she was killed in that creek bed?" Monica asked.

"I think she was there for a day, judging by the mud residue on her body. I think she was abducted and killed quickly by manual strangulation, then spent some time with the killer before he deposited her body in the creek bed."

"You think he did all that decorating with the flowers and stuff at the scene?"

"I do, judging by the amount of wilting. But it probably took him some time to gather those materials."

"They're native plants from the immediate area," I said.

"Yes. They're common plants that could be found all over the county."

"Any prints?" Monica wanted to know.

"Not so far. But we did find a small amount of very degraded DNA under the victim's fingernail."

"Degraded?" Monica echoed. "She hasn't been there that long."

"The perpetrator painstakingly washed the body." Constantine lifted up her right hand, showing short, thin nails. "We found some glue residue and suspect the victim was wearing false fingernails. He took the time to strip them off with a solvent, so that degraded the bit of skin cell DNA we found there."

"Did it match anyone?" Monica asked.

Constantine put the corpse's hand down and crossed his arms. "Here's where it gets weird. Some elements of the DNA we found are similar to those of the original Forest Strangler, Stephen Theron."

My heart lurched into my throat.

"What do you mean?" Monica's brow furrowed.

"We don't have enough for a complete profile, but we did compare what we could salvage to the original Forest Strangler's DNA. And we found a mutation that was also found in Stephen Theron's DNA, an RTN4R variant. That same mutation is found in the DNA we recovered from this body. It's called the Lyssa variant, after the daughter of night who caused madness in ancient Greek myths."

"How common is that mutation?" I felt lightheaded and surreptitiously grabbed the edge of the table for support.

"It's exceedingly rare. It was discovered while trying to find genetic causes for psychotic illnesses, but it's only been conclusively found in a handful of cases."

"Are we looking at a relative of Stephen Theron?" I asked quietly.

"Not necessarily. The other cases that came up in a search of the literature weren't related to him and were tied to a study of murderers on death row."

I nodded, my throat dry.

Monica frowned. "So our perpetrator has the same marker that the Forest Strangler did. So if we get a suspect who has that marker . . . that's circumstantial, but I like this for building a case."

My heart pounded.

The killer had DNA like my father's.

The killer could be my father.

———

"You're quiet."

Monica chewed her milkshake straw as she drove. We'd stopped at a gas station for snacks, and the milkshake machine had been operational, if mediocre. The gas station had a hand-lettered sign announcing that the store was closing at six p.m. I thought back to the girl on the news who refused to work the night shift with a killer on the loose.

I leaned into the open window, feeling stunned and hollow. "I don't know what to make of what Constantine said about this Lyssa variant," I admitted.

"Fuck if I know," Monica said. "For right now, I'm treating it as a weird coincidence."

"Okay." I sounded doubtful to even my own ears.

"Or maybe not. Maybe our perpetrator realized, for whatever reason, that he had this genetic weirdness. Maybe he had mental problems, went for treatment, and found this out. Maybe he researched other people who had it and came across Stephen Theron. Maybe he got obsessed and emulated the Strangler."

"Maybe." I slurped my milkshake. It was comforting to think that.

"It's clear our copycat feels some connection to him. Maybe that made him feel special. I mean, a guy like Cas wants to feel special, right?"

"It's as good a theory as any."

"Well, at least until the FBI profilers come up with something." Monica crunched on her straw.

"They keeping you in the loop?"

"I don't think they've done much yet, to be honest. I think they're just gathering data."

"Chief doesn't like them stomping on his territory."

"Nah. He wants the spotlight. He wants us to catch him." Monica glanced sidelong at me. "I mean, that's the plan, of course."

I frowned.

"You aren't down for a future of writing books and made-for-TV movies about the Forest Strangler, Part Deux?"

Shit. I was used to being anonymous. "No. I don't think that's something I want."

"That's why you're a good cop, Koray. You just do the work."

"You can leave me right out of that."

"Well, it's a good thing the boss likes the limelight. Let him soak it all up."

I made a face. My phone dinged a notification, and I fished it out of my pocket. "Oh, hey. Cas uploaded something new on YouTube."

Monica pulled over to the shoulder of the road. I held up my phone and pressed PLAY.

Cas leaned toward the camera, looking wild-eyed and intense.

"Guys. The cops are after me. They fucking ransacked my apartment. They had no right . . . ," he stammered in rage. "Those fucking assholes were in my home, going through my stuff!"

He rubbed his hand over his mouth. "I didn't do anything. I followed up on a tip. All I did was exercise my freedom of speech. I could be helping the police, of course, but they're chasing me down like a criminal . . ."

He started ranting again, and I looked over his shoulder. Looked too clean behind him. Matching lamps on either side of a bed. Had to be a hotel. The two lamps cast competing shadows: there was the top of his head, cast against a wall, and then another silhouette.

I pointed it out to Monica. "He's not alone."

She nodded.

Cas continued: "You know what I think? I think they're after me. I think they think I killed that girl."

"Hm." Monica sat back.

"What the fuck?" I muttered.

He looked left, then right, then shut off the camera.

"Well, that was some unnecessary drama." Monica slurped air bubbles from the bottom of her cup.

"You think he's doing that for likes?"

"Probably. I mean . . . I don't like him for this kind of crime. Do you?"

I tapped my Styrofoam cup. "He's got a serial killer channel going. He clearly craves fame. I'd argue that he might have motive. And he has that attention to detail. He knows every last bit of what the Forest Strangler did. So maybe he's got the means to duplicate the Strangler's signatures and his MO."

"Maybe. I don't know if he'd be able to keep his mouth shut about killing anyone long enough to actually do it. I dunno. I feel like he might live in a fantasy world, sure, but I don't know if he could actually execute."

"Yeah, I'm not sure."

Monica took out her phone. "I'm gonna get a warrant to obtain the IP address that uploaded that video to YouTube."

"When the fire chief releases his apartment, I'll have our people look through Cas's stuff for a strand of hair or something they can use for DNA analysis. See if he has that mutation. We can rule him in or out, get him center stage or sideline him."

"We might have chain of evidence problems," Monica realized. "With the fire department and bomb squad stomping in and around his place, his defense team could argue that a DNA test on a strand of hair we find in his comb is inadmissible."

"Yeah," I admitted. "They could. But we'd just have to get another warrant for his DNA later."

"And hopefully we can get some information on who his informant is."

"If he even exists."

I stared out the window, gazing at a field.

Could Cas really be the killer?

He seemed like a weird guy involved with the drug business. He had problems, sure. But were those problems big enough to turn him into a killer?

I had no idea.

I reached into my pocket where the warm souvenir necklace lay.

18

THE INTERLOPER

When I got back home, an unfamiliar car was out front. I paused halfway down the driveway and parked.

I radioed in for a plate check.

"L4, those plates are registered to Jerry Rollins." Dispatch sounded surprised.

I stared ahead. I didn't see anyone in the car. I didn't see anyone on the porch.

"Dispatch, please send a cruiser to my home address."

"Roger that."

Part of me wanted to put the car in reverse, to back up to the mouth of the driveway and wait for backup. The other part of me was furious that Rollins was here—why?—and I wondered what the fuck he was doing in my sanctuary. Rage lit through me. This was my land.

How *dare* he?

A hand slammed down on my car door, through the open

window. Rollins looked down at me. Automatically, my hand slid to my right side, to my holster.

"Wait, wait!" Rollins said. "I just want to talk."

My eyes narrowed. "What the fuck are you doing here?" I drew my gun, shielding it from him with my body.

"I just want to talk. Look . . ." He was sweating. "I'm gonna lose my job. I wanted to ask you to reconsider, to tell IA you were mistaken."

"Rollins. Go home. This is inappropriate."

"I know it is. I just . . . I don't have anything else but that job." Tears glossed his eyes.

I felt no sympathy for him, only an exhilarating burn of rage. How dare he come here and throw himself at my feet, to ask for mercy, when he'd been spending years being a complete and total shithead? Only now, when he'd been caught, was he willing to pretend to try to be a decent human being.

"Koray, please. I'm begging you."

For a moment I imagined what it would be like to draw down on him, to shoot him. I imagined what it would feel like to stand over him and watch the light draining from his eyes.

I wanted to do it.

I don't know what look my face held, but his meek expression contorted to rage. "I can't believe you're going to do this to me," he yelled. "You can't—"

He reached to open the car door.

I turned to him. My pulse beat low and evenly. "Don't you dare. Don't you fucking dare." My voice was a hollow growl.

A crash sounded behind him, from the woods.

He turned, startled.

I couldn't see through his body, but I felt a shadow pass over us. Something dark and strangely familiar. My skin crawled, knowing I was in the Forest God's presence.

I threw the car in reverse and sped back up the driveway, tires spitting gravel.

By the time I reached the road, a sheriff's car had paused with its turn signal on.

I holstered my gun and popped my door. I was sweating, knowing I'd left Rollins there with . . . with that thing.

Deputy Detwiler opened his door and crossed to meet me. "Dispatch said you had an unwelcome visitor."

"Yeah. Rollins is here, and he's trying to intimidate me into getting his charges dropped."

Detwiler sucked in his breath. "Damn. Okay. Are you all right?"

"Yeah."

"Why don't you pull out and I'll go in. You can head on to the office if you want, or you can come in behind me."

"I'll follow you in case he continues to be belligerent." And the Forest God was there. Fuck, I didn't want to feed Detwiler to Veles.

"Right. Thanks, El-Tee."

I was conscious of how green Detwiler was, but he was following the book very carefully. That boded well for his future . . . if we both didn't get devoured by that thing in the woods.

I backed out onto the road, and Detwiler headed down the drive first. I fell into line behind him.

Detwiler pulled up behind Rollins's car, with me behind him, blocking Rollins in. We stepped out onto the driveway.

"Rollins," Detwiler called. "Come out. I need to talk to you."

No answer. I listened, but there was no sound from the forest. No birds, no squirrel chatter. Nothing. My skin crawled.

Detwiler spoke into the radio pinned to his collar. "Base, his vehicle is here but he's gone. Going to look for him on foot."

"Acknowledged, D6."

Detwiler called out again. "Rollins, you aren't making this easy for yourself. Get back here and let's talk about what's going on, okay?"

Detwiler moved to the edge of the forest, his right hand resting on his weapon. He walked noisily into the woods, calling for Rollins.

I walked some yards behind and to his right, listening. I didn't add my voice to his; it was better if Rollins didn't believe I was on the field. I was hoping the Forest God had just scared him, or else I'd imagined him, but I didn't need to fuel Rollins's anger.

I paused. A set of wet footprints crossed a flat rock. Was Rollins—

"El-Tee," Detwiler said quietly.

I made my way to him.

He was standing in a little thicket, looking at something on the forest floor.

I joined him, following his gaze.

Rollins lay sprawled on the ground. Detwiler crouched before him and shook his shoulder. When there was no response, the deputy turned him over.

"Rollins."

Rollins's brow was smeared with fresh red blood. His chest rose and fell with shallow breaths, and his eyes were closed. The blood stained a rock below him.

"Rollins, man, c'mon. Get up."

He didn't react. Detwiler pried up his eyeball and shone a flashlight into each pupil. They didn't contract.

"How bad is he hurt?" I crouched beside him.

"Looks like he tripped and hit his head on that rock." Detwiler spoke into his radio. "This is D6. I need an ambulance at my 20."

I looked down at Rollins. He looked very much like Tom Sullivan, nearly dead, with the life hesitating around his eyes.

I felt a sting of satisfaction at that.

Fuck him.

Fuck him for being a filthy cop. Fuck him for abusing his power and poisoning the ideals I upheld. I still held those principles. They were slippery, but I was trying. Damn it, I was *trying*. And Rollins had never tried.

But most of all, fuck him for fucking with me.

———

The ambulance came and went.

My house was crawling with cops.

I gave a statement.

By now, the sun had set and the rarely used porch light was the best illumination in the place, casting white light out into the forest. Moths fluttered around the bulb, beating themselves against its glow. I'd checked the doors and windows. To my relief, everything seemed secure.

Chief arrived, still in his dress uniform from a press conference. "Hey. You all right?"

I nodded. "I don't know what he thought he was going to accomplish by coming here."

He patted me on the shoulder. "He's an asshole. That's all there is to it, kiddo."

Detwiler stepped up to the porch. "Report from the hospital, Chief. They say he's got a severe closed head injury. He's in a coma."

The hospital . . . shit. "I should call Nick."

I picked my phone out of my pocket. I'd missed three calls from him.

Headlights appeared in the driveway, behind the line of cars. They shut off, and Nick jogged down the driveway.

"Anna," he said. "Are you okay?"

I leaned into his embrace. "Yeah. Just a guy with a grudge."

"You should stay with me," he said into my hair.

"That's a good idea," Chief said.

"Okay," I agreed reluctantly. "I'll get my things."

I opened the front door. All the lights were on inside, as the deputies had insisted on doing a sweep of my house, just in case.

My gaze fell to the kitchen windowsill, where I'd placed the white violets the night before.

The violets were gone, replaced by a neat line of three acorns.

———

I didn't mention the acorns to anyone.

I packed my bag, turned out the lights, and locked the front door behind me.

Nick and the chief were having a low conversation by the door. Chief liked Nick. The department tended to be an incestuous tangle of romantic relationships, and he approved of me staying out of that mess by finding a suitable guy from the outside.

"And a *daaahktor*, no less," he used to say to me in a New York accent.

They stopped talking when I arrived at the porch, nodding to each other. I walked with Nick up the driveway to his SUV.

"Jesus, Anna." He shook his head and flung an arm around my seat to back out of the driveway. His voice was short, with a tone

I'd never heard before. I'd always known him to be patient and even-tempered.

I looked into the forest as we left the house, scanning for some sign of what had chased—or pushed—Rollins. I stifled a shudder.

"Why didn't you call me?" I could hear him struggle to keep his voice from sharpening.

I bit my lip. I didn't want to tell him the truth: *I didn't think of it*. I wasn't used to having anyone to call, to having someone to rely on. I paused, imagining a situation in which calling Nick would've been my first impulse. I felt warm, imagining that trust.

But what I said was: "I was just . . . It was a lot."

"I love you, you know." The abrasion in his voice faded when he said it.

My heart flopped behind my ribs. I wanted to reach out to him, but I paused, lifting my hand.

He stared straight ahead at the road, and I could tell by the set of his jaw he was upset. "You're scaring the shit out of me, and I need you to communicate, all right?"

I rested my forehead on my hand. "I'm sorry. It was just a whirlwind of things. I didn't hear my phone."

"I'm not . . . I'm not mad at you," he said. "I just wish you'd let me be a part of your life. I don't want to just pick up the pieces."

"I know. I'll try." I wondered if that was why he was back . . . to pick up the pieces? That was what he did, professionally. I wondered if he saw me as a project, somehow, and it was just his instinct to try to glue broken bits back together.

Or maybe . . . he really and truly loved me. Maybe it was as simple as that, and I was overthinking it all.

I reached for his hand, and he rubbed his thumb over my knuckles. We rode in silence for a bit, back toward the county seat.

"I like your new car," I said. It smelled new, too. Leather and plastic and chrome.

"Thanks." He grinned. "It's been on custom order for a few months and finally came in."

"You never struck me as an SUV kind of guy."

He shrugged. "I got stuck last winter on the way to work. Rear-wheel drive, while cool in the summertime on asphalt, sucks in a ditch in January."

I nodded. That was an eminently logical decision for a logical man. Maybe he was at an age when he wanted to take fewer risks, settle down.

Maybe with me.

Nick's town house was well lit and immaculate in the way rarely used spaces can be. It hadn't changed since we broke up. The kitchen looked like it came from a magazine: stainless steel and granite, with an expensive coffee maker and even more expensive chef knives in a block. The living room, with its massive leather sectional, curled around a humongous television. Above the television stretched a shelf displaying his collection of minor-league baseball caps. A frame hung on the wall with a picture of a dog in it. The picture had come with the frame, but Nick had always insisted that he liked the picture and hadn't bothered to change it. I took my shoes off before I padded across the cream plush carpet.

Nick carried my bag to the bedroom. The same blue duvet cover still covered the bed, but a different selection of books occupied the left nightstand. He used to read history, but the stack included titles on psychopharmacology, academic journals on trauma, and a coroner's memoir.

On the right side of the bed, where I used to sleep, there was only a lamp. I felt a pang of regret at that emptiness. He quickly put my bag on the right side of the bed.

"Have you eaten?" he asked, not making eye contact.

I shook my head. We were circling each other carefully, scanning for threats. It was palpable.

"What do you feel like?"

I paused. That was a twenty-thousand-league-deep question. What did I feel? Did I want to clutter up his nightstand again with a paperback novel stuffed with pressed leaves, a phone charger, ChapStick, and hand lotion? Could I even contemplate filling up that space right now, with my past coming back to haunt me?

"Thai," I answered finally. Why was it so hard to make decisions in his presence? My heart fluttered, and hope clotted in my throat.

He nodded and plucked his phone out of his pocket to order.

I sat down on the edge of the bed. I pulled open the drawer on the right-side nightstand. There was nothing in there but a velvet ring box, the ring he'd proposed to me with. The ring I'd rejected.

Then, I'd rolled over in bed and he was sitting up against the pillows with the box open and a serene expression on his face. I was terrified. I scrambled out of bed and fled into the dark. I always fled into the dark. I left him alone.

I closed the drawer. Maybe he wasn't seeing anyone else. Maybe I should just accept that he was telling me the truth: he loved me still.

I came out to the living room and sank into the couch. I opened my mouth to talk to him, to apologize, to acknowledge the hurt I must have caused, but my voice was frozen. Instead, I reached for the remote and clicked on the news to let other voices fill the room.

A criminologist was talking to a cable news host about serial killers.

"A serial killer is an object of fascination and revulsion. It doesn't surprise me someone decided to copy the Forest Strangler. They're elevated to the level of antiheroes in the media, and some antisocial, disaffected soul is trying to get their fifteen minutes of fame by riding on Stephen Theron's coattails."

The news host steepled his fingers. "And what about this copycat? Do you have any insight into the Strangler's motives?"

"I think the copycat is doing this for fame. What the Strangler did was a deeply personal act with unknown significance. Opaque. This guy . . . he's a nobody, doing it for fame or thrills. He's transparently chasing attention."

"Just terrible." The host turned to the camera. "Up next, in sports—"

I clicked the television off and stared at the blank screen.

Nick came to sit beside me.

"I'm working that case," I blurted.

He stared at me. "I don't like you putting yourself in danger like that."

I blinked. "You never had a problem with my work before."

His hand slid over his mouth, and he looked away. "You could get hurt."

"I could get hit by a bus tomorrow."

"You look like his victims, you know." He pushed a strand of blond hair behind my ear and I pressed my cheek into his hand. "I don't want to lose you."

I shook my head. "You won't. I swear."

He took my hands. "Anna, please. I've almost lost you. And I can't lose you again. Please leave this alone."

Internally, I bristled. I hated the idea of being controlled.

But his eyes were glassy, and his voice cracked when he tried to speak again. I had underestimated how much my being shot had affected him. And I didn't want to disappoint him.

I nodded. "Okay."

He enfolded me in his embrace. I felt safe there, secure. But also guilty for lying to him, because there was no way I could leave this case alone.

19

MY FATHER'S DAUGHTER

My dad woke up.

Margie told me in hushed tones in the kitchen of the safe house while my mom was taking a nap.

I was eating a bologna sandwich and asked about him.

"He's going to pull through," Margie said.

I had to remind myself to swallow.

"Don't worry. He's never going to get out of prison. Not ever."

I stared down at my sandwich. "I want to see him."

She pushed hair out of my eyes. "I know you do. And this all has to be really confusing. But it's best you don't."

I flicked my gaze down the hallway. "What's going to happen to us?"

"The media attention will quiet down. You and your mom will change your names and start over someplace else."

We tried. She tried. Mom dyed our hair brown. She cut my hair off at my chin, and I fought back tears. We moved to a town a couple of states away. We were given new names, and it was assumed we would bloom where we were planted, away from my dad's shadow.

Mom didn't speak about Dad. She was hollow, moving through the motions of life. She became a medical transcriptionist, and we lived in a little yellow house with thick drapes. She had prescriptions for pills, many pills, and she haunted the house like a thin ghost, except for her intermittent rages.

I snuck information about my dad. I watched television when she wasn't home, read newspapers in the town diner. I learned my dad would stand trial for the killings of twenty-seven women.

I didn't want to believe it. But I had seen it with my own eyes. I knew what he'd done, but I wasn't fully convinced that it was really him. I'd seen the monster in his face.

I tore out newspaper clippings of my father's picture. In the black-and-white photos, his eyes were exactly the same shade of gray as in life.

Mom caught me with those clippings. She tore them up, screamed at me, and locked me in my room.

"You have a good life now!" she shrieked. *"Can't you be grateful for it?"*

I stared at her, blinking, lip quivering.

She leaned down, her face at my level, and shook me. "You could have been one of those girls, don't you understand?"

I ran away when I was thirteen. I packed a bag and fled to the woods outside of town. This wasn't a forest I knew, but I knew any forest would welcome me. That was my domain as much as it was my dad's. With my pockets full of holed stones and acorns, I vanished into the woods. It was summer, and I drank from the cold streams and slept in thickets, just yards away from deer.

I was unafraid. I don't know why. I should've been afraid that the monster tied to my father—the Forest God, who had made him do those horrible things—would come for me. I should've been cowering at home like a good girl, throwing myself into the new life I'd been given.

But I didn't want it. I wanted to be among the trees and leaves. That was home. When I lay down on the ground, my spine melted into the earth. My fingers tangled with tree roots, and my hair mingled with blades of grass.

The forest whispered to me, and I closed my eyes, listening to it, straining to hear.

A voice trickled up to me.

Elena.

You are mine.

You belong here.

I looked into the afternoon woods, feeling a sense of peace and sunshine warm on my face. I felt love . . . and felt loved.

A fawn that had lost its spots walked across the clearing. Its mother was behind it, tail flicking. I held my breath; they were so close. So very close.

And then my memory became fuzzy. Sun dazzle and leaf shadow melded in my sleepless mind. I thought I glimpsed some-thing in the shadows behind them: a pale figure with antlers, standing upright and shrouded in fur. It wasn't human. It wasn't animal. It was something strange and unearthly. Was this what my dad saw? Was this the Forest God, Veles? Here, now, it seemed part of the forest. In the forest, there was no good or evil. There was no human morality here. Just . . . life and death. And that was all.

Who are you? I wanted to know.

Your father called me Veles. One of the old, forgotten gods.

I lay there listening to the deer chew grass.

The figure placed a hand on my head. *I revealed myself to your father. And I reveal myself to you.*

Tears prickled my eyes. It was such a gentle touch.

The figure raised his hand. I heard, or imagined I heard, as I was too lightheaded from thirst:

I love you, Elena.

His voice sounded like my dad's. My heart swelled, and I sobbed. Why couldn't Mom say that to me? When I opened my eyes, I couldn't see him. But I knew he was there, in the shadows, in the tracks of deer on the forest floor. He was in the leaves shading me and the moon's glow. He was the fawn and the dead snake in the hawk's grasp. He was everything, and I was steeped in him.

A park ranger found me after three days. I ran, but he caught me. I kicked and fought and spat like a feral animal.

I was brought home to my mom. Though she smiled tightly at the ranger, when she looked at me—filthy and covered in leaves and needing to be restrained—cold hate burned behind her eyes. I gazed at her with his gray eyes.

She knew what I was—my father's daughter—and she could no longer stand to look at me.

"What the actual fuck?"

Monica sat behind the steering wheel of the unmarked sheriff's office Crown Vic, eating pretzels from a bag. Salt covered her black blouse like snow. She offered the bag to me, and I dipped in for a handful.

"I don't know what Rollins was thinking. I mean . . ." I shook my head.

"Fucker went off the deep end, coming to your house to intimidate you like that. You were lucky he didn't try to hurt you," Monica said.

I crunched my pretzels thoughtfully. "Nick said he made it out of surgery to put in a drain. He hasn't come to yet."

"Maybe he'll head out on a medical retirement and be out of our hair."

"Maybe." I changed the subject. "So we think Cas is hiding out at the Relaxation Inn on I-70?"

"Yeah. Out of our jurisdiction. But I called the staties next door and they're watching the place. They checked the records, and Cas hasn't used any of his bank cards. But the desk clerk remembers a Goth-looking guy and his girlfriend checking in. They're waiting for us to arrive before knocking on their door."

"Hopefully, this will go smoothly, and we'll have him in our jail by this afternoon."

We rocked up to the hotel at ten a.m. It was a typical interstate exit: a couple of gas stations, a handful of fast-food restaurants, a truck stop, and a hotel. Everything was well lit and clean to make the place inviting to travelers.

Monica parked the car beside another unmarked car in the hotel parking lot, facing the other direction. She rolled the window down to speak to the driver.

"Thanks for keeping an eye on this," Monica told the two men in the car.

They nodded back and made introductions. The driver, Trooper Pauls, still looked like a cop while in plain clothes: he was in a polo shirt, khakis, and sunglasses and looked like he spent every spare moment working out. His partner, Smithson, did a little better, in a T-shirt, jeans, and a ball cap. He looked as if he spent only slightly less time working out.

Trooper Pauls advised us, "Front desk reports they checked in early Thursday a.m. That blue Volkswagen over there is registered to a Lisa Ramos from Nashville. Ramos checked in at 1600 with a guy matching your suspect's description. No one has seen them leave. They've had the DO NOT DISTURB sign on the door. We've been here since 0700."

"Cameras?" I asked hopefully.

"Not operational." Pauls made a face.

"Where are the exits?"

"Here and an alarmed fire exit beside the pool." Both were visible from the lot.

"You wanna knock and see if anyone's home?" Monica cracked her gum.

"Sure."

We climbed out of the cars. Smithson headed over to the emergency exit.

Monica and I accompanied Pauls to the front desk.

The front desk clerk, a young woman who looked to be in her early twenties, smiled cheerfully at us. I noticed the can of pepper spray on the desk beside her and wondered how often she worked alone. "Good morning. How can I help you?"

Pauls slid his badge across the desk. "I'm Trooper Pauls. This is Captain Wozniak and Lieutenant Koray. We spoke on the phone?"

"Of course." She nodded and handed over a key card. "The room number is 204. The rest of the floor has checked out, though there are families staying in the rooms above and below. I've instructed housekeeping to avoid the area."

"Understood. We don't think this guy is particularly dangerous, but that's good info," Monica said, and the young woman beamed.

"There's coffee in the conference room," she chirped as we

headed down the hallway to the elevator. I peered into the conference room, seeing only an elderly couple gnawing on stale bagels. Monica swept the vending area, and Pauls went to the pool. We reunited before the elevator. Lisa and Cas had to be in their room.

I had mixed feelings about Cas. I felt guilty about stealing the locket, and I wasn't sure I liked him for the killer. But things lined up a bit too much, and I sure didn't love the idea of him spending time alone with a girlfriend who could be in danger.

"He might try to stream this," I warned as we stepped on the elevator.

The trooper patted the body camera he clipped to his polo shirt. "We have our own. We'll mind our p's and q's, ma'am."

We wordlessly advanced down the patterned carpet to room 204, just beyond the elevators. Monica and I stood to the right and left of the doors, Pauls in the middle.

He gave a sharp rap. "State Police. Open up."

I pressed my ear to the wall, hand on my gun. Someone shuffled around inside.

"State Police. We have a warrant for the arrest of Cas Russo."

The shuffling intensified.

Pauls opened the door with the key card, and we swept in.

"Get down on the floor, right now!" he bellowed.

A young woman stood in the middle of the floor with her hands up. She was wearing sweats, with her long black hair up in a ponytail.

"Where's Cas?" Monica demanded.

I swung to the left, to the bathroom, shoving open the door. I ripped aside the shower curtain. He wasn't there.

Monica was peering into the closet, and Pauls looked under the bed. The young woman was on the floor, sobbing.

"Where is he?" I asked.

"I don't know," she said. "Last night he went for a walk and he just didn't come back."

"What time?"

"I don't know . . . right after the local news."

"So, like, eleven thirty?"

"I think so."

Monica pulled her off the floor and sat her on the bed while Pauls and I swept the room for cameras.

"Who are you?" Monica asked.

"I'm Eva Ramos. I'm a fan of Cas's." Her face crumpled and she began to cry.

"So . . . how do you know him?"

"From his YouTube channel. I'm a top fan."

"How did he get in touch with you?"

"He messaged me. Told me he needed a place to stay, that the cops were after him for messing up a crime scene."

I realized there was no computer here. "Where's Cas's computer?"

"I don't know . . . I guess he took it with him."

"Did he have a backpack? Luggage?"

"Um. Backpack."

I opened drawers, rifled through her clothes. Pauls found her purse next to the television and pulled out her credit cards and driver's license. "Lisa Ramos's name on the credit cards and the car registration, but the driver's license is for Eva Ramos. Jesus. She's seventeen. Did you use your mom's cards and car?"

The young woman stared at the floor and nodded.

"What?" Monica rubbed her forehead. "Do your parents know where you are?"

She winced. "Don't tell them. They'll be furious. They think I'm at my cousin's."

"Do you know that Cas is thirty-two?"

"I mean, yeah."

"Did he try to have sex with you?"

"Um . . . we had sex, yeah, but I wanted to."

Pauls was talking softly into his radio, asking for social services.

Monica sat down beside her. "Do you know where Cas went?"

"No." Her eyes filled with tears. "I can't believe he just left me after I helped him out."

I crossed to look out the window, staring down at the truck stop outside.

"Monica."

Monica came to stand beside me.

"You think he hitched a ride with a trucker?"

"It's a definite possibility. He'd have a better chance as a single dude getting a ride with a trucker than some family stopping for a burger."

Pauls frowned. "I'll have the truck stop pull video and send out Cas's description to every state weigh station to see if someone sees him."

I chewed my lip. Cas was proving to be more slippery than I gave him credit for. But was he slippery enough to copy my father?

20

SLEEPING IN TREES

"The FBI says you're not keeping them in the loop."

I jerked my head up. I'd totally lost track of the conversation, and I bit the inside of my cheek to bring myself back. Fuck. I was in my boss's office and he sounded fairly pissed.

Chief paced across his office floor. He was wearing one of his most expensive suits, which still smelled of dry-cleaning chemicals, with a pair of glittering gold cuff links.

"I'm totally keeping them in the loop," Monica said, from one of the chairs arranged around the coffee table. "They're just not giving us anything to work with."

"I know, I know," Chief growled. "And I have full faith that you'll catch this guy without their interference. But we have to keep up appearances."

"Mm-kay," she agreed. "What would you like us to do?"

"They want to have a meeting, have you meet their serial killer expert," Chief said.

"Okay. Is he like a profiler or something?" Monica asked.

I leaned back in my chair. I was certainly content to let Monica, as lead investigator, interface with the Feds.

"One who worked the original investigation," Chief replied.

I paused. My heart thundered in my ears.

Was this someone who could recognize me?

Fuck. Fuck. Fuck.

I took a deep breath. No, that wasn't possible. I was decades out from that. No one knew who I was, where I was, once upon a time. I'd passed my background check when I joined the department without so much as a parking ticket. Then I'd been unaware of my past. But now I knew that my adoption records had been doctored and sealed by Dr. Richardson long ago. Miraculously, she'd even managed to keep my fingerprints away from any databases. No one knew, and no one was going to know.

A knock sounded at the chief's door.

Monica and I stood as two men in suits came inside. I barely looked at the first man, just registered that he was middle-aged and bearded. My attention immediately fell on the second man. He was older than I remembered, maybe a couple of inches shorter. His hair was thinner and gray, but his eyes were the same.

"I'm Supervisory Special Agent Russell," the first agent said, shaking Chief's hand. "And this is retired Special Agent Parkes."

I arranged my face into a neutral expression and shook hands with Russell, then Parkes, as Chief introduced us. Parkes's gaze landed on my face for a moment, and I worried that he held my hand an instant too long.

"Pleased to meet you," I said.

"My pleasure," he answered, and released my hand.

Did he know? No, there was no way he could. It was my imagination. If he recognized me, my life would be destroyed. My career would evaporate, and this investigation would be blown to smithereens due to my conflict of interest. I'd have to go on the run, hounded by press. And Nick . . . he'd know what a monster I really was.

We arranged ourselves in chairs. I took one catty-corner from Parkes. I rested my elbows on the arms of the chair and folded my hands in my lap. I did my best to fade into the background, imagining I was sinking into the chair and blending into the green paint on the walls.

Russell accepted a coffee from the chief's secretary. "I work in Behavioral Sciences, and we're trying to come up with a profile for your killer. Parkes worked the original case, so we're picking his brain to see if there are some nuggets that we can generalize to the copycat."

Chief leaned back in his chair with his coffee. "I'm curious to see what you have to tell us."

He was offering nothing up.

Russell nodded. "Let's start from the beginning, with the original Forest Strangler."

Parkes took the floor. He put a laptop down on the coffee table and set it to project on the wall behind it. A black-and-white image of a little boy with a crew cut appeared on the wall. "Stephen Theron was born in 1953 in the Upper Peninsula of Michigan. His father was a World War II veteran and factory worker, and his mother was a second-generation Polish immigrant. His parents moved farther south when Stephen's father got a job at a chemical factory."

The picture changed to a picture of an older boy standing between a man and a woman in front of a classic car. I'd never seen these pictures before. I watched as the photo changed to a young man with an intense gaze in a school photo.

"Stephen was an average student, with nothing remarkable in the available records. He was drafted into the Army in 1972 and married his first wife right before shipping out."

A very young version of my father in uniform stood beside a woman with long dark hair in a mini dress.

"He married Cheryl Casperger in 1972, but they divorced immediately upon his return. Interviews with Casperger suggested he had a temper. He broke the windshield on her car, and she fled to her parents' house. They had no children, and she had no contact with him after the divorce."

The next slide was my father in uniform, a posed military photo of him from the shoulders up. "Stephen saw action in Vietnam. He was honorably discharged, though interviews with his comrades suggested he was very withdrawn among the other men. He often slept in banyan trees. He didn't say much, and he had the tendency to disappear into the jungle. He was a scout, and he was reportedly very good. On at least two occasions, he detected enemy soldiers advancing on his unit's location miles in advance, and gave his unit the chance to mount an offense.

"After his discharge and divorce, Stephen traveled for a year. He went to Europe, stayed in some hostels. From what we could gather, he managed to slip behind the Iron Curtain and wound up wandering the forests of Eastern Europe. He wound up at the legendary Sedlec Ossuary, the Bone Church, in Czechoslovakia."

The slide changed to a chapel seemingly constructed entirely of bones, with skulls leering from chandeliers and spines draping the ceiling. It was over-the-top macabre in a heavy-metal way.

"This reportedly made quite an impression on him. He came to the church daily to pray, for hours. The ossuary was locked at this time, and he broke in to do so. We only learned of this because he was apprehended by the local Communist authorities for trespassing. They stripped him of his papers, but he managed to escape."

A photo appeared of my father with long hair, wearing sunglasses and a long coat, and carrying a backpack. He looked like a hippie, which amused me.

"Since it was winter, the police assumed he'd freeze. Coincidentally, there were some reported deaths of women in the area. Details of these Cold War–era crimes are sketchy, but three women were found nude, buried in snow, with elaborate dresses sculpted in snow and ice around them. The police called these women the 'Ice Princesses.' We can't definitively tie these crimes to Theron, but the MO is strikingly similar."

A grainy photograph of a woman's head appeared above a buried body. She was surrounded in a voluminous snow dress decorated with icicles. Her lashes were frozen to her blue-white face. It looked like a scene out of a storybook, except for a small seep of brown blood around the high neck of the faux dress.

"I think this is where he began killing. He'd seen a lot in Vietnam, and I think he took refuge in the forest, a rural place he knew. The ossuary deeply affected him, clearly, and I think that's where he broke.

"But he somehow wound up back in America in 1982, just in time for his father to pass away of a heart attack. He was emotionless at the funeral, which angered his mother. She threw him out of her house. In subsequent interviews, she insisted, 'That man is no longer my son.'"

The photo changed to a grainy obituary.

"Stephen moved out of state and took a job in a tool and die factory. He met his second wife, Sheila Fredericks, at a bar in a nearby town. They got married quickly, and I speculate that was because Sheila was pregnant."

My parents' wedding photograph was shown. They were feeding cake to each other very civilly. My mom was very pregnant in a lavender dress with puffy sleeves. My dad was in a suit. He'd cut his hair a bit and looked pretty respectable.

"For the first years of the marriage, we think Stephen did not kill. He and his wife settled down with their daughter, Elena Marie, on a rural property an hour away from the nearest town."

A picture of my childhood house flashed on the screen. I was in a yellow dress, standing between my mother and father on the front step of the brick ranch.

I looked at the photo with an expression of mild interest. I didn't look at Parkes. I wondered how many photos of me there would be in this slideshow. My pulse beat slowly, evenly, in my ears. I knew, on a marrow-deep level, I was in more danger here than any scenario I'd faced as a law enforcement officer.

I should have been feeling panic, but I felt a deep stillness instead. I did as prey did in the forest when a predator is about: I went still. I fell into that, listening to Parkes speak.

"We think his first victim in the U.S. was Samantha Williams, a waitress at a truck stop."

A picture of a young blond woman appeared on the screen, a high school yearbook photo. Her long hair was curled in a spiral perm.

"Her body was found about a mile from a logging road. She died in the fall but wasn't found until the following spring, so her remains were badly predated and disturbed. We really weren't able to get a sense of the staging at this crime scene."

A crime scene photo flashed up. Under a blooming dogwood tree, a skeleton lay. A shock of muddy blond hair was still attached to the scalp. There was something in the eye sockets, something that looked like black river stones.

"That death was viewed as a one-off, and it was assumed a truck driver passing through had a hand in her death, but the crime was unsolved."

Another crime scene photo appeared. This was a woman in a tree, in summertime. Under the shade of the tree, a violet-mottled arm could be seen dangling out of a nest built with sticks.

"We think this was the second victim, Leila Napolitano. This caught the attention of authorities, and an investigation was conducted, but no leads arrived."

The picture changed to more photos: a bloated woman beside a riverbank, her arms full of cattails; a woman in a meadow, a crown of desiccated flowers around her head, her hands folded across her belly.

"We knew then that there was a single someone behind these killings. It had to be someone who could spend time with the corpses, who had freedom to go missing for long periods of time. At first, local authorities suspected the boyfriend of the third victim, Stephanie Schmidt. Gary Walker had no alibi and was last seen arguing with his girlfriend in a parking lot before she disappeared. He broke down and confessed under questioning, but it turned out to be a psychotic break. He was committed to a mental facility, and there wasn't a crime discovered for another nine months."

A picture of a young man in an ill-fitting suit was shown. He was in his twenties, flanked by lawyerly people.

"It was hoped that incapacitating him would stop the killings, but it didn't. A new body was found in 1984."

More pictures of women clicked across the screen: women dreamily holding wilted seasonal flowers as if they were captured from Rossetti paintings. Decay bloomed in their cheeks and sometimes stole their fingertips. Animals often disturbed them, gnawing on the carefully arranged remains. Rib bones poked out from a side, and once, a head had disappeared. I sank into the pictures, these images that hadn't been exposed to the public, half listening to Parkes's voice in the background.

My gaze fell on a young woman curled up on a raft of oak branches. Her hair was carefully braided with cattails, and she clutched besoms of dogwood in her fists.

"This was number eighteen, Teresa Stanger," Parkes was saying. "She, too, had been abducted at night. Stephen likely came upon her after she had a car accident, or perhaps he caused it. She was taken from the scene. And this follows his MO . . . He would find women who fit this general appearance out of sheer blind luck when they were alone and would abduct them. We found ether in his truck, and we think he strangled them shortly after abduction. The bulk of the time was spent on the staging, being alone in the woods with the body."

More photographs flipped by, both beautiful and gruesome.

"Well, he certainly had a type," Monica observed. "Where did that fixation come from?"

"We initially thought it had something to do with his wife, who was blond," Parkes said. "Or maybe his daughter, who was also blond."

I looked at him calmly, arranging my face into an expression of bland curiosity.

"But we realized he'd killed women of that type before, in Europe. Though he had an uncannily close relationship with his daughter, Elena, we don't believe he intended to kill her until the end."

"So he abused her?"

"He didn't sexually abuse her. But she was certainly traumatized when she led us to his hiding place and we discovered his last three victims in an abandoned house."

The slide switched to the exterior of the decaying house, then the scene inside. Flashbulbs rendered the interior severe and somehow artificial, like an overwrought haunted house that had been decorated too gruesomely to be believed. "Theron killed with more frequency in the end. We were led to him because he tried to snatch a woman in a parking lot and we got a partial plate. His luck had finally run out."

"Wait." Chief leaned forward in his chair, eyes narrowed. "You let a child walk into that?"

All eyes fell on Parkes. His jaw worked before he spoke. "It was an error in judgment. A severe error."

"Jesus." Monica rubbed her temple. "That poor kid. Her therapy bills had to be astronomical."

I sat still, watching, listening to my pulse beat low and evenly. I made the corner of my mouth turn down in disapproval.

Parkes leaned back in his chair and crossed his arms over his chest. "She was really messed up. The Bureau connected her with a therapist who specialized in victim trauma, but her mother was adamant that she wanted to start over somewhere else. She and her daughter walked away from witness protection. She reportedly put the child up for adoption when we caught up with her later. She wouldn't tell us where, and no judge would force her to."

"What the actual hell." Chief stared at him. "And who lets you people be in charge of anything?"

Parkes's shoulders slumped. Russell jumped in. "It was a different era, and mistakes were made. We're doing our best to be transparent."

"Okay." Monica lifted her hands. "What do you think the

copycat is taking away from this? Who is this guy, and why is he emulating this dude?"

Russell answered. "Our preliminary profile suggests this is a Caucasian man between the ages of twenty-five and forty. We suspect that he may have problems with sexual performance, much as we speculated with the original Forest Strangler, since none of the victims were raped and no semen was found at the scene. As a result, we think he might have problems with women. If he has a relationship, it's with someone who he can control, someone who he keeps isolated. Or he may be involved with online relationships to an inordinate degree."

Monica frowned. "Well, Cas Russo was shacking up with an underage girl."

"He might be a good candidate. He's the right age range, and he's got a fascination with serial killers."

"Maybe," I said. "But I don't like him for this. He likes to talk. I can't imagine he'd be able to keep his mouth shut about a crime like this."

Parkes nodded. "I think it's likely to be a man who's self-contained and self-controlled. Maybe older. It's someone who feels a kinship to this guy on a serious level."

"Cas might feel that," Monica said. "He had all kinds of serial killer memorabilia around his apartment. Our IT is in the process of trying to decrypt his hard drive."

"We'd be happy to lend our resources to that."

"Of course," Chief said. I wasn't sure how fast or slow that was going to happen.

Parkes continued. "Serial killers are classified by the FBI to fall in four categories: control-oriented, hedonistic, mission-oriented, and visionary. Control-oriented killers want to dominate and have power over their victims. Hedonistic killers kill for pleasure. Mission-oriented killers want to remove certain types of people from society, stemming from bias. Visionary killers tend to be psychotic, thinking they're serving a higher power.

"It's my theory that the Forest Strangler doesn't fit neatly in a category. He seems to display some elements of a visionary killer. Given his fascination with the Sedlec Ossuary, he may have had some kind of spiritual experience there. And there are elements of ritual in how he poses the bodies.

"Visionary killers tend to be psychotic and hallucinate. They think they're serving a higher power. Think of Son of Sam, who insisted the neighbor's dog instructed him to kill."

"Yeah," Monica said. "Visionary killers are disorganized, though, and are opportunistic predators. They lose interest in their victims after they're killed. Theron was very organized, and his MO is very disciplined and intricate."

Chief gave Monica an appreciative nod.

"That's true," Parkes said. "And so Theron exhibits some characteristics of a control-oriented killer. He was meticulous, kept souvenirs. But I'm not seeing much desire for control over his victims. He killed them quickly and didn't torture them.

"Theron was never forthcoming about his motivations, so we sought alternative explanations for his behavior. When DNA testing became more reliable, samples of his blood were analyzed. In recent years, an unusual genetic marker was found that's been the source of much academic speculation."

"Is this the Lyssa mutation?" Monica asked.

Parkes paused. "It is."

"State crime lab found some partial DNA from our perpetrator with the Lyssa mutation in it," Monica said.

Russell frowned. "That was thought to be a contributing factor to Stephen Theron's psychopathy, but there haven't been enough cases to draw solid conclusions. It's mostly a scientific curiosity at this point."

Chief frowned. "How common is this?"

"Rare. Very rare." Parkes sat back in his seat, gaze unfocused. "It's possible that someone found this anomaly in their own DNA through genetic testing, looked up the Forest Strangler, and got obsessed."

Conversation stilled around the elephant in the room.

"Well, there's the rumor about the Forest Strangler's body going missing," Monica said. "When he was executed, his body vanished. It was assumed that it was whisked away for medical research, but nobody owned up to it."

Parkes shook his head. "It wasn't us."

"What kind of a show are you guys running?" Chief blurted. "Losing bodies now?"

Russell lifted his hand. "Whoa. That was not on us. That was the Department of Rehabilitation and Correction. And nobody's seriously suggesting that a guy in his late sixties is walking around committing crimes."

He looked around the room. "Are they?"

"It's as good as any other theory," I said.

"What about relatives? Do any of Theron's relatives have the Lyssa variant?" Chief asked.

"Unknown, but unlikely," Parkes said. "His parents are long dead, and so is his brother. We'd be looking at cousins, who wouldn't be a whole lot more likely than the general populace to have picked up that trait. My understanding is the mutation only appears in people who have two parents who both express the mutation."

"He had a daughter," Monica said.

Parkes shook his head. "No. She wasn't a psychopath. She

didn't have any elements of the homicidal triad: she didn't start fires or wet the bed. She loved animals and had empathy. Though she was close to her father, she was horrified at what he'd done."

I nodded thoughtfully, resting my chin in my hand as if I were watching a scene on television. I couldn't get emotionally involved in this, I couldn't . . .

Parkes reached down to turn off his computer. "I hope to hell she doesn't see this on television and get traumatized all over again. Wherever she is, I hope she's living a quiet, peaceful life far away from all this."

"I hope so, too," Russell said. "But we need to cover all our bases. She needs to be found and her activities accounted for."

Parkes opened his mouth to respond, but Russell made a slicing gesture with his hand. "We need to do this by the book this time around. Period."

My pulse thundered in my ears, obliterating the conversation. They were going to come looking for Elena . . . for me . . . Voices washed over me as I struggled to maintain composure.

"I'll look for her," Parkes said at last. "It's a digital age now. Nobody can remain hidden."

For an instant, our gazes crossed, but his passed beyond mine without recognition.

For now.

I didn't know how much time I had, but I felt as I did decades ago, running in the woods with a monster on my heels.

21

UNDERWATER

I stood on the edge of a quarry in late afternoon, watching as a crane pulled an SUV out of a muddy lake, trunk first. The SUV was late-model, loaded to the gills, pouring water out of its open doors. The quarry was a favorite swimming hole of a group of teens. One of them cut his foot on a piece of metal in the water. The squad got called and discovered an SUV at the bottom—Rachel Marie Slouda's SUV.

Hauling it up was slow, inexorable going. The weather was humid, and my stitches, which were beginning to dissolve, itched. It was as if late summer were determined to cling to every hour it could.

I glanced at the distant road. Media was there. How in the fuck did they know these things? We'd kept radio silence.

"I wonder if someone's feeding them info." Monica cracked her gum.

"Sure looks like it. There's no way to keep them from seeing that SUV as it comes up, too."

"Nothing to do for it."

I glanced behind me, where forensic techs were swarming over tire tracks, and muttered to Monica: "I'm surprised a car that loaded with tech didn't squawk out its location to satellites."

"Mmm. Let's see what we get."

The soggy SUV was placed, clunkily, on the rocky shore, where a squad of men in coveralls converged to unhook the frame from the crane's line. It was pretty beat-up; I was guessing it went off the cliff to the deeper parts of the old quarry, rather than being simply driven into the shallows. The front end was crumpled upward; it must have hit first. We descended to look at the car. Both front tires were flat, and the SUV's cherry-red paint was encrusted with mud.

I peered inside the SUV. The front computer panel had been smashed.

"That probably fucked up the GPS, if it happened when Rachel was abducted."

Monica looked at her notes on her phone. "Last spot the cell tower pinged her cell phone was on the interstate at 2337 the day she began her trip."

I donned gloves and reached inside to wrestle open the cracked glove box. Water leaked out with soggy registration papers and manuals. I pushed those aside and pulled out a plastic bag. Peering inside, I saw dozens of boxes of ADHD medications: methylphenidate and dextroamphetamine. I also counted a half dozen containers of esketamine inhalers. That was new on me. I knew from DEA bulletins that prescription-grade ketamine was available for depression treatment, but I had no idea it was actually available in our neck of the woods.

None had prescription stickers on them. Though they were wet, the boxes looked legit to me and not counterfeit. I was thinking these came from her job.

"I've got a trick-or-treat bag full of prescription drugs," I announced.

From the back, Monica chirped. "Got her purse."

I joined her at the back. The purse had bounced around the SUV and been thoroughly soaked. I was surprised to find it still in the vehicle, since the doors had been opened and the windows rolled down. It probably should've been sucked out, but the strap got tangled around the driver's seat's floor bracket.

Her phone was in her purse, dead as a brick, along with a standard assortment of cosmetics, tissues, and receipts. I didn't attempt to unravel the waterlogged receipts; I'd leave that to forensics. But I eyeballed a nice roll of cash that had to be at least three thousand dollars.

And Rachel had been carrying a gun. It was a newish-looking 9mm, no scratches or signs of wear on the blued steel. Blued steel showed nicks and scratches pretty damn easily, and this gun looked like it had never been used. By the weight, it was loaded.

"Did she have a concealed-carry permit?" I asked Monica.

"Checking." She punched a number in her phone and had a short conversation. "No. But records show she bought a gun three days before her disappearance. Aha. She was afraid of somebody."

"Or running drugs from the hospital pharmacy and needed protection." I liked that this case was seeming more mundane.

Monica sighed. "Let's go talk to the boyfriend again."

———

Rachel's boyfriend, Mason Finch, sat in the interrogation room, holding a canned energy drink. We'd left him in there, alone, for a good fifteen minutes, watching him through the one-way glass. He was very still, in a depressed way. His hair was shorn short, and he was wearing a camo T-shirt and jeans.

"Where'd they find him?"

"At his parents' house, shooting cans in the backyard. Mom didn't want him to come with us. Dad wasn't home."

"Was he a good shot?"

"Not really."

Monica and I played rock paper scissors for who got to talk to him. I won and let myself into the room.

"Hi. I'm Lieutenant Koray. I don't think we've met?"

"I'm Mason Finch."

I shook his hand. "I'm so sorry for your loss."

"Thanks." He stared down at his drink. "I can't believe she's gone."

"Thanks for coming in to talk to us again. We recovered Rachel's car and some of her things. Some questions have come up. Since you were the person closest to her, we thought you might be able to shed some light."

"Sure."

I was going in soft. "Did Rachel mention any personal conflicts she was having lately?"

His brow knit. "What do you mean?"

"Any conflicts with people at work, arguments with friends or relatives?"

He seemed to think for a moment, his eyes moving right and left, as if he was searching for an answer. "She got a promotion recently, to charge nurse. That ruffled some feathers, since she hadn't been at that job long."

I flipped open my notebook. "Did she mention any names?"

"Um. I think she said someone named Crystal had been snarky to her about her pay raise. But I don't remember anybody else."

"Okay. Did she mention any patients who scared her?"

He lifted his shoulders. "She worked in labor and delivery.

There are always weirdos . . . grandmas who try to bust into the rooms, dads who want to name their kids after video game characters."

I made a note. "Did she have any patients who died or who were injured in birth?"

He looked up at the ceiling. "No. I don't remember anything like that."

"How about her friends?"

"Her friends are a nice group of girls. They party a little bit too hard sometimes but they're good gals."

"Where do they like to hang out?"

"They hang out at Cosmo's. She likes the carrot cake and the chocolate martinis."

I noted that he used the present tense when talking about her. "Did she have any run-ins with any guys there that she mentioned?"

He shook his head. "Nah. I mean, there are often guys there. But they really aren't the kind of guys who are interested much in women."

"Got it." I tapped my pen on the notepad. "How about her family?"

"Her dad is kind of a drunk, and her mom's pretty overbearing," he said. "Rachel moved out as soon as she turned eighteen. He's honestly sort of an ass, but I can't see him really doing something like that."

"She get into any arguments with them lately?"

"They weren't really happy that we were engaged." He made a face. "I didn't do that whole asking-her-father-for-permission thing."

I scribbled down a note. "Why not?"

"Because she's her own person and it's not 1920 anymore." He sat back in the chair. "Sorry. But that's just stupid."

"Right." I cracked a smile. He considered her to have autonomy, a point in his favor. I liked him less for her murder.

"Was she involved in anything like drugs, legal or illegal?" That was the million-dollar question, and I wanted to see if he'd be straight with me.

He frowned. "In college, she did a little Ativan and sold it on the side for spending money."

"She had a prescription?"

"Yeah. She hasn't taken it for a while now. But she was considering going back on it before the wedding to lose weight."

"We found some prescription ADHD meds and ketamine in her SUV. Lots of it. And several thousand dollars in cash."

I let that hang.

He rubbed his face.

"Shit. I suspected she might have gotten into stuff. She lost twenty pounds. And she seemed to have an awful lot of money for the wedding." His lip quivered, and I could tell he was trying not to cry. "But I didn't want to think . . ."

That might be an avenue. If she wasn't shy about misusing drugs, she might've run afoul of a dealer. But . . . drug dealers didn't kill like this. This could be someone she knew intimately, copying the Forest Strangler to cover the killer's own rage. Strangulation was a very intimate act. Or it was a total stranger who had ensnared her at random to play a role in his fantasy. This was no cold, professional slaying.

"There's a guy she works with. I don't like him." He sucked in his breath. "He works in security. He always seemed like he was on something when I saw him. He's a party guy who tries to date a lot of the women at the hospital."

"You got a name?"

"Braden Mariner. It's just a bad feeling, but . . ." He spread his hands.

I felt like he was being straight with me, so I pushed forward. "We also found a gun in her purse, one she bought a few days ago."

To my surprise, he nodded. "I went shopping with her for that. She drove a lot at night. And she was going to quit her job to become a travel nurse . . . more money. I didn't want her driving alone at night without protection."

"Did you take her shooting?"

"Yeah. We did the waiting period, the whole thing, and shot it at the range where we bought it. All legal."

"Of course." I nodded. "I just wanted to let you know what we found and to try to find out if she was feeling threatened by anyone. I wanted to talk to you because you know her better than anyone."

He took a deep breath, and it looked as if he were fighting off tears.

"Can I ask you something dumb?" he said.

"You can ask me anything." I put my pen down and placed my hands on the table in a gesture that would inspire trust.

"Did you find her engagement ring?"

"No. It wasn't on her when we found her. We're still processing her car, though."

"It's not that I want it for the money or anything. She picked that ring out, and I wanted to have something to . . . remember her." His voice dropped low, and he looked at his hands.

"If we find it, I will personally make sure that it's returned to you."

He nodded.

"There's something else I'd like to ask you to do, just a pro forma thing to get the investigation moving in other directions. Would you like to submit your DNA for a sample?"

He looked up. "Anything. I want you guys to find her killer."

"Good man. I'll be back."

I picked up my notepad and went out of the room to get a DNA swab kit and forms. I passed by Monica in the mirror.

"He didn't do it," I said.

"Nah." Monica agreed. "Let's get him cleared and move on."

I came back with a DNA kit and forms but was stopped in the hallway by a man in an expensive suit. "Lieutenant Koray?"

"Yes?"

Screeching echoed in the reception area. I heard a woman ranting about her son, and I immediately knew where this was going.

"I'm Rob Lewandowski, Mason Finch's lawyer."

"What can I do for you?"

"You can release him from questioning. He has nothing further to say to you."

"Actually, Mr. Finch has been very cooperative, and we're happy to have his assistance."

"Please take me to my client."

"Did Mr. Finch hire you, or did his mother?"

Another aggrieved howl sounded at reception, and Lewandowski struggled to keep from rolling his eyes.

"I see."

I put my hands, with the forms and test kit, behind my back. Monica walked behind me, cracking her gum, and smoothly relieved me of the kit and the forms.

"I'd like for you to know that Mr. Finch has not requested an attorney in my conversations with him."

"Doesn't matter, you know that. I'm here now."

"Of course. If you'd like to wait here, I'll bring him out to you."

"Actually, I'd like to go see him now." He was getting suspicious.

"Certainly. Please come with me." I had him follow me down the long hallway to the interrogation room. A payroll clerk rolled her chair out into a doorway to hand me a piece of paper.

"Hey, El-Tee. Can you sign your overtime slip for me?"

"Sure can. Thanks." I patted my pockets for a pen, didn't find one, and the clerk handed me one. The attorney shifted his weight from foot to foot. I signed the slip on the wall and handed it back to her.

"Oh, whoops. I put the wrong date."

"No problem. Just fix it and initial beside."

"Thanks." I made the correction and returned the form. "Can't miss out on time and a half."

"You know it," the clerk said.

I heard a door open and close around a blind corner, then saw Monica walking in our direction. The payroll clerk winked at Monica.

Monica and I exchanged nods. She was carrying a manila folder with all the forms and the test I needed.

I ushered Lewandowski back to Finch's room. "Mr. Finch, an attorney has arrived here for you."

"What? I didn't ask for an attorney."

"Your mother called me." The attorney sat down.

Finch put his head in his hands. "Tell her to fuck off."

"You have to protect your rights. You didn't sign anything, did—"

I let myself out of the room and headed down the hallway. I stopped at the water cooler to watch a woman in her fifties slam her fists down on the reception counter. "I want to see my son!"

I drank cold, clear water and watched a deputy escort the woman to the parking lot.

His mother calling a lawyer, in and of itself, was no indicator of guilt. Some parents lost their shit when their kids got in trouble.

"Full assault helicopter mode," Monica said.

"You get the sample?" We could've gotten his DNA from his energy drink, but that would have been inadmissible, since we didn't have a warrant.

"Signed, sealed, and delivered."

We bumped fists.

"Nice work. We owe Brit from Payroll lunch."

Monica chewed some ice from a cup. "Now I'm wondering about the victim's father."

"How did it seem when you talked to him?"

"He seemed really intense. I chalked it up to the situation, but I think we should talk to him again. Though I'd really expect him to pull the plug on an interview a lot sooner than Finch did."

"There's no shortage of asshole dads in the world."

That felt like an immutable, inescapable truth of the universe.

22

MEMORY DRIP

Nick was working the midnight shift and had asked me to stay at his place that night. But I'd told him I needed to get clothes from my house and that I would stay there. Rollins was in the hospital. He wasn't going anywhere.

As much as I basked in Nick's declaration of love, it bothered me that he hadn't been honest with me the other night. He hadn't been at work when he said he was. But then again, I didn't have any right to demand honesty from anyone.

I shook my head. *Trust.* I needed to learn to trust. Even as I lied to him about quitting the Strangler case. I told him that I was working on a drug task force.

Was it so impossible to believe he loved me? We dovetailed together so nicely, like two dark creatures swimming parallel in water, almost touching, never interfering with each other's pursuit of goals. We craved our solitude and reveled in our togetherness. I could accept him as he was, remote and sharp, and not place any further expectations on him. Was it too much to expect that he could love the same in me? Or did he really desire the picket fence, the 2.5 children, and the woman who went with it? Whether I was Anna or Elena, I knew I couldn't be her.

I rolled down my gravel driveway to my silent house. The porch light still burned from the night before, with moths orbiting furiously.

My stitches felt like itchy splinters trying to work their way to the surface of my skin. I let myself into my house, finding everything as I'd left it. I started a hot bath and dumped a good deal of bath oil in to hopefully soften the brown sutures that swarmed my body like flies.

I undressed and laid the necklace on the vanity where I could see it when I sank into the hot water up to my chin. Idly, I picked at a disintegrating stitch on my arm. Pink scar tissue was already forming beneath. I tried to tell myself that I was just molting. Soon I would be feeling as good as new without skin stretched so tight over old wounds.

I leaned back in the bathtub, feeling the cool enameled cast iron on the back of my head. I realized I hadn't turned on the lights.

I dozed, in that steamy water, in the dark. I was nearly found out. I'd seen Parkes for the first time in decades. Part of me, the part that was Elena, wanted to run up to him and throw my arms around him. I wanted to know if he had another dog and when he'd retired. If he had children and a spouse. But he was a stranger to Anna.

I was surprised he hadn't recognized me. Had things gone that hazy with time? Professional age progression sketches of missing children were never really as accurate as hoped. Some things stayed the same, though. Millions of women with blond hair and gray eyes wandered around the U.S. I was nothing more than happenstance.

Until Parkes found me. I knew the FBI's reach was vast. Could I slip through their fingers once more?

I exhaled, and my breath turned to steam. When I was a child, it was still possible to disappear, in that era before DNA analysis was commonplace, before the internet and lightning-fast sharing of records. I had disappeared once; I didn't think I could do it again.

Unless . . . unless I let Dr. Richardson zip my mind back up once more. Maybe then I could pass a lie detector test if I were confronted, plead ignorance . . .

I shook my head, my blond hair sliding in the water. I'd opened that door, and I could feel the water flooding in, and there was nothing I could do to stop it.

I leaned back in the black water and let it suffuse me.

———

"My name's Barbara Richardson. I'm here to help you."

The woman handed me a teddy bear. I stared at it. I was too old for teddy bears. Wasn't I?

I was in a white padded room with no windows. Everything there was artificial; even the stale air I was breathing. Surrounded by plastic, I was withering away beneath twenty-four-hour fluorescent light.

"Did my mom send you?" I asked her. She was petite, with glasses and blond hair styled in a helmet-like bob. She didn't wear a white coat or scrubs. Instead, she wore slacks and a blouse with a floppy bow at the neck. She looked more like a lady from the bank than a doctor at the psychiatric hospital.

"She did. She wants you to feel better."

"She wants me to behave."

"That too."

She wasn't lying to me at least. I sat on the floor with my knees drawn up under my chin. "What are you going to do to me?"

"I'm going to take you to live with a new family. Someplace safe."

"Mom doesn't want me anymore." A wave of sorrow washed over me. I was truly alone.

"It's not like that." The woman sat on the floor beside me. "Your mom has a lot of problems."

I sobbed, pressing my forehead to my knees. Both my parents had abandoned me. And my mother didn't have the courage to tell me this herself.

"I'll be good," I whispered. "I'll be good."

She patted my back. "It's hard to leave hurtful things behind. But I think I can help you."

I wanted to trust her. I nodded.

"Okay," she said, drying my tears with her sleeve. "Are you afraid of the dark?"

I shook my head no.

"Good. You're a brave girl."

She dimmed the blinding lights, then sat across from me. She turned on a small flashlight. "I want you to focus on this light. Take a deep breath and focus."

I stared at the light. Soon, the rest of the room fell away.

"You are safe. You are loved. You are divinely protected," she said.

I wanted so badly to believe that.

"I want you to imagine a safe place. A place where no one else has ever been; a place for you and you alone."

I imagined myself on a grassy hillock at twilight. Fireflies seeped out of the forest, and birds flew home to roost, moving across the sky in great black shadows. Stars were beginning to prickle out, and a moon had risen low in the east. At the foot of the hill, a forest stretched in all directions.

I imagined standing and walking down into the forest to a cave, hidden away from everyone. Over countless sessions, my feet wore a dirt path from the hill to the cave and back again. Piece by piece, I transformed my memories into coins that I dropped into the pond there. Some days, it was only a penny. Other days, I dropped handfuls of change into that water. My memories sank to the depths, and I never heard them strike the bottom.

Plink.

Plink.

Plink.

Months later, Dr. Richardson took me by the hand for a walk outside the facility. I was used to her leading me to a small court-yard enclosed on all sides by walls, a place where there was no-where to run. A single tree stood there, surrounded by benches and thick grass that smelled like chemicals. We'd sit on the benches and watch clouds. Dr. Richardson would ask me what I saw in the clouds, and I would tell her.

My answers must have been good, because she took me for a walk on the grounds. There was a walking path through a grassy lawn studded with sugar maples losing their leaves. I relished the feeling of the yellow leaves crunching underfoot. Blackbirds washed across the bright blue sky, slashed with airplane contrails.

She let go of my hand.

I stood still, closed my eyes, and listened to the wind tangle in the trees. I felt the sun on my face.

"What do you see in the sky?"

I looked up, stared at the contrails.

"I see stripes."

"Stripes?"

"Yeah. Like stripes on a cat."

"Very good."

"Can you tell me about when you were a little girl?"

I took a deep breath and looked inward. My memory was fuzzy. In my mind's eye, I saw two parents taking me to the beach, helping me pick up shells. They were smiling and laughing, helping me build a sandcastle. The memory was dreamy, hazy. I described it to Dr. Richardson.

"I am very sorry that your parents are no longer with us," she said.

I smiled. "They're in heaven. But they still love me." They'd died in a car accident. It was no one's fault, just bad weather. But it had destroyed my world, and that was why I wound up in the facility.

She put her hand on my shoulder. "You've done very well."

I looked up at her. I wanted to please her. I felt warm, knowing that I had.

A few days later she helped me pack up my clothes and Louie, the teddy bear. I climbed into her car and she drove me many hours away to a house in a quiet suburb. We pulled into the driveway near dusk. Lights shone inside.

She turned the engine off and looked at me. "Your new family is inside."

I sank into the seat, clutching my backpack to my chest.

"They're very nice people. They've always wanted a daughter of their own."

I stared out the window. Fireflies rose up out of the grass.

The front door opened, and a big floppy hound dog bounded into the yard and trotted up to my car door.

I opened the door. The dog wagged his tail. I reached out to pet him.

A man and a woman appeared on the front step. The man was round, balding. The woman was a couple of inches taller than him, with curly brown hair and laugh lines.

"His name is Rocky," the man said. "After the movie."

Rocky licked my face, and I smiled.

The man and the woman approached me. "Hi," the woman said. "My name's Mary Ann. This is David."

I looked up at them shyly.

"What's your name?"

"Anna," I said.

The Korays were lovely people. I learned later that Mary Ann had suffered six miscarriages and they'd stopped trying for a child. Dr. Richardson had provided them with a report that I was mentally distraught after the deaths of my parents but provided no other alarming detail.

The Korays invited us in for a spaghetti dinner. They showed me the house and a room they'd prepared just for me. It was painted yellow, with a bookshelf of Mary Ann's favorite Nancy Drew books. But my attention was snagged by a calico cat purring on the pillow.

I gently petted her. "Who's this?"

"Her name's Patches."

Patches purred at me and showed me her belly.

I slept that night with Patches and Rocky. My adoptive parents enrolled me in school and Girl Scouts and ice skating. I made friends with the kids down the street. My parents doted on me. I did well in school, winning a scholarship to college. I wasn't sure what I wanted to major in; I thought I might want to become a veterinarian or maybe a botanist.

I was in my college dorm one evening, watching television. My roommates and I had returned from a party and were more than a little tipsy. We were sitting on a futon, eating chips and watching late-night trash television. Beth clicked on the news channel to see the weather.

"Maybe class will get canceled for snow," she said.

"Class never gets canceled," Rhonda insisted.

"It could happen," I insisted. I was pretty woozy, staring at the glow sticks Rhonda was waving around.

The meteorologist wasn't on. Instead, the news was covering a night scene of what looked like a rave or tailgate party, cars clustered around what might be an arena.

"The Forest Strangler was executed today at twelve fifty-eight a.m.," the newscaster said. "After three attempts at lethal injection, the execution was taken off public display. But the warden confirms he is now dead."

I leaned forward. So that was a prison and not a sports arena. I stuffed my face with salty chips.

"Stephen Theron, the Forest Strangler, was responsible for killing twenty-seven young women in the Midwest in the 1980s and early 1990s. He was known for elaborately staging the bodies in rural locations."

A picture of a man with gray eyes in an orange jumpsuit appeared on screen. My eyes narrowed. "He looks familiar."

"Oh, he's one of those serial killer weirdos," Beth said. "My boyfriend read a book about them."

I hadn't seen him before . . . I thought.

"He never gave interviews, and psychologists are still unclear about his motives. But the world breathes a sigh of relief that the Forest Strangler's nightmare has been put to rest."

I stared at the television, at that familiar face. Something stirred in me, but I chalked it up to having too much to drink.

I forgot about that face, continued to focus on college and all it had to offer. I studied hard during the week, but on the weekends I partied with my roommates. We felt the invincibility of youth, assuming nothing bad could ever happen to us because nothing bad had ever happened. We drank a little too much, visited the clubs and danced.

Our favorite club was the Poison Club, a dive bar off campus. It was the sort of place that gave hand stamps to underage patrons like us and had no running water in the bathrooms to wash them off. Grunge music played with a reverberating bass beat we could feel in our chests.

I generally ignored the guys. They were fun enough to flirt with, but I had my eye on a boy in my chemistry class who didn't know I was alive. My roommates were more interested in the men, but we always left together, without them. We kept an eye on each other, and all was well.

We were dancing at the club one Saturday night when I opened my eyes to see that Beth was gone. I grabbed Rhonda and we went to look for her. She wasn't on the dance floor, wasn't at the bar. We checked the ladies' room. No luck.

"Where is she?" Rhonda shouted in my ear.

We asked the guy doing hand stamps at the door if he'd seen her. He pointed down the street. "She left with some dude."

Beth and I headed out onto the sidewalk, ears ringing. We looked up and down the block, calling for her.

I paused outside an alley, spotting movement behind a dumpster. I shouted for Rhonda.

A man had Beth pinned against the wall. She was sobbing.

Something snapped in me. Without any conscious thought on my part, I swept down the alley. I reached down and plucked up a bottle.

"Let go of her!" I yelled.

The guy looked up. He looked like any other guy at a frat party, any guy at the club: some clean-cut guy with generic good looks. He shoved Beth back, reached to haul up his pants.

I smashed him in the head with the beer bottle. I struck him once, twice, and the bottle shattered. Wrath coursed through me. In that moment I wanted to kill him. I wanted to stop him from breathing the same air as the rest of the world. I kept hitting him, hearing nothing but my pulse in my ears.

I think I would have killed him, too, if Rhonda hadn't grabbed my arms. He clutched the waistband of his pants and yelled at me before he stumbled away. I had no idea what he said. I just stood there seething, holding the remains of that bottle.

Rhonda let me go and turned to Beth. Beth rubbed the tears at her face and tugged her skirt down to cover her thighs. Blood was smeared down her legs.

"Jesus, Beth." I knew better than to ask her if she was all right.

"Let's get you to the hospital," Rhonda said.

Beth couldn't speak. She could only sob. We supported her to the mouth of the alley, and Rhonda ran back to the club to call for help.

People walked by, pretending not to see us. I wrapped Beth in my arms and she just shook.

An ambulance came to take her to the university hospital. They did a rape kit and gave her some tranquilizers. They said she would heal. I didn't think so. Beth had been an eighteen-year-old virgin.

Beth didn't want to call the police. She didn't want anyone to know. I tried to convince her. That guy needed to be stopped.

But Rhonda took me out to the hall. "You can't force her," she said. "She's been forced enough."

We took her back to the dorm, arriving shortly before dawn.

Beth stayed in the shower for an hour. I knew the water had to be cold. We wrapped her up in towels and put her to bed.

Rhonda and I sat together on the couch. Rhonda seemed numb. I struggled to keep from screaming.

Every day after that, I looked at the men on campus, wanting to catch sight of Beth's rapist. I was like a predator searching for prey. Beth skipped three days of class. We kept the bedroom dark and warm for her, bringing her food she didn't touch.

This was our first experience out in the big, glorious world. And she had been punished for it.

Beth never filed a police report. She didn't tell her boyfriend and broke up with him without explanation. She went through the motions of going to class for the rest of the semester, looking over her shoulder. She never went out after dark again, and I'd hear her slip from bed in the middle of the night to check and make sure our door was locked.

I never saw the man who attacked her. I planned great, detailed fantasies of what I would do to him, starting with cutting his dick off and feeding it to him. In the dark of our bedroom when I heard Beth sob at night, I wanted to utterly destroy him.

I assumed the rapist had gone to the ER to get stitches, but he never showed up the night we were there. Not that we knew. I scanned the campus police reports in the student paper and saw no mention of a guy cut up with a beer bottle. He was like the bogeyman: there and gone.

Beth left after that semester to go home. She kept in touch with letters, and I learned that she had transferred to a community college close to her parents' house. We never talked about what happened again.

But I changed my major to criminology. I felt no other outlet to my outrage other than to try and stop men like that from hurting women like Beth.

My parents indulged me, perhaps thinking I'd read a popular book about criminal profilers. I read that one, too, and everything else I could get my hands on. I was a stellar student, winning a scholarship to graduate school. I finished a master's degree and had ambitions of joining the FBI once I had enough law enforcement experience.

When I graduated, I cast a net for hiring agencies within five hundred miles. I was offered a position on the Canadian border with the Border Patrol and a position as a deputy with the Bayern County Sheriff's Office. It should've been a no-brainer, but I didn't relish winters in International Falls. And . . . there was something about Bayern County.

I didn't realize it then, but it was home. When I drove there for the interview after passing the peace officer training exam, I was enchanted by the forest. It was spring, when the damp earth smelled of life. I pulled off the road at a state park on the way back to inhale it. Everything about the land—the roll of the hills, the susurrus of the trees, the buzz of the red-winged blackbirds—felt familiar.

It felt like home.

I'd only intended to stay for two years, to gain the experience I needed to join the FBI and lead a glamorous life in New York or Los Angeles. But I was lulled by that place, hypnotized.

And I came full circle to where it began, waiting for my memories to rattle, trickling in like melting ice in spring.

And for him to find me, that dark god of the woods.

23

LETTER FROM THE PAST

I awoke in the dark, eyes shut, listening.

The forest roared beyond my house, through the open windows, and I yearned for it.

I opened my eyes, climbed out of bed, and walked out onto the porch. The woods seethed. I walked across the yard to the edge, that ragged demarcation line between where I mowed and the faraway wild.

Something in the woods had almost killed Rollins, something or someone that felt familiar. And that was impossible. I shook my head and turned to go back inside.

Was that what had left me acorns, poison ivy, and a bird's nest? Maybe, or maybe it was just my imagination, connecting disparate happenstances into a constellation of synchronicity. Maybe they came from someone else, someone more human.

But my toes flexed and dug into the dirt. I turned back to face the trees. I had to confront whatever this threat was, whether it was in my own head or slithering through the forest.

"Are you here?" I breathed.

Leaves rattled overhead. Clouds obscured the sky, and I smelled rain coming. A cool breeze slid through the trees.

I took a step forward. I wouldn't hide any longer.

"Why have you come?"

It was a demand, a challenge. The wind rose and branches churned above me. I wondered if my father had summoned something, a monster from the depths of a forest far from here. I shook my head. That was a child's thought. My father was that monster, and I had created the framework of something supernatural around it. He believed in the Forest God. As a child, I had come to believe, too. But it was his delusion, his alone. I struggled to separate myself from it, tears streaming down my face. My father had made up the Forest God to excuse his own killing.

But my father was dead. Executed.

And something was in the world now—something that was killing.

Rain spangled the darkness, light at first, then a downpour. I let the rain pelt me, rinsing my tears away. The rain in itself was an answer. It was an arrival. The Strangler had returned. Of that, I was certain. The Forest God had reawakened.

And it must have a new killer in its thrall, one I hoped was in this physical world; one I could find.

"I will stop you," I whispered to it, but my voice hissed like lightning.

It was up to me. I understood why I had been drawn back to this place, to the unfinished business of my childhood. On some level, I'd come back here to right wrongs, to atone for my father's sins. The dark forest called me. I was tangled in its roots, its child. But I was here to stop it.

Thunder growled at me.

I peered into the woods, and dark shadows seethed among the curtains of rain. My heart pounded. Part of me hoped to confront it—now, when I felt towering and resolute. But another part of me wanted to run and hide, to run back into the house, to lock the door behind me and cower under the covers. I was both adult and child with it, one foot in the past and one in the present.

A slithering sound crept over wet leaves, and I sucked in my breath. Shadows churned ahead of me, gathering close and coalescing into something solid. A misty shape with antlers approached me. The antlers shone in the dim light as if they were leafed in gold, cradling a blacksnake in their tines. Eyes like distant moons glowed in an inhuman face, bone pale and cadaverous. The creature pushed aside branches with long fingers shading to black, as if they'd been stirring something rotted. I glimpsed dark fur, smelling rust and decay and green leaves.

I sucked in my breath, tangled in terror and wrath. My hands balled into fists.

This was the forest come to claim me, as it had claimed my father. Some part of me insisted this was a dream, or some latent drug hallucination, but most of me didn't care. I had to face it.

"Serve me," he said. "Serve me as your father did."

"No." I lifted my chin. "You have no power over me."

"Don't I?" His chuckle sounded like a hundred grackles shrieking.

I bit my lip, tasting blood. I didn't want to admit his influence over me, the knowledge that I was a killer. Maybe I was *the* killer, and the Forest God had already been working through me, the way he had worked through my father, an awful spiritual contagion . . .

"Stop," I meant to shout, but it came out as a whisper. Rain and blood dripped down my lip.

He loomed over me now, touching my chin the way a father might caress a beloved child. But I was aware that this force was ancient, older than mankind, and my entreaties to him meant nothing. The snake in his antlers dipped down to flick its tongue at my brow. I forced myself not to flinch—not from the snake and not from him.

He shook his head. "If you will not serve me, others will."

He melted back into the woods. I took two steps in to chase him but stopped. My hair stood on end, my feet buzzed, and the air sizzled. The marrow in my bones instinctively recognized the danger.

"Veles!" I shouted after him.

I crouched down and covered my head as lightning closed a circuit from earth to air, striking a tree before me. The tree crashed down, blocking my path.

I stood slowly, smelling ozone.

I was alone.

———

I woke up to the sound of the front door creaking open.

I blinked. I'd lost time again. I had been in the forest, but that was at night. I dimly registered morning light leaking beneath the drapes.

While my brain struggled to connect the dots, my body acted automatically. I rolled over to reach the gun in my purse on the floor. But it was just Nick; I could tell by the jingle of keys and the squeak of his sneakers on the kitchen linoleum.

He came to the bedroom to sit on the edge of the bed. He looked bone-tired. I clasped his hand.

"Are you okay?" I asked.

"Yeah. Tough night." He ran his hand through his hair. He smelled like antiseptic and blood.

I lifted his hand to my lips and kissed his palm.

He smiled, but it faded. "I wanted to tell you about Rollins."

"Yeah?"

My thoughts traced back to the forest, of the shadow of Veles. It felt dreamlike now. My T-shirt, hair, and lounge pants were dry, and my feet were clean. It had been a dream, my subconscious telling me something. My shared delusion with my father. Or the traces of PCP still in my blood.

"He regained consciousness. Briefly. He seemed confused and incoherent, which isn't out of the norm for a serious concussion. We were going to get another CT to assess bleeding and swelling, but he left his room."

"What happened?" My thoughts raced.

"He ran out into the parking lot and got hit by an ambulance." He didn't have the energy to adorn the news with gentle words. It was just the terse, sharp truth.

"Oh my God."

Nick stared at the floor. "It was a mess. We tried, but he didn't make it."

I closed my eyes. "Jesus."

He squeezed my hand, trying to soften his words. "I thought you should hear it from me first."

"Thank you." We sat there for a moment in silence. I knew he was exhausted and that he wanted me to release him from the need to do emotional maintenance. I let go of his hand.

"There's something else," he said, as if the words were dragged from him. "Something weird. I found this in his hospital room, on his pillow."

He fished in his pocket and handed me something. I stared at it.

It was a piece of antler, a spike about as long as my thumb, broken off at the base. I lifted it to my nose. It smelled like fur and bone and a fresh break. It was useless as evidence, compromised by Nick's touch and now mine.

"Where did it come from?" I whispered.

He shook his head and shrugged. Weariness was evident in the sagging line of his shoulders. "I'm gonna go shower."

I nodded. He stood and headed to the bathroom.

I got up and made some coffee, placing the antler on the kitchen windowsill. I stared out the window at the forest. Rollins was dead. It seemed surreal. But I couldn't say I felt sorry. *That* bothered me.

And it bothered me that there was some kind of artifact left in his hospital room. Had the piece of antler been tangled in his clothes after the attack in the woods and come loose somehow? Or had someone left it there for me? It was impossible to imagine Veles stalking through fluorescent-lit hallways. No, whoever had left that had to be human. Right?

I drank my coffee and stared at the damp forest, trying to chase last night's dream from my head. The dream was interfering with my objective analysis of the situation. I squinted, seeing that a tree had fallen in the middle of the night.

Just a tree that I heard while asleep and incorporated into my dream, I told myself. I hadn't gotten out of bed at all. That was why I didn't remember getting back into bed.

I frowned, seeing mud on my palm. I rubbed it away against my T-shirt.

I thumbed through the mail I'd brought in from the mailbox the night before. Catalogs, advertisements, credit card applications. I flipped through them and deposited them in the recycling, until I reached a plain envelope with a computer-generated delivery address and no return address. The postmark was from the nearby city.

I opened it. There was only a sheet of copy paper inside that said, printed in Times New Roman font:

I know who you are.

I dropped it like a hot rock, breathing quickly. I stared at it on the kitchen counter as if someone had let a scorpion into my house.

How was this possible?

My first instinct was to take it to the crime lab, but I couldn't take that risk. I covered the page with a catalog and gulped down my coffee.

I offered Nick some, but he wanted to crawl into bed. I tucked him in and closed the door behind him. He didn't sleep, though; I could hear the squeak of the bedsprings as he turned over and over.

I went back to the kitchen, removed the catalog, and stared at the letter. I needed to know who had sent this.

I headed to my SUV to dig out an evidence collection kit. I spread the letter and envelope out on a clean piece of paper and dusted the letter with a fluffy brush.

I lifted the prints with transparent tape and taped those smudges onto clean pieces of paper. Several were mine, and I pulled those off the paper, leaving behind smudges. I was left with a bunch of dusty whorls and loops on the envelope that probably belonged to postal employees and a couple of really nice index prints on the paper. Those were also mine.

There was absolutely nothing else on the paper.

I frowned, staring at it.

I paced the kitchen. There was no blackmail demand. At least, not yet.

I could only wait to see what happened.

24

CHASE

I got the rundown on Braden Mariner, the security guard at the hospital where the victim, Rachel Marie Slouda, worked. No priors, which didn't surprise me, since he was working security. He'd done a brief stint in the Marines after high school, with an honorable discharge.

If he was involved in a drug ring, I didn't want to interview him now and tip him off. Instead, I parked an unmarked car outside the hospital where Rachel worked. The only unmarked car available at the moment was assigned to Vice, an aging sports car that had a creased right fender and smelled like weed and cheeseburger wrappers. When I drove, a distracting tree-shaped air freshener dangling from the mirror wiggled until I ripped it down. I let the hula girl glued to the dashboard stay.

The hospital was a smaller one than Nick's, a level II trauma center that could handle most ordinary medical emergencies but would send people to Nick's hospital for things like cardiac surgery. It was two stories tall, maybe constructed in the seventies.

I sat in the parking lot watching a uniformed security guard escort a woman in a lab coat to her car.

I frowned. People were fearful.

I saw that replay itself twice more, with different guards. I wondered if they'd put out a policy not to allow anyone to walk to their cars alone.

Finally, Braden Mariner got off first shift. He was a tall, lanky guy with fashionable stubble who walked out to his car with a drink in a Styrofoam cup and a plastic bag. He slouched when he walked. Odd for an ex-military guy. Possibly he was subconsciously looking to disappear . . .

I zeroed in on the plastic bag, similar to the one I'd found in the victim's glove box. Maybe it was the kind the hospital used for patients' personal effects, or it may have come from the pharmacy. He got into a sedan and put the bag on the passenger's side.

The hula girl wiggled on the dashboard. She thought it was interesting, too. So I decided to follow him.

He drifted through the streets of Maysville, hitting up a drive-through. It seemed like he was killing time, since he was looking at his watch. I followed at a discreet distance while the hula girl swayed her hips in an ever more enthusiastic dance.

Rachel Marie Slouda's murder still didn't feel like a drug killing to me. No drugs or money had been taken from her car. But perhaps someone with my father's appetites happened to have gotten involved in the local drug scene. I felt as if my experience with PCP had drawn me closer to that demonic force in the forest . . . What if I wasn't the only one? What if someone else had had the doorways of their mind blown open by a bad batch that connected to something strange?

Mariner turned down an alley and parked beside a dumpster.

I stopped at the mouth of the alley. His behavior looked sus as hell to me, so I radioed for backup.

"This is L4. Anyone in the Maysville area for backup on a 10-48?"

"This is S12, on the DL, just headed through the Chill 'n Slush. You want anything?"

I grinned. Sergeant Calvert from Vice was only three blocks away in an unmarked car. Things were going my way today. "No, but could you keep eyes on a black Audi in the alley between Maple and Sycamore? I'm at the south end."

"Copy that. I'll be there in five."

The hula girl swayed, reminding me of the way a cat wiggled before it pounced.

A white car with tinted windows headed down the alley toward Mariner's vehicle. They pulled up to each other, driver's-side window to driver's-side window. I saw a hand flash some cash and the bag exchange hands.

I pulled my car down the alley, blocking the entrance, scarcely believing my luck. "S12, I've got a suspected 10-49A," I said into the radio.

"Copy."

Mariner's car was facing me. He tried to back up but saw that the other end of the alley was blocked by a white panel van. Calvert, I presumed.

Mariner's head turned and he floored the gas, aiming his car straight for me.

The hula girl shuddered.

"Fuck," I muttered. All I could do was set the parking brake and stand on the brake pedal as Mariner slammed into the front of the car.

Metal and rubber squealed. The seat belt slammed into my

chest. Fortunately, Mariner hadn't had enough space to pick up much speed, and my airbag didn't deploy—if this rattletrap even had them.

The hula girl bobbed furiously.

I wrestled my seat belt open, popped my door, and drew my gun at Mariner's windshield.

"Freeze."

Mariner lifted his hands and pressed his head to the steering wheel. I circled the car carefully, spying the wad of cash on the passenger seat.

"Bayern County Sheriff's Office," I announced. "Are you hurt?"

"No," he mumbled.

I glanced up the street. Calvert and his partner, Sykes, had the other guy down on the ground. He'd apparently tried to run on foot, but they snagged him. Calvert lifted a plastic bag.

"It's Christmas morning here," he called, holding up prescription boxes.

I nodded, blowing a strand of hair out of my face. They'd found drugs. Merry Christmas indeed.

"I need you to step out of the car, please," I told Mariner.

He complied, and I cuffed him.

I read him his rights, and Sykes hauled him off to the van. Sykes was dressed like a club guy, complete with a shiny shirt that showed too much chest hair and pants that were far too tight. He made a bizarre pair with Calvert, who was dressed in electrician's coveralls.

"You going to a party?" I murmured.

"Today is alllllll party," he said, grinning.

Mariner refused to speak without an attorney, but his buyer couldn't stop talking. He offered to turn informant. Since this was Vice's beat, I deferred to them.

I plucked the hula girl off the dashboard of the wrecked car and pocketed her. She was good luck, and there was no way I was gonna let a girl like that wind up in the junkyard.

After the wrecker and prisoner transport came, I filled in Calvert and Sykes outside at a table at the Chill 'n Slush. Cops usually got a forty percent discount at restaurants, but the manager at the Chill 'n Slush insisted we eat for free when he saw my badge dangling on a lanyard.

I slurped a strawberry milkshake that gave me an instant headache.

"We've been finding some pharmaceuticals here and there," Calvert said. "We suspected a local pharmacy was supplying a trickle of drugs to upper-class and professional clients, people willing to pay for purity."

"Interesting. I never figured people were all that discriminatory."

"Most aren't. But we're seeing more and more folks who want to make sure that they're not going to OD. Lot of ADHD drugs for day-to-day use, and pharmaceutical ketamine as a party drug," Sykes affirmed.

"I'm curious about Mariner for the murder of Rachel Marie Slouda," I said. "Will he talk?"

"Depends on what we try to offer him." Sykes picked his chest hair out of his gold chain. "We could drop charges if he talks. I mean, we've got him on narcotics charges and vehicular assault, assault on a peace officer . . ."

"If the prosecutor wants to play ball, I'm willing to reduce charges," I said. "What I really want is his DNA to rule him in or out for that murder."

Calvert grinned. "We'll get him to sing. Or spit."

Sykes and Calvert tag-teamed Mariner, and it was a thing of beauty to observe.

On the dark side of the one-way mirror, I watched Sykes be the good cop . . . and Calvert come back to be the better cop.

"You had about four thousand dollars' worth of street value in prescription amphetamines and ketamine. For distribution charges alone, you're looking at five years in prison and ten thousand dollars in fines," Sykes told him.

"Wait, what?" Mariner's lawyer said. He looked like a dude who had just been called from the golf course, with a sunburn and a pink polo shirt. He turned to stare at his client.

"You were within two hundred feet of a school dealing drugs, dude," Sykes said sympathetically.

Mariner leaned back in his chair and looked up at the ceiling. His eyes were hollow. "Fuck me."

"And there's also the matter of you striking a peace officer with your car," Calvert chirped.

"He didn't know she was a peace officer," the lawyer countered.

"Even if that's so, felonious assault alone gets you two to eight," Calvert said.

I watched Mariner carefully. He sat with his arms crossed like a little boy who'd been sent to the principal's office. Sweat glossed his brow, and sweat stains spread under his arms. He looked like a man who knew his life was ending.

"What do you want?" the lawyer asked.

"I want details on this operation. And a DNA swab. Prosecutor will go down to possession six to eighteen only."

"What do you want the DNA for?"

"One of his colleagues, Rachel Marie Slouda, was murdered recently. We're shaking all the trees."

The attorney looked at his client. "Can we have a moment?"

"Certainly."

The Vice guys came back to join me behind the glass.

"If he rejects this sweet deal, I think we have to consider him a viable murder suspect," I said.

Sykes shrugged his shiny shoulders. "If he rejects it, then we get a warrant for the DNA. We'll get it one way or the other. They have to know that."

The attorney rose and knocked at the door. Sykes answered it, and they spoke briefly.

When he returned, Sykes shook his head. "No deal."

"What?"

"No deal. Now we hit him with every charge we can, and we lean on his buyer to provide details on the drug operation. He'll be cooling his heels in jail until you can get a warrant for his DNA."

I picked up my phone and started dialing, promising, "I'll harass every judge in the county."

Sykes did a pretty convincing disco pose. "You did good, Koray. Give us a yell if you ever want to work with Vice. It's an ongoing party."

I grinned. I feared Vice was far too much of a party for me.

But they let me keep the hula girl at least.

———

I stared at the candle on Dr. Richardson's coffee table. The rest of the world had faded to black around me, and the only things that existed were me and the flame, burning steadily.

"Come back now," she said, counting backward from ten to one.

The world came back into focus. Feeling cold, I pulled a blanket that smelled like dust around my shoulders.

Dr. Richardson turned on the lights, and we sat in silence.

"Are you remembering?"

I nodded.

"How does it feel?"

"Like there's a shadow set of memories behind things I thought I knew. That things aren't quite real."

She leaned forward. "Do you feel that you're disassociating? Not fully inhabiting your body, not feeling?"

I nodded. "I feel as if I'm observing most things, not participating. Sometimes, floating above them. And sometimes . . . I'm missing time." I told her about the incidents where I'd been losing hours, forgetting where I'd been.

Dr. Richardson frowned. "That's understandable, though, given the work we're doing to open up your mind. Your brain is struggling to process it all, and I've seen this sort of thing happen before in some of my patients. Admittedly, that's a very small sample size."

"That's reassuring." I felt tension drain out of me.

"How often does this happen?"

"Off and on. Mostly at night." I told her about the dream of Veles.

"Veles." She set her pen down on the notebook. "I don't think you mentioned that name before."

I exhaled. "My father said the forest had a spirit, some kind of consciousness. A god. When I was a little girl, I'd make daisy chains for Veles or leave acorns on my windowsill. Offerings."

And I paused, the full gravity of the realization settling into me. "Just as my father made offerings to him. Those women. They were offerings." Parkes had been right. My father was a visionary serial killer communicating with some higher power in his head. Fuck. And was I now sharing his delusion?

Dr. Richardson and I occupied that space, just breathing for a few minutes.

I took a deep breath and told her about Rollins, how he had tripped and fell in the forest, how I couldn't help but wonder if he'd seen the same monster I had.

I didn't tell her about stealing the necklace from Cas Russo's apartment. I was too ashamed. But I haltingly mentioned the gifts that were appearing for me and the antler found in Rollins's hospital bed.

"Have you considered the likelihood that Rollins simply tripped and fell and that this all was an unlucky coincidence?" she suggested.

I lifted one shoulder.

"Human minds seek out patterns. We try to make sense of things by giving them meaning. Sometimes this isn't always warranted. Sometimes things just *are*, and we never make sense of them."

I nodded. "I guess it's possible."

She looked at me levelly. "Do you really believe that an entity your father was involved with killed Rollins?"

It sounded absurd coming from someone else's mouth. "Maybe."

"A forest spirit would have been a natural coping mechanism for a child, especially a sensitive child like you. It was a way to externalize the horror of what happened, to remove the responsibility from your father."

My fingers wove into tight knots in my lap.

Dr. Richardson continued, "Since we've opened your memory vault, it's not unexpected this childhood mechanism would arise again. Your adult mind is searching for connections, as it does in the real world when you're working. But now you're dipping into the past and potentially dredging up some artificial connections."

"I think you're right. I'm just reaching for connections," I sighed, feeling relieved and also confounded.

"And that works when you're working a regular case. I'd encourage you to focus on tangible things, verifiable proof. I suspect that, after your drug exposure, you may be experiencing hallucinogenic flashbacks."

I nodded, feeling a little ashamed of myself. "It's hard. With this case."

Richardson paused in writing. "What do you mean?"

"The lead investigator on the Forest Strangler case asked me to help her."

She looked at me over her glasses. "Do you feel that's a conflict of interest?"

"Yes."

"But you're doing it anyway?"

"Yes."

"Why?"

I sifted through my feelings. "Because it feels like something I need to do."

"Because of your connection to the case."

"Yes."

"Is it possible that your own biases might jeopardize it?"

I was still, thinking. It was certainly possible. But I wanted to believe that I had special insight, that there was something only I could bring to it. And that I needed to.

The silence stretched.

"Yes," I answered.

Dr. Richardson was quiet.

"Are you going to contact my boss?" I said it without heat or accusation; I just needed to know.

"No." She closed her notebook. "I have no moral high ground. You know this."

We stared at each other, a stalemate.

I knew what I should do, given this and the threat to my identity: I should quit my job and start over someplace else, leave all this behind.

But I did that before, and this shadow had followed me.

Now there was something more important to lose: a second chance with Nick. Running would mean losing that . . . losing him. I was surprised at how the thought of that loss ached in my chest.

I had to stand and face the shadow.

My phone vibrated. I fished it out of my pocket to stare at it. It was Monica.

"Pardon me," I apologized to Dr. Richardson.

"What's up?" I answered the phone.

Monica's voice sounded distant and tinny. "We've got another body. You'd better get over here as soon as you can."

———

I descended to the forest once more. Today was my day off, but I still had my gear in the back of my SUV. I tied on my hiking boots and donned a sheriff's office windbreaker. The sky was still spitting rain, and I walked down into a ravine, mindful of the mud.

I climbed down, down, finding treacherous footing and clinging to saplings as I went. When voices echoed softly at the bottom of the ravine, I knew I was close.

At the bottom, the cool earth smelled of moss. A couple of deputies wound police tape around trees. I faced the mouth of a sedimentary sandstone cave supporting the weight of an entire forest on its roof. I peered into it and clicked on my flashlight.

Shelf caves were common in this part of the country and usually pretty shallow. I ducked into the mouth and walked twenty feet within, following sets of wet footprints. With each step, I lowered my head as the cave ceiling grew closer. I had the sensation that some people reported while descending into the underworld at Delphi, wondering what message the dead might have to impart.

I tried to ignore how much the coolness of it felt like my memory vault had cracked open and the monstrous memories were escaping. It felt as if this was a place I could have visited before, even if only in dreams.

Monica crouched on the sandy cave floor. When I reached her, I was nearly crawling. Cold radiated from the rock, through the soles of my shoes and against my face, a clammy humidity.

I peered over her shoulder, where her flashlight shone.

A young woman lay on the floor of the cave. She was nude, with her hands folded over her belly. Her long blond hair was combed out in a solar flare, a halo around her head. Pieces of milky quartz were set in her hair like tiny stars. More of those pale pebbles surrounded her, circling the body, meticulously spaced one inch apart.

Her hands held a deer skull, its antlers spreading out beyond her elbows. Bits of moss were arranged in lines down her bruised throat, sternum, and legs.

But her face held my attention. Two black river stones had been placed beneath her eyelids, where her eyes should have been. Her jaw was closed, her lips still. But a centipede crawled from her lips, moving down her cheek.

"Fuck," Monica said softly.

"Fuck," I agreed. "Do we have any idea who she is?"

"There's a missing person report for a girl who vanished from a campsite a few days ago. We're going to check there first, but I don't think that's her."

"Why not?"

"That girl was twenty-one and had facial piercings. I don't see any sign of them."

I looked over the body. "Come to think of it, none of the Strangler victims had tattoos or facial piercings, did they?"

"No. He likes them to be blank canvases."

I stared at the body. I was alone in the dark with Monica, and I felt like I could say it: "You don't think it's him, do you? That he somehow survived execution?"

Monica blew out her breath, and I knew she'd been thinking of it, too. "I mean, he'd be in his late sixties, right? And who survives an execution? But . . ."

I took a deep breath. "I know what the FBI said, but I want to talk to the executioner."

25

CHRYSALIS

After making some phone calls, I took a drive to the state's super-max prison. Hills became steeper, and the land grew more dense with forest. There were more birds here, ducks and geese crossing the white sky in complex formations.

When I pulled into the cracked macadam parking lot, I tried to imagine what it had been like for my father, being in this concrete prison, knowing that the woods were just beyond reach. I wondered if he'd ever caught glimpses of it, in the yard, or if he only saw the sky through windows embedded with chicken wire. This place would have been worse than hell for him, trapped in a concrete box, divorced from the natural world. He would've withered like a plant stuffed in a cabinet, and I could easily imagine him dying here.

I made my way through the reception area, where a guard led me down a hallway constructed of tan-painted cinder blocks lit by fluorescent lights overhead. I was shown to a spartan conference room where a white-haired man in a suit rose to shake my hand. "Lieutenant Koray? I'm Warden Sharpe."

"I'm pleased to meet you, Warden."

"Likewise. I have to admit that you've piqued my curiosity. I was an administrator at another prison during Stephen Theron's incarceration, but I've gathered some staff who might be able to answer your questions."

My gaze fell to the end of the table, where a wiry man in his late fifties in a corrections officer's uniform sat. Beside him was a middle-aged woman in scrubs.

"Lieutenant Koray, please meet Major Don Seamus and Nurse Darlene Rittenhouse."

I shook hands with Major Seamus. His grip was room temperature, not sweaty. When I shook Darlene's hand, it was cool and limp. I sat down opposite them while the warden took a seat at the head of the table, before a stack of manila file folders.

The warden flipped open a file. "Stephen Theron was, by the previous warden's accounts, a volatile prisoner. When he was first transferred here, two inmates jumped him, but he broke the orbital bone of one as he ripped out an eye. The other one, he broke six ribs." The warden licked his fingers and flipped through the pages. "He got sent to solitary for thirty days. The other inmates pretty much left him alone after that."

"Did he see a psychologist or social worker here?"

"Well, he was assigned a social worker, but he never spoke. Occasionally, academic researchers and the FBI would come by to talk to him, but he would never participate."

"He never opened up to anyone?"

"Nope. Usually, when we get a guy in here for a notorious crime, he'll respond to ego stroking. A lot of 'em like holding court, the attention. And it's not like there's much else to do here, anyway."

"Did he talk to his lawyers?"

"Not so much," the major said. "He didn't really fight for appeals, though his attorneys filed them."

"How about other inmates? Any confidants or cellmates?"

"We kept him in a cell by himself," Major Seamus said. "When he was put in with others, the others didn't fare so well."

"How's that?"

"The first guy we put him in with, after he got through his time in solitary . . . that guy died of a drug overdose."

I nodded. Sadly, this wasn't an unusual fate in jail or prison.

The nurse looked at me. She had chin-length brown hair. "That happened my first week at work. The coroner did a tox screen on him, and it came back positive for PCP. We tested Theron, and he was squeaky-clean. Dude must have died in there and Theron didn't call for help. He must've hung out with that dead body for hours."

"He was weird all around," the major said. "The inmates in neighboring cells complained of strange sounds they heard at night, voices coming from his cell. It was like the place was haunted. A lot of COs wouldn't patrol to the end of the hallway in E-6, where his cell was."

I leaned forward. "Did you go?"

"Yeah." He shook his head sheepishly. "I was young and curious. I went down that hallway a few times on third shift. The lights would go out. Sometimes there would be water puddling on the floor. Pipes kept breaking, and Maintenance kept fixing leaks, but they kept coming back. And it wasn't piss . . . it was water."

I paused in scribbling in my notebook.

"I saw it rain in his cell, hand to God."

I flicked a glance to the warden. The warden didn't say anything, just listened with no hint of distrust.

"You're telling me that a serial killer made it rain indoors?"

He wrung his hands on the table before him. "I walked up to the window in the door, shone my flashlight in . . . and Theron was standing in the middle of the floor, nude, with his arms outstretched, and droplets of rain were coming out of the ceiling."

"Did you . . . did you tell anyone about this?" I asked.

"No. Not at first. But I listened, to the inmates and the other COs. Shit happened down there. Radios stopped working, and you'd hear weird voices from them. Wet footprints would go up and down the halls. Along with everyone else, I just decided to ignore it. Unless somebody was getting hurt, I was gonna leave that alone until sunrise." The major nodded to himself.

"I don't know what to say about that," I admitted. Hearing this made me nervous. I was willing to believe Dr. Richardson's explanations, that child me had concocted supernatural reasons for the unfathomable. But for others to feel that darkness . . . I wondered if Dr. Richardson was wrong. And what would that mean? I wanted to close my eyes, to avoid that line of inquiry. But I couldn't; I had to face it head-on.

The warden flattened his hands on the files. "That was before my time, but there's a lot of lore built up about this prisoner. I've found the staff who witnessed his behavior to be trustworthy and reliable people."

I nodded. "Okay, then. He sounds like a very difficult prisoner to manage."

"If you left him alone, it was okay. But I gotta tell you, I'd rather deal with a guy who likes to pick fights than a guy making it rain in the middle of the night in his cell." Major Seamus shook his head.

"Did you let him out into the yard for rec?"

"Yes. And he attempted to escape." The major showed me a photograph of a section of fence. Prisons had several layers of fence, ribbon razor wire, and electricity to provide multiple fail-safes. "He got over the first layer of fence . . . We have no idea how. He was spotted from the tower, and COs were able to take him down without much incident."

I stared at the photo. Beyond the fence lay green forest.

"He was pretty cut up," the nurse said. "I treated him."

"Did he say why he tried to escape?" I asked.

"No." She wrapped her hands around her elbows. "But he gave me the creeps with this thousand-yard stare. He just kept saying . . . 'Almost.'" Her hand slid up to her light brown hair. "I dyed my hair. The only way we can work with inmates is to get close to them. And, yeah, there's a CO in the room. But you're working on people who can kill you in a heartbeat. I was very aware of that with Stephen Theron."

"A lot of women dyed their hair," I said. But this woman was still dyeing hers. Had she always been dyeing it? Or had she gone back to it after the new crimes were committed?

"He never got rec time again," the warden said.

My heart sank. That had to have been devastating to him.

"Can you tell me about the people who visited him?"

"Sure." He looked through the files and handed me a few sheets of a visitors' log.

I scanned the pages. Parkes appeared often. So did several people who used the honorific "Dr." And I recognized the names of his attorneys. Others I didn't recognize. They might be media, people writing books. I flipped through the pages.

My mother's name was on page three.

My mother hated my father. She swore she never wanted to see him again. I wondered why she would've visited him. To see him helpless? To ask him why? To tell him to go to hell?

I paused, pointing at her name. "Do you remember anything about this visitor?"

The major squinted and shook his head. "I mostly worked nights, so I didn't see visitors. Just heard rumors. That there were people trying to tease out his secrets. But he'd just sit there and stare at them."

"Could I get a copy of this, please? And his commissary account and phone logs?" I asked. Anyone obsessed enough with him to try to copycat him might have come to see him or left money on his commissary.

"Of course," the warden said.

I thanked him and focused my attention on Nurse Rittenhouse. "How was his health while he was here?"

"He didn't complain of anything. Other than that time trying to climb over the fence, he didn't get hurt," she said, fidgeting. "He wasn't on any meds, so I didn't see him at pill call. Which . . . I was glad for, to be honest."

I took a deep breath and brought up the reason I was here: "What can you tell me about his execution?"

There was a pause. The major and the nurse looked to the warden. He clasped his hands over the file folders. "He was executed at twelve fifty-eight a.m. on January 6, 2001. The method of execution was lethal injection by sodium pentothal."

"I imagine there were spectators."

"Yes. They had to call in the state highway patrol to keep people from breaking in. Demonstrators are one thing, but this group was something else." The major pushed a newspaper clipping across the table to me. "Media, protestors, and groupies filled the parking lot and the whole access road."

This was nothing I didn't already know. "Did that interfere with the execution?"

There was a pause.

"It seems like there were problems, since it took almost a full hour to declare him dead, and executions traditionally begin at midnight." I deliberately put my pen down and closed my note-book to put them at ease.

The major and the nurse exchanged glances, then looked to the warden again. The warden nodded.

Major Seamus stared down at his hands. "I was there. I'd been a paramedic before I got on at the prison. So I knew how to give IV fluids. I volunteered to be on the death squad."

"Tell me about the death squad."

"A couple months before the execution, the warden asked for volunteers. I signed up because I thought it was something I could do. At least, technically. But I never did it again." He shook his head.

"What happened?"

"It was standing room only in the observation area outside the death chamber. His legal representation, victims' families. So many victim family members . . . we were afraid we'd have to turn people away. Everybody wanted to see the Forest Strangler dead. And I did, too. He'd done awful things, and I honestly wanted that hallway to stop being haunted.

"We brought him into the execution room. I helped strap him down. He didn't resist or say anything. I started the IV line, and one of the other COs opened the curtains. Theron didn't say any-thing, not even with all those eyes on him. He just stared at the ceiling.

"But something was wrong. I looked at my watch. The drugs should have put him out unconscious, but his respiration and heartbeat were still normal. I turned up the flow, thinking that would speed things along. The warden had sent the members of the death squad to a seminar on how to do this, and I knew something was wrong. But I kept a poker face and kept going while the clock ticked on.

"Then his vein blew out. I pulled the line and started the other arm, but I was having a hard time getting it started. The crowd was starting to chatter. One of the other COs drew the curtain. I called for help from Medical." He glanced at Darlene.

"I wanted no part of this. None." She looked up at me. "I could lose my license if anyone found out."

"I'm not interested in seeing anyone lose their livelihood," I assured her.

"I was called to an emergency, and I went. I got the IV restarted in his hand. That's not the way to do that, but it was what I could do. He stared at me the whole time. I told him I was sorry." She rubbed at her eye.

"You did what had to be done, Rittenhouse. Nobody needed to suffer," the warden said reassuringly.

She composed herself. "The IV ran, and his eyes closed. I left."

The major took over. "They pulled the curtain back. I took his pulse and respiration, and they were gone. I called him at twelve fifty-eight. Which was a good thing, because the IV fell right out of his hand then."

"Then what happened?"

"Then it was time to get all those people cleared out. That took forever, with all the traffic. And you don't want to rush victims' families or anything."

"Did an undertaker come for the body?"

The major looked down at the conference table. "We were told the university was going to pick up the body, to dissect his brain or something, since the family didn't want it. Usually, when people die, the family claims the body or the state pays for cremation.

"So we waited out on the loading docks. The traffic was filtering away, and we had Theron zipped up in a body bag out there in the cold. An ambulette van went through Security, backed to the dock. Two men who looked legit climbed out. They had forms and ID and all that. We loaded the body into the ambulette—which looked totally normal inside, too—and they drove off.

"I thought we were done. I stayed out on the back dock, smoking and watching it snow. The whole situation rattled me more than I wanted to admit, and I was glad to get things back to normal.

"Then the gatehouse radios. They say they've got some folks there from the university for Theron's body. I tell them that they already were here. Only they weren't." The major's eyes narrowed. "We'd been fucking had. Someone called the state highway patrol, quietly, and they searched for that ambulette. Story I heard is they found it a couple of days later, abandoned in a parking lot. And for some weird reason, some sick fucks stole the body."

I glanced at the warden, who said: "I don't have any of the state highway patrol's records. And there's a lot of things missing here." He didn't want to admit, *The old warden redacted that shit*, but his expression said it all.

"And the old warden . . . ," I ventured.

"Died of a heart attack three years ago."

"I see."

I looked at the major and the nurse. "I have to ask you, because

I have to ask you. You are absolutely, one hundred percent sure that Stephen Theron was dead?"

The nurse exhaled, looking close to tears. "I left the room before he flatlined. That's all I can say."

The major looked me in the eye. "I've seen dead bodies before. He was dead."

I wasn't sure if I could trust his word on this. He believed my father had made it rain in his cell, after all.

But hope and dread flared within me. Maybe, somehow, my father had survived.

———

I asked to see my father's cell. Not because I needed to for the investigation, but because I needed to see it for myself.

I'd visited prisons before, and anything out of the ordinary is immediately cause for attention. Especially women.

Maximum security facilities kept tight control over inmates, and there tended not to be inmates roaming around as much as at minimum security facilities. Minimum security inmates could be trusted to be runners, do laundry, and serve food. That wasn't the case for this facility. I walked down a hallway with Major Seamus, and all the inmates were behind bars.

I'd long since perfected the thousand-yard stare necessary for walking through the county jail. The idea was to look straight ahead, with my gaze softened a bit, so I wasn't staring at anyone in particular but was alert to any movement. Prison was the same as jail, with inmates shouting detailed descriptions of what they'd like to do to me if they got me alone, pithy observations about the nature of the universe, and random shouts for sympathy.

I ignored them, following Seamus as he led me to a wing of

single cells with solid doors. Windows reinforced with steel pierced the doors, above the slots for food. Prisoners smacked the windows and shrieked, but we ignored them. They were a rowdy bunch for protective custody.

The major led me to the end of the short hallway and pointed to a door on the right. "This is E-6." He pulled keys from a ring and unlocked the door.

"It's not occupied?"

"Honestly, it smells weird in there, probably from the water damage. Inmates don't like it, so we don't fill it unless we have to."

He opened the door and I walked inside.

The cell was perhaps six by nine. A single cot was bolted into the wall, and a stainless steel one-piece toilet was riveted into the back wall. Like other prison cells with doors, the hinges were hidden to prevent suicide by hanging. Florescent light burned above, covered in a protective cage.

Indeed, it smelled damp, like black mold and moss and a thousand other rotting things. Even though the green paint over the cinder blocks looked fairly recent and the cement floor was clean, this was not a sterile, institutional place.

I glance up, spying a moth flitting against the cage. I wondered how a moth had wound its way this far into the building.

I imagined this place at night, when men slept and screamed. It inexplicably felt to me like a chrysalis, a place where my father would have gone dormant in preparation for . . . what?

That was too much of me wanting to believe he was alive, that he'd flown from this place with wings into the woods, where he belonged.

"Nobody's asked to see this place since that FBI agent, years ago," the major said.

"Which FBI agent?" I asked, though I knew the answer.

"Parkes. He was in and out here a lot, even after he retired. That guy never left this case alone."

"I've spoken with him. He was the one who told me about the missing body."

Major Seamus nodded. "Odd duck, that man."

"Yeah?"

Seamus frowned. "He spent hours with Theron, asking him questions. I don't think he ever answered. They said that sometimes they'd just sit in silence. Gave the visitation staff the willies."

"Sounds like he gave everyone the willies."

"Yeah. I'm glad he's gone." Seamus shrugged. "No man with a direct pipeline to the devil should be walking this earth with the rest of us."

A drop of water dripped down from the ceiling to kiss the top of my head. I reached up to touch it, stifling a shudder.

26

KNOWING

I sat in the car and thumbed through the list of visitors, phone calls, and people who left my father commissary funds. My mother had only visited him once, but Parkes had been to see him forty times. It actually surprised me that my mother had visited him at all; I thought she would've done anything to distance herself from him. As for Parkes . . . that seemed like a lot, even for someone involved in the investigation. Maybe he was looking for answers, ones he never got. I intended to track down the rest of the visitors. Maybe somebody who was obsessed with him stole the body. Maybe someone admired him and wanted to be like him.

But if so, why wait so long? My father had been dead for decades. If someone were unhinged enough to copy him, why wait?

And if my father was alive . . . why wait?

I didn't think that digging this far back would yield a viable suspect, necessarily. But I wanted to know, to understand what happened to my father. I was abusing the hell out of official processes to do it, but . . .

. . . I needed to know.

I started the car and headed back to the freeway. I wanted to talk to Parkes about the investigation, but I was afraid he would recognize me if we had too much one-on-one time. It made me wonder: Did he send me the letter? He would've been the only person who might recognize me after all this time. And the prison visitor logs suggested he was more than a little obsessed with the case.

I decided it wasn't him. He would've spoken to me directly. The letter was an attempt at intimidation, clear as day. The letter might or might not have had anything to do with the gifts I was receiving. Whoever was doing these things, whether they were human or not, knew who I was.

Dr. Richardson knew my identity. But I mentally crossed her off the list. She had too much to lose if my story was told. If my secret was kept, she kept her job.

Was it someone like Cas Russo? Possibly. I didn't doubt that some internet conspiracy theorist, author, or journalist would've loved to find out who I was. I doubted it was someone working for the media, though. That kind of intimidation wasn't the style of legit journalism. A serious journalist would've invited me to talk in a neutral location. A shady one would've just knocked on my door and tried a gotcha interview, filming for effect.

I thought about my adoptive parents. They didn't know, or at least I didn't think they did. Dr. Richardson had told them I was an orphan and they never questioned it, especially since I had false memories to relate. Still. I worried that if someone had discovered who I was, they might have begun by sniffing around the circumstances of my adoption. And they might have told my parents.

I closed my eyes, fear churning in my gut. If my secret got out, their lives would be ruined, too.

I put my personal cell phone on speakerphone as I drove.

My adoptive mom picked up on the second ring. "Hello?"

"Hi, Mom." I hadn't seen my parents since Christmas. It felt at once natural and also weird to call her that now. "I forgot . . . what time is it where you are?"

"It's almost ten. We were just getting ready for bed. We saw on the news what was happening in your part of the state . . . about that killer?"

I winced. News of the Forest Strangler had reached Japan.

"You're being safe, aren't you, dear?"

"Of course, of course." I rushed to a new subject: "How's school?" My parents had gone to Japan to teach English. It had been a dream of theirs, and I was happy they'd been able to chase it in their retirement.

"It's wonderful! The kids are just fantastic. Did you get the picture your father sent you?"

"The one with you and all the kids in the garden? Yes!" My parents were surrounded by two dozen smiling children in uniform.

"The apartment is small. It's a lot to get used to, but freeing in other ways. Not having so much stuff, you know?"

"I bet. Do you have a dishwasher?"

"No. Not even a washer and dryer!" my mother chortled.

I heard my father announce in the background: "I'm the dishwasher! And the laundry guy!"

I grinned. "I'm glad you guys are doing well."

"How are you, sweetie?"

I paused. I didn't want them to worry, and I hadn't told them about getting shot at work. I should have. But I didn't know how now. "Work's pretty intense. I'll have to tell you some stories when we get together."

"I can't wait! Do you think you could take some time off and meet us in Osaka?"

"I'd really like that. I've got some cases to tie up first. But when I can get some time off, I'll book tickets."

"You'll love it here," my mom said. "There's so much to show you! The temples, the restaurants, the gardens . . . It's all wonderful."

We chitchatted about the food in their neighborhood, which made my stomach rumble. When the conversation paused, I asked, "Hey, I wanted to check in with you about something . . . Before you left, did anyone come around asking about my adoption?"

There was a pause on the other end of the line. "No, sweetie. Let me ask your father." A muffled conversation rumbled in the background, and my mom returned to the line. "No. Why? What's going on?"

One of my mom's fears was that the family of my fictional parents would try to take me away from them. "I was getting some genetic testing done for work. Nothing's wrong or anything. They're doing some interesting things with DNA now in the lab. It's just a work project."

"Hm. Okay. Yeah, nobody's asked us."

"I know it was a closed adoption, but do you remember anything about the agency that placed me?"

My mom paused. "Your adoption paperwork is on file with our family attorney in Springfield. You remember him, Lowell Parsons?"

"Yeah. I remember him. He was the guy who came by your New Year's Eve parties with the disco records?"

"Yep. That's him. He'd have the details."

"Is there anything you remember about my birth parents?"

"They died in a car accident. You remember that."

"Yes." That shadow memory now seemed so two-dimensional.

"Your psychiatrist reached out to the adoption agency, and they connected us with you. And the day you came home was the best day of our lives."

"It was the best day of mine, too." I meant that.

"Honey, are you searching for your roots? It's okay if you are. I just don't want you to ever feel bad about asking any questions . . ."

"Not really, Mom. Just playing with this DNA project. I have all the family I could want, you and Dad."

I heard my mother's smile on the other end of the line. "We love you, sweetie."

"I love you, too, Mom."

"Good night."

I sighed, staring at the road ahead when the line went dead. I loved my adoptive parents and I wished that I could drive out and see them. I wished I could sleep in my teenage bedroom, play chess with my dad, and help my mom paint the kitchen a sunny yellow.

Maybe I could introduce them to Nick. They would like him. I had a brief fantasy of the four of us playing a board game around the living room coffee table. It was an image of a safe, ordinary life I couldn't ever have.

Tears came on me quickly, and I pulled off the side of the road to wipe my eyes. I never wanted to hurt my adoptive parents. Not ever. I loved them, and maybe it was good that they were far, far away from this.

From me.

———

I was able to reach my parents' attorney. Lowell Parsons was semi-retired but delighted to hear from me. He promised me that he could still bust his disco moves with a hip replacement and promised to email me the adoption records.

"Your parents wanted everything done by the book," he told me. "So they called me when their adoption agency had a lead. They were ready to be parents and weren't wanting to fall in love with a child who'd be taken away from them."

I frowned and thanked him. I hadn't stopped to consider what my parents would think if they knew I was the daughter of the Forest Strangler. Would they still love me? I wanted to believe they would, but . . . who could? Could Nick? He had much of a devil-may-care attitude about life, but I thought this would be a bridge too far. In his head, he probably wouldn't want to blame me for my father's sins. But the heart is a strange thing, one I'd never deciphered.

I wanted to believe that people would see me as a separate entity from my father. But I knew better. Most people, no matter how good or well-intentioned, would recoil from that proximity to evil. It was why houses where a murder occurred were a hard sell. Someone would eventually buy, but those buyers were few and far between. People who could sleep in a bed above permanently stained floorboards were rare, ruthlessly pragmatic and unsentimental. Were those my parents or Nick?

No. I was not going to deal with this until I found the killer. One foot in front of the other. Gazing into the future was too much for now.

Judge McPherson was still signing warrants while on vacation, and he agreed to let us get DNA from Braden Mariner. I touched base with Sykes, and he said that Mariner's buyer clammed up, even though they offered him protected status as an informant. They'd also been in touch with the hospital pharmacy, and an audit was underway. They'd already found a disturbing amount of missing drugs and were trying to keep things hush to avoid bad publicity.

I managed to get a call in to a contact of mine at the state highway patrol to try to rustle up any files on the recovery of the ambulette suspected to have made off with my father's body.

"Are you kidding me?" Doreen asked. I could hear her taking notes on the other end.

"Anything you might have would be amazing."

"I'll dig around, see what I can come up with. There's got to be a record somewhere. I've gotta say, I'm intrigued."

I grinned. "I knew you would be."

I parked myself on my couch at home after changing into lounge pants and a T-shirt. I put a frozen cauliflower pizza in the oven and started cross-referencing the visitor and commissary list from the prison with people I could easily find. Many were attorneys, some academics who were unsuccessfully trying to write a book about my father. I circled my mother. I found a few journalists and a handful of psychiatrists. Some members of victims' families. I felt bad for those who came to my father for answers, knowing that he never gave them. I started crossing people off the list who were deceased. That narrowed things down a bit more.

My phone rang, and I picked it up. "Koray."

It was Monica. It sounded like she was talking around a mouthful of hard candy.

"Hey, we got a tentative ID on that second victim."

"That was fast." I sat up. "Who is she?"

"Stefanie Childers. She was a sex worker, frequenting truck stops in the northeastern part of the state. I'm looking at her most recent mug shot from a prior arrest, and it looks like her. She's twenty-eight, three priors for soliciting."

"Truck stop. Mmm." I tapped my pen against my teeth. "We think Cas has been hanging around truck stops."

"Yep. We got video back from the truck stop on 71. Caught Cas on camera loading up on chips and energy drinks. He got into a rig in the lot. Highway patrol ran down the plate number and caught up with the driver at a weigh station in Florida."

"Where did he drop Cas off?"

"Here's the thing: the driver dropped him off one hundred miles north, at a trucking plaza off the turnpike, before picking up a load bound for Florida."

"This turnpike . . . is it in Stefanie Childers's territory?"

"Maybe. They're looking for tollbooth footage and video at the trucking plaza. But here's the thing: even if Cas was the killer, and he was at that truck stop cruising for a victim, how would he get her all the way to back to Bayern County? He's got no car. We found his van in a grocery store parking lot about twenty miles from that hotel he was hiding in."

"Yeah." I stared at the ceiling, thinking. "Let's check car thefts and rentals in that area. Especially online reservations. He might be using his girlfriend's identity or her mom's identity for that. Speaking of which, how's she doing?"

"Back home with her parents. Mom and dad aren't happy and want to press charges for statutory rape. Not sure how that will go, but it's in the hands of the DA in that jurisdiction."

"She come up with any new information on where Cas might be going or what he might be up to?"

"Nope. She just said he was on a mission. And I don't love the sound of that."

"Maybe Forensics will get something good out of that cave."

"Hope so, but there's a whole lot to go through, with that and the prior scene. I told the techs to be especially mindful of tire tracks; they might help us narrow down what kind of vehicle the killer is driving. Might connect with whatever Cas is driving now."

"Hopefully, we'll get some clear prints or DNA. That would be the jackpot."

"How did it go at the prison?"

I filled her in. "Here's what I'm thinking . . . Whoever was obsessed enough with the Forest Strangler to rip off his body might be nuts enough to copy him."

"Hmm. That could happen. But I'm not loving the idea that it took whoever that was thirty years ago to start back up."

"Could be that our subject was in prison for an unrelated crime. That's a pretty common thing that explains gaps in serial killer action, anyway." I made a note to start screening my list against people who went to prison.

"You know, I wonder if the original Forest Strangler was just one guy."

"What do you mean?"

"Well, dude was super prolific. What if he had help? And what if his accomplice got cold feet and went to Mexico for a few decades? Or if he wound up behind bars? Now that time has passed, maybe he's back at it."

"I'd think the FBI would've covered that," I said. "I mean, the evidence they had pointed to him because they got his prints, right? And he was chased down to a house with more bodies, right?"

"Far be it from me to second-guess the FBI," Monica said. "But I think we need to at least entertain the notion that the Forest Strangler wasn't acting alone."

I sat back on the couch. I'd never, ever considered this before. It wasn't unheard-of for serial killers to hunt in pairs.

"Well, fuck."

We agreed that I'd continue to look into the original Strangler's case to see if there were any ghosts of the past who could speak to the present. Monica would work through the current evidence, and we'd keep each other posted.

We hung up, and I got ready to close down for the night. I did one last check of my email, when I saw that an email had come in from a supposed "Strangler Fan." The email address was a throw-away Gmail account. The subject was "Knowing."

I opened it, expecting a rant from a serial killer afficionado. I'd gotten a few of these and ignored them. But this one was just for me.

I've been watching you for a long time.

There was an attachment, a photo. It was taken using green and black night vision tech, likely with a telephoto lens. The picture was of me sitting on my front porch. It must have been taken in spring; I could make out the redbud at the corner of the house flowering. I was sitting with my arms wrapped around my knees, looking off into the distance, away from the camera. I thought I remembered that night, when the spring peepers had awoken. I wanted to listen to them in the dark.

That asshole had been to my house. And he'd been watching me for months. Fuck.

I changed views to the email header and checked the IP addresses of the servers it had traveled through. It seemed to originate near Chicago, or someone wanted it to look that way. It was relatively easy for someone with enough knowledge to manipulate these things.

That was far enough away from me that it wasn't anyone in my immediate vicinity, which made me feel better. The mail with a local postmark had concerned me. Assuming that whoever sent it wasn't just covering his tracks.

But, again, just that statement of knowledge. No demand.

I drummed my fingers. This had been sent to my departmental email, and as such it theoretically existed forever. I couldn't hide it from IT if they went digging. Thousands of emails traveled throughout the department, and they went looking only when necessary. Still.

I hit REPLY.

I typed out:

Who is this?

I almost hit SEND, but I didn't. I backspaced over it and deleted the draft. I didn't want any conversations about my identity to take place on a departmental server. Instead, I created a new, anonymous email account, then emailed the original address back.

Who is this?

I hit SEND, wondering if I would hear back. I didn't want this person to escalate and involve anyone at work.

"Well, Chicago, let's see if you have anything to say to me."

I turned out the light and went to bed.

But I drew the curtains first. Let that bastard guess whether I was asleep or sitting up with a gun in my lap, waiting for his creepy self to skulk around the foundations of my forest kingdom.

27

THE LAST SURVIVOR

Nick pulled the last few itchy, stubborn strands of stitches from my skin. What remained were tiny pink scars. I swept my hair over my shoulder as I sat on the edge of the bed in a towel. My bruises had faded from violet to a lighter green, like moss. I thought it was interesting how living bodies could show exactly the same shades as corpses. My jaw was speckled with a few small spots, but they might have simply been acne scars.

"Those will fade, become white eventually," Nick murmured, his fingers lightly brushing my skin, exploring those tiny scars scattered in a constellation across my body. "Keep them moisturized. If you want a referral to a derm, I know a guy . . ."

I turned to face him, and he trailed off. His warm breath stirred a strand of hair covering my face.

I leaned forward and captured his mouth with mine. He hesitated for only a moment before sinking into the kiss. His fingers slid up from my arms to cup my face. The kiss grew searching, and I ached for him. I ached for the feeling of my hands roving over his warm skin, for that thrill of lust, of knowing he wanted me the way I wanted him.

But I also ached for that sense of normalcy we had, of Saturday mornings stretched out in bed, in the sunshine, drinking coffee and doing the crossword puzzle. I'd missed having him beside me, warm at night. Even when we worked opposite shifts, I missed seeing evidence of him in my life: the half-drunk milk in the refrigerator or a forgotten pair of shoes under the couch. He was my stability in life, a North Star, even though I didn't want to admit I needed one. Now, with the ghost of my father haunting me, I wanted to connect with someone real, with flesh and blood.

We made love that night, finally, sinking into familiar skin. We knew each other's bodies, how a touch or a sigh could move one another. When we finished, I lay curled up on his chest while he stroked my hair.

Neither of us spoke, too afraid to break the spell of what was moving between us. I thought of the ring in the nightstand drawer, sparkling silently in the dark like a forgotten star.

———

My father wasn't the only ghost walking the earth.

My biological mother was still alive.

I trawled empty public records. I went back to the county clerk records in the county where we had lived with my father, then where we'd lived in the safe houses, and then her parents' in Florida. None came up with anything.

I sent Agent Parkes a politely worded email to ask if he knew where Sheila Theron currently lived. I didn't want to deal with him face-to-face.

He replied back in short order:

> Lt. Koray:
>
> She was placed in witness protection, due to media harassment. I can get a message to her, if you'd like, but I can't disclose her location without a court order.
>
> Are you thinking she knows the whereabouts of Elena Theron?
>
> Parkes

I froze at the mention of my old name. Maybe I could get Parkes to divulge where he was on that part of the investigation.

Where my mother was concerned, I didn't really love going through an intermediary, but I had no choice. There was no way I was going to get a court order.

> Agent Parkes,
>
> Please let Sheila Theron know that I'd like to talk to her, off the record, about the case, and that I would do my utmost to preserve her anonymity.
>
> I do wonder if she knows where the daughter might be. Does she have any light to shed on that?
>
> Koray

I waited, but eventually heard back:

Unfortunately, Sheila doesn't want any contact from law enforcement at this time.

She doesn't know where Elena is, since there was a closed adoption. But I've been in touch with some old contacts, and I think I'm picking up the trail.

If there's something you're looking for, please let me know and I'll try to help.

I narrowed my eyes at the screen. He was rooting around in my background. I wasn't sure how thoroughly Dr. Richardson had swept away my footprints. I tried to tell myself that if Parkes knew where I was, he would have acted by now. Right?

With respect to my mother, he wasn't stonewalling, but he wasn't helpful, either. I wasn't interested in turf wars, like my boss. But it looked like some damage had been done to interdepartmental relations.

And to my relations, too, within the department. It was very quiet after Rollins's death. According to the flyer on the bulletin board, the family was holding the funeral next week. Normally, when there was a death, everyone in the department was expected to attend. I wasn't sure about this. I thought I had to go. But damn.

I was getting coffee from the kitchenette as deputies in the hallway described Rollins's body: "It's gonna have to be a closed casket funeral. There's not enough left of him to put together to look decent."

"Do you think it was suicide?"

"Maybe. He sure as fuck had some kind of freakout at Koray's place."

"That's some creepy shit, dude. Who goes to someone's house like that?"

"Well, there was a personal shotgun in his car and a box of shells."

"Fuck."

"Fuck. What's gonna happen now?"

"I dunno, but rumor from the union rep suggests his wife might try to seek some damages. Says the department pushed him to going mental with too much OT."

"Oh, that's bullshit. Rollins never saw an OT sign-up he didn't like."

"Right. But the department might throw some dollars to keep this quiet."

I waited until they drifted down the hall before emerging and slinking back to my desk.

I stared at my desk.

There was a snake skeleton sprawled across my blotter.

It was a medium-size snake, about three feet long, its spine curled in a great cursive swoosh. Featherlike ribs spread from the spine, and the skull looked up at me with jaws slightly parted. Its teeth curved backward toward its neck in a smile.

If I'd found this on a hike, I'd have taken it home and treasured it. But seeing it here, at work . . . Fear coursed through me.

I called over my shoulder. "Hey, who left this here?"

Nobody claimed responsibility. I snapped on a pair of gloves, grabbed a fingerprint kit, and headed to an unused storage room with the snake. I parked it on top of a file cabinet.

The snake's skeleton was incredibly intricate and textured, though it had been flawlessly defleshed. I seriously doubted I'd be able to get prints from it. But someone was messing with me. And I was determined to try.

260

I dusted that thing from skull to tail, to the point where it was sooty black and covered with adhesive tape in the effort to lift a print.

I got nothing.

I bent down to face it, eye to eye.

"Why are you here?" I whispered. "What do you want?"

The snake continued to grin at me.

I scooped it up into a paper evidence bag and stashed it in the bottom drawer of my desk.

I washed my hands in the ladies' room, steadied myself with more coffee, and forced myself to refocus on my mother. It was difficult, as I thought I could hear faint hissing from my bottom desk drawer.

No. I would not give in to this. Not here. Not now. Whether it was left for me as a sign by one of Rollins's buddies, or it was left by my stalker, or it was a missive from Veles himself, I would not.

I tried a different tactic to get my mother's location: I contacted the Social Security Administration. My father was legally dead, and someone had to be collecting his Social Security death benefits. A few calls, flashes of the badge, and favors got me a name and a last known address before death benefits expired: Rebecca Conley, with an address in a neighboring state. It surprised me that she was so close.

I wondered if she'd gotten remarried, had more children. I wondered what she'd done for a career. I didn't expect she'd know who I was. Maybe some mother's instinct? I wasn't sure. It had been a long time. And maybe she'd just shut the door in my face.

Either way, I had to know.

I could get down there and back in a day. I filled out an itinerary and dropped by my boss's office to get a departmental credit card. I knocked on the open doorframe.

"Chief?"

He was sitting behind his desk, staring at the television on his wall, with an ill-tempered look on his face. The FBI was on television, talking about the Strangler. Agent Russell was behind the podium, confirming how seriously the FBI took threats to public safety. Parkes was beside him, among the people in suits lined up to lend gravitas to the press conference. A K9 handler with the state highway patrol moved to join the lineup, but his Belgian Malinois dog turned and growled at Parkes. The handler pulled the dog back, moving out of the camera frame. Seeing Parkes look off-balance cheered me somehow.

Chief gestured for me to come in and turned the television on mute.

"Could I get your signature on this and a 'Get out of Jail Free' card?" That's what we called the departmental credit cards.

"Sure." He scanned the document. "You're hip deep in the Strangler research?"

"It's a weird case. And fascinating."

"Every parent with a blond daughter was locking them up in their rooms. It was a bizarre time." He scrawled his illegible signature on the paperwork. "And they're doing it again. I'm getting panicked calls from concerned citizens to impose a curfew."

"You were here when that happened the first time?"

"I was a brand-spanking-new deputy." He leaned back in his chair. "Fresh outta the training academy and convinced I was going to be the one to catch this guy."

I sat down across from his desk. "I kind of get that."

"That motherfucker was slick, though. I give him that. He left nothing behind; the crime scenes were squeaky-clean. And they were so surreal . . . You've seen." He waved his hand.

"You saw the crime scenes?" I leaned forward.

"Two of them. The one by the river and the one in the field off Route 35. I was just there to work crowd control, but I looked." He shrugged. Cops were nosy; we all knew that.

"What was it like?"

"Like something out of a fairy tale, honestly. Like something a movie would've come up with. It was like he sort of . . . revered those women. It didn't surprise me at all to hear that he hadn't raped any of them. It was some weird kind of deification, almost. But that's my two cents." He slurped his coffee. "I think he was a man with more problems than could be worked out with mortal psychology. Something in his brain was wired completely differently, on a different frequency. And it was working for him . . . He didn't get caught for a long time."

"He was out there for years."

"The bodies would show up seasonally, but not in a frenzy, except toward the end. There were a lot of victims in the last six months. I guess what they say about serial killing is often true: they have to escalate to maintain the thrill." He laced his hands over his belly.

"The FBI said someone ID'd his truck plates and he was tracked down that way. What happened with that?"

"So there was this Halloween costume party the high schoolers were doing, an annual thing. They had it up on a creepy barn that belonged to one of the students' relatives. Mostly harmless: some underage drinking, kids scaring the shit out of themselves by playing with Ouija boards and doing whatever kids did in the eighties."

"I can only imagine."

"So, with a serial killer on the loose, you could imagine how much these kids were wired for sound. They did a haunted forest maze kind of thing. One of the girls got separated from the group, and she swore someone tried to grab her in the woods. Her boyfriend showed up, and the guy took off. We got a partial description, a boot print, and a partial print on the girl's earring."

"You sound like you were there."

"Yup. I got to wrangle drunk teenagers who were barely younger than me." He chortled. "Most of them knew me from high school, so it was, um, challenging to establish any kind of authority. I responded first, and the detectives showed up later. Wanda Cruise, the girl, sold her story to the media. She made a good nickel off that."

"I read her interviews. She said that it was like she was falling down into a black pit and screaming was her only way out." It was hard to tell what was embellished and what wasn't, in her accounts. They seemed to change a bit over time, becoming more lurid.

"At the time, she thought it was her boyfriend messing with her." The chief wore a trace of a smile. "Afterward, it became the cloak of Satan sweeping down on her."

"Eyewitness testimony being the fragile thing it is."

"Later that night, he tried to snatch a girl in a shopping center parking lot. She was wearing a blond wig and dressed up like a princess. He grabbed her. When her wig slipped off, revealing that she was a redhead, he let her go. We got partial plates on the truck, connected the partial print from Wanda's earring to one of the earlier crime scenes, and from then it was a quick jump to Stephen Theron."

"Who was the girl he tried to kidnap?" I asked.

"Jennifer Dryden. We didn't release her name in the media,

but she got married and changed her name. She got harassed a good bit by the weirdos who wanted to know what it was like to survive a serial killer." He rolled his eyes. "Fortunately, Wanda was able to give them the details and they eventually left her alone."

"The media is a thing," I said mildly.

"The media is a weapon." He fished through his desk drawer for the departmental credit card and handed to me. "You can use it for good or ill."

"I might look those ladies up," I said.

"You should." He leaned back in his chair, lacing his hands behind his head. "I have faith that you'll work this case and get him. And then you and Monica get to be on CNN." He grinned and gave me finger guns.

I grinned back. I most definitely did not want to be on CNN. But I'd be happy to give my boss all the airtime he wanted.

Sadly, Jennifer Dryden had passed away from cancer ten years earlier and Wanda Cruise had died of an overdose four years earlier. All I had left were the dusty VHS tapes in the departmental archives.

I sat in the basement, slurping my coffee, watching grainy video footage on an old CRT television. Jennifer seemed shell-shocked, very quiet in her interviews. She answered the questions asked of her but offered little else. I could see that, in every fiber of her being, she didn't want to be part of this nightmare. I empathized.

Wanda was different. This tape must have been made after the incident, since she was dressed in acid-washed jeans and a bright pink T-shirt. When she was questioned, the detectives waded through details of what everyone was wearing, the construction of her costume as Bo Peep, and how much she'd had to drink. It didn't sound like anyone was anywhere close to sober.

"I was walking in the woods behind the barn, calling for Jeff." She paused for dramatic effect. "And someone came up behind me and grabbed me. I screamed, but a hand fell over my face. I felt like I was being enveloped in cold, just so much cold." She shuddered. "I couldn't see, I couldn't think . . . I could just feel my heart racing. I knew this wasn't Jeff. This was . . . evil."

"Then what happened?" the detective asked.

"He tried to drag me away. I screamed like my life depended on it. Because it did. I heard Jeff shouting, and the guy let me go. He dropped me into the mud."

"Did he say anything?"

"No."

"What happened next?"

"My costume was ruined. I was hysterical. Jeff came and I told him what happened. He just thought I was drunk, but I told him that it was the Forest Strangler. It had to be." She nodded triumphantly.

"Do you know why he let you go?"

She frowned and picked at her jelly bracelets. "I mean, the guys were coming. I think he just got scared and ran off."

She was lying. She was a small woman; it would've been nothing for my father to drug her with ether, like the others, and carry her away before anyone knew she was gone.

"Wanda?" the detective probed.

Red spots rose on her cheeks. "I pissed myself, okay? I peed all over him and then I threw up. Just don't tell anyone, okay?"

I paused the tape. My father had rejected her as a victim, as an offering to Veles. She'd defiled herself and was no longer worthy. Jennifer had been rejected for being the wrong hair color, not the avatar of a sacrifice that he held in his head.

Veles demanded sacrifices, but only the ones who fit the profile. Just the ones who looked like me.

28

BLOOD AND OTHER SECRETS

"Hi, this is Dr. Meyer. Can you hear me?"

A man in a cardigan sweater peered back at me through my computer screen. I'd set my laptop up on my coffee table and was sitting on the floor before it to bring it to eye level.

"Yes, thank you for meeting with me," I answered. I'd arranged an online meeting with an expert neurogeneticist on the Lyssa variant.

"Of course." He grinned. "I'm always delighted to get the chance to talk about rare genetics."

"As I mentioned in my email, I'm doing some research about the Forest Strangler case, and it was said that Stephen Theron had some genetic abnormalities you discovered. Can you tell me more about this?"

He leaned forward, an academic excited about the chance to talk about his pet project. "I was always curious about how genetics impact behavior, so I did a study of DNA of death row inmates early in my career. Like most studies trying to connect genetics to criminal behavior, I came up with no results of statistical significance."

"Right. Biology isn't destiny."

"Exactly. We were looking for markers that might help to predict schizophrenia, which impacts about one and a half million people in the U.S. Prison systems are good about taking DNA samples now to solve cold cases, so it was a natural database to want to use for this kind of work, since people who are mentally ill often get caught up in the criminal justice system rather than receive mental health services."

I nodded. "I see that on the local jail level, too. There aren't enough beds at mental health facilities for prisoners."

"Right. So we started looking at the DNA and frankly weren't having much luck. But then we found something really odd in the case of Stephen Theron. He had abnormalities in a genomic region associated with schizophrenia. This variant led to overproduction of a protein involved in brain development. This protein regulates the growth of neurons and memory. We were able to obtain his brain scans and saw that he had an abnormally high density of neurons in some regions of his brain."

"So . . . Stephen Theron was destined to be schizophrenic?"

"No. Like I said, genetics only lays the groundwork. We need activating events in life to bring those factors to the forefront. And what we saw in his brain wasn't consistent with our classical ideas of schizophrenia. It's as if his brain was working a lot harder than a normal brain." Meyer shook his head. "I really would've liked to research his brain over time, sample some tissue, but . . . the state refused to let me or anyone else I know in academic circles analyze the body."

I changed the subject. "How do you think this would've changed his perception of the world?"

"That would be something we might have been able to determine with interviews. But the guy didn't speak, and he didn't leave behind any journals or letters. He didn't even testify in his own defense. We were never able to figure out what was going on in his head. But if I had to guess . . . I'd imagine his thoughts might be pretty alien to the rest of us, making connections that no one else saw, constantly thinking multiple thoughts at a time. His neurotransmitters were probably pretty intense, so he might have felt things that no one else did. But that's just me guessing."

I could understand that. "So you found this mutation in Stephen Theron."

"Yes. We dubbed it the Lyssa variant in a paper. I will send that to you, if you'd like."

"I assume you're a Greek mythology afficionado? I read that Lyssa was the daughter of Nyx, the goddess of night and the blood of Uranus. She was a goddess of rage and madness . . ."

"Well, there's that. But I actually named it after my cat." A sheepish look crossed his face. A pair of black ears over green eyes peeped up into view, from where his cat had to be sitting on his lap. "Don't tell anyone."

I grinned at the cat. "Is this her? She's beautiful."

"Yes. Lyssa's twenty-three years old now." Meyer rubbed her chin as she slow-blinked at him. "I know we won't have her for much longer, but she'll be immortal, in her way."

I waggled my fingers at the cat, who regarded me with interest. "She has to think we're talking about her."

"She is the center of the universe, after all." Meyer grinned. "But back to the Lyssa variant: we started looking for it in other inmates. We surveyed thousands of profiles but came back with only four others."

I leaned forward. "Four?"

"Yes. All murderers who had been executed before the start of the study. Three men here in the U.S. We were also given access to a DNA profile of Kateřina of Komárov for another historical study from hair and skin cells collected from a hair ornament. One of our graduate students ran her through the profile, and she possessed the Lyssa variant, too."

"I don't know who she is."

"She's referred to as the Czech Elizabeth Báthory . . . tortured and killed between fourteen and thirty of her serfs to death. Our graduate student tried this on a lark but was surprised to find she had it." Meyer shrugged in amusement.

I thought of my father roaming the Sedlec Ossuary . . . and beginning his killing career there.

"So . . . is there any other genetic or geographical tie?" I asked.

"We don't have a large enough sample size to be able to draw any valid scientific conclusions. We do know it's a recessive gene. You'd need two copies of the gene to be affected, meaning each parent would need to have at least one copy themselves. This would be vanishingly rare."

I nodded, scribbling down notes. "So . . . how prevalent do you think it is in the general population?"

"I can't say for certain. But guessing . . . maybe five thousand people in the U.S. could have full expression of the variant. Many thousands more could be carriers. Most don't know and go about their daily business. Again, biology isn't destiny."

"What's next for you in this research?" I asked him.

"Well . . . we pretty much hit the end of the road. We didn't have enough funding to do large-scale studies. There aren't any pharmaceutical companies interested in doing this sort of research on such a small population." He spread his hands, and Lyssa put her head in one of them. "The research, though interesting water cooler talk, is pretty much a failure."

"I'm sorry to hear that," I said sincerely.

He smiled wanly at his cat. "Yeah. Well, unless another Lyssa variant comes up, we're at a dead end."

———

"There's something I'd like you to do for me."

I closed my eyes and focused on the feeling of the phone against my ear. What I was asking Dr. Richardson was a big ask, and one she could refuse.

"What is it?" she asked, her voice professionally conciliatory.

"There's something . . . something I can't get out of my head. One of my father's phantoms." I licked my lips. I'd rehearsed what to say, but I couldn't be certain that she'd agree with me. "This isn't like the Forest God, though. This is something that could be proven or disproven. I want you to test me for the Lyssa variant."

There was a pause. I squeezed my eyes tighter shut.

"Of course. I think it makes sense to talk about this further in a safe space, of course. But I can perform the test."

My breath came out in a hiss. "Thank you."

I could think of little else until I arrived at her office. I wanted to know if I harbored my father's genetic abnormality. I wanted to treat it as some sort of litmus test. In the very likely event that I didn't have a fully expressed abnormality, I could disavow any further influence of him upon my blood or psyche. It was a psychological crutch, I acknowledged. But I needed to individuate myself from him some way. And this was the easiest way I knew how.

I refused to think of what it would mean if I had the fully

expressed Lyssa variant, what would happen if those were frag-
ments of my own DNA where the bodies were found. I'd lost some
time, and I wondered if I had somehow returned to haunt those
crime scenes after the deaths, like I had when I'd shot Tom
Sullivan . . .

I shook my head and gripped the steering wheel. No. I was not
going crazy. I was in control. And I could prove that I was with
this test.

"I know this is completely weird," I told Dr. Richardson. "But
I appreciate you humoring me."

She drew blood from my arm. Once she'd filled two vials, she
removed the needle and gave me a Band-Aid to put over the crease
of my elbow.

She put the vials on her desk and stripped off her gloves. "And
you feel as if this would be meaningful how, exactly?"

I sat back on the couch, sinking into it. "I want to know how
much of this madness I've inherited."

"This marker hasn't been studied thoroughly. While it is cor-
related with psychopathy in certain populations, there hasn't been
enough randomized research to establish a firm causal link. And
if you are a carrier, it hasn't expressed itself. It's not going to af-
fect you."

"I know."

"But this is symbolic to you?"

I nodded. I wanted the results to show there wasn't a bomb in
my head, ticking, waiting to go off. "I want a piece of paper to
show me that I'm not him."

"I think you're placing too much importance on this, frankly.
It doesn't determine your destiny or your worth as a person." She
peered through her glasses at me. "You've led an exemplary life.
You are in control, not your father, no matter what the test says."

I leaned forward, elbows pressed to my knees. "I need for you to run this test."

She stared at the vials on her desk. "All right."

I nodded in satisfaction. I had pushed her into doing it.

"There's something I have to tell you," she said. "Someone came looking for you—for Elena—yesterday."

I froze. "Who?"

"Agent Parkes from the FBI. He said he was trying to find Stephen Theron's living relatives."

I laced my cold fingers together. "What did you tell him?"

"Nothing. I am bound by patient confidentiality. I told him that I never saw you."

I exhaled. "Thank you."

She nodded. "Of course. It's the least I could do. And how is this investigation affecting you?"

I stared up at the ceiling. "It's like . . . excavating something ancient. Something that I knew on one level, some muscle memory level, but that I didn't know consciously."

"Retrieving memories can be like that."

"I'm learning more than that. More about what made my father tick. Not that I can really tell anyone."

"What couldn't you tell them?"

I laughed bitterly, sighed, and shook my head. "I can't tell them that my father was intertwined with some kind of ancient, monstrous entity."

"When we last talked, we discussed that Veles was likely a coping mechanism, one that you used as a child to make sense of the world."

I told her what I'd seen in the woods, the dread that seemed to be seething just beyond my eyesight. I told her about the shadows that moved, the exhalations I heard in the dark. I was haunted, and I could feel Veles was coming closer. I was afraid—afraid that

Veles already had his claws in me and that I was a lost cause. I let all that darkness pour from my mouth in a stream of ichor, until there was nothing left and I stared at the accumulated pool of it on the floor.

We both stared at it, seeing only my reflection.

"Let me see if I can understand," Dr. Richardson said slowly. "Something inexplicable—what your father called Veles—drove your father to murder?"

I nodded, rubbing my forehead. It sounded stupid to have someone else say it like that.

"And this influence still exists after your father's death."

I nodded.

"And that you, and others, are interacting with it now."

I nodded.

"And it may be responsible somehow for the current deaths."

I nodded miserably.

"I suspect you're trying very hard to push this evil away from yourself. That's what you're doing with the test. And you're trying to push it away from your father as well."

I sat with that. An objective outsider would certainly see it that way.

She took a deep breath and looked me in the eye. "Anna. I think you've become too closely involved in this case. I think that the excavation of your memories, the current murders, and your recent drug exposure are all having negative effects on your mental health. Any one of these things could be overwhelming, but all three . . ."

I shook my head. "Don't start this."

"Don't start what?"

"Don't start telling me that I'm crazy." My eyes narrowed. I was either tainted by evil like my father, or I was crazy. A bright flash of anger lanced through me.

"That's not what I'm saying at all."

"If I am, you made me that way."

She flinched. I knew where to fling that arrow to hit that target of guilt.

I stood to leave.

"Anna."

I turned.

"I want you to know that I want to help you. In whatever way I can." She seemed very small then, elderly and frail.

My gaze softened. "I know. But I have to see this through. I hope you understand."

She nodded sadly. "I think that this, despite all my interference, was inevitable. You have to confront your father, whether in the flesh or in spirit. This is your shadow work to do, your reason for being. And that process can no longer be postponed."

I nodded. I thought that we finally understood each other.

I went out to the parking lot and climbed into my SUV. I took a deep breath to steady myself. I didn't like how that conversation went with Dr. Richardson. I felt guilty for being harsh with her, for demanding that she comply with my requests. It was manipulative as hell, and part of me wanted to go back inside and apologize to her.

I tried to put my key into the ignition but fumbled, and my key ring fell to the floorboards. I groaned, moved the seat back, and cast around on the floor.

My hand closed around them, but I froze. I was staring at the OBD port to the lower left of the steering column, under the dashboard. There was a device plugged in, one that I hadn't installed, an unobtrusive piece of plastic a bit smaller than a cigarette lighter.

I grabbed it and plucked it out. I sat up in my seat, gripping it so hard in my fist that the corners bit into my palm. This was real. This was hard evidence that hadn't been conjured up by my paranoia.

It was a GPS tracker.

Someone was following me.

———

I contacted the manufacturer of the tracker and was on hold for nearly an hour before I was disconnected. I switched tactics, sending them a tersely worded email with the device's serial number and my badge number. I wanted to know who had purchased it. I wouldn't allow them to ignore me.

I returned to Nick's town house to gather my things. He was gone, but he'd given me a key, which felt like a declaration of love. I brought with me a bag of things that I could leave there, bits and bobs of my energy to remain in his space. I wanted to slowly come back into his life, and I had brought these things here as talismans.

I'd seen no sign of another woman in Nick's town house. No lost bras kicked under the bed, women's clothes in the closet, or scented candles left around the bathtub. Perhaps I'd been wrong and Nick wasn't seeing anyone. Perhaps he had, and it wasn't serious enough for her to take up space here. I told myself I wasn't jealous, but I needed to know where I stood in his affections. I needed . . . him. To feel like we could return to where we had been before.

I tucked a change of clothes in the bottom drawer of his dresser and paused, sitting on the edge of the bed. I opened the nightstand on my side of the bed and opened the ring box.

I took the ring out of its velvet box and slipped it on my finger. It fit perfectly. And it was lovely: a single, square solitaire set flush in a band. Nick knew that I never would've wanted anything flashy, anything that would have snagged on my clothing or gotten in the way at work. The ring felt right.

I took it off, put it back in the box, and closed the drawer.

Perhaps . . . someday we could trust each other that much, to put our whole lives in each other's keeping. Maybe I could stop lying to him.

I went to the bathroom to put my toothbrush and some hair ties away. I opened the medicine cabinet.

My eyes narrowed. The medicine cabinet was full of amphetamines. Boxes of prescription amphetamines, stacked on top of each other between toothpaste and razors.

I plucked up a box and stared at it. There was no prescription information on it. This one was half-used. The lot number was the same as one of those that had been stolen from the hospital where the first victim worked. I double-checked it on my phone, heart pounding.

I replaced the box and stared at the stack.

Nick worked strange hours, in twelve-hour shifts. He needed to be awake, alert. But I never expected that he would abuse prescription drugs. He, of all people, should know the risks.

But it made sense: his lack of sleep, his unexpected irritability, the circles under his eyes.

My heart hammered. I closed the medicine cabinet.

I searched his house.

I knew how to do it without him having any idea that I'd been there. I searched his closets, furniture, cabinets, and his garage. The only things that I found that were different than when I'd been here six months before were an empty box from a wine-of-the-month club, three new minor-league baseball caps, and a set of new grill tools. He'd also changed brands of laundry soap.

I discovered no more amphetamines or suspicious quantities of cash but found a fireproof lockbox at the bottom of one of his closets that I couldn't open without a key. I lifted it and gently shook it. It felt and sounded like there might be a gun in there, and maybe papers.

I put everything back and paced his floors. My mind drew connections to the hospital pharmacy drug ring where the first victim worked. That was a different hospital, but maybe the drug ring was larger than I thought.

I chewed my lip. I needed to warn him. Confront him. Tell him to stop.

But how could I do that when I was keeping so much from him? He trusted me enough to give me the key to his house. The drugs weren't hidden . . . Had he wanted me to see?

My thoughts churned as I let myself out and locked up.

I resolved to deal with this later.

I had more secrets of my own to uncover.

29

THE NIGHT TRAVELER

I liked being the night traveler.

I encountered few cars, and the moon shone above me as I drove. It was cool enough to open the windows, and I relished the feel of the wind on my face. As miles flashed by, I drove in silence, over land studded by quiet houses with no lights on. This far away from the cities, the Milky Way spilled over me in a glorious river of stars. I hung my elbow out the window and splayed my fingers in the air.

Time slipped through my fingers as the miles flashed past. Each time I glanced at the clock, time moved startlingly forward. I think I should've been concerned: driving in this disconnected state was probably dangerous. But there was no one else on the road, I rationalized to myself. And I had to get to my mother.

I wondered how my mother chose where to settle, if she'd made that decision, or if witness protection had made it for her. I thought she would've gone to Florida, where her parents lived. There was sunshine enough there to erase my father and ocean enough to wash him away.

But she'd stayed in the Midwest. Here, in land that was so similar to what I'd known as a child. Maybe she hadn't been able to let go of that, not as easily as she had let go of me.

I felt a stab of anger. She'd left me. She'd left me alone, to the world, wiped clean, and expected me to fend for myself. Maybe I looked too much like my father and she couldn't stand that. Maybe she just wanted to run. It was asking a lot to expect her to live under the shadow of a serial killer.

But I wanted more from her. I wanted an explanation. I wondered if I would ever get it—and, if I did, if it would satisfy me.

I bit my lip until it bled. I wasn't sure what would mollify me. Maybe nothing. Maybe there was nothing she could say or do that would make her brainwashing and abandonment of me all right.

But I still wanted her to try.

I stopped at a rest stop to pee and get some caffeine from the vending machine. While I was in the ladies' room, I heard the outside door open and footsteps in the lobby.

Instantly alert, the way that every woman traveling alone is alert, I washed my hands and waited. I was wearing my service gun under my jacket, and my fingers reached inside the jacket as I opened the door.

There was a man there, waiting. The instant the door opened, he rushed me into the ladies' room. I stumbled back and slammed into the wall. The hand dryer went off, roaring in the small space. He was in my face.

"It's just you and me . . ." His hand reached for my breast.

I smashed his nose with my forehead, and he flinched back.

That gave me enough space to kick him in the knee, feel it collapse under my heel. He howled, sinking to the floor.

I blew my hair out of my face, retreated a couple of steps, and drew my gun on him. Fury rushed through me, fury for all those women in Bayern County dyeing their hair and hiding at night, for all the things they had to do to try to avoid exotic and garden variety criminals like this piece of shit who couldn't even let me take a piss in peace.

He stared up at me, befuddled. His pants were still tented up in a confused erection. It angered me to see it as much as my college roommate's attacker, who I never saw again but whose very presence on earth angered me.

He rolled and swung at me. I kicked him in the head and stomped on his groin with all the force I could muster. His scream echoed in this tiny space. I stomped on him again. I wanted to utterly destroy him.

He rolled over on his side, removing my access to his groin. I kicked him in the temple, stomped his jaw as he curled into the fetal position. As he did so, his pocket spilled open, and acorns rolled across the floor.

I froze, staring at the acorns. This was just a random jackass, the kind women run into every day. Right? There was no connection to the Forest God. This was just coincidence.

I scooped up an acorn in my hand and thrust it in his face. "What the hell is this?"

He just whimpered a stream of invectives, calling me a raging bitch who needed to be taught a lesson.

I wanted to kill him. That need flashed through me like lightning. I could wipe this piece of trash from the earth, prevent him from ever offending again. I didn't want to shoot him. I wanted to kill him with my feet, with my hands. He was a total waste of precious oxygen. I wanted to watch the light drain from his eyes and feel it seep away into the earth. No one would ever know, out here in the middle of nowhere.

I hesitated, stumbling backward and breathing heavily. I couldn't do it. I'd be found and my life would end. My prints were all over this place, and there was no way I could escape.

I banged through the ladies' room door. I walked through the front door of the rest stop, flipping the sign around to CLOSED.

I sat in the car, hands on the steering wheel, considering what to do. I could call the highway patrol and tell my story. They'd likely believe me because I was a cop, but they would think I over-reacted by using too much force.

I waited in the dark with my window rolled down, listening to the crickets. I wondered if maybe I had killed him.

After about twenty minutes, the man came limping out of the rest stop building. He was hunched over, his face already purpling under a bruise.

He walked toward a blue SUV, his eyes darting right to left.

I sucked in my breath and wolf whistled at him.

He dropped his keys, then scrambled on the ground to retrieve them. I watched him get into his car and drive away.

I wanted to think that I'd taught him a lesson, that he wouldn't offend again.

I wasn't sure.

I pulled out of the rest stop to follow him.

He stepped on the gas. I kept a few car lengths behind but matched his speed. I sped up, moving close to his bumper, and turned my lights off.

He freaked the fuck out, swerved onto the nearest exit, and zipped away.

I felt the delicious ache of satisfaction, driving that dark car in the dark. I was flying down the road, anonymous and powerful.

I wondered if my father felt this way.

I turned my lights on and slowed down.

I drove in contemplative silence for another hour. The guy deserved to be dead; I had no doubt of that. But I hadn't been prepared. If I had prepared, and wasn't leaving prints all over the scene, I wondered if I would have killed him . . .

I thought so.

I felt no guilt about that. The difference between me and my father was that I wanted to kill people who deserved it.

I remembered the acorns on the ladies' room floor. What was that? A coincidence? A warning? An offering? Lots of people gathered acorns this time of year. Maybe it meant nothing.

My phone dinged an alert. Cas Russo had dropped a new podcast. I plugged my phone into the car and listened to Cas's voice as I drove. He hadn't graced me with video or I would've pulled over to glower at him.

"Hello, darklings. This is Cas, your fugitive friend. I apologize in advance for the shitty quality of this missive, but I'm on the run, and recording facilities beyond fast-food restaurant bathrooms are few and far between. Not that I'm complaining about those: the echo is quite nice. Sort of like singing in the shower.

"Lots of people have messaged me to ask me where I am and how I'm involved in this investigation. Firstly . . . I'm on the run, so I'm not going to tell you that. Obviously. Some of you have been lovely help, and I wish I could give you appropriate shout-outs. Maybe sometime later down the line."

I frowned. Monica was combing through the list of Cas's followers to figure out who he might have roped into helping him next and who might possibly have been the tipster he talked about.

I hoped she had access to his messages by now. I wanted to see the net close over him so that we could focus on other leads. But tech companies could be ridiculously slow in responding to requests from law enforcement, so I wasn't holding my breath.

"People are asking me: Cas, are you the Forest Strangler? And to answer that, I have to tell you all about my connection to the Forest Strangler from the time I was young."

I gripped the steering wheel. Was that asshole going to confess?

"The Forest Strangler was executed when I was a teenager. I remember being fascinated by the visual masterpieces he created in his crime scenes. Truly, he was an artist trying to express himself in the world, and his work was gorgeous."

"So was Hitler's," I murmured.

"His medium was death, but he respected that death. So much reverence went into his crimes. You can see how much he loved those girls, every one of them. He spent hours, maybe days, with them, posing them and creating this fairy world that was his alone.

"I began experimenting with morbid photography. I convinced some of my friends to pretend they were dead and photographed them for art classes and my own private collection. I loved this kind of artistic expression, but I was frustrated because I couldn't quite re-create the stillness of death. No matter how much makeup I applied, no matter how much I changed the lighting, they still looked alive. Maybe it was just because I knew, and that knowing totally fucked with my perspective."

Monica texted me: Hey. You listening to this?

I texted her back: Yup

He's going to confess. Hot damn.

Cas droned on. "So my interest in the dead went other ways. I started ghost hunting and ran into some pretty strange situations.

I've combed through reports of serial killers and ordinary murderers, trying to capture that magic of when people were alive . . .
and then not."

I sucked in my breath. That golden moment. Holy shit. Cas
knew about that.

"But I'm just a voyeur, you know? I like to watch. I like to muse
about them in smoky rooms with a glass of bourbon. And that's
what got me into trouble with the Forest Strangler case. I got that
tip and didn't send it to the police. Instead, I went myself, to see if
it was as beautiful as the others, to maybe get some of my own
pictures.

"I wasn't disappointed. It was something to see, that meticulously arranged scene, a story unfolding there.

"But I didn't create that scene. If I had, I certainly wouldn't
have come back in broad daylight and gotten caught. I'm guilty of
poor taste, morbid curiosity, shitty timing, bizarre appetites, and
a total lack of manners.

"But I'm not the Forest Strangler."

The recording ended.

He's teasing us, Monica texted.

Maybe, I answered.

I put the phone down and stared into the night.

Cas talked a good line. But did he have what it took to be a
killer?

I wasn't sure.

———

I reached the town of Carlisle, where my mother lived, by dawn.

It was a sleepy little river town. Barges drifted down the brown
river, and bridges crisscrossed over it like the dirty laces of boots.
I tooled down the streets, finding an assortment of fast-food joints,

a grocery store, gas stations, and a fruit stand. Seemed like a quiet enough place.

I pulled through one of the drive-throughs for coffee, then consulted the GPS for my mother's address. Maybe I was stalling, but I told myself that I didn't want to go rolling up on my biological mother while she was still asleep. Even though my mother had always been an early riser, I promised myself that I'd wait for a decent hour. Nine o'clock.

I closed my eyes, then opened them. The clock moved forward an hour in only a breath.

My phone rang. It was Monica.

"Hey, don't you sleep?" I asked.

"Not much," she admitted. "IT cracked Cas's hard drive."

"Oooh. Tell me." I stared at the dregs of my coffee.

"As he alluded to in his podcast, there are shit tons of pictures of dead-looking girls. We can't tell yet if they're really dead or who they are."

"You think he was trying to get ahead of that by making excuses on the podcast?"

"Probably. But that's not the most interesting thing."

"Yeah?"

"Cas has some crazy detailed files on the Forest Strangler. Like . . . they rival what the FBI told us."

"Mmm?"

"He knows a lot of shit about a case that's not public knowledge. He knows Theron's body vanished, for example. He's been trying to track down people from the case . . . He has addresses for the principal investigators, with timelines and shit."

The hair lifted on my arms. "He was tracking down, like, Parkes?"

"Yeah. He has Parkes's home address. He has addresses for

Theron's widow, even. And he's been looking for the daughter. He's got evidence she wound up in a mental institution. Trail seems to go cold from there, but it's really disturbing."

I paused, reminded myself not to panic. "So, does he know anything we don't?"

"Not so far, but I'll keep digging."

"Any information on his supposed tipster?"

"Nothing concrete yet. They found a few encrypted emails with spoofed IP addresses. IT's working on it."

"Okay. Keep me posted."

"Same."

I hung up and stared at the blisteringly bright morning.

Maybe Cas was the one who had figured out who I was, who was sending me those messages and leaving me little gifts.

And I was not confident at all about his ability to keep his mouth shut if he had.

My watch beeped. It was nine a.m.

Time to meet my mother.

30

FAMILY PORTRAIT

I drove down a street in a working-class neighborhood. Small ranch houses sat on lots fenced with chain link. Mature trees shaded backyards with metal swing sets, tomato patches, and the buzz of lawn mowers.

Parking on the street a few doors down, I looked at my mother's house. No cars sat in the driveway. A crab apple tree grew in the front yard, with a large maple in the back. Neatly trimmed azalea bushes obscured part of the front of the brick house.

Anxiety bubbled in my chest. I hadn't decided what to say to her, not yet. Part of me wanted to arrive on her doorstep as Elena. But I was Anna now, and I should stay as Anna. I had a job to do. I finished my coffee and popped a mint.

And . . . if I appeared as Elena, I wasn't sure I could go back to being Anna. I took off my father's necklace and put it in my pocket.

I screwed up my courage and stepped out of the car. I put on my sunglasses, squared my shoulders, and walked across the cracked pavement to the front door.

I rang the bell and crunched the mint with my back teeth as I waited. Maybe she wasn't there. Maybe I had the wrong address.

The door opened, and a woman peered at me through the locked screen door. She was shorter than I remembered, dressed in a T-shirt and leggings. Her hair had gone white, and she looked at me through plastic-framed glasses. There was no glint of recognition in her eyes, no expression of startlement, distaste, or fear.

I wanted her to enfold me in her embrace and ask for forgiveness. I wanted to feel love.

Instead, I felt a cool breeze move between us, ruffling my hair.

"Mrs. Conley?" I asked.

"Yes?"

"My name's Anna Koray. I'm with the Bayern County Sheriff's Office. I'd like to speak with you about an old case you were acquainted with." I lifted my badge.

She froze. Her gaze scanned my badge, and I could tell she was memorizing the number.

For a moment, I thought that she would slam the door in my face. But she unlatched the screen door.

"Come in," she sighed.

I stepped into the living room. It was painted beige, with two overstuffed couches facing each other and a television at one end. Framed photographs dotted the wall.

"Would you like coffee?" she asked. "I just put the pot on."

"Yes, please."

She disappeared into the kitchen. I took off my sunglasses and scanned the photos. They were of my mother's family. Her new family. A man with a full head of dark hair and a moustache stood with my mother in a wedding dress with poofy sleeves. Other photos showed two children at Christmastime, a boy and a girl. Both looked like my mother. The children grew up, and I saw high school and graduation pictures. The girl had long brown hair, down to her waist, and soft dark eyes. In all the pictures, my mother looked . . . warm. Her smiles touched her eyes.

A lump rose in my throat. She had what looked like a picture-perfect life. I wondered if she had ever told anyone about me, or if I was entirely erased.

"Do you take cream or sugar?" she called from the kitchen.

"Black's fine, thank you," I answered.

She returned with a cup and gestured for me to sit. I sat on a couch opposite her. She was crowned by that wall of photos. She sat stiffly on the couch, and her bare toes curled in the carpet.

"I'm sorry to bother you, Mrs. Conley. But I hoped you could shed some light on a current investigation."

She lifted the cup to her lips and lifted a brow.

"Were you formerly known as Sheila Theron?"

Her nostrils flared. "No one knows that."

My gaze flicked to the photographs. "Not your family?"

"None of them." She lowered the cup. "I would like to keep it that way."

"Understood. I'll keep this in strictest confidence." I opened my notebook. "I assume you've seen the news, that someone is copying the Forest Strangler."

She flicked her gaze to the television. "I don't watch that sort of trash."

I nodded. "Well, to fill you in, there have been two deaths, in a manner very similar to the Strangler's MO. The killer seems to have intimate knowledge of the Strangler, so we're tracking down folks who were close to him, who might remember someone around the fringes of the investigation who struck them as odd."

She cupped the mug in her hands and tapped it. "Everything was odd about that. Everything. Now it's like a dream."

"Take me back to that time. What do you remember about him?"

She frowned into her cup, as if she were scrying for answers. "I fell in love with Stephen because he was quiet, even-tempered. He was everything my ex wasn't. He had a job. If anything, I thought he was a bit boring, you know? What we had wasn't a great love story or anything. We were more like roommates, especially at the end."

"After he was arrested, did you speak with him about the crimes?"

She paused, seeming to think. I was using this as a litmus test to see how honest she'd be with me. I knew she'd gone to the prison. Would she tell me that?

"I went to prison to see him, after he was sentenced," she said at last. "I was furious with him for destroying my life. I wanted answers."

"What did he tell you?"

She looked up at the ceiling. "He said I wouldn't understand. And I told him that, damn right, I didn't. I didn't understand how he could just do what he did and then come home and act like he'd just been out for a walk in the woods. How he could pretend to be a human being when he was so monstrous inside. I yelled at him until I was hoarse, while he just sat there. Eventually, my time was up."

I was disappointed at this, but not surprised that my father hadn't confessed. "Did you speak with him again after that?"

"Once."

I paused. She hadn't appeared on the visitor logs again. My brow creased. "While he was in prison?"

"No. It was afterward." Her gaze was distant as she conjured the memory. "It was when Lenny—my husband—was working the night shift. I got a phone call in the middle of the night. It sounded like him, whispering from very, very far away. I didn't know how he'd managed to find me, after all that time."

"When was this?"

"April of 2001."

"So . . . after he was executed?" My brow wrinkled. My father had been executed in January.

"Yes."

"What did he say?"

She closed her eyes. "He told me that I wasn't good enough to be sacrificed. That I was weak. He said he expected more from me. He said it with such wrath . . . He was furious. Before I could say anything, he hung up."

"Did you report this?"

"I called Witness Protection. They tried to trace the number but couldn't find any record of calls made to this address. They told me I'd dreamed it and to call back if it happened again. It never did."

I tapped my pen on the paper. Was it possible my father had survived? He'd been declared dead. Likely, this was a dream or random caller that had nothing to do with the case. Still. It added to the pile of creepiness. I changed tactics.

"Your husband was actively operating from 1983 to 1995. Do you remember if he had any close confidants then? Friends he might've traveled or gone hunting with?"

She shook her head. "He was always a loner. He didn't go on trips with friends like other men did. He'd disappear in the woods for days. He worked shift work and would have a week off every month. Sometimes he'd take our daughter with him. But most of the time he was alone."

I tried to sound like a cop, asking the next logical question. "Do you think your daughter saw anything?"

She barked out a short, unpleasant laugh. "She certainly saw too much at the end, when she found him in his hideout with those other filthy girls."

"The FBI mentioned that," I said mildly. But a flicker of anger lit in my chest that she was throwing me under the bus. And that she was jealous of those poor women who my father lavished attention on.

She pressed her lips together before speaking. "I don't know. Part of me wondered. He gave her one of his trophies, though. A necklace. She adored it, rarely took it off."

"That seems . . . odd."

"They were close. Closer than a father and daughter should've been. She knew about his secret hiding places, where she led the FBI. It wouldn't have surprised me if she'd seen bodies like that before. They were alike, you know." She said it coldly, taking another sip. This was the mother I knew, angry at being on the outside looking in.

"Do you have current contact information for Elena?"

She shook her head. "Elena was adopted. I didn't keep the records."

I tried to bite back the sharpness from my voice but failed. "She was your child."

She shook her head. "She wasn't my child. She was Stephen's child. And if she was involved, I did her a favor in giving her a new life."

I swallowed the accusations I wanted to make as if they were glass shards. "Your husband and children don't know about her?"

"No. That was another lifetime ago. Lenny knows I was married before, but that's all." She said it with such finality. I couldn't reveal myself and ask for anything from her. She was cold, distant . . . and she thought I was a monster like my father.

"I can understand that." I tried to sound sympathetic, but I thought I failed.

My mother shrugged. "Honestly, I'm surprised that you came. I already told everything to that FBI agent who was here yesterday."

I froze, and blood roared in my ears. "Agent Parkes?"

"Yes."

"Ah. He's also working with us on this investigation." I made it sound casual. My mother didn't know where I was; there was nothing she could have told Parkes.

"He asked about Elena, too. But nothing about my ex-husband."

The front door banged open. The younger woman from the family photos zipped in. She was wearing a baker's uniform.

"Hey, Mom." She crossed to the couch and kissed my mother on the cheek. She glanced at me. "Hello."

I nodded at her and opened my mouth to say hi, but her mother interrupted my attempt at an introduction. "What are you doing home so early, Raina?"

"Today's Roxanne's bridal shower, remember? I've got to get everything ready."

My mother's face shone with a love I'd never known, like the sun had come out and lit on that woman. "You can use the folding chairs from the garage."

I stood up awkwardly and closed my notebook. "Thank you for your time, Mrs. Conley."

"Of course."

"I'll see myself out."

I fled to the front step and took a deep gulp of air. I leaned against the faux brick façade next to the azaleas, trying to steady myself.

My gaze fell on the mailbox beside me. Outgoing mail was clipped to it to be taken by the mail carrier.

I snatched a greeting card from the stack and walked away with it under my jacket.

When I got to the car, I cranked the engine. I couldn't wait to be out of there. I waited until I was blocks away before pulling over and pressing my forehead to the steering wheel.

I knew what I wanted to happen. I wanted her to apologize for what she'd done, to welcome me back in her life. I wanted to have that connection from my past, despite the horror my father had visited upon us.

But she'd erased and replaced me instead. She implied I was privy to my father's murders. What had she told the FBI about me when I was an unsuspecting child? Was she the reason I'd been kept in that mental institution?

Who was the real monster here?

Had Parkes seen it, too, when he looked into her eyes? Had he seen it then, or did he see it now?

I picked up the lavender greeting card. I didn't have a warrant for what I was about to do, and screwing with the mail was a federal offense.

I donned a pair of gloves and ripped off a corner of the back envelope that included a good part of the adhesive strip. I tore off the strip and put it in a clear evidence envelope.

I opened the card and read it. It was from my mother to her mother-in-law, wishing her a happy birthday and a nice time at the beach. *Love, Rebecca.*

I never remembered her telling me that she loved me. Hell, she didn't even say goodbye when she abandoned me to the mental facility. She threw me out like trash. She couldn't fucking wait to start her new life with her new family.

I flung the card to the floorboards and labeled the clear evidence envelope for DNA testing. I couldn't use this for the investigation: it was poison fruit from a poisoned tree.

I sure as hell suspected my father wasn't the only goddamn monster here. Intellectually, I knew the likelihood that my mother had the Lyssa variant were vanishingly small.

But I wanted to know. I wanted to prove to myself that it wasn't me, that my mother was irrevocably broken, and always had been, when she brainwashed and abandoned a thirteen-year-old girl.

31

CORNERED

It started raining when I pulled over at a truck stop to get gas and a sandwich. Fresh signs announcing the presence of surveillance cameras had been placed on the front doors of the store, behind the checkout, and between the gas pumps. I put my food and gas on the "Get out of Jail Free" card and was halfway back to the car when I got a notification from my personal email account.

I slid behind the wheel and opened it. The asshole who knew my identity had responded.

I've seen everything.

I've seen you.

Leave this investigation alone.

If you don't, I will tell what I know.

I'll tell them you're the Strangler's daughter.

And then nobody can save you.

I typed back with my thumbs:

Why would anyone but the Strangler want to derail this
investigation? And why would anyone believe you?

I hit SEND.

I watched the rain pelt the windshield.

I had no intention of stopping this investigation. But if I didn't,
and this guy revealed my identity, the whole case was toast.

I ran my hands through my hair. Shit. It was one thing that
this guy knew who I was, and another thing that he knew I was
working the investigation. How would he know that? I wracked
my brain. I'd been at the crime scenes . . . Press would have
seen me there. I'd stayed away from cameras when the chief
made public briefings, since I didn't want Nick to see me on
the evening news and know I was lying to him. I didn't think it
was anyone involved with the old Forest Strangler investigation . . .
I hadn't been in touch with them until after I'd received the
threats. Cas might've guessed. He'd seen me at the first scene.
Shit.

I considered what to do while I drove back home. Maybe there
was a way that I could keep my involvement in the investigation on the down-low, avoid those moments when cameras would
be around. But I didn't know how to do that without spilling my
guts.

I had to get to this guy first.

———

I made it home by midafternoon. I felt grungy and grabbed a shower. I dragged my laptop to bed.

The attorney had sent me my adoption records attached to an email. I paged through those. My mother had given up custody of me to the state, and my adoptive parents had adopted me from there. All adoptions in our state were closed adoptions. Interestingly, my mother had signed the paperwork as Rebecca Smith, and I was named as Anna Smith. That must have been the name she used before she married her current husband. There was no mention of me spending time in a mental institution. Just a few straightforward pages.

I drummed my fingers. These should have been sealed by the court. Had my stalker found this somehow? And how had he known about my mother's name change? Had my father known, and was that how he'd managed to call her . . . if that wasn't a dream?

There were too many what-ifs at this point.

I scanned my work email. There was an automated response from the GPS tracking company, promising to get to my request within forty-eight hours. I ground my teeth and tried to message them through the chat function on their website, but it was down. Figured.

A zip file from my contact at the highway patrol also arrived. The message accompanying it said above the confidentiality notice only:

You owe me a cheeseburger, Koray.

I grinned and unzipped the file. I skimmed over it, intending to read it in full depth later. I saw pictures of the ambulette that had stolen my father's body abandoned at a parking lot in the nearest city and copies of the forensic records. Fingerprints had been found all over the ambulette, which wasn't surprising, since the doors were found open and it looked like it had been robbed after it was abandoned. The state highway patrol had quietly followed up on all the prints, finding a couple of small-time crooks who had liberated the fixtures for scrap metal. Several sets of unknowns were found, but those hadn't been run since 2001.

I sent copies of the unknowns to our forensics team to see if AFIS would yield some hits. The fingerprint database had grown exponentially since that time, and maybe a hit could be found now.

I couldn't, for the life of me, figure out who would want my father's body. Unless my father had concocted some elaborate plan to spring himself from prison. I scanned the call log and the visitor list again. I wasn't convinced he could play dead, not unless someone snuck some drugs to him. And who would want to help him?

I skimmed through the report. His body was supposed to have gone to a local university for dissection. No kidding people wanted to know how his brain worked. That was the million-dollar question.

I shut off the laptop and lay down in bed.

Maybe Veles wanted him back.

Maybe I was looking in all the wrong places.

I tossed and turned in the dark. Storms washed in and out, rain rattling through the gutters. When the storm front subsided, I slept. I had shallow, fitful dreams of my father in the execution chamber when rains swept down, flooding the chamber and chasing everyone away until it was just him and me in the room.

"How did this happen to you, Dad?" I asked him, standing up to my hips in cold water.

He looked up at me from the table. Water rose over the top of the table, giving the illusion that he floated on it. The light fixture over our heads flickered luridly.

"It was a long time ago, and a faraway place. I was alone in the woods, and I wanted to live. I struck a bargain."

He closed his eyes, and the water closed over his head.

I awoke to my phone ringing. I crawled across the bed to pick up my phone on the nightstand. Dimly, I registered the gray light before dawn seeping under the curtains.

"Koray," I mumbled.

"It's Monica. We're getting ready to move on Cas Russo."

I sat up straight. "You found him?"

"Yup. He's currently chilling at a fan's house just over the state line. We got a warrant for his arrest and coordinated with the local sheriff's office in Park County. You wanna go along for the ride?"

"Yeah," I responded without thinking. "I'll be ready in ten."

I hung up before realizing what that probably meant for whoever was stalking me. If it was Cas stalking me, he was likely to spill his guts as soon as the cuffs were on his wrists.

I took a deep breath. I'd made the decision. I just had to see it through.

———

Monica came by to pick me up in an unmarked car. I was waiting for her on the porch, holding a coffee. I'd stuffed my hair under a baseball cap and had my sunglasses dangling off the neckline of my sheriff's office windbreaker. Maybe I'd be less recognizable if anyone was watching.

My porch was covered in chestnuts.

I stared down at them, hundreds of them, as I sipped my coffee. The rational part of my mind insisted they'd been blown there by the storm last night. The irrational part of my mind saw nothing but the eyes of the corpse of the first victim, staring back at me a thousandfold.

Monica rolled up and popped the door for me to climb in. She glanced at my porch. "What's with that?"

"I don't know," I said truthfully.

She grabbed my sleeve. "Hey. Are you okay?"

I stared at her. I wanted to tell her everything, how I was losing what was left of my mind. Who I was. What I was afraid was following me. But all I could do was nod. "Yeah."

She frowned at me. I didn't think she was buying it.

I shoveled two boxes of cheese puffs off the passenger seat. "What the hell is this?"

"Breakfast of champions," she muttered as she slapped a magnetic gumball light on the top of the car. "You remember. When we had that staff meeting earlier this week about the new payroll codes. Brit was selling these for her kid's T-ball team."

"Staff meeting?" I didn't remember.

"I mean, it was a snoozer, but there was food. Chief brought donuts."

I looked out the window and rubbed my temple. I didn't remember that. Not a bit. Fuck me. I felt nauseous.

Monica tooled up the driveway and lit the gumball light up. She left the siren off, but we zinged down the two-lane road fast enough for my stomach to lurch. I reminded myself that we'd be on a proper highway soon.

"How'd you find him?" I asked.

Monica grinned. "IT broke the encryption for his passwords

on his computer. Dude had two-factor authentication turned on to change any of them, but he doesn't dare turn on his cell because he knows we're just waiting for that cell to ping a tower. Wanna guess what his favorite password was?"

"Something crass about the female anatomy?"

"Nope, surprisingly. It was Charles Manson's birth date. They got into his messages. Found out he's been corresponding with some ghost hunter over the state line, and he invited Cas down to hide from the cops."

"He's just racking up charges with fleeing and eluding," I muttered. "Never mind interfering with an investigation."

"Oh, he's getting mileage out of this. He's centered himself in a serial killer–adjacent investigation, and he's gonna coast on this notoriety for years. If he's not involved, he'll spend misdemeanor time and fines and go write a book."

"And if he is involved?"

"When we get his DNA back, we'll know." Monica jabbed a thumb at a file folder crammed between her seat and the console. "Gotta say that I'm not amused by the pictures from his hard drive of the apparently dead women."

"Any word on who they are?"

"We're doing some facial recognition, but no hits yet. There seem to be at least six different girls. If he'd used the same model and posed her in different scenes, I'd chalk this up to just a fetish. But I'm not sure."

"Can I see?"

"Sure. I got some stills in the file."

I reached for the envelope and leafed through the printed-out images. Superficially, they looked similar to the Strangler's work. A girl with blond hair lay in a cornfield, hair tangled in cornsilk, holding sheaves of corn in her arms. Another was lying in a drainage ditch, half covered in duckweed with mud painted on her hands and feet like gloves and boots.

"He's put these girls close to areas of human habitation," I said. "Places where someone would happen upon them at some point . . . Farmers walk their fields, and that drainage ditch can't be far from a road. Any previous cases turn up that match these girls?"

"No. Which makes me think they could be staged."

I squinted at one of the pictures. One girl didn't have creases across her neck. It was far from a foolproof method, but underage girls generally didn't have those. "I think this one's a minor."

"We can add another charge, then. He keeps rackin' 'em up."

I thumbed through the file. "Any word yet on the DNA profile of the security guard at the hospital or the first victim's boy-friend?"

"Mariner's not a match. Neither is the boyfriend. No markers on either. But victim's father is a piece of work." Monica made a face.

"Yeah?"

"Yeah. Refused to cooperate in any way. Struck me as very possessive. Didn't like the boyfriend, didn't like his little girl moving on with her life. If this were a single murder, he'd be at the top of my list, but with a second victim . . . ehhhh. I don't want to rule him out, but he has an alibi for the approximate time of death for the murder of the second girl."

"A good one? Like, not just his wife insisting he was home watching television?"

"He was at a sports bar from six until two a.m., at which point he got tossed out by the bouncer."

I sighed. "Did the state lab come up with anything from the second crime scene?" I found one of the photos from that scene and stared at it.

"They found semen from an unidentified male in her body. That semen doesn't have a marker, so it's likely to be from a client or boyfriend. They're running it through DNA databases for potential matches."

I looked at the stones surrounding her. "Any good prints?"

"Not yet. Each one of those rocks looked like they were scrubbed with steel wool. Looks like he wore gloves again."

"Even the strangulation injury? No DNA there?" Our only connection to the killer was that degraded DNA from the first scene. Whose was it? Could Cas have the Lyssa variant?

But more than that, I wanted to know that another set of DNA or prints hadn't turned up. I had been missing too much time, and I didn't entirely trust myself not to be creeping around crime scenes, as I had done after Tom Sullivan's death.

"Yep. No contact DNA."

I exhaled, staring at the photo of the young woman surrounded by a halo of milky quartz stones. I hadn't been there, thank God. I focused on the stones, shining like stars in the half-light. I compared it to Cas's work.

There was a difference. There was something . . . sexual about Cas's work, about how suggestively the corn ears were gripped, the slight parting of the womens' lips. Something about how the breasts were thrust forward, the backs arched, and the legs parted. The angle of the photography seemed lascivious.

My father's work wasn't about sex or about art. For Cas, I think it was, very much. I wasn't seeing that element in the recent confirmed killings. Those were like my father's work: reverent, in their way.

I could be wrong. Feelings and intuition were often wrong.

But I felt like this killer was tangled up with the entity my father knew in the forest, and that Cas wasn't. No matter how much he wanted to be on the inside, he wasn't. He was always going to be a bystander, a groupie, an onlooker . . .

. . . right?

"Has FBI gotten anywhere?" I asked casually.

Monica rolled her eyes. "Russell keeps poking me for updates. He's really freaked out about following procedure to the letter."

"Well, given the way the original investigation went, I'm not surprised."

"We seem to be giving them more info than they're giving us. All I know is that Parkes is shaking Theron's family tree for the Lyssa variant."

"I thought he didn't have any family left."

"Theron's parents are dead. But he had a brother who died wrapping his car around a tree. That guy was in his early twenties when he died. It's possible that both he and or Stephen managed to father some children who might possess this mutation."

"That's a totally reasonable assumption," I said.

"We know he had a daughter, though. Parkes hasn't found any information on her through the commercial DNA databases."

I swallowed. To my knowledge, I hadn't given any DNA as an adult to any agency. The sheriff's office hadn't required it as a condition of employment. The most I'd done was pee in a jar for random drug tests. It was possible, however, that someone had taken blood from me while I was in the hospital as a child. That was before DNA databases, but I didn't know how closely guarded those records were. I was regretting asking Dr. Richardson to test my DNA for the variant now. I knew those results were supposed to be kept confidential and not submitted to commercial or law enforcement databases, but . . .

"FBI doesn't like women for these kinds of murders," I observed.

307

"Maybe. But we can't rule anyone out." Her jaw was set in a grim line. "I've got a feeling this has something to do with Stephen Theron himself. I'm hopeful that some relative turns up who submitted DNA as part of a prior crime investigation."

"Yeah?"

"Parkes says he's real close to finding the daughter. Maybe she'll be able to unearth some family skeletons."

"Like, does he have a name or something?" My tongue stuck to the roof of my mouth.

"He wouldn't say. Just that he's close."

I stared out the window. What would I do if they figured out who I was? I was screwed if Cas didn't confess when we took him down.

I filled Monica in about my journeys to the prison and the Forest Strangler's former wife.

"You think there's a possibility he's still alive?"

I opened my hands in an exaggerated shrug. "Maaaaybe? I think the possibility is very, very small. My theory is that his body was stolen by some groupies, like Cas. Maybe his brain would've gained a tidy sum on the black market. I imagine there are people much richer than Cas who would get off on having a serial killer brain in a jar."

She wrinkled her nose. "Gross."

"And like we were talking about before, there's always the possibility that he didn't work alone. Maybe he had help and that help decided to liberate his body. Maybe that guy got distracted by prison or something for a few years, or he had some kind of life-changing event. And now he's back, doing the same thing."

Monica looked sidelong at me. "You find any evidence for that?"

"Not a shred. Just spitballin'."

We rode in silence for a while, before Monica spoke again. "The FBI didn't identify any accomplices in the original cases. But I'm not too impressed with their handling of that, with the way they traumatized that girl."

I shook my head. "I feel like Parkes means well, but there were a whole lot of irregularities in that case, start to finish."

"You think that maybe the wife could've been in on it?"

I stared out the window, at billboards on lush farmland advertising the need for drivers to repent for their sins or face certain damnation. "Mmm . . . nooo?"

"I mean, how many times do we catch guys who are killers and the wives know, but we can't prove it? Wasn't there some serial killer case where the guy kept body parts in a locked freezer and told his wife not to open it? Who doesn't suspect that?"

"I don't remember that one."

"Don't you think that some of these women wake up in the middle of the night and realize they're sleeping with monsters?"

I chewed my lip. "Well, we see it enough in child abuse cases."

"Yeah. Just . . . don't be too quick to rule her out. She might know a lot more than she's saying."

My mother was older, sure. But she certainly didn't seem frail, though I didn't think her capable of overpowering a younger woman. Maybe she'd drugged them? I chewed on it but decided to put that aside until I got that DNA test back. If she had the Lyssa variant, too . . . well. That would tell me something. I couldn't tell anyone else, but I could avoid looking at her more. I'd already looked at her too closely, and it hurt.

I checked my personal email to find a message from my stalker. Monica's eyes were on the road as she annihilated the cheesy puffs.

I opened the email. In response to my questions:

Why would anyone but the Strangler want to derail this
investigation? And why would anyone believe you?

My pen pal replied:

I know everything about you. I know who you are, what
you're afraid of, and what you see in the woods at night.

There were three attachments. The first was a scanned copy of
a sealed name change certificate, filed in a court, with my old
name, Elena Theron, changed to Anna Smith. The second was a
copy of my adoption certificate, establishing that I'd been adopted
by the Korays.

And the last attachment was a photograph of me in a forest,
captured in mid-step. The same night-view green as before tinted
the shot. I squinted at it. I was wearing a black track jacket and yoga
pants. If I zoomed in, I could see speckles of stitches and bruising
on my face.

I froze, eyes scanning the scene. That had to be . . . right after
I got out of the hospital. I stared at the forest. It felt so familiar,
but I couldn't tell which forest it was. Was it the forest behind my
house? Maybe. There was a green blur that might be a cedar tree.

Could it be the forest surrounding the house where I'd killed
Tom Sullivan? I scanned for maple trees, remembering how the
seed pods had been scattered when I was there.

Or was it another forest entirely, a place that I didn't remember?
Fuck. Fuck. Fuck.

I glanced at Monica, who was slowing down to take an exit.
"It's right around here," she muttered around cheese dust.

I closed my email. Shit.

I didn't like Cas for the Strangler, but I was liking him for my stalker. He'd been digging too much into that case, and it was possible he'd found me. That business about knowing what I saw in the woods . . . that could be a bluff. Nobody could get that far into my head, right? I knew damn good and well I shouldn't have come here, but I wanted to look him in the face.

And after that . . . I didn't know. I couldn't see past that wall of rage, the fury at the bomb he'd flung into my life.

We rolled through a town with two stoplights, over roads studded with rural mailboxes. We pulled into a well-lit gas station where two sheriff's cars from Park County idled.

Monica and I got out and introduced ourselves to the two deputies. One, who went by Rudy, was close to retirement age, while the other, Max, looked barely old enough to shave but sported wraparound mirrored sunglasses.

"Did anyone get eyes on him?" I asked.

Rudy nodded. "He was seen sitting on the porch of the house around noon. It's a dead-end road bordering on some woods. We've got an unmarked car at the mouth of the road, just chilling."

Max stuck his head out of the window. "You think he's the guy? The Strangler?"

"Not sure," Monica said. "But he's sure inserted himself into the investigation."

Max grinned. "I hope we get your man, ma'am."

"So do I. Thank you for your help."

Rudy tipped his hat. We climbed into our cars and followed Rudy out to Old Starr Run Road.

Rudy waved at the deputy parked at the mouth of the road. She nodded, then moved her car to block the road entirely after we entered.

If Cas fled on foot, I felt sure we could catch him.

My heart beat slowly and steadily as we approached the house.

It was one of three houses on this road, a two-story farmhouse. Its white paint was peeling, and the windows were obscured with mismatched materials: a pirate flag, beach towels, and a shower curtain.

We parked on the road. Rudy and Monica headed to the front porch. Deputy Max and I circled around to the back. A sagging addition to the house had a back door leading to an obstacle course of cinder blocks, yard ornaments, and a hammock. I stepped over a dead chicken covered with flies.

Rudy hammered on the door and announced a warrant for Cas's arrest. I scanned the windows, pressing myself against the exterior wall with the back door in view. I unholstered my service weapon, pointing it to the ground. Max stood before the door, his gun aimed at it. I thought that wasn't advisable, but this wasn't my party . . .

The back door burst open and Cas lurched out. He was sweating, dressed in black, clutching a backpack.

"Freeze!" Max and I shouted at once. More shouting echoed in the house.

But Cas wasn't alone. A big dog lurched out of the house with him, launching himself at Max. The dog clamped his jaws around Max's leg and felled him instantly.

I reached down for the dog's collar. He was strong, and Max yelped. I dragged the dog off Max and redirected him to the chicken. The dog happily tore into the carcass.

My gaze swept to Cas. He was running for the tree line for all he was worth.

"Cas! Stop!"

He didn't, so I chased him into the forest.

He was easy to follow: I could hear his breath whistling past his teeth and his feet crashing into every leaf, pine cone, and twig on the forest floor. He careened like a pinball into the woods, plunging mindlessly as a prey animal and rattling yellow leaves from the trees he smacked into.

I was behind him, noiseless, leaping over logs and dodging tree trunks. I gained on him quickly.

At last, he thought he was safe, and he slowed. He was at the edge of a sandstone cliff, the kind where trees clung to the stone for dear life, reaching up for the sun. I heard water far below them, suspecting a river.

I snuck up behind him and pressed my gun to the back of his head.

"Cas. Give it up."

He shrieked, and as he turned his head, his gaze fell on me.

He started laughing. "Oh, shit. It's you."

"You seem surprised."

"I mean, I know who you are. Finally. I've wondered for years."

My lips peeled back on a sneer. "Who am I?"

I strained to hear him over the blood pounding in my ears. "You're the daughter of the Forest Strangler."

32

THE BLACK ROOM

I ripped the backpack from his hands, hissing: "And you are not my father."

My finger flexed on the trigger. The birds stopped singing. I was aware of a roaring darkness behind me, the shadow of Veles. Cold loomed over us like a thundercloud. I smelled rain coming, mirrored by the lazy river snaking a hundred feet below us. A stone rolled from behind me, past us, over the edge of the cliff, rattling as it went. But someone was behind me.

I knew Cas felt it, too. His eyes dilated. He looked past me and his jaw dropped. The overwhelming scent of leaf mold washed over us.

A shadow fell over my shoulder like a protective cloak, cool as night and just as opaque. The Forest God was with me, and his wrath radiated to Cas, not me.

The blood drained from Cas's face. I relished this moment, the expression of terror.

He flinched, tried to step away. His sneakers slipped on the wet leaves covering the ledge. His hands splayed out, reaching for air.

And he fell.

He looked back at me, shock written all over his face.

I watched him as he fell a hundred feet, down to the sandstone shore of a shallow river. He landed with a soft crush, the sound of a bird's egg falling from a nest to a sterile lawn.

I waited, watching him. His eyes were open and he didn't move. Blood leaked from his ears and behind his head, growing in a red halo. He was an egg cracked open, the life diffusing into the air around him.

I inhaled this, this victory, this death. I had the killer who had pretended to be my father. My secret heritage was safe. It was over.

Behind me, I heard the hiss of laughter, the sound of wind moving through the tree canopy.

I did not turn to face the Forest God. I waited for him to subside of his own accord, melting back into the woods. A flicker of daylight warmed my face; then I knew it was safe to turn around.

I circled back through the forest, taking a detour to hide the backpack in a rotten stump, then covered it with leaves.

I returned to the house, running the last few meters to burst into the yard, breathless.

"Call an ambulance!" I shouted at Rudy, who was wrapping a bandage around Max's profusely bleeding leg.

"On the way," Monica answered. "Where's Cas?"

"I was chasing him, and he fell . . ." I pointed at the forest.

I wondered if that was how it had happened with Rollins, too. If that monster revealed himself and Rollins stumbled in the shadows. Or had the Forest God chased him down? I think he was capable of both, depending upon his whim.

I led the squad back through the woods. They had to go upstream

315

about a half mile before there was a safe place to climb down the muddy cliff to recover Cas's body with a gurney.

I stood from afar, watching them, while Monica smoked. She lit one cigarette after another from the butt of the previous one.

"I hope this shit is over," she said at last.

"I hope so, too," I answered, with sincerity.

Darkness fell swiftly in the woods.

Deputies swarmed the house. Animal Control came for the dog who had bitten Max, who was easily lured into the truck with peanut butter. I felt sad for the dog, but hoped he would get released soon.

I was sequestered in a bedroom, where I answered the Park County deputies' questions while they fed me a steady stream of coffee. This bedroom was painted black, with an impressive collection of occult books on a bookcase, interspersed with black candles and a shiny assortment of crystals. I sat in a chair someone had hauled in from the kitchen. An altar had been built from a shelf that wasn't quite level on the wall. It was full of candle wax drips and jars stuffed full of coins and plant matter.

After I answered questions, I waited while they interviewed the homeowner in the next room. I could hear almost every word.

"We hunted ghosts in Gettysburg together. We really haven't kept in touch since then. So I was surprised when he hit me up for a place to stay."

"What did he say?"

"He said the cops were railroading him and he needed a place to get his shit together."

"And you knowingly harbored a fugitive?"

"I thought it was bullshit. I mean, Cas is the kind of guy who always has a persecution complex. He thinks that a cabal of lizard men runs the government and spy on him, for chrissakes. He was a little weird back in college, but to hear him talk when he got here, I knew he was nuts."

"What sort of things did he say?"

"That he had made spiritual contact with the Forest Strangler. He'd had some kind of séance or something and connected with him."

"Did he talk about killing anyone?"

"No. He talked about the Forest Strangler killing people, but he never talked about 'I did this.' It was hard to tell if he was talking about himself in the third person or just really obsessed with this guy's history."

"Was he on any drugs?"

"He took some PCP while he was here. Not very good shit, to be honest. He shared. Gave me a bad trip."

I crossed the room and knelt at the bookcase. Maybe Veles had reached out to Cas. Maybe Cas had opened the door to something he couldn't understand and awakened my father's slumbering monster.

I pulled a book on demonology off the shelf, paged through it. It was an anthropological study documenting modern examples around the world. A page at random read:

> *In such societies, a possession is a way to rebel against the established order without consequences. It is a way for the possessed to transgress in the most awful ways, and to remain blameless.*

It was clear Cas was capable of believing. Back in the woods, I'd felt the presence of the Forest God so clearly. But now, among other people . . . I wasn't so sure. I felt haunted by him. Not in the way my father had been haunted. I believed that my father's will had been taken from him, that Veles acted through him. Perhaps that was a true possession, and I merely flirted at the edges of it. Enchanted. Maybe that was how it had begun with my father.

I rubbed my temple.

But I had to ask myself . . . what if he wasn't real? What if I was feeling the echoes of PCP and Dr. Richardson rewiring my brain? What if Veles was just a subconscious excuse to exercise my most antisocial impulses in accordance with what I had learned from my father?

I didn't turn on the light as the sky darkened. I had the sensation of floating in this room painted entirely black. I heard rodents crawling in the ceiling and wondered if the homeowner had considered them to be supernatural.

I hadn't intended to kill Cas. It was an accident.

It wouldn't have been an accident if I'd pushed him.

And I hadn't pushed him.

It was an accident. It was Veles.

And I was blameless.

The door opened and Monica stood in the doorway.

"Hey. You doing all right?"

"Yeah. I guess." I blinked against the light.

"Should I leave you alone?"

"Yeah. For right now."

I stared down at the floor, and she closed the door.

———

The investigation wore on late into the night.

I haunted the kitchen, staring out into the dark backyard. Park County deputies combed the woods for Cas's backpack. Max remembered that he'd headed out the door with one, and they assumed Cas had hid it somewhere. Judging by the flashlights, they were nowhere near the right spot. They were following a straight line from the house to the cliff and likely looking along the muddy riverbank where his body fell.

I didn't know what Cas had saved on that computer, but he probably had at least my updated birth certificate, photos, and name change documents on there. And I hoped to hell that no one would find them.

"Hey."

Monica came to join me in the kitchen, snagging a cold coffee from the counter.

"How's it going?" I asked.

She shook her head. "You know, I wonder if he killed himself. If he felt the cops closing in and he just didn't want to go to prison."

"You still think he's our man."

"Yeah. I do." She stared into the dark. "In talking with the homeowner, he's been involved in some weird-ass shit over a long period of time. He was able to identify one of the girls in Cas's photography project."

"Is she alive?"

"No. She died of a drug overdose four years ago. Her body was found undressed in her apartment. No foul play was suspected then, but we may need to revisit that."

"I'd think the cops would've noticed any strangulation marks."

"You'd think. Maybe they were hidden in the pictures with makeup. Nothing's outside of the realm of possibility."

Nothing really was. I was in uncharted territory now, falling into that dark beyond the window.

"Look, I'm worried about you." Monica's voice was low, not carrying beyond the kitchen.

I crossed my arms over my chest. I was worried about me, too, but I couldn't tell her. "What about?" I asked neutrally.

"You've been through a lot. Maybe it was too much to ask you to take on this case with me. There's been so much death and stress, and you're putting in an exhausting number of hours."

"I'm okay. Really." What was she seeing? Did I seem crazy? Was she beginning to suspect I was more than professionally interested in this case?

"Girl, you almost died. And then there's the biggest case of our careers dropped in our laps."

"I'm seeing my shrink. A lot."

"And that's good, but you seem really . . . intense lately. I don't know what you're going through, but . . ." Her brow knit.

I swallowed a lump in my throat. "Are you taking me off this case?"

She blinked in surprise. "Hell no. I just wanted to talk to you as your friend. I know that something is going on with you, and I want to help."

I exhaled. "I mean, I appreciate that. I do. This case is over now. I promise that I'll take some time off."

"Go to the beach with your doctor boyfriend or something, okay?"

I nodded. "I promise."

"Pinky swear?"

I extended my pinky finger, she linked it with hers, and we shook. This was the kind of promise I would have made with a classmate as a little girl, before the world got dark and complicated. But it made me smile.

She took a swig of coffee and made a face. "You should head back, though."

"You're staying here?" I was surprised.

"Yeah. I'm gonna get a motel and hit the local drugstore for a toothbrush. I want to make sure everyone does everything by the book."

"Park County doesn't need me anymore?"

"Nah. They know where to find you if they have questions. Sheriff said you could go."

"How are you gonna get back?"

"I'll hitch a ride with one of the Feds. They'll be here in the morning." She gazed out the window with me. "And then I'm gonna get about a week's worth of uninterrupted sleep."

Someone yelled for her upstairs. She rolled her eyes and disappeared.

Rain swept in, and the searchers returned to the house. There was talk of getting a dog from the FBI to look in the morning. I thought the rain would rinse a lot of the scent away, but I didn't want to take any chances.

I grabbed a trash bag from under the sink, folded it into my jacket pocket, and walked out the front door. I shut off my cell phone. I started the car, navigated my way out of the crowded parking situation at the end of the road, and made my way back to the main road. I turned right, watching my rearview mirror to make sure I wasn't being followed.

I turned right down the next county lane. It was dark, and I saw only two houses. Neither had any lights on. I drove about a mile, beyond the sight of those houses, and pulled off just before a small bridge crossed the river. A dirt road led around the back side of a barn that had collapsed in on itself, and I drove down there. I was out of sight of everyone but hip-deep in poison ivy. No one would bother me.

I got out of the car. Rain glistened on my face. I turned north, toward the way I'd come, and plunged into the forest.

I didn't need the stars to navigate. I wound my way back to the dead-end road where Cas had died. Rain trickled through the forest around me, echoing on leaves, branches, and earth.

Soon I found the stump. I cleared the wet leaves off it and re-trieved the backpack. I put it inside the garbage bag and walked back the way I'd come, retracing my own wet footprints.

I got back to the car and put the bag in the trunk. Putting the car in reverse, I navigated out to the main road and then headed to the freeway.

I was determined that Cas Russo's secrets were going to die with him.

The sky opened up, and sheets of rain swept across the high-way. I felt my eyes growing heavy and thought Monica had the right idea. I pulled off the road at an exit with a small town, picked up some fast food, and checked into a motel.

I checked my email and saw a departmental notice about Rol-lins's funeral. I'd missed it. I wasn't sorry, exactly. I felt like I should've been there. But I was relieved to have an excuse not to have been.

I took a warm shower, hung up my soaked clothes, and lay in bed in the dark, listening to the rain. I texted Nick:

I'm too tired to drive back from the drug task force raid. Yes, I was still maintaining that lie. Got a hotel and I'll be back in the morning.

He texted back:

Sleep well. I love you.

I hesitated. But . . . all this was over. I could breathe once more. I texted:

I love you too.

I fell into the sleep of the dead. I had closed a door today and was ready for another to open.

322

33

THE WRONG GUY

I made good time getting back to Bayern County in the morning. I dropped the departmental car in the lot, then transferred the gear to my own SUV. I put the black trash bag in the back.

I got home to find flowers on my kitchen counter. A note from Nick read: *Dinner in? I'll cook.*

I smiled. He'd asked the florist to make the bouquet a bit wild. Orchids wound with trailing ivy and curled pieces of bark. He knew what I liked. I hesitated for a moment when I saw that the stems were placed in a clear vase filled with black river stones. I couldn't help but think of the stones replacing the eyes of the second victim.

I sucked in my breath, suddenly suspicious of Nick. That was a special kind of paranoia, wasn't it? I was trying to shift my guilt and fear onto him. What would have Dr. Richardson called that? Some kind of projection?

Nick was the best, kindest person I knew. He could accept a

broken person like me. He did more than that. He loved me. And I would not allow my paranoia to accuse him of things he didn't do.

I needed to talk to him about the amphetamines in his medicine cabinet. He might regret bringing flowers to me after that discussion. But it wasn't like I'd been squeaky-clean in all my dealings lately, either. I wasn't really in a position to accuse him. How many crimes had I committed in the last few days? How many lies had I told?

I certainly wasn't going to arrest him. But we had to address this, to keep him safe and make it go away.

I put the black trash bag on the kitchen table, pulled out Cas's computer, and booted it up. It asked for a password and I entered Charles Manson's birth date. To my delight, it let me in. Cas's hard drive was stuffed with notes on ghost hunting, photos of naked women, movies, videos for his podcast, and arguments he'd had on the internet saved as text files. Some of the photos of naked women were like what Monica had showed me from his desktop: a woman draped in curtains of ivy, and another in repose at the base of a tree, posed with sunflowers.

I clicked past those and found my birth certificate and adoption records.

"Fuck you, Cas."

I closed the lid and took it outside. I found a hammer and took all my frustration with the Strangler case out on the laptop. I shattered the housing and rent the hard drive to bits with the claw of the hammer. My arm rose and fell in a steady rhythm while my heart beat steadily in my ears.

I put the pieces and the backpack in my burn barrel and set them on fire. When the fire cooled, I dumped the twisted plastic bits, metal, and charred zipper into an oil pan. I buried those parts at a random spot in the woods. The ground was soft, and digging was easy. I put the remains to rest beneath a sassafras, enjoying the warm fragrance as I worked.

Cas's evidence was in the dirt. Rollins was in the dirt. Nick and I would get past the amphetamines. He wasn't a street addict; he was trying to save lives. My lies would fade in the rearview mirror; nobody knew. All was right with the world, or soon would be.

When I was done, I returned to the house to wash the ash from my arms in the kitchen sink. I glanced at my cell phone on the counter and saw Monica was calling.

"Hey, it's me. I've got some bad news from Forensics. Cas doesn't have the Lyssa variant in his DNA." There was a pause. "You okay?"

"Yeah," I said finally. "Talk to you later."

I stared at the phone, then at the burn barrel.

Cas was an asshole, but he was innocent of the murders.

My gaze fell to the kitchen window, where a milkweed pod had been wedged between the sash and the glass. It was beginning to dry out, and its silky guts were spilling out into the air like gossamer lies.

———

Nick came home with groceries. He was determined to make mushroom Stroganoff; he'd found the recipe online and was eager to try it out. When Nick had free time, he enjoyed trying out elaborate recipes. Most of the time, I was perfectly content with a bowl of cereal, so Nick's attention to detail was a treat.

I sat at the kitchen table as he worked. Before Monica's call, I'd been looking forward to seeing him, even with the knowledge that I'd have to confront him about the drugs. But now . . . now he was a distraction from the unforgivable mistake I'd made with Cas.

Nick was blithely chatting about his day: ". . . And you would not believe what this kid had shoved up his urethra."

I raised my eyebrows. This was a game we played: he'd tell me about strange things found in orifices, and I'd have to guess. I rarely got it right.

"Mmmm . . . how old was he?"

"Fifteen."

"Hm. I'm going to say . . . a swizzle stick."

"No." Nick shook his head while he chopped mushrooms. "A plastic lizard."

"What the hell?"

"We could see it on X-ray. Like this." He lifted his hands up, fingers splayed.

"Damn. That has to take some practice."

"Right? This is not a starter toy. But he's General Surgery's problem now."

I made a sympathetic noise and looked out at the woods, where the grave of Cas's laptop lay. I'd fucked up. Big-time. And there was no fixing this.

"Anna?"

I turned my head. "Hmm?"

He set down the knife. "I was asking you about work."

"Ugh. It's just . . . a lot."

He reached over to take my hand. "I just want to say, after all this crazy shit with Rollins and the serial killer stuff on the news . . . I'm glad you're safe. I'm glad that Rollins is out of the picture and that you're not working that case anymore."

I couldn't meet his gaze. I shook my head. "Let's not talk about it."

"Would you rather talk about the marble I picked out of a grown-ass man's nose?"

"What?"

"Dude was twenty-four. Thought he could see if the marble would fit."

"The human race is doomed." I was pretty sure of it by now.

Dinner was delicious, and he promised to reprise the recipe. We ate on the couch, in front of a movie Nick had been wanting to watch about a bank heist. I stared at the screen, my thoughts churning static in my head.

Cas was innocent.

I had broken every rule I held sacred. I'd lied. I'd destroyed evidence. And worst of all, I had allowed Cas to die. I could've saved him. I could have reached out and grabbed his shirt, kept him from falling. But I didn't. Because I wanted him erased, what he knew to vanish. I didn't want to give up my life, my career, my relationship, because of what Cas had uncovered.

In my bones, I'd felt the influence of the forest, of Veles, whispering in my ear. But it didn't matter. I'd made the decision to let him fall. It was my choice, independent of any spirit murmurings.

"Anna."

I blinked. The credits had stopped rolling, and I was staring at a black screen.

I turned to look at him.

Nick was putting his shoes on. "I think I should go."

"No, you don't need to go," I said automatically.

He fixed me with a sad look, then headed toward the kitchen.

I got up to follow him. I grasped his elbow. "Nick, wait. We need to talk."

He paused, confusion on his face. "Okay."

I drew him back to the couch and took his hand in mine. "I'm sorry I've been distant."

"It's okay. Things have been complicated lately." He reached out to brush a piece of my hair behind my ear.

I took a breath. "I need to talk to you about something I saw when I was at your house."

His fingers froze behind my ear. "Yeah?"

"I was putting away my toothbrush and saw the amphetamines in your medicine cabinet."

He didn't break eye contact, just nodded. "Yeah. I've been taking those to stay awake at work."

"We're investigating a ring of hospital pharmaceutical thefts. I don't want to know if you're involved, but . . ."

He withdrew his hand from my ear as if he'd been burned. "Are you insinuating I'm selling?" Anger and hurt flashed in his eyes. "I've seen what that shit does to people . . . to kids. And you've got to know that I don't need the money."

"Nick, I'm not judging you."

"Sure sounds like you are."

"I know you'd never sell drugs. I'm just telling you so you can extricate yourself from this. I don't want you to get hurt or in trouble."

He pinched the bridge of his nose. "Okay, okay. I'll stop. I'll let you watch me flush every last one of them. It's just not what it looks like . . . not what it started out like." His hand slipped down to cover his mouth, and he stared into space. He looked haunted, I told myself. Not possessed by the drugs.

"I can't let anything happen to you. I just need you to be safe, because it would break my heart if I lost you." I whispered, aching. What I told him was true, and I wanted him to see it.

"Thank you." He looked at me and his voice shook. "I mean it."

I lifted my hand to press it against his cheek. As I did, the collar of my shirt slipped open. I didn't notice it at first, but Nick's gaze fell on the pendant lying at the hollow of my throat. That symbol of all my secrets and anguish that I couldn't share with him.

"I have something to tell you," I said. I had decided: I was going to tell him everything. No more secrets between us.

He reached for my throat, his thumb brushing the heart-shaped locket. Emotions washed over his face: sadness, fear, and anger. He jerked his thumb back as if he'd been burned. Maybe, on some subconscious level, he'd sensed the evil I had come from, the evil that I was. I felt exposed, as if he saw the horrific person I really was, deep down.

He bolted to his feet. "I've gotta leave. I can't do this." His voice was strangled as the words tumbled over each other.

He grabbed his coat and left, the screen door banging behind him.

Stunned, I watched him leave.

I was alone in that house perfumed with orchids and mushrooms, feeling tears dripping down my chin in the darkness.

I didn't know what happened. This had to be my fault, all my fault. I'd been afraid to tell him the truth, to let him in, and maybe he felt attacked for his drug habit, and . . .

I downed my glass of red wine from dinner and then his. Then I poured more wine from the bottle into my glass. The edges of my pain grew softer, fuzzier, like moss on a sharp rock. Soon the bottle was empty, and the room swam in my periphery.

I put on shoes and my holster, then walked out onto the porch. The night was clear and humid, and I stalked into the forest. The canopy held the humidity close, and I felt like I was breathing in dark soup glittering with fireflies and smelling of mud.

"What do you want?" I screamed into the dark. It wasn't an incantation; it was a demand. Veles owed this to me. He'd destroyed my life, contaminated it in every way.

The dark swirled ahead of me, and starlike eyes glowered down at me.

"Why do you want those girls?" I roared, tears rolling down my cheek. "What did you do to my father? And why won't you fucking go away?"

Were those pale antlers tangled in the branches? Eyes blinking slowly, like a cat? His voice was like rain on gravel. "Your father met me on a dark road. He bargained for his life. He promised to feed me, to honor me as men throughout the centuries have paid tribute."

"He was your servant."

"Yes. And now I have returned for you."

I growled at him, though my heart pounded. "Never."

He laughed, the sound of dry leaves pushed in a breeze. "You are already mine."

I drew my gun and fired in the direction of his eyes. The darkness dissipated, and the mocking rustle of leaves remained.

There was no blood, no bone chip or broken antler, no sign that there had been anything there.

How did I fight a god?

I returned to the house, putting my gun down on the kitchen table. I scrubbed my hands, smelling of gunpowder, through my hair. I put on a pot of coffee to get my head on straight.

I had nothing left to lose except this case. I had to solve it. Because no one else could. Maybe I could track down who was serving Veles . . . but then what? He would just find another, right? And he'd continue to torment me because I reminded him of those girls? Because he wanted me as a sacrifice, and my father wouldn't let him have me?

My phone was blinking notifications. With dread, I picked it up.

A message from Forensics, about the envelope sample I'd sent them. It was positive for the Lyssa variant. And she wasn't just a carrier; she had a full-blown expression of the mutation.

My mother was as much of a monster as my father. I inhaled deeply.

Dr. Richardson had tried to call me. I called her back.

"Anna. Thank you for returning my call."

"What's going on?"

"Is this a good time?"

My mouth turned down. No. I'd lost my boyfriend, was seeing supernatural monsters, had violated my oath of duty several times, and was responsible for an increasing body count. "Yeah."

"Your DNA results came back. Your DNA was positive for the mutation, fully expressed."

"I figured." With my mother and my father both testing positive for the fully expressed mutation, I didn't stand a chance.

"Are you okay?"

"Yeah. I . . . Can we talk about this at our next appointment?"

"Of course. I—"

I hung up.

I sucked in my breath. My parents were monsters. I was a monster, too.

No wonder Veles wanted me.

If he didn't already have me.

34

THE RETURN OF THE DEAD

I dove into research about Veles. I'd thought it was a nonsense name my father had conjured, but I discovered that he was an obscure Slavic god of the underworld. He was depicted, variously, as a serpent in the darkness at the foot of the Tree of the World, a hairy beast, and a psychopomp or shepherd of the dead. He was said to love the rain and fight with a thunder god, Perun. The serpent Veles was said to wind up the Tree of the World to the heavens, where he snatched Perun's wife. While escaping, he took various forms: transforming into trees, animals, and people. When he was finally killed by Perun's lightning, he gave up what he'd stolen, bringing the rain of seasons changing.

But he was reborn again and again, in new shapes and guises.

"He's a force of nature," I whispered. I thought of the women my father had brought to him. Were these meant to be wives, offered to please him?

I scrubbed my hand across my face. I had little use for spirituality and had always considered myself to be an atheist.

But now there were monsters. Weren't there?

I saw monsters all around me. I sent a few of the river stones from Nick's floral arrangement off to Forensics, to see if they were similar to the ones found on the second victim.

I left a message at the only car dealership in town about Nick's SUV. I wanted to find out when he'd ordered it, if he was telling me the truth. His new car had room to dispose of bodies and those easily hosed-off floor mats.

It seemed crazy to do these things. But my life was disintegrating, and I knew that I was, too.

I paced the floors of Dr. Richardson's office. She'd insisted that I come in right away, to "process." I was still wearing my father's necklace, drumming my fingers against it as I walked. My father was one. My mother was one. I was one.

I stared out a window. It was usually covered by thick blinds, but Dr. Richardson had drawn them aside today, revealing a massive aloe plant that cast curling serpentine tentacles like the head of Medusa.

I was a killer. I knew that. I had killed and been to blame for deaths these past weeks.

"Tell me," I begged her. "Tell me if I'm a psychopath like them."

Dr. Richardson spoke carefully. "I believe you experience empathy. I believe you feel grief over the losses of relationships: your boyfriend, your biological parents. I know you feel deeply. As a child, you didn't set fires or harm animals, and you still don't."

I felt a twinge of relief.

"However," she said, "in the last few weeks, since you shot Tom Sullivan and your memories were reopened, you're not upholding the standards of your profession. Situations you've told me about have been, at best, gross abuses of power. At worst . . . there's intent to harm."

I sank to the couch.

"And you've described to me the influence of a supernatural entity. Some of those symptoms fall under psychosis."

"You don't believe me." I looked at her, clear-eyed.

She tipped her head. "It's not a matter of belief or unbelief. It's not a judgment, either. Just an observation about how your mental state seems to be degrading. And I feel I'm to blame for that, for . . ." She blew out her breath. ". . . for reaching into your head and playing God with your memory. That's an unforgivable crime. I have damaged you."

I took a deep breath. "You can fix me. Right?"

She pressed her mouth into a line. "I don't know. I believe where we are now is beyond the limits of my ability to assist. I would like to refer you to a colleague of mine—"

"No," I said automatically. "I don't want you discussing my case with anyone else, either."

"I won't. But . . ." She looked down at her lap.

"What? Tell me."

She looked me in the eye. "I think it would be worth asking yourself . . . Do you have an alibi for the times of the murders?"

I blinked. "What?"

"This is hard to say, but I want you to listen carefully. I'm concerned that, since your mind can be so easily partitioned . . . that you might be partitioning other things from yourself. I want you to go back and see if your whereabouts can be accounted for."

I stood up and turned back to the window. "I'm not the Strangler."

I heard the squeak of her chair as she turned away from me. Papers rattled in her file cabinet. "Where were you when the first woman was killed? The second?"

My heart pounded. I sifted through my memories. I didn't

have an alibi. I was missing time. But I couldn't have done it. I would've remembered. My fingers slid behind the aloe plant, to the window latch. I slid it open noiselessly, as if my hand were disconnected from my body. I also found the security sensors next to the latch; they were the adhesive kind that registered as operational when the edges touched. I deftly peeled them away, placed them beside each other on the sill, so they still made contact and the system would register the window as closed.

Wouldn't I have remembered?

But there was Lyssa variant DNA found at the scene. It could have been mine. Or my father's. Or my mother's . . .

I turned back to Dr. Richardson. She twisted up from her perch over the file cabinet. I knew I couldn't trust her anymore.

I walked toward her, and she flinched.

I kept walking, to the door.

"Please destroy all my records," I said. "Our client-therapist relationship is terminated."

I closed the door softly behind me, though my hand shook.

———

I couldn't believe that my father's god was working through me. Could not.

I couldn't believe that I had inherited that task from my father. Would not.

I would prove that someone else was murdering those women. I would find the killer and I would go back to the life I had before, as a good cop.

I sat in my SUV, checking messages. Nothing from Nick, and my heart sank at that. But I was too afraid to call him. The way he'd left . . . I wasn't sure he wanted me to chase him.

The state highway patrol had come back with fingerprint results from the ambulette. In the intervening years, AFIS had caught up with a set of prints belonging to a Carl Curry. He lived a couple counties over in Springfield. Didn't seem like he'd wandered too far from his old stomping grounds, which wasn't really unusual.

I decided to talk to him. The only thing I had left to cling to was the theory that Veles had more than one puppet. Maybe I could find them.

Carl Curry was forty-eight years old. He would've been twenty-six when my father was executed. He had priors for aggravated assault and bank robbery. He'd been in and out of prison for twenty years, with a handful of years of freedom here and there. There had been no Strangler murders during those times, though.

If it was him, why start now?

At the very least, he could tell me what happened to my father.

He'd registered with his probation officer as working as a dishwasher for a diner on the east end of town. After a couple hours on the freeway, I cruised down city streets with the skyline as a backdrop. I didn't blame him for moving to a more urban area. In rural areas, everyone knew everyone else's business. Here, maybe he got a clean slate.

I walked into JessAnn's Diner and sat at a sticky booth in the far corner. The waitress brought me a coffee, and I ordered a cheeseburger and fries. It had been years since I'd eaten meat, and I felt like I could cheat today. I asked the waitress if Carl Curry was working.

"He gets off in fifteen." She looked me up and down.

"Please tell him I'm a friend of Nora's." Nora Chaplain was the name of his probation officer. I didn't want to out him at work if they hadn't done a background check.

"Sure thing." She headed to the kitchen.

It was possible that Curry would run out the back and I'd never see him again. But I was hoping that, since I was playing it cool, he'd talk to me.

By the time my cheeseburger came out, a man in a damp apron slid into the booth across from me. He was one of those guys who lifted a lot of weights and had no neck: his head sprouted directly from his shoulders. A tattoo of a cartoon character covered his right forearm.

I looked him in the eye. I didn't know if I'd sense Veles on him if Veles was driving. My judgment was that faded.

He looked back at me. "Nora sent you."

"I'm Lieutenant Koray with the Bayern County Sheriff's Office. I want to talk to you about something that happened a few years ago. Off the record."

Curry looked at me suspiciously. "I don't do shit anymore. I got a little girl. She's fourteen."

"I get it. I'm not looking to mess anything up for you." Well, not unless he was the Forest Strangler. "I just have some questions."

He crossed his arms over his apron. "I'll see if I got answers."

"I'm trying to figure out what happened to the body of Stephen Theron."

He rubbed his forehead. "Aw, shit."

"Do you know what happened?"

He sucked in his breath. "This off the record? No names?"

"Yup."

"I can't go away for another crime. The judge said I won't see the light of day."

"I understand."

He looked at the wall, then back at me. "About twenty years ago, I was involved in a racket for a funeral director."

"What kind of racket?"

"Well, he catered to people with certain . . . predilections. Wealthy people who could pay."

"So . . . necrophiles?" I tried to sound nonplussed.

"Among other things. There are people who want to fake their own deaths for life insurance, to escape their wives, stuff like that. There was even a guy who wanted to bind books with human skin, and another who liked severed heads in bottles. Totally weird shit, but there's a market for it."

It reminded me of Cas's collection of serial killer memorabilia. Maybe if he had deeper pockets, he would've gone for something like that.

I saw Curry looking at my plate and I pushed the French fries close to him. He took one and chewed on it. "So, someone with big bucks wanted to buy the Forest Strangler's body. I didn't know why, but I suspect it had something to do with preserving the brain. We were supposed to drive up with an ambulette, put the body on ice, and deliver it to the funeral home. The client would pick it up, and we'd get paid."

"How many of you guys were in on this?"

"Just me and this other guy I'd worked with before. Reliable dude. The funeral director got us some papers and shit, and we rolled on in there, picked up the body, and rolled on out. Smooth as glass."

"And you took the body to the funeral home?"

"Well, we were going to, but this is where shit gets weird. Really weird." He licked his lips. "You ain't gonna believe me."

"Try me. I've seen some shit."

"Okay." He shrugged and took another French fry. "So we were instructed to take these back roads to avoid the cops. It was snowing. We were on this gravel road in the middle of fucking nowhere when a deer jumps out in front of us. Chris slams on the brakes, and we go skidding. We don't hit the deer but wind up in the ditch. I go back to check on the body, make sure it's still on ice.

"There's ice everywhere, and the body is sitting the fuck up. I shit you not. It's sitting the fuck up in its body bag."

My heart lurched into my throat.

"I scream for Chris, who's outside the ambulette, looking at how deep we're in the ditch. I open the back doors, and he's face-to-face with this body sitting up. He laughs at me, tells me it's just rigor mortis. He goes to unzip the body to show me.

"But the corpse's eyes are fucking open. He's looking at us. We are both fucking screaming like little girls. We back away, and the Strangler climbs out of the back of the ambulance. He's real unsteady on his feet, barefoot in the snow. Like he's in a trance, he goes over to the woods, walks into the woods maybe fifty yards . . . and then he fucking collapses in front of this giant oak tree.

"Then this chill settles over the forest. We freak the fuck out. We run back to the ambulette, shove it out of the ditch, and get on the road."

He shook his head. "We decided that we wanted no part of that shit. None. Maybe the execution got fucked-up and he wasn't totally dead, you know? We talked about going back and killing him. He'd seen us, after all."

I thought back to what I'd been told of the execution. It wasn't outside the realm of possibility that the execution was more fucked-up than I knew. They checked his vitals only once. What if he wasn't actually dead? What if his vitals had just crept below detection level . . . and . . .

I clung to this. I needed to believe that there had been a medical mistake. Not that my father had come back from the dead.

He paused to smear a fry in ketchup. "And a guy like that needs killing, you know?"

"I know." I *knew.*

"We ditched the ambulette in a parking lot and went our separate ways. Fuck that guy and his money. Some things are not to be fucked with."

"Can you tell me where you last saw him?" I asked.

"Sure."

I passed him a piece of paper and a pen. He marked the roads and drew the gravel road. He marked three curves and a heap of stones and then a tree, back from the road.

"Right here," he said with certainty. "He collapsed there."

"Thank you," I said. "You've been a lot of help. By the way, where were you the nights of the fourteenth and the nineteenth?"

He narrowed his eyes at me. "I was here on the fourteenth. Working. And I was at my daughter's birthday party on the nineteenth."

"Thanks." I slid him two hundred-dollar bills and headed for the door. Informants always got paid.

I chewed on what he'd said. He didn't have any reason to lie. If anything, he was motivated to tell the truth to avoid getting in trouble with his probation officer.

I looked down at the crude map in my hands. Or he could be guilty and just bullshitting me.

I thought I believed him, but I wanted to see for certain, the place where my father had come back from the dead . . . or walked away from it.

35

FAMILY TREE

I drove ribbons of country back routes for miles, reaching the gravel road in Curry's diagram by twilight. On one side of the road were fieldstones pulled from a grassy meadow that had been farmed once upon a time. The field had been cleared at one point, then allowed to go fallow. Now black walnut saplings had taken root, and the thistles and purple ironweed were shoulder-high.

The other side . . . that was forest. I pulled over and stopped. The canopy of an oak tree spread in the distance. Walking down the steep sides of the ditch, I tried to imagine what it must have felt like for my father to awaken in the back of the ambulette, disoriented and full of drugs. Of course, he would have headed for the familiar, to the woods . . . to home . . .

The oak's leaves had started to turn red near the crown, where the evening chill had begun to touch. The oak, once I got closer, looked a little sickly. Some of the branches had died off, and I spied a girdling root around its base that was slowly strangling the life from it.

I fell to my knees before the tree, in the red leaves, as my father had done.

I scarcely dared hope that my father was still alive, that he had walked out of this forest. I wanted to speak to him once more. I wanted to hold him in my arms and gaze at him and ask him why. I thought he would tell me. I was his daughter, after all. And he loved me.

I brushed my hands through the leaves at the base of the tree. If my father had died here, he would've decomposed long ago. Many of his bones would've been scattered by animal predation. If I were a good cop, I would ask Forensics to come, to sift through the dirt with painstaking slowness.

But I was not a good cop. Not anymore.

I'd brought a trowel. I dug into the top foot of the soil, casting aside rocks and clods of dirt. If there was something there, I would find it.

As the last daylight drained away, my trowel hit something. It didn't ring, not the way metal did when hitting rock.

I excavated carefully around something white.

My heart lurched into my mouth.

I lifted up out of the ground a human jawbone.

I pressed my head to the dirt and sobbed.

My father was dead. My hopes of having some kind of understanding or reconciliation with him were extinguished. As were my hopes of charging him with the recent murders. My heart broke at the thought of him having those moments of freedom, of stumbling into the dark that he loved, and passing away. He'd held on that long, until there was dirt under his bare feet and the shadow of a tree above him.

"Why, Dad?" I sobbed. But there were no answers. Only a thin ribbon of a DeKay's snake sliding beneath the leaf litter.

After I had cried myself out, I carefully reburied the jaw.

I would tell no one. Whatever monster he was, he deserved to be buried in the woods. If I told anyone, I'd have to defend my chain of inadmissible evidence. My father's remains would be boxed up in an anthropology department at a university until the end of time, imprisoned.

I wanted him to be free.

———

I had to believe I could get my life back, that I could be Anna once more. Maybe I couldn't ever have Nick again, but I could have my work. I could return to being a decent human being who helped people. That's who I'd been for many years . . . and who I wanted to become once more.

I didn't think that Dr. Richardson would destroy her records. Not really. She had kept all those records of me from childhood all this time. And she thought that I might be the killer. There was nothing stopping her from going to the authorities with her notes except for the threat of revealing what she'd done. But now . . . now she thought I was doing harm, and that might exceed her own self-interest. I couldn't trust her, and I couldn't risk it.

I drove to the office park, arriving by three a.m. Dr. Richardson gave at least lip service to protecting client privacy, and she didn't have cameras up, despite the serial killer panic gripping the state. But I was still careful. The front door was alarmed. I parked around the back of the building, then slipped along the shrubbery to the window with the aloe plant . . . the window I'd unlocked.

To my relief, it was still unlocked. I opened the window, mindful not to disturb the security sensors I'd tampered with. I climbed in, pulling it shut behind me.

The room was lit only by the dim glow from the street filtering in. I pulled the blinds, plunging myself into near total darkness. I reached for the candle on the coffee table and the book of matches beside it. I lit the candle, inhaling the generic vanilla scent.

In my mind's eye, I stood before my memory vault, holding that candle, peering into the shadows. I walked forward, to the pool from which nightmares rose.

The pool was still now, and shallower. I only saw coins below in the clear water.

The monsters had escaped.

I blinked and I was back in Dr. Richardson's office.

I had to focus. Get what I needed and leave.

Richardson's file cabinet was locked, but that was an easy thing to bypass. I wasn't very good with locks, but most old file cabinets operated the same way. I pulled out my pocketknife and inserted the blade, jimmying it until the lock was released. I didn't care if she saw evidence of me breaking in; she'd know I had been there when she saw my file was missing. I needed her to know that the evidence she had against me was gone and she needed to seize the moment to fade into retirement nicely and quietly without fucking up my life any more than she'd already done.

My phone rang, and I jumped. I picked it up. "Koray."

"Detective Koray, this is Fred Kapp from Kapp's Automotive. I understand you had a question about a sale?"

"Yes. I'd like to know when this car was ordered and sold." I read him the VIN number from Nick's SUV that I'd saved on my phone.

There was a pause as Fred tapped at his computer slowly, sounding like he was using two fingers. "Ah, yes. I remember that one. Doctor in town ordered it last spring. Took a lot of time to get all the chips in, but it's a beautiful car. It was sold to Nicolas Kohler on August 27."

"Did he trade in his car?"

"Yes. A silver Alfa Romeo."

I paused. Everything Nick had told me was true. Part of me wanted to tell the dealer to hold the car for me to look at it.

"Has the car been cleaned?"

"Um, yeah. It's been detailed and put on the lot. We've already had a couple test drives in it."

"Thank you. If I need to see it, I'll be in touch." While it was likely that detailing had removed some potential evidence, I didn't have enough for a warrant.

I set aside my feelings about Nick to return my attention to Richardson's files. They were organized alphabetically by patient last name. Most were covered with a thin layer of dust and labeled with yellowing file stickers. I located my own very fat file and stuck it under my arm. It wasn't dusty.

I paused, squinting at a file name that snagged my attention: Nicolas Kohler.

What? My thoughts tumbled over each other: She was Nick's shrink? Surely that couldn't be *my* Nick? Had I ever told her Nick's name? Maybe she didn't know that we knew each other.

I pulled the file. It was a thick file; she'd been seeing him for years.

I opened the creased manila, and my breath caught in my throat. This was my Nick. She'd been seeing Nick since he was ten, when his name had been Nicholas Stanger.

My fingers slipped up to the necklace around my throat. Nick's mother was Teresa Stanger, my father's fifth victim, the original owner of the locket. He had to remember the locket . . . When he saw it, he fled . . .

Tears dripped down my nose as I flipped through his file. He'd been referred to counseling by victims' advocates . . . likely the same way I'd come into contact with Dr. Richardson. I glanced at the file cabinet, finding a handful of last names I recognized. My God. She'd counseled most of the children left behind by the Forest Strangler.

I rubbed my nose with my sleeve and read Nick's file. He last saw his mother when she left for school, leaving him with his babysitter. He was ten years old. She never came home.

His father hadn't been in the picture, and he'd been raised by his grandparents. He'd taken their last name and switched schools. He did well academically, gotten into medical school, but struggled with depression and anxiety. Dr. Richardson suggested the possibility of a major depressive disorder and warned of problems in relationships.

Dr. Richardson's notes said: "Despite best efforts, I've been unable to provide closure to this individual. He's unable to make sense of the death of his mother, obsessing over the original crime. I've attempted to use CPT, hypnosis, and EFT therapies to try and reduce his level of distress, but no satisfactory reduction in emotional distress has been noted. Hope that being a doctor and serving others will resolve his pain through positive action."

I flipped to the back of the file. Her notes ended a few months before I met Nick. I could only assume he was no longer seeing her.

But my mind spun. What were the chances that Nick and I would meet? Maybe he had come back here after school, as I did, to face his old ghosts.

I sat on the floor and wept for him, for the far-reaching evil my father had wrought that poisoned everything it touched.

I replaced Nick's file and took my own. I returned home exhausted and fell into a thick sleep. I dreamed of seeing Nick in a forest. No matter how hard I ran, he was always just ahead of me, and I could never catch up. He finally changed into a stag and disappeared into the night, leaving me alone.

I awoke to my phone ringing. I grabbed it.

"Don't you sleep?" I growled.

"No. We've got another victim," Monica said.

"What?"

"A hundred miles away. Near a pond in Springfield. I mean, I guess this rules out the security guard or his buyer as our killer, since they're still in jail."

"Where is it?"

Monica paused, and doubt softened her voice. "Are you feeling up to it, though?"

"Yes." I couldn't let her take me off the case. "I'm good. Let's get to work."

"I'll text the directions. FBI's already out there, nosing around with the locals."

"Great. I'll see you there."

I brushed my fuzzy-feeling teeth. When I went to get dressed, I paused.

My bare feet were filthy.

Fuck. I must have been sleepwalking in the woods again. I jumped in the shower to spray the mud off my feet, got dressed, and headed north. I felt disconnected from my body. I knew where my father had been laid to rest and that he'd tasted a moment of freedom before dying. I was grateful for that. But I also despaired at what I'd learned about Nick, at what he'd suffered at my father's hands. I wished he were still alive so that I could scream at him, hold him accountable, even if a malevolent god whispered in his ear through tangled strands of DNA.

Monica's directions led me to a sunlit grassy field. I pulled off behind other cars and waded into the field. Grasses came up to my thighs, and the wind stirred the tassels, punctuated by black-eyed Susans and yellow prairie dock. The grasses were beginning to yellow in anticipation of autumn. This seemed like a landscape I'd seen as a child, a pocket of golden beauty hidden from the world at large. I walked downhill to an algae-covered pond, where people huddled around a woman's naked feet.

Monica waved and climbed up the rill to meet me.

"What've you got?" I said by way of greeting.

"Fresh victim this time. Dead not even twenty-four hours. The flowers aren't all wilted. Her body's decorated with black-eyed Susans and blue asters. The black-eyed Susans could have come from here or pretty much anywhere. There aren't any asters in the field, so they had to have come from somewhere else. And there's a magenta flower we've sent pictures to the university's extension service to identify."

"Any news about the victim?"

"She's older than the previous ones. Or else the killer ran out of fresh young flowers to pluck."

We approached the crime scene, and my heart launched into my mouth.

A woman lay at the edge of the pond. Her body was covered with black-eyed Susan petals, as if she'd been a decoupage project. She was indeed older than the previous victims, a young sixties, perhaps. Her hands were wrapped around a bouquet of blue asters still fresh enough to summon honeybees. An evidence tech gently untangled one hand to take fingerprints. Bees buzzed lazily through the crime scene, crawling on the woman's face. Her eyes had been replaced by the decapitated flower heads of black-eyed Susans, and a ring of bruises circled her throat.

But the face.

I knew without a doubt this was Dr. Richardson.

My heart hammered and my hands sweated.

My God.

Where had I been last night?

After I left her office, I'd been alone. In bed. I thought. My panicked mind raced back to my filthy feet.

Agent Parkes was beside us, writing in a notebook. "She's a departure from the pattern. I'm thinking she might have had some personal connection to the killer."

I closed my eyes. They were going to know that I knew her. Dr. Richardson had sent a letter to the chief concerning my fitness for duty. I had to tell the truth . . . part of it.

"She looks like my psychiatrist," I said softly.

Parkes paused in his writing. Maybe he'd think that was a co-incidence. Unlikely . . .

Monica put a hand on my shoulder. "Are you sure?"

I nodded. "Dr. Barbara Richardson . . . her offices are in Spring-field on Gibson Avenue."

"Holy shit." Monica wrote down the info. "Are you okay?"

I lifted a shoulder. I didn't trust myself to speak.

"It's okay to get out of here. I'll keep you posted."

But I couldn't leave. I crouched down to peer at her, mostly because I didn't want to make eye contact with Agent Parkes. I stared at the magenta flower on her chest, delicate and balloon-like. It had been placed over her heart.

"That flower," I said. "That's from a pitcher plant."

"Oh, yeah?"

I nodded. "I remember seeing those as a little girl. They like shaded woods. Damp places."

"Are they common?"

"No. They're rare. I think they might be endangered." I'd seen these plants near the collapsed house where I'd last seen my father. This felt like a message to me, like a hidden story told in a Victorian flower bouquet.

"We should start looking. The flowers this guy's been picking are common ones. But this . . . it might give us a lead."

The evidence tech came back. "We got an immediate hit in AFIS. The victim is a Barbara Richardson. She's a psychiatrist. Clean record, current licensure."

Monica nodded. "I'll get a court order to get into her records. She might've had a client connected to the case."

My world was unraveling. Any hope of saving my job, my identity as Anna, was vanishing.

I stepped back from the scene, watched the techs continue to process it. One of them approached me, a young man in a crisp navy windbreaker.

"Hey, I looked at those rocks you sent."

"Yeah?" I held my breath. At that moment, I wasn't sure what I wanted. Part of me wanted Nick—not me—to be the killer.

"They're dissimilar from the ones at the scene. The ones at the scene were actually well-worn coal, likely local. The ones you sent were tumbled basalt, the kind used for decorative and craft purposes."

I nodded. "Thank you."

Nick wasn't involved in the crime, but my paranoia had implicated him. The undertow of this case had me fully in its grip.

The coroner's office eventually loaded the body into a body bag, then carried it to the road. A nest-like indentation remained in the grass, trampled flat by feet, next to that still green pond. Dragonflies zoomed over the water, and red-winged blackbirds buzzed their summer calls.

Parkes stood beside me, saying nothing as the scene was cleared.

"What was it like, working this case the first time?" I asked him. My voice sounded distant to my own ears.

"I felt like Alice falling into a strange world. Not Wonderland, but something darker and more terrifying." His creased face was pensive. "I wanted to believe that I'd never be back there again."

I glanced at him. "You didn't need to come out of retirement."

He sighed. "And I didn't want to. Nobody wanted to come back to this."

He gazed at me then, with a flicker of what might have been recognition. But he turned away and walked to the cars near the road.

I stared at that algae-covered pond. I was in too deep. Drowning.

Veles had taken me. I was convinced of it. Like my father, I was now his puppet, carrying out his desire for flesh.

"This stops now," I whispered. "This ends with me."

36

LIGHTNING

I returned to where it had all begun, to the house in the woods where the pitcher plants grew.

I drove into the sun, heading south and west. My thoughts were an acrid jumble. I had to confront the Forest God, in that place where he drew so much of his power. I'd demand that he release me and go skulking back into the shadows of fable, or I would kill myself.

I knew I had little chance against something so ancient. But all I could do was remove this instrument from his control.

I thought of Nick. I wished I could explain to him what had happened. He was the only one I felt I truly owed an explanation to. He was the person who knew me best, but he still knew so little. And I wanted to protect my adoptive parents from this, from what I was.

His file said that he had always sought closure. At the very least, I could give him that. The woman he loved, Anna, had slipped away from me. I realized that I'd lost sight of her over the past weeks. I'd become Elena, my father's daughter.

I activated the voice recorder on my phone and confessed. I confessed who I was, how I had discovered it. I confessed my inappropriate involvement in this case, the deaths I'd brushed up against and was responsible for. I confessed that I couldn't remember where I was when the last three women were killed. Over the course of two hours, I told everything. About Veles, how I was going into the woods and how I wasn't going to come out.

And I confessed to Nick that I loved him. And that I was sorry. I should have trusted him with the truth about who I was. I shouldn't have lied to him about working this case. And now it was too late. What had he thought when he saw that necklace? Did he recognize it? Did he think I was following in my father's footsteps, collecting his souvenirs? There was no way to know. But I could at least tell him the truth.

I finished the recording, zipped the file up, and sent it. There was nothing else to say.

If I survived this confrontation with my father's monster, I would walk into the river and inhale the deep, silty water. I'd feel the mud sliding into my lungs, and I'd extinguish my parents' legacy. I would be unornamented with flowers, floating along the currents until I rotted, unseen.

———

I pulled my car into the driveway of my childhood home around sunset. The house was boarded up, abandoned. No one had been willing to buy the house after we left. Too much emotional baggage. It looked it: curled asphalt roof shingles, plywood over the doors and windows. Saplings had grown in the yard, while honeysuckle had overtaken the grass.

But people had been here. Graffiti and cigarette butts littered the area. Likely, this was the place where high school kids went to smoke and scare the hell out of each other. A bouquet of yellowed cattails had been nailed over the lintel of the door. I stared at it, thinking of how much that looked like the Strangler's work.

I rummaged in the back of my SUV. I kept all manner of odds and ends there for investigations; some digging through gloves and evidence bags and extra ammunition brought me a claw hammer and a flashlight.

I set the hammer to work against the front door, peeling the soaked plywood back. The wooden door gave way with a kick, and I was soon standing inside my old living room.

It smelled of mildew; the ceiling was black with it. The carpet was stained black and green, and the walls bloomed with pockets of mold. Footprints across the carpet were brown with rot.

A familiar plaid couch stood in the living room, in front of a console television. The glass was broken out of it, and an opossum stared at me from its nest within.

I moved to the kitchen, dark and cavernous. Water dripped somewhere, and something rustled behind the rust-colored refrigerator. Squirrels moved in the attic, the characteristic scrape of their claws on beams. Creatures scuttled through the drywall.

I turned down the hallway, to my old room. It was mostly as I'd left it, except for the mildew and the colony of bats huddling in the drapes. The drawers had been opened and tossed, and a soggy stuffed animal lay on the floor. Perhaps someone had broken in here years ago and found my necklace. Then sold it. What else had they stolen of mine? Plastic pastel horses, sticker books, drawings from art class?

I felt violated. Nothing was mine anymore. Everything I was or had belonged to someone else.

I reached into my pocket and put on the necklace my father had given me. I was going to go to the grave with it.

I left the house, the door open behind me. I wanted the creatures of the forest to take up residence in it, to take it down to the ground and erase the memory of it.

I filled my pockets with ammunition and strode into the woods as the last golden line of sunset filtered through the trees.

The forest was quiet as I moved through it. My feet still remembered the now-overgrown paths my father and I had taken. I wondered if I'd ever gone with him on those kills, if I had locked those memories away.

It might explain my mother's disdain for me. Perhaps she knew. Perhaps she'd seen me come home with blood on my hands, scrubbed them clean, and despaired of what she could do to repair such a damaged child. Maybe that was why she took me to Dr. Richardson, why she abandoned me and started over. Maybe that was the best she could do.

There were too many maybes. I needed answers.

As night fell, I confronted the abandoned house where my father had killed those women. Clouds swept in, obscuring the stars, giving a soft, insulated quality to the forest. The house was in even worse shape than I remembered. Only the rusted chimney stood intact. Half of the structure had collapsed entirely, sliding into the ground with poison ivy crawling up to the ruined roof. Rain began to speckle the leaves, and they shook in response. Beside it, pitcher plants bloomed the color of blood with gaping mouths.

I approached the door. It had crumpled in on itself. I struggled to open it, and it finally yielded with a crack.

I shone my light within. This place, too, had been vandalized. It had been stripped bare of anything I remembered, everything except that cast-iron stove that was too heavy for anyone to move. It had disintegrated almost entirely into rust, shattering when I touched it with my fingertips.

Beams overhead were broken and covered in moss. Beyond them, a sliver of night shone, spitting raindrops.

"*Veles*," I roared. "*Face me.*"

The forest shuddered. The black air thickened, solidified. The rasp of rain on the roof melded with the shudder of thunder.

A shadow darkened the doorway.

My breath froze in my throat. Veles had come to confront me. I'd thought that my bullets and words could stop a monster, but I realized, too late, that that was foolish. How could I fight a ghost?

A floorboard creaked beneath its foot, and I realized this was not a spirit. It was a man, flesh and blood and capable of exhaling into the dark.

"Dad," I whispered.

Love and fear and fury and revulsion expanded my chest. There was so much I wanted to say, so many answers I needed to demand . . .

I turned on my light, eager to see his face. But, to my shock, Agent Parkes stared back at me.

His brows drew together. "What are you doing here?"

I immediately snapped back into cop mode. "I'm following up a lead."

His mouth turned down. "No you aren't. You've come home, Elena."

I sucked in my breath. "How did you know?"

He rested his hand on the doorframe, stroking the moss that grew there. "I've known since before I saw you in Chief Nelson's office. I've always known who and where you were."

I lifted my chin and rested my hand on the butt of my holstered gun. "Then why didn't you tell anyone?"

He tipped his head. "I thought Dr. Richardson had done her work well. That you had forgotten everything."

"I did. For a time. And then I remembered."

"So I see."

Thunder rolled over the land, and he took a step inside the door. His fingers tangled in a grapevine leaking into the house, and his eyes glittered when he looked at me.

Instinctively, I drew my gun. "Why are you here? Were you following me?"

He paused, his fingers tightening in the vine so much that sap glistened on his knuckles.

"Answer me. Answer me, or I'll drop you here and bury you beneath the floorboards." My voice was a growl. I wasn't sure if I was bluffing or not. I could kill him and dispose of his body in a way that it would never be found. But would I? I knew I was walking into the river. Would I take him with me?

When he answered, his voice was the rumble of thunder. "Years ago, when you and I and your father were here, you dropped the gun and fled. Your father and I fought, and he escaped. I was too far into this case, into your father's head. That night, I saw it all clearly."

Lightning flashed, illuminating his face in profile. I saw a chalky face there, for just an instant . . . the face of Veles. I saw it reaching out for Parkes all those years ago, leaking like ichor from my father's mouth into his. Blood pounded in my temples, and my hold on reality swam, trapped between a vision of the past and the awful present.

"My father . . . was he working alone? Not . . . with anyone?" My voice sounded very distant, as if it came from the bottom of a well.

"He was alone." I don't know if it was Veles or Parkes who answered me; it didn't matter. "I just picked up where he left off."

So I hadn't been involved. Breath hissed from my throat as the vision expanded to the new victims in the past weeks, lovingly

arranged and laid bare for the evil. Parkes had continued my father's work as the new Forest Strangler.

As if he could hear my thoughts, Parkes nodded. He stared at
his hand as if it were a garment that could be taken off and on.

"Why were you silent all this time? Why were there no killings
in decades?"

He smiled and took a step forward. "Oh, there were. I just hid
them well."

Fuck. As a federal agent, he knew how to accomplish these
things as well as I did.

He continued. "I made the last three obvious."

"You tipped off Cas," I realized.

"He was an inconsequential bit of bait."

"Was it you or Cas who put that tracker on my car?"

He lifted a brow. "I don't need technology to track you."

"The emails . . . was that you?"

"That was me. I wanted to remind you of who you were. Of who
you could be, carrying on your father's work." Parkes offered me
his hand.

Every bit of heredity in my body wanted me to take a step
toward him, to allow that malevolent spirit to work through my
blood as it had worked through my father's. But every part of me
that I had created—every bit of identity that had been hard-won
through my adoptive family, my love of Nick, and my career—
begged me to take a step back.

"I won't."

"I already have flowers chosen for you if you refuse. They will be
the most beautiful and rare of all, the blooms of the pitcher plant . . ."

Parkes was fast. He was on me. Fighting with me for the gun.
It went off with a blinding flare, and the flashlight spiraled away
into a corner. While Parkes wrested my service pistol from my

grip, I reached into his jacket holster, grabbed his own gun, and lurched back.

We stared at each other over gunsights, half-blind and panting, before he rushed me again. He was trained at least as well or better than I was, and he had the advantage of strength. I fired, but the weapon was twisted away from me. I jammed my fingers behind the trigger to keep him from firing on me. I screamed as bones in my fingers and wrist shattered. He punched me in the ribs, once, twice, three times . . .

I growled and bit him, forcing him to release my hand. He shot me.

I landed on my ass, stunned by hot blood searing my abdomen. I kicked at him. I scrabbled behind me for a weapon, and my hand closed around a rotted piece of wood. I slashed out at him, swinging, connecting with a knee.

He stumbled. I lurched to my feet and front kicked him. He stumbled back into the stove, crashing into it with the smell of rust. It rained down on him, coating him in a cloak of rust.

He grinned at me. "You can't escape." He didn't say this in Parkes's voice. He said this in that low, rasp of water in a drainpipe.

Thunder crashed. In his eyes I saw the gleam of the Forest God's glare and the outline of antlers.

I gripped my piece of wood.

I lunged for him, intending to stake him in the chest like the monster he was. But I paused. The hair stood up on my arms, and I smelled ozone. I remembered what I'd learned about Veles's enemy: lightning.

Instinctively, I stepped back.

Lightning crashed down the metal chimney, into the stove . . . into Parkes in a brilliant flash of white. He screamed, and I smelled burning meat and iron.

I held my breath, heart pounding. A small fire bloomed from the belly of the stove, where some creature had built a nest. Parkes was tangled in a seared, twisting mass of rust, fused to it. His flesh reddened and crackled. He hissed softly.

I lifted the wooden stake and plunged it into his throat. Anything to stop that awful sound. Blood bubbled, and his head flopped to the side.

He was dead.

I stumbled back and looked down at my belly. My hand was covered in red.

If I didn't act quickly, I would be, too.

I walked out into the storm, lightheaded. My chances of getting back to the car were slim. I dug my cell phone out of my pocket, tried to dial 911. But I couldn't get a signal.

I focused on putting one foot in front of the other, plodding. Rain hammered me.

I collapsed to my knees, then facedown in the mud. I listened to the rain tap on my back, felt the blood ooze out into the cold earth. Moss was soft as a blanket under my fingers.

At least I'd done it, I thought. I had been victorious in the storm battle.

I grinned into the mud as I lost consciousness.

37

FIRE

I awoke under white light.

I focused my gaze on Nick, startled to see him. He wasn't wearing his surgical scrubs; he was in street clothes. His hand on my forehead was cool.

"Hey. How are you feeling?"

I looked right and left. I was hooked up to wires and a monitor. My gut ached and I hurt all over. My right arm was in a cast. I was in a hospital somehow.

"Like shit."

"Well, you've got four cracked ribs, a broken wrist, two fractured fingers, a punctured lung, and lost part of your spleen. So, yeah, I wouldn't be surprised. If you'd been out there for much longer, you'd have been dead." His mouth thinned.

My brows drew together. "How did I get here?"

"You sent me a voice note." His gaze was soft. "I figured out where you'd gone, and when you didn't respond to my calls, I contacted Monica. She was able to trace the GPS on your phone and sent emergency services. After the GPS I put on your SUV stopped working, it was the only way I could find you."

"It was you," I breathed.

"Yeah. I'm not proud of it. I was worried about you, that you were still working this case. I was afraid you were going to go missing, too." He exhaled. "I'm sorry."

I looked away. My secrets were laid bare. He knew, and now Monica knew.

"Hey. Look at me. I only told Monica where you were and that I was worried."

I forced myself to look at him, but my words were glued to the roof of my mouth. "You . . . didn't tell her the rest?"

"No. It's not mine to tell. I have more things to confess to you." He ran his hand through his hair, looked away, and then looked back at me. "I know who you are . . . I've always known."

Air exited my throat in a squeak. "You knew?"

"There's no way of making this sound good, so I'll just say it: I knew because I came looking for you." He stared down at his hands. "My mother was Teresa Stanger."

"I know." I licked my lips. "I saw your file in Dr. Richardson's office the other day."

He smiled and shook his head. "That's how I found you. Rooting through her antiquated paper files."

"Why? Why did you seek me out?"

His voice was small and quiet. "I spent years trying to make sense of what happened to my mother. Years of fury and hate. I thought that by becoming a doctor I might be able to find a new purpose. It didn't work. I kept circling back to when I was ten and the cops came to tell me that my mom was dead."

362

I placed my hand on his tentatively. "I'm sorry."

"I thought I might understand if . . . I got to see you. I thought you could explain to me why he did what he did. I thought that you'd be able to give me some closure. So I tried to engineer the most innocent of meetings."

His gaze became unfocused. "At first, I meant to ask you directly, to be up front about who I was and what I needed more than anything else in the world. But then I met you. And . . . I wanted to get to know you more than I wanted answers. So I didn't say anything. I didn't say anything and I fell for you. Or the other way around."

I bowed my head. "I'm sorry."

"But you did tell me, you know? You told me everything in that audio file. Everything. The monster, how it contaminated him, how it spoke to you." He rubbed his stubble. "I listened to it, and I understand it now."

"Really?" I asked skeptically. "But why did you leave?"

He blew out his breath. "I wasn't ready to see my mom's locket."

"You remembered it."

"Yeah. And I lost it when I saw it. I was . . . furious." His voice lowered to a whisper.

My heart fell still. He had every right to hate me, down to the cellular level.

"I understand," I said quietly. My vision blurred. It was hard to love the poisoned apple from the poisoned tree.

"I thought that . . . I thought that you were continuing his work. I couldn't stay there. As irrational as it was, I had to get away. I needed space to think."

All I could do was nod. Closure was strangling me, and I couldn't speak.

"I think I'm beginning to understand now. And I'd like to continue to try to understand."

My tears tapped down on the hospital sheet. "What are you saying?"

"It's hard to explain. But you've given me a gift. Some peace? You explained it to me. There was so much I wanted to know." He smiled at me wanly. "It was everything I ever wanted before I met you."

I watched him carefully. He was fucked-up. Every bit as fucked-up as I was.

"I owe you an apology," he said. "For lying to you. For expecting you to wave a magic wand and fix me. For putting you in a shitty position with your job. For tracking you. For everything."

I shook my head. "No. I forgive you. I don't want there to be secrets between us. I want . . . I want us to try again. To be there for each other."

My heart hammered. I'd never asked him to stay before. Not after the failed proposal, not when he fled when he saw his mother's locket. I'd seen into his soul, and it was a mirror of my own. We had both been victims of the Strangler, of the monster. When I looked into his eyes, I knew he understood me. There was no fury there, only love.

This was the first time I'd seen that understanding in another. I started sobbing, hiccupping. I couldn't take it, the weight of that love.

He kissed my temple and was about to say something more when a knock sounded at the door. I looked up to see Monica and Chief.

I watched Nick as he left, wondering if he'd change his mind. Would I ever see him again, after he had time to decide that the two of us together was a terrible idea?

Monica sat on my right side and the chief on my left. I struggled to keep my heartbeat even on the monitor. I didn't know what they knew, and here I was, hooked up to something really similar to a lie detector.

"How you feeling, kiddo?" Chief asked.

"Like I got run over by a truck," I admitted, sucking back a string of snot and scrubbing tears from my face.

"You would've made out better in a fight against a truck," Monica murmured. She sat down beside me but didn't take her eyes off me. Her suspicion weighed on me, and I deserved it.

"Where's Parkes?" I asked warily. I knew I'd killed him. Right? I just had to confirm that he was really and truly dead.

"In the morgue," Chief said quietly. "Well, what they could peel of him from that iron stove, anyway. What the hell was that?"

"Lightning," I said. "A one-in-a-million hit." Veles had been struck down by Perun, the god of lightning, as he had been since the beginning of time.

"What the hell were you doing there?" Monica asked.

That was the question they couldn't answer. That was the suspicious thing they needed to get to the heart of.

"The pitcher plant flower," I said. "I'd seen it in pictures of that place. When I saw it at the Richardson crime scene, I knew there was a connection." My heart monitor continued its steady beeping. No liars here, right?

Chief and Monica exchanged glances. The tension drained away immediately. I had put their question to rest and could feel things returning to normal.

"That must have been where Parkes got the flowers, too." Monica put a bag of chocolate candy on the right side of the bed and opened it for me. "We had some plant nerds compare the DNA of the flower from Richardson's body to the stand of plants there.

They're biologically identical to the flowers that were in Parkes's car."

"We got some contact DNA from the second body that matches Parkes." Chief pulled a teddy bear out of a bag and put it on the nightstand. "And get this: he has the Lyssa variant DNA marker. Fully expressed, same as the original Strangler."

I stared at him. "That's got to be a one-in-a-million chance."

"Like getting struck by lightning."

I leaned back into the pillow and stared up at the ceiling. "Fuck this."

"We're piecing together what happened with him," Monica said. "The Feds are mum and distancing themselves from the situation, emphasizing that he was retired and no longer part of the Bureau. But we got his personnel file. Turns out he had some erratic-as-hell behavior since the original Strangler investigation. Missing evidence, arguing with other agents. He threatened a witness five years ago and was pressured into retirement."

"He probably snapped at some point, tried to keep it under wraps," Chief said.

"He said there were others," I said. "He said he'd killed and hidden them well."

Chief and Monica exchanged glances. "We need to go through his files. Figure out where he was, when. Who was missing in those jurisdictions."

I paused to think of a way to explain this horrible truth I'd felt oozing in the marrow of my bones. "I think he took up right where the original Strangler left off. I think he got too far into Stephen Theron's head and was contaminated by that evil."

"That's the risk of getting so close to this all this shit. It rubs off." Monica unconsciously rubbed her hand against her jeans.

Chief glanced out the window. "It's always about power, whether it's institutional power or power over another person. There's the temptation to abuse it."

"How the hell did he get that far?" Monica shook her head. "How did he convince himself that he was a god?"

Chief looked at her, then me. "When he realized he was a god, intoxicated by that control over another, it was time to stop."

Power. I had it, as a cop. I was acutely aware of it, from the very first time I killed a man. Maybe power was a bad thing for someone like me.

"We'll get the files handled," Chief said, patting my shoulder. "You just rest up and get better."

I tried.

I carefully answered the FBI's questions. I told them that Parkes had confessed to me. Agent Russell spent much of the questioning with his head in his hands. This was a massive black eye for the Bureau. But there was no making it go away.

The news made the media rounds. The second Forest Strangler had been an FBI agent. My boss was front and center on cable news, describing how his heroic staff had chased down the killer. I was glad it was him on the news, not me.

I'd been admitted to the hospital under a false name, to keep the media away. I was good with false names. No one discovered that I was Elena. Perhaps a god of some sort smiled down on me.

I thought about Nick, over and over. We had a whole lot of deception between us. But he was, of anyone alive, the only person who really understood me. Maybe I could do the same for him.

I texted Nick and asked him to come back. He stayed in a nearby hotel and sat with me as I recovered. He brought me pizza.

We didn't speak of the Strangler case or our past. History was understood. Instead, we did crosswords and he read aloud to me a book about the history of the Roman Empire that put me to sleep every time.

We might have been monsters, but maybe everyone had a monster within them. Our job was to be sure those monsters slept.

I didn't go back to that house in the woods where the murders happened. Instead, I slipped out of bed in the middle of the night to go to the edge of my forest near my house to listen for the Forest God.

I heard nothing but the crickets chirping as summer slid into fall. I healed, but not perfectly. My right hand was arthritic, and my ribs were uneven and tender.

I quietly checked in on my mother. I parked my car outside her house and stared at her front door. Part of me wanted to knock, to demand answers. To demand recognition. Maybe even love.

The other part of me wanted to expose her to her do-over family. I wanted to tell them that she was a monster. I wanted to destroy her life, explode it, brick by brick. I gave a lot of thought to how I might make that happen and still preserve my privacy. It was possible. I just had to drop an anonymous tip to someone in the press. If her cover were blown, she would be hunted mercilessly.

I watched as she went out to the porch to smoke one night after midnight. She didn't turn on the porch light. I thought her gaze landed on my car. Maybe our eyes met. Maybe they didn't. I didn't trust my own imagination.

But I wanted her to know that somebody, somewhere, knew what a monster she was.

I stared at her with the same cold gray gaze that belonged to my father.

She extinguished her cigarette under her shoe and went back into the house.

I held Nick's hand as he got clean at my house. He took a couple of weeks off work and told everyone that we were taking a trip. No one at the hospital ever knew, though it seemed as if he were painfully shedding a skin. He'd been careful not to take enough amphetamines to put himself at risk of an overdose, but it took time to wear out of his system. He slept deeply, so deeply that I'd sometimes put my head on his chest to hear if he was still breathing. I didn't think he'd slept this deeply in years. When he woke, I fed him and forced him to drink water.

"I had the most fucked-up dream." His elbow was planted on the table and his forehead rested in his palm.

I placed another pancake on his plate. "What about?"

"I dreamed you had this snake as a pet. This giant snake. You found it in the woods and brought it inside. It lived under your bed and grew bigger and bigger. It started to eat people. Like the mailman. It slithered up the road and went into town and started devouring people, Godzilla-style."

"That's some dream," I remarked.

I wondered at Veles. If Dr. Richardson were still alive, I would've asked her if he were perhaps some kind of entity plugged into the collective unconscious, reachable by DNA or drugs or some kind of spiritual awakening.

She would likely have told me, nicely, that this was an insane idea.

DEA got involved with the pharmaceutical ring investigation, and it blew up in a way that made the evening news for weeks. The security guard, Mariner, had had keys to the hospital pharmacy and been helping himself. Drug inventory control had been lacking, and one of the staff doctors had written many fraudulent prescriptions. Nick had bought from a blind drop twice with cash, but the investigation didn't discover him. Nick had been savvy enough not to write any fraudulent prescriptions himself, so there was no direct trail to him. More than a dozen personnel were fired and a half dozen arrests made. Since accusations were made about proper controls for the hospital pharmacy, its accreditation was on the line.

Drugs had cast a long shadow on the county. The PCP lab run by Cas and the maintenance guy at his apartment complex blew up into a major statewide investigation. Mariner had stolen one of the chemicals used to make PCP, piperidine, from the hospital. He was facing decades in prison.

I burned the memorabilia I had of my father and my psychological file in my fireplace. I cast the ashes out into the forest. I gave the necklace to Nick, who stared at it in his palm. He remembered that his mother had always worn it; it had been a gift for her college graduation, once upon a time. He told me she used to keep pictures of him inside.

When the season changed and the fall leaves lit in brilliant flames of color, when the smell of frost was close, I stared into the forest. Our new rescue dog, Gibby, leaned into my thigh, wagging his tail. He was the dog seized by Animal Control from the house where Cas had hidden, the one who'd bitten Deputy Max. I'd been able to pull some strings and get him released from doggy death row, and he greeted each day with buckets of dog slobber. He was high-strung but a work in progress. As we all were.

I took a step toward the forest, reaching out with all my senses. Was Veles truly gone? Had the Forest God been chased away by the lightning in that dilapidated shack?

I knelt down. I had left an offering there the night before: a perfect apple. I shoved aside the leaves to find it was still there, untouched.

Whatever had been in the forest was no longer listening to me.

Gibby barked at me.

"Yeah." I smiled at him. "Let's go."

I turned away from the shadow of the forest, toward the sun and the light and the memory of darkness.

ACKNOWLEDGMENTS

Many thanks to all those who made this book possible.

Thank you to my excellent editor, Jen Monroe, for taking a chance on my story. Thank you for your keen editorial vision and insight while molding this book. I'm so thrilled that you loved it as much as I did, and very excited that you shared it with readers.

Much gratitude to the whole team at Berkley for standing behind me and this book, with special thanks to Candice Coote for all her help throughout the process.

Thanks to my wonderful agent, Caitlin Blasdell, for championing this book in the world. I'm so lucky to have you in my corner, and I appreciate all you do. Thank you for hanging in there with me.

A personal thank-you to Jason, Marcella, and Michelle. Telling tales is strange work, and I'm glad to be on this road with you.